CLASSICS MUTILATED

CTRL-ALT-LIT

Edited by **Jeff Conner**

Illustrated by **Mike Dubisch**

Cover painting by **Menton3**

SAN DIEGO, CA
2010

To English and History teachers everywhere.

Book Design by Robbie Robbins

www.IDWPUBLISHING.com

ISBN: 978-1-60010-830-3

13 12 11 10   1 2 3 4

IDW Publishing is: Operations: Ted Adams, CEO & Publisher • Greg Goldstein, Chief Operating Officer • Matthew Ruzicka, CPA, Chief Financial Officer • Alan Payne, VP of Sales • Lorelei Bunjes, Director of Digital Services • Jeff Webber, Director of ePublishing • AnnaMaria White, Dir. Marketing and Public Relations • Dirk Wood, Dir., Retail Marketing • Marci Hubbard, Executive Assistant • Alonzo Simon, Shipping Manager • Angela Loggins, Staff Accountant • Cherrie Go, Assistant Web Designer • Editorial: Chris Ryall, Chief Creative Officer, Editor-In-Chief • Scott Dunbier, Senior Editor, Special Projects • Andy Schmidt, Senior Editor • Bob Schreck, Senior Editor • Justin Eisinger, Senior Editor, Books • Kris Oprisko, Editor/Foreign Lic. • Denton J. Tipton, Editor • Tom Waltz, Editor • Mariah Huehner, Editor • Carlos Guzman, Assistant Editor • Bobby Curnow, Assistant Editor • Design: Robbie Robbins, EVP/Sr. Graphic Artist • Neil Uyetake, Senior Art Director • Chris Mowry, Senior Graphic Artist • Amauri Osorio, Graphic Artist • Gilberto Lazcano, Production Assistant • Shawn Lee, Graphic Artist

Table of Contents

🙟 🙝

Foreword

By

Jeff Conner

This collection represents a multitude of takes on the so-called Monster Lit phenomenon, a trend that's spreading through the book trade like gossip at a church picnic. To recap, Monster Lit is the pub biz tag for breeding public domain classics and/or historical figures with outré genre elements, usually of the horrific supernatural persuasion. The absurd genius of "mashing" the English-speaking world's most popular dead author with its equally popular undead abominations that aren't vampires was brilliant, a laudable piece of literary pranking that—in a rare alignment of commerce rewarding art—was gobbled up by book buyers like Halloween candy laced with spicy brains.

Given the notable mass-market success of that first foray into repurposed prose, it didn't take long for a "remix recipe" to emerge, namely take one Public Domain Classic, insert choice of Generic Monster, mix well in favorite Word Processor, and serve to sales-starved Publishers.

Of course, the reality is that publishing is more art than science and such formulas don't adapt well to endless corporate replication. Public domain classics are like oil, there's only so much out there, so what happens when they run out, and all the good monsters have long been taken?

Can Monster Lit survive its inherent expiration date? This collection provides the answer. Here at Classics Mutilated Industries, we're endeavoring to rescue Monster Lit from its own termination by reframing the concept as a whole new concept: CTRL-ALT-LIT, literature remixed. This bit of editorial doctoring calls for injecting a healthy dose of Mashup Culture into Monster Lit's left ass cheek. So bend over, corporate publishers. It's our belief that CTRL-ALT-LIT can avoid the fate of other publishing fads and evolve into a vibrant, self-sustaining category all its own, like franchise fantasy, techno-thrillers, and celebrity tell-alls.

But just what is Mashup Culture, you ask? A simple demonstration provides the best answer: simply Google "Single Ladies (In Mayberry)" and watch the

YouTube video—all will be revealed. (*Mashup* is also a term for hacker-made multi-function apps, basically the software equivalent of what's happening in the arts, especially music.)

Indeed, for over ten years now an underground global community of DJs and producers (music hackers, if you will) have been "mashing" together two or more songs and then playing the results at local clubs or putting them on their websites. (*Glee* had a mashup episode this year, signaling that the scene is either far from over or totally over, depending.) Because these unauthorized mixes use copyrighted material they are literally bootlegs, hence the term "bootie" to describe these types of illicit releases.

The best bootie mixes are startling juxtapositions of diverse musical elements, reflecting a prankish humor and refreshing energy that is strikingly reminiscent of the early Surrealist and Dadaist movements (e.g., "readymade" and "found object" reconfigurations; an anarchistic art stance that later influenced punk rock). It's this bootie vibe that informs CLASSICS MUTILATED collection and our CTRL-ALT-LIT movmement. (Deeper "remix fiction" is still too esoteric, even for this project.)

Of course, attentive readers of science fiction and fantasy will recognize that the recombinant genre blending at the heart of Monster Lit is very much like "fan fiction," a staple of SF fandom since the 1930s. Now a well-established form of self-expression and community participation—and an obvious precursor to the contemporary mashup movement—these self-motivated "franchise hackers" diligently craft new mix-and-match adventures for their favorite characters and franchises—without regard for copyright or NSFW content (e.g., gay-centric "slash" fiction with titles like "Brokeback To The Future").

And while bootie culture has spread globally, there is a thriving form of fanfic found only in Japan in the form of the somewhat low-profile *dōjinshi* communities. In this grey-market publishing phenomenon, artists and writers use copyrighted material for their own projects and then sell small, self-published quantities to fans and collectors at special conventions. The practice is tacitly encouraged by the country's mainstream publishers because the *dōjinshi* scene is an effective way for young creators to learn their craft, and it produces a lot of fresh content.

Another view of copyright enforcement is described in a recent article in *Der Spiegel* by economic historian Eckhard Höffner posits that the reason why Germany surpassed England's industrial and technological innovation during the early 19th century was due to its lax copyright laws (and corresponding strong ones in Great Britain). The theory has it that cheap bootleg editions of technical books and journals (an early form of "open source") allowed the German populace freer access to practical knowledge, leading to greater innovation as a society. And because strict copyright enforcement kept English book prices high, and thus out of reach to all but the aristocracy (who hadn't much interest in new technology in the first place), that country fell behind. This bolsters the "information should be free" ethos of many Internet communities, which is still different than downloading copyrighted material without paying for it—that's just theft. Really.

But it's no revelation that technology has always impacted society and the arts, or that the digital revolution has created many new arenas for expressing one's creative (often subversive) impulses. In this light, Monster Lit is just another in a long line of fringe phenomena that has been discovered, and in some cased absorbed by the mainstream—like hip hop fashion, extreme sports, waxing, or even the ecology and civil rights movements.

From the start, CLASSICS MUTILATED was designed as a "corrective" for cash-in Monster Lit, a vampire and zombie free one. The project started with commissioning talented writers, not adhering to a shallow formula. Asking smart creators to bring their own visions and sensibilities to our bootie party seemed like the best way to achieve our goals, and just about anything was fair game (as long as it wouldn't attract corporate lawyers, since this isn't Japan or 1830s Germany, at least not yet).

And now you can feast on the tasty results. Some stories use "classic" Monster Lit as a point of departure, while others approach their mashups from their own singular perspectives. And while the styles and stances may vary, the results are always highly entertaining and totally original.

Case in point, Joe R. Lansdale's masterful "Dread Island," which features Huck Finn narrating a strange new adventure involving familiar anthropomorphic creatures and a notorious ancient tome of inter-dimensional evil. Only Lansdale could effortlessly combine Mart Twain, H.P. Lovecraft, and Uncle Remus into one compelling, novella-length tale.

And speaking of compelling, "Little Women in Black" is undoubtedly the most rigorous example of Monster Lit ever written. Rick Hautala's deft "collaboration" with Louisa May Alcott is an authentically subversive work, created by slipping shards of new text into Alcott's original prose, transforming an extended Christmas interlude into something eerie and sinister. (We also have Mr. Hautala and writer Christopher Golden to thank for the "Classics Mutilated" moniker.)

Lezli Robyn's "Anne-droid of Green Gables" is a great example of Monster Lit *sans* monster, instead using Steampunk to recraft Lucy Maud Montgomery's beloved 1908 "orphan lit" novel. An entirely different but no less effective revision of a classic, Nancy Collins extends the adventures of Herman Melville's Capt. Ahab in "From Hell's Heart"; it's so heartening to discover that the crusty captain still wields a mean harpoon. Taking on Norse mythology, Chris Ryall's "Twilight of the Gods" features the outcast god Loki (you know him from the Thor comics), as done in the style of a very popular dark fantasy series.

Presenting one of the most anticipated match-ups in fantasy, Sean Taylor's "The Fairest of Them All" which pits Snow While and Lewis Carroll's Alice (via a certain enchanted mirror) in a magic-infused battle royale. Another pitched battle occurs in Thomas Tessier's "The Green Menace" which finds Sen. Joseph McCarthy, the infamous Red-baiting demagogue, fighting an insidious homeland invader that even *his* paranoid brain couldn't imagine.

Mixing historical figures with fictional characters is another hallmark of this collection, and one of the most evocative examples is Kristine Kathryn Rusch's "Death Stops for Miss Dickinson," which recounts the famed poet's heretofore secret graveyard hook-up. And speaking of graveyards, John Shirley's "Frankenbilly" has Henry McCarty, aka Billy the Kid, encountering the "real" Dr. Frankenstein in the old west, with electrifying results.

Spotlighting a more recent outlaw, Mark Morris's "Vicious" details a pivotal moment in the too-brief life of John Simon Ritchie, aka Sid Vicious, the notorious Sex Pistol. Rio Youers' "Quoth the Rock Star" concerns another gone-too-soon rocker, namely the singer/poet Jim Morrison, and his strange encounter with Edgar Allan Poe (or at least something like him).

Mixing non-fiction techniques with fictional fact, Marc Laidlaw's "Pokky Ma" is an investigation into the fate of a passionate young naturalist whoe intense study of the odd little "pokky" creatrues leads to a bizarre tradgedy. Also set in a world like ours (yet thankfully not), the writing team of John Skipp and Cody Goodfellow unleashes "The Happiest Hell on Earth." Also employing documentary techniques, their story reveals how Dr. Moreau's man-creatures survived the House of Pain, only to be even more cruelly exploited as live-action cartoon characters. (Does the name "Darn Old Duck" ring a bell?)

And so CLASSICS MUTILATED goes out into the world, claws held high, turntables on stun, leading by example, showing those other be-yoches how Monster Lit/Mashup Fiction should be done.

Let the mutilation begin. CTRL-ALT-LIT has arrived.

Jeff Conner
Los Angeles, California
August 28, 2010

CLASSICS MUTILATED

The Fairest of Them All:
A Symphony of Revenge

By

Sean Taylor

First Movement—Once Upon a Time

They were nameless, though they had no trouble distinguishing one another. Short and squat, they smelled like the caves they mined, but that didn't bother them. They had done so and been so for more than two hundred of the humans' years, and they looked neither older nor younger than they had a few decades ago.

The one who knew himself as the leader, and perhaps the eldest—it had been so long and who knew really—walked the tunnels in thought.

The woman, the human woman, was waiting for them at the cottage. No more than a cleaned-out cave by her standards, no doubt, but for them it was as close to a cottage as they could tolerate. Before finding her, he had simply called the place home, but she had named it *cottage* and because they loved her, he could abide the change of terms.

"Good day today, brother?" the one with the red beard said as he passed.

"So far," Leader said. "Enough gold to justify another day of digging."

"That's not what I mean."

"Oh?"

"You'll turn gray from the worry I see on your face. You've got wrinkles on your wrinkles this morning."

He laughed, a coughing sound laden with rock dust. "I'm thinking about Snow."

"We all do. She's quite a beauty."

He shook his head. "Not like that. Something's wrong. There's a darkness growing in her and I fear we can't stop it. It's an ill wind, brother, and I fear for her safety."

"She's fine. The Queen thinks she's dead."

"The Queen is not a fool. She knows more than we hope. At any rate, what she doesn't yet know, she will learn soon through her dark arts." He cleared the dust again and patted his chest with a rock-like fist. "Snow is not safe and will not be until her mother is killed."

His brother dropped his voice to a whisper and cut his eyes askance. "Are you suggesting...."

"I'm suggesting nothing, brother. Merely stating a fact. Whether or not it is our role to play the assassin, who can know?"

Redbeard shoved his stubby finger in the elder's chest. "Be careful what you say. She has eyes and ears all throughout her kingdom, even as far as these Deadlands. If you don't want a price on your head too, I'd keep my tongue from waggling, or failing that, cut the damn thing out to keep it still."

He laughed and stepped away from the finger in his chest. "At any rate, it's not a matter for today. And there is more gold to be found to keep our little Snow's neck lined with jewels."

Redbeard raised his fist and opened it. Leader did the same then clasped it, and the two nodded twice and let go.

Both turned when the tallest of their brothers, though still a stump of a man by human standards, tripped along the path toward them, panting and dragging his pick behind him.

"Brothers!" he said. "We found something you need to see."

Leader reached up and grabbed his brother by the shoulders. "Calm down."

"What did you find?" asked Redbeard.

"We're not sure."

"Not sure? Then why are you running like a cowardly troll?"

Tallest grabbed his elder brother's dirty arm and pulled him closer. "It's a mirror, but we don't know what kind."

"What kind, what kind," said Redbeard. "What a stupid brother. A mirror is a mirror. There are no kinds. They're for women to crow about their vanity and little else."

"Not this one." Tallest crouched toward his brothers' faces, his breath hot and sweaty in their eyes. "This one has a girl inside it."

The cave stank of sweat and urine, and she cleaned it daily on her knees, then cooked whatever forest creature the little men captured and killed for dinner on the way home from the mines. She sang as she worked, a melody she remembered from when she was a child, perhaps no older than five or six. It was increasingly difficult to remember. The years had been far too unkind since her mother's death.

Her father's second wife had been a beautiful woman, practically a goddess of a high order, but only on the outside. Inside her throbbed a heart of poison. She hated her stepdaughter from their first meeting, pretending to enjoy their time together and planning whenever she could events that would take the girl and her nanny away from the castle, leaving her alone with her new husband.

She'd grown up lonely, and no matter how they smelled or how atrocious their table manners, the little men had become her friends, and she loved them.

Still she shuddered.

She'd seen the way the eldest of them and the redheaded one looked at her across the table. She'd heard that dwarves remained unmarried and merely mated when nature called for more of their species to arrive. Like something wild, something that was more a part of the forest and mountains, not part of her civilization of culture and glamour and pomp.

But that place had forsaken her. After her father's death, her stepmother had grown more openly vile toward her, insisting on marrying her off to a distant prince from a nation of barbarians, so she had run away.

To retaliate, her stepmother had thrown the blame of her father's death onto her and labeled her guilty of treason, then offered a reward for her death.

"Just a little longer," she said to no one, gazing out at the reddening sun as it dipped into the edge of the world. "I wonder what we'll have for dinner tonight."

As she spoke, she walked to the row of beds sitting in the dark shade of the overhanging rock. Once there, she reached down to steady herself with one hand then sat down, her knees poking up even with her chest thanks to the small frame.

The door burst open and a small dog with white matted fur bounded in and leapt into her lap, pushing her back onto the bed. Her feet hung off the edge and touched the floor, flat-footed, and the top of her head pressed against the head rail. The dog snuggled into her chest and licked her lips and nose.

"Stop, Aspen. Stop," she giggled, covering her face with her hands. "That tickles. Stop."

Of course the dog didn't stop.

"And you probably tracked mud all over the clean floor."

She finally managed to push the dog off her chest and sit up again. Clean floor, she thought. Not very. Even freshly swept it was just a base of flattish stone cut out from the base of a mountain and etched with a grid to make it look fancier than mere rock.

The little men had done that for her. They would have been content with a hole cut out from a rocky ledge, but for her they had created a floor. A pattern. A little bit of culture and glamour and pomp. For her. The same reason her larger wooden dresser and bed were adorned with spheres and cubes and statuettes of dragons and harts instead of the simple blocks of their own furniture. And the same reason her top drawer was filled with golden chains and colorful stones from the mines and the rest with fancy dresses they had traded for with the villages beyond the mountain. For her.

They loved her.

And she loved them.

But that was no longer enough.

For any of them.

The faces were staring at her. Ugly. Wrinkled. Filthy. Prunes with noses, she thought. No. Rotten prunes with noses. She imagined that they'd smell horrible too if she could be close enough to fall prey to their odor.

But the glass that had been her prison for years was in this case a grace, protecting her from the trollish monsters.

In her father's kingdom, years ago, he had gone to war with the creatures, and ultimately run them off his lands into the mountains.

But her father's kingdom was long gone, lost for centuries in the world on the other side of the glass. Her family had grown old, died, rotted and nested forests in their remains while she remained a captive of a witch who had stolen her away and sent her to this land of nightmares and hallucinations.

"Alice," said a voice she recognized instantly. "What are those horrid creatures?"

"Long ago, when I was much younger and not younger at all, my father called them the darshve. He told me how they were creatures born from the sides of mountains and baptized to life in the blood of our ancestors. Monsters of the rock and greed."

She turned toward the voice and smiled.

A white rabbit, dressed in armor save for his face and head stood before her, bowing.

"What news, Ulysses?"

"Alas, none, Alice." The rabbit frowned. "I wish I had better news. But I've traveled as far as the ocean to the East and as far as the swamps of the Jabberwock to the West, and no one has any knowledge of another doorway into your home world. It appears that when the looking glass was destroyed behind you, that was the only path to your old world."

"No!" she screamed and flung her hands against the mirror between her and the darshve. "There is a way, rabbit, and you will find it for me. I will not be slave to this witch any longer than I have to." Alice turned and glared not at her companion but through him to the door of her chamber. "And when I do escape, she will die."

She glanced toward the wooden desk beneath the mirror. On it sat a book bound in leather. Ulysses caught her gaze and asked, "And the book?"

"Sadly, no. There are paths to and from other worlds, but none back to mine." She released a heavy burden of a breath. "Yet."

The air between them wriggled. Then rippled out. She touched the center of the motion and pulled back.

"Damn."

"Her?" asked the rabbit.

Alice nodded.

"I'm not going this time," she said and sat down on the floor, crossing her legs in front of her. "She can rot before I let her collar me again with her beckoning."

"But Alice...."

"Hush, rodent." Alice glared at him this time. "Leave me alone."

The rabbit bowed, saluted, then turned on his left heel and strode from the chamber. When he was gone, Alice gripped her stomach and doubled over.

"No ..." she said through gritted teeth. "Not this time, witch."

But the pain in her gut became a fire. In a few moments she crawled onto her knees, then lay her face down against the stone floor. Her stomach churned.

"No...."

She pressed both palms flat against the floor and raised her face a few inches from the stone.

"I will not obey you."

Her gut twisted and bile danced in her throat. She coughed. Three drops of blood splattered from her lips to the floor.

"I will n—"

Her stomach opened, pushing blood and water and acid and bile and pain and fire through her throat and thrusting it onto the floor in a puddle of green and red and brown.

"One day, witch," Alice said, reaching to wipe her mouth free of debris and mucous.

But another churning sent her hand to the floor to brace herself as her stomach emptied its filthy contents into the puddle again.

A voice in the air whispered, "Mirror, mirror on the wall…."

Second Movement—There Lived a Princess

"What's wrong with her?" asked Redbeard.

"She's beautiful, almost as pretty as Snow," said Tallest. "And she's young."

"Where is she?" Redbeard again. "Is she real, or the mirror a conjurer's trick?"

"Quiet, both of you," said Leader. "She's in pain." He tapped on the glass. The girl turned to face him and retched a third time. "She's real. That pain isn't a conjurer's game. No one could fake that. Look at her face."

His brothers crowded him at the mirror and he pushed them away.

"One side," he said. Not waiting for them to move, he pushed them away from the mirror and traced his thick, calloused hands around the oval edges. He tried to dig his nails between the glass and iron rim. There was no rim, as if the glass and frame were somehow molded from one piece of material. But it couldn't be, he thought. As a miner he knew raw materials, and iron was as different from glass as he was from the human woman living with him and his brothers. "There's conjuring here, but not necessarily only inside the mirror. This is made and bathed in magic. This is no ordinary mirror."

The smallest of his brothers, a golden-haired one with a mere few inches of a beard, shoved through the melee to the front. "Let's take it to Snow!"

"To Snow?" he asked.

"Yes, she loves trinkets and jewels, and a magic mirror would be the perfect thing for her to use when she brushes out her hair."

The others sighed and oohed approval.

"This is not a trinket, brother."

"No. It is a magic trinket," said Redbeard. "And our brother is right. Snow would love us even more when we give her this."

Tallest puffed out his chest and made himself a few inches taller. "And with the year of maturing coming soon, we will need to find women of our own kind or find something more wonderful than mere jewels to woo Snow."

"Here, here," said the others, in a sort of off-unison.

"Quiet," Leader said and stomped his boot into the dirty trail. "I say this is a bad idea. This mirror is enchanted and until we know what it does, it is far too dangerous to remove from this mine. But, we are brothers, and we will do what we will do. Who knows what role even this cursed looking glass may play in the evil that rides on the air through our Deadlands? We will put it to a vote and we will play our parts."

He let go of the mirror and leaned it against the wall of the cave. It teetered twice then stopped. The girl in the mirror had disappeared while they had argued, he noticed, though her chamber remained in view. Curious, he thought.

He sat on his knees and drew two circles in the dirt. He poked two dots outside the top of the left circle and one dot with a line across the top at the bottom of the right circle. Then he stood up again and walked to the wall opposite the mirror. He raised his pick and cut several slivers of stone from the wall. Then he put the pick down and gathered up the shards of jagged rock. He walked from one brother to the next and handed each a fragment until he had given away six of them, then kept one for himself and threw the remaining pieces into the dark tunnel.

"You know our way, brothers," he said. "Cast your vote."

They formed a single line and as each walked by the circles, he placed his stone in one of the circles. Redbeard placed his in the circle with the two dots, as did Newbeard and Tallest. Stumpfinger dropped his in the other circle. Then Finder.

That made two votes for each.

After Finder, No-Talk dropped his shard into the two-dot circle, then Grunt-Mouth did the same.

Leader gazed at the circles. Four votes to two. His vote was the only one left. Not that it would matter.

He sighed, then grumbled and stepped forward and carefully placed his stone fragment in the circle adorned by one dot and a solid line. Then he turned around and addressed his brothers.

"Let it be as we agreed. When we leave today, the mirror will go with us as a gift to Snow. Whatever danger befalls us and our love, let it be on our heads."

"Here, here," said his brothers. Then they each shook on the decision with open palms and two nods.

After they were done and finally returned to work, Leader carried the mirror to the mouth of the cave and laid it out in the sun. He slipped out of his tunic and spit on the cloth, then proceeded to wipe the dust and dirt and mud from the mirror and the frame.

That's when he felt the symbols etched into the iron.

Old letters. Older almost than his own people. From just after the time of the great wars. The Dark Days, as the humans called them. His own people called them the Time of Great Adventure but even the oldest of them couldn't remember the time. Only that they had been free to live anywhere in the land, not confined to the Deadlands.

He cleaned vigorously for nearly an hour, passing the time with a tune that Snow had taught him. He had tried to whistle as she had tried to teach him, but he just couldn't get the knack for it, and had to suffice with humming, though even that was difficult for his throat and mouth to conjure. In his own tongue, the old stories and songs were immensely disagreeable to human ears, and he had refrained from making the noises while in Snow's company, but he did enjoy grunting and burping out a story from the old language in private as often as he could.

Although—and the thought struck him as odd—Snow's songs were growing on him. Far too sweet and kind for his race. He knew that. But still they were pleasant, and they seemed to relax him.

There was no hurry, and he let the job take him another hour before he was able to at last make out the symbols around the glass.

Only, he couldn't read them. Not only were they older than his father's father's father, they weren't in his tongue.

But neither were they in any human tongue he knew. And admittedly he knew them all. The need to barter had dictated that knowledge.

"'Tis a bad sign, it is," he said, then spit again on his tunic to clean the glass itself.

Dinner was ready when the little men arrived home, just vegetable soup this time, since her friends had returned so late from the mines. But they didn't mind, and they each smiled at her in an odd way as she greeted them at the door and reminded them to remove their boots at the door.

"Such a proper woman," the one she called Smiles said as he entered. With a thick red beard and an almost permanent smile, the name seemed to fit him. Not that he'd acknowledge for himself outside her presence, she knew. His name would change among his brothers as often as his beard or disposition.

The tallest came behind him and she kissed his head. "Good evening, and how was your day at the mine?"

He only grinned and looked away.

The one who took care of the others entered last and nodded toward her then bowed slightly. "We have a surprise for you after dinner, Snow," he said.

Another necklace, she thought, or perhaps a new gown from beyond the mountains. That's what had kept them today.

The gifts were nice, but so inferior to her trifles at the palace. Still, that was a world and a witch away, and there was no use letting it ruin her mood in front of her friends who worked so hard to make her happy.

"Oh?" she said, feigning an excited squeal. "Perhaps we should skip dinner and just let me see it now."

"If you want to," said the little one she called Grandpa because his blonde beard reminded her of her grandfather's portrait hanging in the hallway outside her chamber at the castle.

"No," gruffed the leader of the group, a squattish stump of a man she called Squash for no other reason than it seemed to fit him. He coughed then relaxed his voice. "We will wait. Our stomachs are empty, and food and beer will make the giving more enjoyable for all of us."

"I certainly can't argue with that, Squash," she said, curtsying as she spoke, then let him take her lean fingers in his stubby hand and escort her to the table.

Once dinner was eaten and the dishes cleared away for her to wash, Smiles and Grandpa grabbed her hands and whisked her from the table toward the door. They led her outside, the others following as a group. She couldn't get back without trampling through them, so thickly were they packed around and behind her. Only Squash stood off at a distance, watching cautiously as he smoked his pipe. The foul odor of the ground bitterroot was nauseating from even a distance, but she dared not say anything to him, as it seemed to be his only real vice aside from typical dwarfish issues with hygiene.

The group led her to the edge of the garden they had dug out for her. Leaning against the rock-hewn gate was a flat package about four feet tall and wrapped in a cloth tarp.

"Open it," they cried, almost in unison.

Except for Squash, who remained a few feet away, still smoking his obnoxious pipe.

"Okay," she said and knelt down to unwrap the gift. As she did, her skirt fell away to one side, exposing her knee and she noticed that all the brothers grew quiet at once. When she looked, they were all staring at her smooth, white skin. She quickly recovered her leg. "Sorry about that."

Just as quickly, the little men started to grunt and whisper and jabber with each other as she returned to the gift and lifted the edge of the tarp away from the top corner of the package.

"Hurry, hurry, Snow."

"Yes, we want to see your smile when you learn what we brought you."

"Hurry, hurry, hurry."

So she did. She ripped the tarp away and exposed the gift, twirling around with a flourish as she did. Almost in a dance, just for the benefit of her little friends.

Then she stopped.

Cold.

The gift.

It was a mirror.

A very, very expensive and old mirror.

Inside the mirror was a young woman, blonde, staring out at Snow with the same intense gaze with which she was staring at the girl in the mirror.

She'd only seen a mirror this extravagant once before.

Only once.

Nearly fifteen years ago.

In her stepmother's chamber.

It had the same girl inside.

But the girl hadn't aged a single day.

The girl, Alice thought, the girl, the girl she thought she'd never see again. The hideous little blessed bastards had brought her directly to the stepdaughter of the wretched woman who had imprisoned her behind the glass and left her to die.

Only she hadn't died.

No. She had instead conquered the people in that looking glass world and become the queen of her new domain. It had taken many hundreds of years and cost thousands of lives, but when she found the book and formed an alliance with the elder gods, she had finally defeated and beheaded the evil queen who stole the hearts of her subjects to sacrifice to the dreaded Jabberwock.

Captive to the Queen, the beast had not been native to the land, but a dumb offspring of the elder gods from beyond. And when they had discovered how one of their own, albeit it one not a god as such, had been enslaved, they tore the life from the land and left it parched and mostly dead.

But time causes all things to change and when the creatures from beyond had moved on, Alice merely waited, biding her time as the green returned to the soil and the fragrance to the air, and even the creatures of the woodlands and seas forgot of the darkness of the war and saw only the bright new beginning of their new Queen Alice.

Not only that, but she had also used her time in exile to befriend and nurse even that dumb Jabberwock until it would eat live rodents from her hand without so much as drawing a single drop of blood from her human skin.

It refused to leave with its own kind. It was for the best, she knew. Its presence in her court secured the loyalty of the people.

And she had reigned for a glorious epoch, it seemed, but even a kingdom isn't necessarily a home, she had learned, and over time, all thoughts of political victory had simply faded away, replaced by the singular focus of returning home to kill the witch responsible for her exile.

No queen could be slave to another and still be queen, she had said to her subjects many times, and for that, the witch would have to die.

And her own stepdaughter would be the sword to raise against her.

Only there was the matter of the runes.

Alice stared at the dark-haired girl, envious for a moment for her pale, young skin. Already thousands of years older than she had been when she had fallen prey to the witch, Alice's own skin looked as young as the girl's but carried the calloused tightness of years of struggle.

The creatures were helping the girl to her feet again. She had fallen aback at the unveiling of the cursed looking glass and landed in a disheveled heap in the dirty path. Alice laughed. Then thought it best to smile instead. No sense in looking maniacal toward the only person who had a chance of freeing her from the multiple lifetimes of trapped torment.

When the girl was up and steady she returned to the mirror and cautiously placed her hands on the glass. Alice nodded and placed her own hands opposite those of the girl. The girl gasped and Alice said, "It's okay. It's safe," though she knew the girl couldn't hear her across dimensions.

Using the frame of her matching mirror in her own chamber as a guide, she traced the outer edge of the glass where it met the iron frame. The girl looked at her, confused, and Alice traced the edges again, this time pointing as she did to the characters etched into the iron.

"Come on, little witch-child, don't be a fool," Alice mumbled, tracing the mirror's edge a third time. "It's not that difficult, child."

The girl shook her head, as if to directly counter Alice's comments, and Alice felt her mouth tense and her anger find a home in her brow. She forced a smile and reminded herself to be patient, that she'd waited for more than a thousand years and a few more minutes or hours or even days more couldn't hurt her further.

Alice stepped back and settled into her chair. How, she wondered, just how could she get through to this stupid girl and her hideous helpers?

"Ulysses!" she yelled.

In the chamber she waited for the thumping of padded paws. She was not disappointed—nor was she often—and within moments the armored white rabbit appeared in the doorway.

"Yes, my queen?"

"I need parchment."

"Yes, my queen." The rabbit stood up straight, as straight as a creature of his sort could, and puffed out his chest, pushing the armor out full and gleaming. "May I ask why?"

Alice crossed her legs and puffed out a loud, heavy breath. "This fool of a girl is as dumb as an ox, and can't understand that I need her to read the runes around the mirror's frame."

"Have you asked her nicely?"

Alice cut her eyes at the rabbit, one of the few of her subjects who could get away with such sarcasm. "That's why I need the tablet." She motioned the creature forward and when he was close enough she rubbed his head. "She can't hear me through the portal. I'm going to write her a message, you brainless ball of fur."

Ulysses pulled away and straightened his fur. "You know I despise that," he said. "I am the Captain of the Queen's Guard, not a pet for you to coddle and coo."

Alice laughed. "And I'm the queen you guard, Captain Ulysses, and the one who named you and set you apart from the rest of the forest creatures who grew dumb when the former Queen's magic died with her. If I wish to cuddle and coo you, believe me, I shall."

Undaunted, the rabbit said, "I will return with a tablet, Alice."

Alice smiled, sincerely for her friend, unlike the forced and irritated smile at the dunce of a princess she was dependent upon. "Thank you." She petted his head again, just once, and tussled the fur there. "And I promise to reward you greatly when I escape from this world and reclaim my own homeland."

"And in the meantime, my queen?"

She leaned back in her chair again, uncrossed her legs, then pushed up against the oak arms until she was standing. "In the meantime, my friend, I will return to the mirror and try to educate this illiterate princess."

"By your leave, Alice."

"Do they not educate young women any longer in my homeland?" she mumbled as she took her place in front of the mirror and watched as the girl and her darshve companions did the same to her.

Third Movement—In a Land of War

Leader gazed at the fair-haired girl, learning her face, remembering it and comparing it to all the faces he had made himself remember during his life.

There was no match, but there were faces like it, faces that were etched in lines of sadness and colored with despair. Faces that time had painted with pain and outlined in anger.

But there was also something of the childish nature in her stare. Something like a human infant's smoothness. Something that reminded him of a young hart taking its first steps.

There was a deepness to the face. But a youngness as well. An infant face with a world of age behind it. The pieces did not fit. Young faces were filled with young life. Old faces were the only ones full of oldness.

The fair-haired girl was not normal. She was….

He struggled for the word. He hadn't needed to speak it or even remember it for a long, long time. A word from the old language, one he wasn't able to translate into any human tongue.

"Atyanshvar," he said, surprising even himself when he spoke the word aloud.

"At yon what?" asked Snow.

"Atyanshvar," he whispered this time.

His brothers stepped back from the mirror. They squatted on their knees around Snow and nodded. "Atyanshvar," they said together, like a prayer.

"I don't understand," Snow said.

The girl in the mirror, the one who was atyanshvar, the only he'd ever seen, the only seen in the last seven generations of his people, the girl stared at them as though she were trying to understand them.

"What did you say, Squash?" she asked.

"It's a word from the old tongue. It means…." He pulled on his beard. "There is no human word for it. I'm sorry."

"This thing, is it the mirror?"

He paused for a moment. If he let Snow know the truth, she would be unduly worried. But if he kept it from her, she could be in peril unaware. In the end, he simply shook his head and said, "The girl inside the mirror."

Let her at least know what was transpiring. If he truly loved her, he should; he would not let her face fate unprepared.

"She is old, but she is young," he said.

"Atyanshvar," his brothers nodded and said again.

"Nonsense," said Snow. "You dwarves have gone soft from all the dust in the mine," she said with a laugh, then crouched in front of the mirror and touched its face again. "She's barely beyond a child. Can't you see well? I am her elder by four or five years."

Leader came forward to stand beside her, his gray-mossed head level with her shoulder. He said nothing.

"I wonder if it's a door, or if it's just a window."

The girl inside the mirror heaved her small chest and crossed her arms. She smiled, but the corners of her mouth crawled down.

"I don't like it," he said.

"Pish," Snow said. "I bet she's sad."

"What makes you think that?"

"All girls who are alone are sad, Squash. I've seen only that rabbit with her, and I believe she is trapped somewhere. Maybe not inside the mirror exactly, but somewhere, and if we can see her, we need to help her."

Leader let his frown curl upward to a flat line but said nothing.

"Don't want to be a hero?" Snow asked.

Immediately Redbeard, Newbeard, and Tallest surrounded her, pushing him aside. "We want to be a hero, Snow," they clamored. "We'll be *your* hero."

She stroked their beards, each in turn, and kissed each on the forehead. He noticed the askew glance Redbeard and Newbeard shared, and he knew then that Newbeard was maturing into an adult of the species.

"The rabbit returns," he said, stepping between the young one and Snow.

"What's he doing?"

"Watch."

And they did. The white rabbit hopped to the girl and handed her several pieces of parchment, then stepped away and waited at her side. The girl all but ripped a quill from a desk beside her and shoved it into a small vial of black liquid. She opened the book beside her and fanned through page after page until she stopped. Then she smiled, nodded, and finally began to write, stopping only to check the book or look up at them through the glass.

Her eyes, he thought. They didn't echo the smile that settled in her lips.

After a few moments, the girl tossed the quill onto the desk and looked over the parchment. She nodded twice. Shook her head twice. Then nodded thrice more.

She rose from her chair so quickly that even he leaped back a few steps from the mirror along with Snow and his brothers. Shoving the parchment against the glass, she blocked her own image from their sight.

"It's some kind of writing," said Snow. "But I don't recognize it."

Leader stepped forward. "It's one of the old human tongues. From the time before my father's father's father."

"Can you read it?"

"I can," he said.

"And?" she asked, the lovely skin on her nose and lips scant inches from his own stubbed fig of a face.

Before he could answer, the parchment was jerked away and the girl fell to her knees. She lurched forward, facing the glass, her hands hitting the stone floor of her chamber hard. She screamed silently but kept her gaze locked onto Snow's face.

Snow, of course, seemed unable to turn away, her own stare captured by that of the screaming fair-haired girl.

Without warning, the girl vomited up flame and bile, her hair falling forward to soak in the mess.

Snow screamed and as Leader and his brothers watched, her legs gave way and she hit the ground in an awkward knot of legs and arms.

"Mirror, mirror on the wall, who's the fairest of them all?" The words broke the air between Alice and the glass, swirling in the space above her in colors she hadn't known in her birth world on the other side of the mirror.

She looked up, feeling more animal than human on her hands and knees, hoping for another glimpse of the dark-haired princess.

"No!" she screamed. "No! No! No!"

Her stomach lurched and the pain and fire climbed up her throat and found its way to the floor a second time.

"I was so close! So damned close!"

As she cried, the mirror's image faded and the view of the princess and the darshve was replaced by that of a beautiful woman with golden curls and a bosom that heaved with every breath. She sat in a large antechamber, surrounded by male slaves of several races, wearing only loin cloths, collars, and bracelets of iron. More cattle than men. Fit only for their queen's whims, whether to love or destroy.

Alice fought the image and tried to focus her thoughts on the princess, but the more she fought it the more her stomach emptied the impossible concoction of fire and bile onto the floor.

After thrice more ejaculating the painful mixture, she finally submitted to the witch's will—"For the last time, bitch!" she said through gritted teeth—and the anguish at last stopped.

As it did, the witch's room grew clear and focused in the glass.

"—est of them all?" she asked again.

Alice steeled her will to stand and face the woman.

"Well?" the woman said.

"You are very beautiful, Queen of the Kingdom That Once Was Mine. But there lives one whose beauty surpasses even yours, one whose natural comeliness outshines all that the dark arts have done to augment your loveliness."

"You lie!" the woman yelled and jumped up from her stool. She lifted it and threw it at Alice, but it merely bounced harmlessly away from the glass.

"One day you'll lose your temper and break the curse that traps me here, witch."

The Queen turned toward her slaves, sweeping her hand, nails extending like claws, in one wide motion. "Get out!" she spit. "Get out now!"

The men exited as one, none apparently willing to remain in the woman's company.

"I cannot lie, Queen of All My Family Used to Rule." Alice pushed her lips into a grin. "You know as well as I do, witch, that the curse with which you bespelled me will not permit me to lie to you."

"Cease your prattle, girl."

"I'm almost your equal in years, Stepmother." The word tasted like poison as she spoke it. But it went out like poison too, as was her intention.

"Enough," the golden beauty said. "Who is this wench who rivals me?"

Alice leaned in so close to the glass that she could almost kiss it. The Queen did the same, and the two held the silence for a moment.

"Well?"

And now it begins again, Alice thought. She laughed before answering.

"I command you to tell me, Stepdaughter."

Alice smiled again. "You know it is the daughter of my stepmother's fifteenth husband. You know in your heart that the beauty of your stepdaughter Snow will never fall second to your own."

The witch shrieked. Alice nodded and watched the golden curls fade away.

Snow pulled the cabinet from the wall, careful not to dump the clay dishes and bowls crashing onto the floor, and looked behind it. The mirror was nowhere to be found. The darling little troubles had hidden it away from her after she fainted.

She had awakened from the heat of the sun on her face. Her skin itched and had been pulled tight across her forehead and eyes, burning slightly to the touch.

The sun.

It had been too high for morning.

No, morning had come and gone, and the little men with it. She was alone in the cave and had little time to discover the secret of the girl in the mirror.

So she ignored the cleaning and instead searched throughout the cave for the mirror. She had to see the girl again. To help her. To learn what the words on the parchment had meant. With any luck, to set her free.

She could not let the girl go through torment like that she had seen, not again.

She was in exile, yes. Presumed dead, yes. Living in a cave, yes. Penniless, yes. But she was still a princess, damn it. And she would act like it.

The furnishings lay across the stone floor overturned and in piles as she examined every nook and hidey-hole large enough to fit the mirror. She even checked the floor for loose stones that could hide crannies and caverns below.

Nothing. Not inside anyway.

It had to be in the shed, then.

So out she went.

She took out the hammers and axes, then the picks and shovels, buckets both with holes and without, animal skins too numerous to remember how many and lay them on the ground outside between the shed and the garden. Then came bags of seed and watering baskets, followed by wineskins and mostly empty barrels of homemade ale.

At last the small structure was empty.

But there was still no sign of the mirror.

Had Squash taken it back to the mine?

"Damn him! He had no right." She kicked the wall. "Ouch!" she cried when her toe stubbed the stone wall, and she lost her balance and fell on her behind.

However, instead of hitting hard ground, she landed in soft, freshly shoveled dirt.

"Those sneaky little devils," she said aloud, and pushed herself off the ground.

She walked outside, crouching to avoid hitting her head on the way out, then returned with one of the shovels, really more a spade for her, but it accomplished the task. On hands and knees, never minding the filth staining her dress, she dug until she reached a layer of straw and twigs. Tearing away the nest-like cover, she soon caught a tiny reflection of her dirty dress.

"Those darling, sneaky rascals," she said.

Inspired by her success, she tore into the rest of the straw and made a hole large enough to pull out the mirror. Heavier than she expected, she struggled to lift it, but got it high enough finally to prop it on her knees and waddle out into the yard like a duck.

The sun looked down squarely from the western sky and she knew that her time was short.

Quickening her pace, she lifted the mirror higher, aiming for her thigh and hip, but it slipped and tumbled from her hands, landing glass side down on the rocky ground.

Snow fell to her knees and cried. She had destroyed the mirror, and her only chance to help the girl trapped inside. She dropped her hands, clasping them in her lap, in the fold of her dress, and let her tears drain down the dirt and dust on her face.

She looked less a princess than a scullery maid, a cinder girl, a common household servant now.

After several minutes, however, she stopped and crawled toward the looking glass. If it wasn't broken too completely, she might be able to fashion the pieces together again somewhat and perhaps even enough to do some remaining good for the girl inside.

When she reached it, she took a deep breath and flipped it over.

The damn thing was still intact. Not even scratched.

"It's a magic mirror," she chided herself.

She looked for her reflection but the dirt was so thick on the glass that she couldn't make out more than a dull shadow of something through it. Desperate to see the girl again, she gathered the hem of her dress, spit on it like she'd seen her friends do, and began to wipe it as clean as she could.

She was greeted not by her own reflection, but by the image of the blonde girl. No longer in pain, no longer coughing up fire and blood and bile. The girl simply sat in a wooden chair, gazing ahead, smiling at her.

Snow waved.

The girl returned the gesture.

"What do you want me to do?" Snow asked.

The girl shook her head.

"I don't understand." Snow lowered her eyes, focusing on the ground. "I want to help you, but I can't understand you."

The girl began to speak, but Snow couldn't make out the words. After a few minutes, the girl wrote the symbols again on the parchment tablet as before. Snow again shook her head.

"I can't read that. It's too old."

The girl yelled at her silently and threw the parchment on the floor.

Snow looked away and began to cry again.

"Don't cry, Snow." A hand on her shoulder, stubby and squat. Squash. "If this is the role we play in events, then we must play them as fate prescribes us." He took Snow's hand and helped her stand.

"You're home early," she said.

"We never reached the mine today. No sooner did we cross the mountain path than we saw the Queen's army on the march. At least three hundred fighting men behind her and she rides a dragon at the helm of the battalion. We hid in the woods for hours until we were certain she had passed rather than lead her here. There's precious little time, though, until she finds this place."

"My stepmother's army?"

"She is coming for *you*, Snow."

Snow dropped to one knee. Squash rested his hand on her shoulder.

"The girl. She is telling you to recite the runes along the frame."

"But I don't know—"

"She translates them into an old human tongue from hundreds of years ago. I know it because my father's father taught me the old tongues. But most of my kind has forgotten them."

"So you can recite it?"

He took Snow's hand. "No. I'm sorry. It must be read by one of royal blood." He squeezed gently. "But I can help you recite it."

Fourth Movement—And She Lived Happily Ever After

No sooner had Snow uttered the runic incantation than did the Queen's army top the mountain. The Queen led the charge, sitting across the neck of her dragon, a monstrous black and gold brute with a wingspan of several cottages and claws like broadswords. Beneath them her army marched toward the Deadlands, their boot steps resonating in unison so loudly that they could be heard all the way to the cave.

Even with the battle still nearly seven king's acres away.

Leader didn't care, though. He was busy dragging Snow away from the mirror, which had begun to pulse like a ring of water, flickering in ripples of glass and light and color. After a few moments, the glass grew still again.

"Is that it?" she said.

"Sadly, no." He stood between her and the glass, facing away from her, puffing out his chest to guard her from as much as his squat stump of a body would allow. "Remember this," he said, almost in a whisper. "This was not the best way, but it was the only way to save you."

"I don't under—" she started, but stopped.

A hand emerged from the glass.

Then the crown of a fair-haired head.

Then finally, the girl herself rose from the mirror and stepped away from it onto the ground.

She smiled at Snow, then glanced down at the surface of the mirror. Leader leaned in but saw nothing in its face but his own reflection.

The girl didn't look away. "Farewell, Ulysses. I shall miss you, old friend."

He couldn't resist the urge to peak again to see what he was missing. His whiskers itched from the need to see. Still, nothing returned his gaze but his own confused stare.

The girl turned, took a deep breath, looking into the sky.

"Home at last," she said and strode toward Snow.

Leader held his ground between them.

"If you've come to harm her ..." he said, deciding the threat was just as effective if unfinished.

"Harm her?" The girl laughed. "She saved me from an epoch of captivity. I've come to thank her."

She took another step toward Snow, but he held his ground.

"What did she open?"

"Just a portal for me to return home. I lived in this kingdom long before you were born, not long after your people were created from the mountains. Before your kind was banished to the Deadlands."

"I thought as much."

"It was my father, little darshve, who drove your kind away and made the land safe for humans."

"That was many, many years ago. Why return now, princess of ancient times?"

The girl lowered herself and knelt so that her face almost pressed against his own. "Because, creature of greed, this kingdom is my home, and was mine before it was stolen from my father by the one who now plays at being its Queen."

"Your time has past. You have a new kingdom." He pushed his face so that it touched hers, and she wrinkled her nose and backed away. "This is no longer your world."

"It will be," she said and sidestepped him, reaching for Snow's hand. "Regardless, my name is Alice, and I am in your debt, princess."

Snow took her hand, and Leader glared at her. "Should I know you?" Snow asked. "I feel like I should somehow."

Alice laughed. "Had time not been stopped for me, I might have been your grandmother of many ages past. But as it stands, we will have to be satisfied being half-sisters."

He saw Snow's legs about to give way, and he steadied her.

"Sisters?"

"Yes. The witch who thought she killed you is also the one who stole my father from me. She killed him after she married him. Then trapped me inside the world beyond the mirror so she could have the throne to herself."

Leader could stand no more, and he tore Alice's hand from Snow's. "Enough. That witch, the Queen, comes now with an army to murder your half-sister. What can you do to stop that, Ancient Queen Alice?" he sneered.

She laughed again. "More than is needed, little beast man."

She pushed him aside and stood over the mirror, then recited a verse of runic tongue, and the mirror flickered and rippled again.

This time however, it did not stop.

Nor did a human hand emerge.

Instead a tendril rose above the glass, tapering into a mouth full of knifelike teeth, followed by another, then another, nearly thirty in all, and then a sinewy leg of muscle and visible bone, then two arms of similar makeup, each thin like tree limbs but taller than a full-grown oak, each ending in a tangle of claws long as Norse boat oars. Protruding from its back were two massive wings of thickened, dried blood.

When at last the beast stood completely in the world Leader knew as real, it towered over the cave and rivaled the mountain in height.

Leader and his brothers scrambled in the creature's shade for whatever cover they could find. Alice merely stood between the behemoth's gigantic legs and helped Snow regain her footing.

"Beware the Jabberwock," Alice said. "The bastard child of the elder gods."

High atop the Jabberwock, Alice watched as the foot soldiers of her ancient enemy ran for their lives. None survived, of course. Those who weren't trampled beneath the feet of the elder gods were gathered up by the biting tendrils and consumed alive, their screams blanketing the mountainside until only the Queen and her dragon remained.

She had tried to escape, flying away to the Northern lands, but the Jabberwock had been a mere trifle among the creatures of the oldest world, and kingdoms were but a footstep for the largest of them, and there was no place in the world she knew to escape their reach.

In the end, Alice simply waited for the elders to return from across the sea with the beast and the witch in their grip.

When they did return, the ancient creature tore the wings from the dragon and fed them to the youngest among them. Then they lay the beast on the ground before Alice and placed the half-dead form of the witch-queen beside her steed.

"What are these magnificent creatures?" the defeated woman asked.

Alice smiled. "They are my allies."

"They will destroy this world like they destroyed the one beyond the mirror."

"All worlds return to the green in time, witch."

The witch spit in Alice's face. "But you'll be long dead, girl. There's no magic here to keep you young."

"I've lived long enough, more than anyone should be allowed. It's enough for me to die in my homeland."

The witch shook her head. "I don't think so. You're corrupt now, just like me, just like your father would have become if I hadn't killed him."

Before she realized she had moved, Alice's hand snapped like a vine and struck the woman full in the face. "Don't mention my father, bitch!" she spat.

"Just like me now," the witch said again, wiping the blood from her lips with the back of her hand then tasting it. "You can't be satisfied with killing me. You have to conquer. Is that not what you've promised your allies?"

Alice looked up to see most of the elder gods already moving across the face of the land, some heading into the lands past the mountains and others walking toward the sea.

Someone tugged at her sleeve.

"Sister?" asked Snow. "Is it true? Have you promised our kingdom to these monsters?"

Alice grinned.

"I have. But I don't intend to keep that promise."

"You have a plan?"

Of course I do, Alice thought. But she said nothing.

"You were always a dim child, Snow," said the witch-queen. "You cannot trust your half-sister. Listen to the dwarves you've chosen to live with. They'll tell you."

Alice watched as the stubby darshve who had tried to protect Snow from her stepped forward. "We all have our parts." He pointed at the Queen. "Even her."

"Well said, little man."

Alice gazed up at the Jabberwock, her eyes seeing something she knew the rest of them couldn't see, her words entering places the rest of them couldn't go. Then she broke the stare and frowned at her stepmother.

The Jabberwock struck her with its claws, slicing the witch into three slivers of human pulp. Alice knelt down and picked up the first piece, the center cut, and cocked her head sideways. "Goodbye, stepmother," she said and tossed the flesh into the mirror, where it disappeared.

"You there," she said, motioning toward the darshve with a short blonde beard. "Help me, and I'll give you position and wealth in my new kingdom."

"I don't trust you," he said.

"Do you trust gold?" she asked.

"How much gold?"

"Newbeard!" her half-sister shouted.

"Enough." Alice stretched. "And human women, none so lovely as my sister, but the choicest females from lands far and near."

The little darshve stroked his beard for a moment, then looked at the old one, then at Snow, then back to Alice.

"And we'll be safe from those things?"

"Yes."

The creature looked at Snow again, then back to Alice.

"Make up your mind."

He nodded, and grabbed the left portion of the dead Queen. As he dragged it toward the mirror, the tallest of the darshve went over to help him. Alice watched as they lifted the flesh and tossed it into the mirror.

"Blood seals the magic."

She walked among the remaining darshve. "What of you, little ones? Would you prefer to live off the mountain dust or dine like princes in my palace with your beautiful wives from exotic lands?"

The others said nothing. But neither did they step forward to help dispose of the Queen's corpse.

Damn them, Alice though. Very well.

She locked eyes on the beast above her. Asked it for another favor, and instantly four of the little men lay dead, gutted at her feet.

"You chose poorly, little darshve." Alice looked at the dead darshve, then to Snow. "There's only one way to save this world, my sister."

The girl said nothing, only shuddered behind the old one.

"You can call them back to their own world, but only from inside the looking glass."

"All of them?"

"All of them."

"How many can enter?"

Alice took another deep breath. "I love this home air. Even filled with death, it calms me and helps me remember the way the land used to be."

"How many, Alice?" Snow tightened her gaze and it seemed to Alice that the girl had finally found some courage. Far too late, but an admirable discovery nonetheless.

"As many as who dare," Alice said. "So long as they go before you. Once you enter or I throw you in, the portal will close. Blood seals the bargain, not just my stepmother's blood but also the royal blood in your veins."

The girl knelt on her knees and called out, "Aspen! Come here, Aspen."

In a few moments, a dirty white dog ran from the edge of the forest to her and leaped against her chest to lick her face.

"Good dog, Aspen." The girl gathered the dog in her arms and carried it toward the mirror. "I'll join you in a moment." Then she set her pet on the mirror's face and it slid into the glass as though it were water.

Alice sighed. "Happy now, half-sister?"

"You'll die a normal death now."

Alice laughed and shook her head. "I've learned a lesson or two from the bo—" She stopped herself. "Damn! The book. I've left the book."

When she gathered her wits after a few seconds, she noticed the girl squatting down and whispering something in the old one's ear. He nodded. Then they clasped each other's hands and stepped onto the mirror.

In a moment, all Alice's allies began to moan in a low tone that shook the mountains. Then they simply faded away as if they had never been in the land at all.

"This isn't the end," the girl said.

"Wait!" Alice said, reaching for them too late as they disappeared through the glass. She turned to the two darshve who remained. "I want that damned mirror hidden in the mountains again and buried beneath a rockfall. No, two rockfalls. She is never to escape." She tightened her glare at the little men. "Never. Even if she learns the power contained in that volume." She bit down on her frown. "Do you understand me?"

She was certain they did.

Snow stared out the window of her chamber at the peaceful green and blue of the castle grounds.

The winters in the new kingdom were moderate, with little to no snow, and the temperatures remained just warm enough to enjoy the cold without freezing, but it wasn't home.

Back home, the trickster, the conniver, Alice, sat in her father's castle, entertained guests in her father's banquet hall. But that wouldn't last. It couldn't. She would see to that. The ancient leather book Alice had left behind would help her, even if she couldn't yet comprehend it. But she had time to learn.

Footsfalls thumped softly behind her.

"Snow?"

"Squash?" she asked. "How was the hunt?"

"Productive. I must admit that I enjoy this new land. And Aspen delights in the fields around the castle. He's like a pup again."

"But it's not home," she said.

"Alas. It is not."

"What did you bring us?"

"Four harts and a boar. Enough to feed all the castle servants well."

Snow nodded. "Tell the cook that I will prepare the stew tonight. I've missed cooking for someone all these years."

"I will," Squash said and turned to go.

But he stopped when she cried out.

"Again?" he asked.

She nodded.

"Don't fight it."

She shook her head. "I'll always fight *her*."

The pain in her gut twisted and burned, and her throat constricted.

The air above her rippled and spoke in the hateful voice of her half-sister. "Mirror, mirror on the wall…."

Anne-droid of Green Gables

By

Lezli Robyn

T he Station Master whistled to himself while the steam engine puffed into the small Bright River station, rocking back and forth on the balls of his feet as he checked his brass pocket watch to verify the arrival time for his logbook. He had been told to expect an important delivery today, and so he was personally going to oversee the unloading of the cargo carriage. There wasn't much excitement to be had on Prince Edward's Island, so he was very curious as to what the package contained; he'd been told to unpack the box with care upon arrival.

The train chugged slowly to a stop, and the Station Master scanned the carriages to see if all was in order before pressing an ornate but bulky button on his lapel pocket. It whirred perceptively and then emitted a piercing whistle to alert the passengers that the train was safe to disembark.

He tilted his hat in greeting to the first young lady to step onto the platform, but she didn't have eyes for him. She was gazing about her with a soft smile on her face, smoothing out her skirts. So he made his way to the back of the train, signaling for Oswald to keep watch on the platform while he began to search for the precious cargo, and wondering why the owner hadn't arrived yet.

On the way he detoured to pull a brass lever on the side of a machine fixed to the platform near the last carriage door. The device wheezed to life, numerous brass and wooden cogs beginning to whirl around, steam pumping out of several exhaust valves as the leather conveyer belt sluggishly sprung into action. He then walked into the carriage and lit the gas lamp hanging just inside the doorway, automatically picking up and placing all the small packages and bags onto the conveyer belt so they would be transferred to the station office for sorting.

He paused when he came across a large trunk in the dark recesses of the carriage, the layer of dust that shrouded it a testament to its long journey on more trains than this one. He grabbed the lantern and held it over the trunk, wiping the corner clean to expose the sender's stamp.

"LUMIERE'S REFURBISHED MACHINES-TO-GO"

Satisfied, the Station Master pulled out his Universal Postal Service key and inserted the etched brass device into the leather buckle locks that were holding the lid of the trunk down. He heard a perceptible whir as the key activated in each lock, and they sprung open. He paused, his hand hovering just above the lid, wondering what he would find in the trunk. It was not often that city machines, even refurbished ones, made their way to the tiny coastal towns.

His curiosity got the better of him. The stamp told him that the trunk would be too heavy to carry off the carriage without extra help, so he knelt down, checked that all of the buckles had completely disengaged, and lifted the lid slowly.

Only to find himself looking into a pair of brilliant green eyes.

They blinked and then focused on him.

His blinked too, very rapidly, his mind a jumble of uncoordinated thoughts.

A small hand reached out of the trunk and took the lid from the Station Master's frozen grasp, pushing it completely open.

The man's mouth fell agape in response, as he stared anew at the trunk in wonder. Matthew Cuthbert had always been a man of few words, but his reticence in this case was a little extreme. A machine indeed!

There, pulling itself into sitting position, was an *android*. The Station Master had never seen one of those sophisticated machines before, and he didn't know how to go about interacting with them.

"Are you my new Father?" the android asked.

He shook his head somewhat absently, gathered his wits together, and rediscovered his voice. "Your new owner will be here soon," he offered gruffly. He gestured towards the carriage doorway. "Shall we go wait for him?"

The android looked towards the doorway and then back to him. "I can go *outside*?"

Again, he was taken aback. "Of course. If you want to meet your new owner you *have* to."

He stood up and hesitated, looking down at the android sitting in the battered travel trunk, and then reached down. A dainty hand rose to meet his, and he was startled by its warmth. For some reason he had expected android skin to be cold. Lifeless.

Like a machine.

But, instead, the hand he clasped in his own felt like that of a child. Somehow that thought put his mind at ease. He helped the android out of the trunk and then stepped out of the carriage, turning back to see what such an advanced machine would make of their humble station.

The android moved tentatively into the light and the Station Master gasped. It was female in form! He had previously thought all androids were made to appear androgynous.

He watched her look up in wonder at the sun when she felt its rays fall upon her face. In the full sunlight her skin shimmered with a slightly golden hue, but that was not her most distinguishing feature. It was her hair—or more the point, her two braids of very thick, decidedly red, woven copper filaments that fell down her back. The worn sailor hat didn't disguise the brilliance of the fine metallic strands, nor did the yellowed threadbare dress detract from the elegance of her form. While too slender to be considered very feminine, and her face too angular to ever be considered classically beautiful, she was a striking figure with her huge expressive eyes and the delicate brass nails that graced her little fingers.

In one hand the android held a carpet bag that had clearly seen better days, but she was holding it with such care that the Station Master couldn't help but be intrigued. He'd never considered the fact that an android could have luggage; it must have been stowed in the trunk with her.

She moved forward, turning around slowly as if to soak everything in, but when she spotted the conveyer belt she walked up to it, curious, and without preamble started fiddling with the various levers and cogs on the side with her free hand, only flinching—but not pulling back—when the steam from one valve hit her.

She had clearly done this before. Her tiny hand fit into the tight spaces to tweak this or that with such precision that within minutes the machine was running smoother, much to the Station Master's astonishment. She kept working until the chugging sound of the machine had turned into a soft purr, and then she turned back to the Station Master, who stammered his thanks.

"Oh, no need to thank me," she replied. "This machine is a primitive version of the sorting machines I used to operate at my previous home every day. It's such a pleasure to be able to work out how things operate, don't you think?" The android didn't give him the time to answer. "I've always thought so. There is something beautiful about seeing a machine work to the optimum of its capacity."

The Station Master couldn't agree more. He couldn't take his eyes off the android in front of him. She was an absolute marvel. He wondered where her new owner was.

He turned slightly and gestured towards the station building. "Would you like to wait in the Ladies Sitting Room until Mr. Cuthbert arrives?"

She tilted her head, considering both him and his offer. "No thank you," she replied. "I'll wait outside. There's more scope for the imagination."

The Station Master smiled. What a charming girl.

Matthew Cuthbert looked at the android from the far end of the platform and hesitated. He had never been much of a conversationalist, and had always found talking to girls to be one of the most awkward experiences in the world, so it was daunting for him to discover his most recent purchase was female in form. He had been told that he was buying a prototype whose model had never been put on the production line, but he hadn't thought to ask about gender.

He couldn't help but be intrigued, however, despite his anxiety. Androids had first been created to replace the child workforce in the factories that were expanding throughout the major cities. For many years children had often been the cheapest and most practical workers because their tiny hands and slight forms meant that they were able to manipulate delicate machinery, and so naturally the androids were modeled after them. But their creators soon discovered that their clientele did not want their new workforce looking like children—innocents. Nor did they like that the prototypes were created with advanced problem-solving skills, because some people believed it gave the androids individuality as they adapted to what they learnt, leading them to want to try new things outside the factory walls. As a consequence, the androids that eventually populated the factories all over Canada were created to be completely unremarkable in their subservience and androgynous appearance.

Matthew couldn't fathom how they could be considered superior in design to the original prototypes, but he wasn't going to complain. It meant he could afford to buy the "flawed" machine sitting on the platform in front of him.

He took a deep breath and walked towards the android—and then right on past. He realized at the last moment that he had no idea what to say to her. *How exactly does one greet an android?*

He reached the end of the platform, and stood there for a minute before turning around to see the android now eying him with evident curiosity. Matthew wondered what such a sophisticated machine would make of him, for he was very unassuming in appearance. Tall, with lank shoulder-length hair that was now more steel-colored than the black of his youth, he had a stooped frame, as if his very posture reflected his wish to not stand out in a crowd. But the shy smile he gave the android when he finally walked up to her was welcoming, and his eyes were kind. Before he even had time to consider how to greet her, the android had stood up and reached out her hand.

"You must be my new father, Matthew Cuthbert of Green Gables." She shook his hand in greeting, still clutching the carpet bag to her side. "I'm Anne—Anne with an *e*. Most people believe that Anne is short for *android*, and so often they leave off the *e* when they write it down. However the *e* is the letter that completes the name. If I met someone else called Anne, but spelt without the *e*, I just couldn't help but feel they were somehow lacking. What do you think, Mr. Cuthbert?"

He blinked, surprised. "Well, now, I dunno." He had a simple intelligence, but he wondered if the android was expressing her insecurities about being accepted. And more important, did she *know* she was doing that? "Can I take your bag?"

"No thank you, Mr. Cuthbert. I can manage. I have to make sure I hold the handle with a 43-degree tilt at all times or it's prone to falling off. An extra degree either way and the bag has an 82 percent chance of losing its structural integrity. It's a very old, very dear carpet bag."

Matthew smiled at the unexpected mix of technical evaluation and human sentiment in Anne's statement, seemingly fitting for a machine made in Man's image. He gestured for the android to follow him, and they made their way to his horse and buggy in silence, Matthew looking at the ground, and Anne looking at everything else.

She appeared captivated by the most commonplace things. Even while one of the very rare and expensive steam-operated carriages rolled on by with the girl from the train gracing its leather seat, protecting her fair skin with her lace parasol, Anne's attention stayed focused on the old draft horse hitched to Matthew's buggy.

"I'm at a loss to see how you power this locomotive," she replied after a moment.

The corner of Matthew's mouth twitched, and he ducked his head to hide a smile, realizing that the android had never seen a horse before, and that this particular one was close to comatose.

He walked up to the horse, rubbing the gelding's neck gently, prompting him to shake out his mane and seemingly coming to life. "There are no steam-generated levers needed to operate this buggy. I just tell Samuel here to pull it for me."

The android blinked. "Samuel isn't a machine?"

"No," he said simply.

"But this creature's purpose is to serve humans?" she asked, her head tilting to the side.

Matthew's hand paused mid-stroke. "Well, yes, I suppose in a way that's true."

"Does it have free will?"

This time it was Matthew who blinked. "He lives and works on my farm."

She didn't miss a beat. "Because he has no other choice."

"Yes."

She nodded to herself. "I understand."

Matthew was struck by how definitive her answer was. "How so?"

"That existence was not unlike my life at the factory." She reached out her hand and gingerly mimicked Matthew's actions a minute earlier, her brass nails glinting in the filtered sunlight as she rubbed the horse's neck.

Matthew watched her for a long moment, then: "Did that bother you? Being told what to do all the time, I mean."

"No. Why would it?"

Matthew didn't know how to reply.

Anne continued on, almost absently. "I like to learn, and to keep busy. I also like to discover how things work. The Supervisor told me that that was a flaw in my make-up, and that I had to be terminated. I didn't know why I was going to lose my job when I had just surprised him by halting production of the main sorting machine in the factory to improve its performance by 6.3 percent, but he wouldn't listen to me anymore." Her hand stilled, and the horse head-butted her to resume. "It was Father who intervened. He told the Supervisor that termination was too final a punishment, and that I could still be of some use. However, I don't understand what he meant by that comment, because I no longer work for the company."

Matthew's depleted bank balance told him exactly how Anne had still been of use to the company, but it was her naiveté that fascinated him the most, not the reason why she had been sold.

The journey home was filled with more discoveries for them both, the android talking non-stop and the man appreciating the fact that she didn't expect him to talk too.

"You and I are going to get along just fine, Mr. Cuthbert."

"Call me Matthew."

"I'm not sure why I know this, or why I know I belong at Green Gables, but I've always thought there was more...."

The android stopped mid-sentence, her crystal green eyes going wide as her eyes fixed on the sky in front of her. For a moment Matthew couldn't take his eyes away from Anne's face, struck by how the sense of wonder really bought her features to life. But her attention didn't waver, so he drew his gaze away from her striking features to look up and see an airship sailing gently through the sky, the golden light of the setting sun lapping against the hull as it gently surfed the clouds.

It was barely perceptible to Matthew, but he was sure that Anne could hear the whir of the enormous steam engine at work, pumping hot air into an enormous canvas balloon that the old seafaring ship was now suspended from.

"What a wondrous invention!" the android breathed in amazement.

Matthew looked back at her in surprise. "How so?"

She turned to him with bright eyes. "This machine gives you the ability to fly, which would be one of the most incredible experiences. Imagine being able to look down at the world! It would create such a sense of freedom, don't you think?"

He nodded. He'd never thought of it that way before.

"Have you ever considered flying in one of those machines?"

"No, I can't say as I have," he replied, intrigued by her child-like curiosity.

"Oh, Matthew, how much you miss out on!" They both looked back up at the airship in shared silence for a long minute.

Matthew glanced at Anne out of the corner of his eye, amazed that such a sophisticated machine could be in such awe of an old seafaring ship that had clearly seen better days. It had been hobbled to a simple canvas balloon and operated by the most cumbersome steam engine he had ever encountered, simply so its owner could maximize his resources and try to keep at the cutting edge of the transport industry. He supposed the idea was ingenious, but the execution didn't strike him as being very safe or too elegant.

"I have worked with many machines," the android said quietly, her gaze still on the airship as it disappeared slowly over the horizon, "but I have never seen one that was so beautiful."

"I have," Matthew responded in his quiet, shy manner. "*You.*"

She turned to him, her eyes now wide. "But I'm just a girl."

The innocence in her statement went straight to his heart. Matthew had never been one to talk much, but now he was literally speechless.

She didn't see herself as a machine!

Although he didn't realize it at the time, that was the moment *he* stopped seeing her as one too.

🜉   🜉

Anne discovered that being accepted by her classmates at school wasn't something she could learn from an instruction manual. When she queried Matthew about how to secure a Bosom Friend, he simply told her to "Be yourself," which puzzled her as she couldn't physically be anyone other than herself anyway. When she asked his wife the same question, however, her curt response was "Forget that nonsense! If you prove your worth, friendships will seek you out. Be kind, considerate, and above all, bite that tongue and mind your manners!"

"Biting my tongue will help facilitate friendships?" Anne asked, perplexed.

"You do beat all, girl! Of course not," Marilla replied, frustrated. "It's an expression—a human expression. But then, I suppose you shouldn't be expected to know that."

The old lady sighed, looking at the android. Ever since Matthew had bought Anne home, the peace and order at Green Gables had been thrown into disarray.

"We have to send her back," she had told him the very first hour he'd returned home with the android.

"But she's such a sweet little thing," he had replied softly as he watched Anne walk around the house for the first time, reaching out her hand to touch the most random of things in fascination: the intricate embroidery on the tablecloth, the leaves of a plant, or the polished wood of the rocking chair. She had never seen such diverse textures before.

"Matthew Cuthbert, the entire reason for buying an android in the first place was so you can have help on the farm. It's unseemly to put a girl to work in the fields, even if she is android in form. And we're both too old to be nursemaids to a flawed machine."

"She's not flawed—just different." Matthew paused. "Give her a chance, Marilla."

"We'd have to put her through school, simply so she can learn the basics of interacting in society."

"So she'll go to school."

"But what is the point of buying an android if we can't get our money's worth out of her? There is still the matter of you needing help on the farm."

"I'll hire Barry's boy out for a couple of hours during the day, and Anne can help me before and after school." He held up his hand to forestall Marilla's next protest. "We can't afford to buy a normal android. And the simple fact is: I like her." He looked at his wife. "I don't ask for much, but I'm asking for this."

Marilla harrumphed, more to cover her shock than out of any deep need to protest. This was the first time her husband had ever stood up to her and held his ground. This machine must have really gotten under his skin. "The android can stay," she stated finally, "but strictly on a trial basis. We have a three-month warranty, don't we?"

"Yes."

"Then if I'm not impressed by that time, we are returning her for a full refund. And I want no protests, Matthew. That is my condition for letting her stay now."

Matthew nodded, satisfied. He knew that despite the condition, he'd just won a great concession from his wife.

And so every morning Matthew came downstairs to the library at five to find Anne engrossed in one of his books, looking more like the child she appeared to be as she acted out the plays with enthusiasm, the dying light of the fire dancing about in her copper hair. They would talk about her latest literary discoveries of the previous night while Matthew ate his breakfast, and then their day would start, the android helping Matthew milk the cows, muck out the stables, and carry out all the hay for the animals until it was time for her to leave for school.

Within a week they had developed a comfortable routine, and Matthew was surprised to discover that for the first time in a decade he actually enjoyed getting up before the birds awoke. However, it soon became clear after a few weeks of school that Anne hadn't been able to make as favorable an impression on her classmates, who were quick to point out how different she was.

"People don't often like that which they don't understand," Marilla had told the android matter-of-factly.

But Anne had read about "kindred spirits" and how true bosom friends are accepting of all differences, and as Marilla had said, she just had to prove she was worthy of being a perfect friend.

So every day she went to school and tried to prove herself by excelling in her classwork. She had much to learn, having only known factory life before Green Gables, but it didn't take long until she was tied with Gilbert Blythe for first honors.

And still the classmates' attitude towards her didn't noticeably thaw. The android couldn't understand why. Wasn't she doing everything right?

"You think you are better than us, don't you, Miss Anne-*droid*?" was Josie Pye's snide comment after Anne won her first spelling bee. She twisted around at her desk to look directly at Anne. "Can you spell *machine*?"

Anne looked at her in puzzlement. *Is this another test?* "M-A-C-H-I—"

"Do you always have an answer for *everything*?" Josie interrupted, frustrated that she could never get a rise out of the copper-haired girl.

"Isn't the correct response to a question an answer?" she asked, still puzzled.

Josie glared at her and faced forward again, not speaking to her until their extracurricular painting class that evening. "I'm sure you are perfect at that too," she muttered.

"I don't know," the android replied. "I've never painted before."

The class set up outside to capture the majesty of the rolling fields of Avonlea on canvas. Nestled in the tree line along the horizon, Anne could see the roof of Green Gables, and so she painted that first, her strokes precise and her measurements exact.

Then she moved to the fields, taking care to note the exact hue of the grass and blending the appropriate golden-hued green. Within fifteen minutes the field was done, complete with fences drawn to scale.

While Anne was busy duplicating the trees on her canvas, the teacher went up to each student in turn to ascertain their progress and study what their diverse depictions of the one view told him about their personalities.

When he approached Anne, his eyebrows raised at the quality of the painting. Then they furrowed. "Well, it's technically perfect," he said, and he sat down to start his painting.

Diana Berry looked up from her canvas as Anne was starting to outline the clouds. The raven-haired beauty glanced at Anne's painting, her blue eyes going wide. "Oh Anne! I wish I could paint half as good as you do!"

"Honey, you don't need to be talented with looks like yours," Gilbert Blythe quipped from somewhere behind them. The other students snickered and the light disappeared out of Diana's eyes. She returned them to her painting.

Anne looked up from her masterpiece to discover the clouds had moved. Quickly she started painting their new position over the clouds she had already started to form.

Then she noticed that the sun had changed position. Its lower angle threw a deeper amber cast onto the field. Frantically she started to mix up a different shade of green to replace the grass she'd painted earlier.

Then she noticed that the new position of the sun meant that Green Gables was completely in shadow, rendering the cottage almost invisible to the naked eye. So Anne painstakingly painted it into a silhouette.

Then she looked up to see salmon pink was starting to outline the bottom of the clouds, and a peach was spreading across the horizon. The sun was setting.

Her efforts to keep up with the changing colors of encroaching night meant her painting strokes increased to inhuman speed—and she *still* couldn't keep up. Every time she looked up, her painting was no longer accurate. The trees were now completely black along the horizon, and the fences cast long shadows across the field.

She stopped, at a loss for what to do. As a result of changing the colors in the sky so often and so quickly in a blur of hand and brush, the layers didn't have enough time to dry, resulting in the salmon pink blending with the earlier lighter blue shades. Her sky was now a mauve color. It was a restful shade, throwing a slightly romantic mood over the painting, but all Anne could see was that it wasn't an accurate depiction.

Josie snickered. "It looks like Anne can't do everything right after all."

"Don't listen to her," Diana said, a little pointedly. "Josie doesn't think of anyone but herself." She looked at Anne's painting. "Why did you keep changing the colors? Not that it looks bad," she added hastily, "but your painting looked perfectly fine before."

"The colors are all wrong."

Gilbert appeared over her shoulder, his usual nonchalant stance dissipating in his interest. "In what way?" he asked.

"We were told to paint this view." Anne gestured in front of her. "But the colors keep changing. This painting is no longer accurate."

"A painting doesn't have to be technically accurate for it to be considered a masterpiece," the teacher interjected, only his blond hair visible at the top of his canvas as he continued to paint. "It's how you interpret the view that brings the painting to life."

"I don't understand," said Anne.

"Take a look at mine," Diana offered, a little shyly.

Anne stood up and walked over, studying the painting for a long moment. "The clouds are the wrong shape."

"Not the *wrong* shape, Anne. Just a *different* shape," she replied. "It's a matter of perspective. Take a closer look."

The android tilted her head to the side, as she always did when she was thinking, and considered the clouds Diana had painted. They were perhaps a little too white. Also the strokes she used to define the texture of the clouds were too coarse to depict the lightness of the gossamer structures.

"Pretend they aren't clouds," Gilbert interrupted her thoughts. "What else do you see?"

Anne considered the shapes of the clouds and nothing else, and automatically started comparing them to images in her memory banks. "They're animals!" she blurted out suddenly, Diana laughing as the android's eyes darted up to the sky. Sure enough, she could see the remnants of some of the clouds Diana had painted. If she looked closely enough, she could see what looked like a rabbit bounding over the horizon. "How did you know to do this?" she asked finally.

"I just used my imagination," Diana replied, blushing delicately at the attention.

"But androids don't have an imagination, do they, Gilbert?" Josie pointed out, twirling her hair around her finger.

"Knock it off, Josie." Gilbert replied. "Nobody's perfect. She just had to know how to look."

Anne didn't hear them. She was still trying to process what she had just learned. "So Diana's painting is better than mine, even though mine is technically more accurate."

The teacher leaned around his easel. "*Better* is not the right word. It's a more *realized* painting." He paused, trying to work out how to explain it. "Your painting shows us how you—or anyone here—physically sees the fields, but nothing more. It doesn't show us anything about *you*."

She analyzed his words carefully, and found herself, as well as her painting, lacking. "So I have failed."

"No, not necessarily." The teacher studied the android for a moment, aware that she'd probably never been confronted with failure before.

"It just means you've got more to learn." He smiled gently. "That is what school is for."

"Where do I start?"

Even Josie was struck by the earnest entreaty in the android's tone.

"Here and now," the teacher responded with a smile. "We've still got a half an hour of light."

The android sat down at her easel, unwilling to let the teacher know he had misunderstood her. She remembered what happened when the Supervisor at the factory had misunderstood her, and she didn't want to be sold again. She looked at her painting.

Where do I start?

"Do you see Green Gables in the distance?" Diana whispered into Anne's ear, leaning over in her chair. Anne nodded. "That is not merely where you live, but it's your *home*. What do you *see* when you think of home?"

Diana watched Anne's eyes blink rapidly for a few seconds, and then flitter back and forth across the painting. She reached for her paints and brush, and started mixing colors.

Diana watched, fascinated, while Anne started applying paint to the canvas once more. Her speed belied her android heritage as an airship quickly took shape amongst the clouds in the painting's mauve sky.

When the flying vessel was complete, she dipped her brush in a combination of pots and leaned forward. For a minute Diana could only see the back of Anne's copper braid as the android painstakingly painted a candlelit window onto the silhouette of the cottage, but then she leaned back and dipped her brush into black pot.

After considering the painting for a moment, the android started to paint a tiny profile of a human in the field closest to the cottage. When she also brushed in a little cattle dog beside the figure, Diana realized that it was Anne's depiction of Matthew returning to Green Gables after a hard day's work on the farm.

The android's hand hesitated beside the image of the man, and Diana wondered if the android understood what a lovely—and homely—image she had just created: the light from the kitchen guiding the man home at night.

But then the android's hand darted upwards, and another silhouette started to take shape at the bow of the airship. It appeared that the figure was looking down at the cottage, and when Diana saw that the silhouette wore her hair in a braid that was lifted by the wind, Diana started in shock.

Anne had drawn herself into the painting, and she was sailing on an airship, being guided home by the cottage light like a seafaring ship would a lighthouse.

Who said androids couldn't have an imagination? Diana thought triumphantly, looking at her new friend's painting with a smile on her face. *Anne might be a kindred spirit after all.*

Matthew pulled out his timepiece and opened the case to see where the clock hands pointed. "It's time to leave for school, Anne," he said quietly, sure that she could hear him from across the barn.

She looked up, blinking in surprise. "Usually my internal clock alerts me before now."

Matthew nodded, bemused. One of the things that endeared him the most about the android was that she could often get so swept up in her enthusiasm and curiosity for the current project she was working on that it overrode her most basic mechanical functions, like her inbuilt alarm clock. He knew that Marilla and Anne's creators considered that a manufacturing flaw, but to Matthew it seemed like a very human characteristic.

He watched her methodically put his tools back in order, and then cover the machine.

"I was nearly finished!" she complained.

"So you will finish it tonight."

"I suppose that is an acceptable conclusion," she replied.

Matthew laughed. *Was the android pouting?* "Well, my dear Anne, if this contraption of yours truly works and I never have to milk a cow again with my bare hands, then I will have the time to start teaching you chess before school tomorrow morning." He smiled at her. "Is that also an acceptable conclusion?"

It appeared to him that her eyes lit up. "More than acceptable, Matthew." She tilted her head, considering him.

Matthew blushed under her scrutiny and busied himself with closing his time-piece and running his thumb lovingly over the initials ornately carved across the lid before moving to put it away. He felt the android's curiosity before she voiced it. "It was my father's," he said quietly. He hesitated a moment, then held it out to her.

Anne appeared to understand the privilege she was being given. She took the pocket watch from Matthew with evident care, turning it around in her dainty hands to look at the initials, almost imperceptible on the old tarnished metal. She popped the lid open, and her eyes grew wide. She had never seen such a tiny machine. Behind the ornately carved brass hands, she could see the intricate wheels turn, and despite the discoloration of age, she thought it beautiful.

Matthew let the android hold his timepiece the entire way to school, the light reflecting off Anne's brass nails as she tinkered with it, drawing his attention to the advancement of her construction in comparison to his beloved pocket watch. The 19th century had seen a huge evolution in machines, and he wondered what the next century would bring if Anne was the pinnacle of this one.

The buggy started rocking more than usual, with Samuel having to navigate more ruts as a result of the storm the previous night, but when Matthew briefly glanced over at Anne he saw the pocket watch clutched protectively in her tiny hand.

She seemed almost reluctant to give it up when they reached the school, but then she heard Diana calling and she quickly handed it over, leaping out of the buggy with her usual enthusiasm and grace. She turned to Matthew to say good-bye, and he told her he'd be there at three to pick her up.

"No need, Matthew," she said. "Gilbert Blythe said he'd walk me to the bend, and I wanted to see the new flowers that have come out since the last rain."

Matthew smiled as he watched her rush off to greet Diana, wondering if she realized how human she sounded.

He shook his head at his folly. *Of course she knows. She doesn't see herself as a machine!*

He laughed as Samuel pulled the buggy away from school, and he returned home with a smile still on his face.

"What time do you call this, Matthew Cuthbert?" Marilla asked when he walked into the kitchen to share a pot of tea with his wife before going back to work on the farm.

He didn't know why, but by Marilla's clock he was always late. He pulled out his pocket watch to check—and discovered it was no longer working.

His heart sank in his chest. His pocket watch had never failed him until today, and it was his last tangible memory of his father.

He looked at it closely and he could see that part of the clock mechanism appeared dislodged behind the face, and when he shook it gently, he could hear something metallic rattle around. It appeared that an irreplaceable component was broken in his beloved timepiece.

Marilla saw the look on his face and asked him what was wrong. After he told her, she asked, "What, if anything, did you do differently with the pocket watch today?"

He thought back on his morning. "Nothing, really. I gave it to Anne to look at, and then let her hold it while we travelled through some storm-created ruts on the way to school." He paused, considering. "Come to think of it, those ruts really were pretty rough going. I wouldn't be surprised if one of them was what did it."

Marilla wasn't convinced. "Did you watch Anne the entire time she had your timepiece, Matthew?"

"I can't say as I did," he replied, wondering what his wife was getting at. "I had to concentrate on the road on account of those bothersome ruts."

Marilla was silent for a long moment, and then she asked, "Do you think the android could have tinkered with it? She seems fascinated with the inner workings of machinery."

"Anne was fascinated by the intricacy of my pocket watch," he admitted. "But...."

"Think about it, Matthew," Marilla interrupted. "My theory makes sense. The pocket watch had never broken down in your lifetime, or your Dad's, *until* the day you let Anne play with it."

He couldn't find any fault with her logic, but deep down in his heart he knew it wasn't true.

When Anne came home that afternoon from her walk with Gilbert Blythe, a posy of wildflowers in her hand, Marilla confronted her. "Did you fiddle with the mechanism in Matthew's pocket watch?"

Anne noted the agitated tone in her voice, and became concerned. "What's wrong with it?"

Marilla took that as an admission of a kind. "So you *know* something is wrong with it!"

"No, Marilla," Anne replied. "I honestly didn't." She looked at Matthew, who was quietly sitting in the kitchen chair, watching the exchange. He gave her a gentle smile of encouragement.

"I need a truthful answer from you, Anne," said Marilla. "Did you play with Matthew's watch until you broke it?"

"No, Marilla," said Anne truthfully, since she had no idea when it broke.

"Then who did?" demanded Marilla.

Anne simply stared at her. She'd been taught never to guess when she didn't know the answer.

Marilla glared at the android, trying to keep her temper in check. "Now listen to me carefully, Anne," she said at last, ominously enunciating every syllable. "If you don't admit that you've done wrong, and that you just lied to me, you will not be allowed to go to Diana's birthday airship flight next month."

Anne's mind quickly considered the possibilities and the consequences. If she did not admit to purposely breaking the watch, Marilla would not believe her and she would not be permitted to ride on the exotic airship. On the other hand, if she lied and admitted to breaking it, Marilla almost certainly *would* believe her and she would be allowed to go. It was very confusing: if she lied she would be rewarded, and if she told the truth she would be punished.

Which was worse—to lie and be believed, or to tell the truth and be doubted? In the end it was not the airship that was the deciding factor, but a desire to please Marilla by telling her what Anne assumed she wanted to hear, and what she obviously already believed.

"I broke the watch while I was playing with it," she said at last.

Marilla stared at her a long time before speaking. Finally she said, "All right, Anne. Cuthberts always keep their word, so you will be allowed to go on the airship."

"Thank you," said Anne.

"I'm not finished yet," said Marilla harshly. "As I said, Cuthberts don't lie. You just admitted that you lied to me. Therefore, you are not and never will be a Cuthbert. I'm going to have a serious talk with Matthew after you're in bed tonight. I think we're going to return you and get our money back. You are *not* what we were promised."

Anne was still staring at the empty space where Marilla had stood long after Marilla had turned and walked away.

Deep down Anne had known she was different from everyone else in Avonlea, and that she had the means to repair the pocket watch if she only just acknowledged it. She didn't know if she had refused to accept the truth about herself and had blocked it from her mind, or if she had simply been programmed to not think about it, but she had to confront it now if she was to ever help fix the damage she had inadvertently caused.

She pulled out her carpet bag, and for the first time since she'd arrived at Green Gables she opened it up.

Inside was a batch of tools, some of them not unlike those she was using to create Matthew's milking machine, only finer in construction.

Her delicate hand reached in and sorted through them until she felt the one she needed and pulled it out, looking at it for a long moment.

She hesitated, then unlaced the top of her nightgown, looking down at the barely perceptible panel outlined on the left side of her chest. Her right hand hovered above it, implement in hand, knowing instinctively what she had to do, but unable to take the next step. Then she thought of the pain she saw in Matthew's eyes when Marilla had decreed she had to be returned to the factory, and she steeled herself, placing the implement along one side of the panel and pressing it in, hearing a tiny whir as three micro-latches started turning. A section of her popped out, and she looked at it for a long moment before carefully hooking the brass nail of her thumb into the tiny crevice and pulling it open.

I'm a machine.

The realization struck her like a punch to the stomach as she stood staring at what she had revealed, unable to process anything for some time. Although deep down she had always known, it was still a shock to see tiny brass cogs, wheels, screws, and copper wires so intricately interconnected to a circuit board buried within her chest. It was a wonder to behold, even for the android.

She realized how primitive the pocket watch was in comparison, and yet she also understood its importance to Matthew, and her determination to repair it for him increased tenfold. She closed her eyes and tuned into the sounds her body made.

Tick, tick, tick, tick...

Her eyes sprung open, and she instinctively moved a bundle of copper wires that were covering the specific mechanism she needed to find. She analyzed the individual components, recognizing that some were similar to those in the pocket watch.

Tick, tick, tick, tick...

She rustled around in her carpet bag and pulled out a tiny toolbox, opening it to reveal delicate jewellery-grade tools. She selected one and used it to sever the connection between the tiny mechanism and her main circuit board without a second thought.

The ticking stopped.

The android's hand froze. She felt a strong sense of loss, and she couldn't focus. She had no idea how long it took her to adjust to the change in her body, because she literally lost track of time, but she finally was able to block out the feeling that she had lost something fundamental to her being when she realized how much more she'd lose if she had to leave Green Gables.

She carefully placed the little mechanism on the table in front of her and used the firelight to study it more closely. At first she had thought she'd wasted her time, but when she put the pocket watch beside it, she was able to compare the components more easily, and she could see they were of similar composition and size; they were just finished off differently.

Then she spotted it: the part she needed.

Using the precision that only an android could command, Anne very carefully detached it and transplanted it into the pocket watch within minutes. When the last part was in place, the pocket watch sprang to life.

Tick, tick, tick, tick...

Anne clapped her hands together in delight, an affectation she'd picked up from Diana. She knew that what she achieved that night was more important than any work she'd ever done on the factory floor—or at least, it felt that way to her.

She looked at the part of herself she'd transplanted into the pocket watch, studying her handiwork, unable to find it lacking. The new part stood out from the rest of the components because it was free of tarnish and more rose gold in color than normal brass. It also appeared more refined in composition, and she wondered if Matthew would mind the discrepancy.

She resealed her access panel and relaced the top of her nightgown before methodically packing her tools back into the carpet bag. She considered whether she should clean the brass and restore the pocket watch back to its original condition. But the cleaning agent she normally rinsed through her copper hair was in the bathroom upstairs, and she didn't want to risk waking the Cuthberts.

She picked up the pocket watch again to take it back to the kitchen where Matthew had usually kept it, and walked straight into someone.

"Anne! Give that to me immediately!" Marilla barked, standing in the doorway with a lantern in her hand. "You have been told you are no longer welcome in our house, and that means you are definitely not allowed to touch our things." She looked at the android pointedly. "Especially ones you've already broken."

Anne didn't trust herself to speak after the trouble her mouth had gotten her into earlier that day, so instead she simply held out her hand.

Marilla was taken aback by the silent acquiesce. She looked down to see the pocket watch still open on the dainty little hand, and she wondered what other heirlooms the android had played with while she and Matthew had been asleep at night.

She retrieved the pocket watch, inspecting it to see if it came to further damage—and her heart nearly stopped.

The pocket watch was working again!

She couldn't tear her eyes away from it; she was so surprised. Then she spotted the gleaming new part at the heart of the clock mechanism, and her breath caught. "Where did you get that?" Marilla asked, looking up at Anne sharply.

The android raised her hand and placed it on her chest where a human heart would be. "Here," she said simply, her head tilting to the side.

She had used a part of herself to repair the watch! Marilla realized what a huge gesture that was. "You didn't break the watch yesterday by playing with the clock mechanism, did you?" she asked quietly.

"No."

Marilla sighed. "Then why did you say you did when I asked?"

"You told me I couldn't go on the airship for Diana's birthday celebration next month unless I confessed to breaking it," Anne said, her big green eyes seeking Marilla's out in entreaty. "So I confessed."

"But that's lying, Anne," Marilla pointed out.

"You wouldn't believe the truth."

Marilla sighed again. "So you thought you were giving me the answer I wanted. You were trying to please me." She looked back down at the repaired pocket watch. "Let us make a deal, Anne: I will forgive you for lying, if you will forgive me for not believing you."

"What is this about forgiveness?" Matthew asked, as he, too, walked into the room.

Marilla ate some humble pie. "You were right," she admitted, and without saying any more she handed over the pocket watch.

Matthew brought the timepiece closer to his lantern to study it. That it worked again was no surprise to him. He had a feeling Anne would try to repair it after watching her dedication while building his milking machine. But what he didn't expect to see was the glint of a new component in the clock mechanism that differed in color from the rest of the watch. He looked over to Anne in shock when he recognized its construction was far more refined than the rest of the watch's components.

Anne's green eyes twinkled. "I'll never be on time for school again," she said, and Matthew realized she'd used a component from her internal clock to bring his father's beloved pocket watch back to life.

He knew what a sacrifice that must have been for the android, and his heart reached out to her, knowing that in a way he held a piece of hers within in his hand.

He walked up to her and kissed her on the forehead, much to her and Marilla's surprise. "You'll just have to learn how to tell the time like us average folks," he said as he stepped back, his voice a little gruff with emotion.

"*I'll* teach you, Anne," Marilla stated. "If you learn from Matthew, you'll never arrive anywhere on time."

Anne had always thought that sailing on an airship would give her a sense of freedom unlike any other experience in the world.

She was wrong.

Yes, it was exhilarating. Yes, she felt on top of the world—quite literally—as she leaned over the bow of the ship, the wind lifting her copper hair as the vessel passed through another cloud bank. But she soon realized that she was just a spectator watching the world pass her by. There was some peace to be discovered in that, but she had no control over that journey; she just had to enjoy the ride.

She knew now that her first true taste of freedom had been when the Station Master had released her from the cargo trunk at the train station three months ago—she just hadn't been aware of it at the time. She had stepped out into a brand new world, with sensations she'd never even known had existed, let alone experienced, and for the first time in her brief life she had the opportunity to be accepted. Appreciated.

Loved.

No longer was she being told how to perform her every action like an auto-mated machine. She had to learn and adapt to the ramifications of her actions like everyone else, and deal with any consequences that arose. There was a great sense of freedom in being in control of her own destiny that she'd previously been denied until she'd met the Cuthberts.

Her keen android eyes searched the fields far below her until she spotted Green Gables nestled along the treeline. As she gazed at it she felt a sense of belonging that she'd never experienced before.

"We would like to adopt you," Matthew said quietly when she had hopped off the airship not long after, halting her excited rambles about how the journey through the clouds had given her such scope for the imagination.

"But you have already bought me," Anne replied, perplexed, as she considered Matthew's shy smile.

"That's true," said Marilla, "and what an expensive girl you were, to say the least." She brushed off her skirts briskly, and then looked directly at the android, who returned her gaze. "But we don't want to *own* you," she added, reaching over to take hold of Matthew's hand. "We want to know if you would *choose* to become a part of this family as the child we never had, and never knew we'd even wanted until you came into our lives."

Anne stared at both of them, and for the first time since they met her, she was speechless.

In that moment she became Anne of Green Gables.

She had finally come home.

Little Women in Black

By

Louisa May Alcott and Rick Hautala

C hristmas won't be Christmas without any presents," grumbled Jo, sitting on the rug before the fire. She had a ball of yarn in her lap and, like her sisters, was busily knitting socks to send to the soldiers. Her hands moved somewhat clumsily because of the linen gloves she wore to cover up the scars, scabs, and open wounds on her hands. Even now, a few of them were bleeding through the thin fabric, making random blossoms of bright scarlet.

"It's so dreadful to be poor," sighed Meg, looking down with frustration at her old dress.

"It's not fair for some girls to have pretty things, and other girls nothing at all," added little Amy, with an injured sniff.

"We've still got Father and Mother ... and each other," whispered Beth from her dark corner by the fireplace.

The three young faces on which the firelight shone brightened at the cheerful words so faint they could have been a thought in each one's mind, but their expressions darkened again when Meg said sadly, "But we *haven't* got Father … and the other dear one we lost and miss so much."

"We haven't lost Father," remarked Jo. "He's just away at the war."

"But we shan't have him for a very long time," added Amy, staring at the fire wistfully.

She didn't have to add the phrase "perhaps never," but each girl silently did as they paused to think of Father, far away down South. He was serving as a chaplain in Mr. Lincoln's Army, so he wouldn't see battle directly, but there were many other dangers of war he must face daily. How, each of them wondered, would all of that have changed him when he returned? How could it not help but change him from the kind, loving father they all knew and loved so much?

Nobody spoke for several minutes, the only sound the rhythmic clicking of knitting needles. Then Meg said, "You know the reason Mother proposed us not having any Christmas presents this year is because it is going to be a dreadfully hard winter for everyone, not just our troops. She thinks we ought not to spend any money for trinkets or silly pleasures when our soldiers are suffering so."

"We can't do much," added Jo, "but we can make little sacrifices and ought to do so gladly, I suppose." She paused, and then added sullenly, "But I'm afraid I don't do it gladly. I miss Father so."

Meg shook her head as she thought regretfully of all the pretty things she wanted and might never have.

"I don't think the little we would spend would do any good for the soldiers," said Amy. "We've each got a dollar, and the army wouldn't be much helped by our giving that away."

"I agree not to expect anything from Mother or you this season, but I so much want to buy Mr. Hawthorne's newest novel," Jo said.

"I had hoped to spend mine on some new sheet music," said Beth with a low, wistful sigh that no one heard but the hearth brush and kettle holder. Her pale face floated in the darkness like the moon, obscured by clouds, wavering and dimming. Meg cast a glance in Beth's direction and shivered as though she had caught a draft.

"Well, I shall get a nice new box of Faber's drawing pencils," declared Amy. "I really do need them."

"Mother didn't say anything about *our* money," cried Jo, "and she won't wish us to give up everything. Let us each buy what we want for ourselves and have a little fun. I'm sure we work hard enough to earn it."

"I know I certainly do, teaching those tiresome children all day when I'm longing to enjoy myself at home," said Meg.

"You don't have half such a hard time as I do," said Jo. "How would you like to be cooped up for hours on end with a fussy old lady like Aunt March, who keeps me trotting back and forth, is never satisfied, and worries me till I'm ready to fly out the window or break down and cry?"

"Don't fret," said Beth with a deep sigh that, when it ended, filled the room with a hush.

"I don't believe any of you suffer as I do," cried Amy, "for you don't have to go to school with impertinent girls who plague you if you don't know your lessons, and laugh at your simple dresses, and label your father as nothing but a poor minister."

"If you mean *libel*," said Jo, laughing, "I'd say so and not talk about *labels* as if Father were a pickle bottle."

"I say what I mean, and I mean what I say, and you needn't be satirical about it," said Amy, pouting with hurt dignity.

"Using that fine logic," said Meg, "you may as well say, 'I see what I eat, so I eat what I see.' "

"It's proper to use good words and improve your vocabulary," Amy replied with a huff.

"Don't peck at one another, children," said Meg, sounding more like Mother—their "Marmee"—than herself. "Don't you wish we had the money Father had when we were little, Jo? Dear me! How happy we were then, and how good we'd be now if we had no worries!"

"You said the other day that you thought we were a great deal happier than the Patterson children," Jo said, "for they are forever fighting and fretting in spite of their wealth."

"So I did." Beth said, shifting her gaze to the fire, sure she caught a gauzy flutter of motion in the darkest corner. "Well, I think we *are* happier, and all it will take to complete our happiness is for Father to return to us safely from the war. For though we do have to work, we are a jolly lot, all in all, as Jo would say."

"Jo does use such slang words," observed Amy, with a reproving look at the long figure now stretched on the rug. "At least I try to use a *vocabulary*."

Jo immediately sat up and, self-conscious of the scarlet splotches on her gloves, put her hands behind her back and began to whistle.

"Don't whistle like that, Jo. It's so … *boy*-ish," advised Meg. "It irritates me so."

"That's why I do it."

"Well I, for one, detest rude, unladylike girls," said Amy.

"And *I* hate affected, niminy-piminy little chits!" Jo responded, her hands shifting from behind her back and clenching into knotted fists.

"Birds in their little nests should all agree," said Hannah, their faithful servant, from the kitchen. Although Hannah had been with the family since even Meg could remember, her austere presence impelled both sharp voices to soften to gentle laughs.

"Really, girls, you are both to be blamed," said Meg, lecturing in her elder-sisterly fashion. "You are old enough to leave off boyish tricks and playing with your pet rat. You should have learned by now how to behave better, Josephine."

"I *don't* like being called *Josephine!*"

"That's why I call you that," Meg replied. "Such manners didn't matter so much when you were a little girl, but now you are grown. You should remember that you are a young lady."

"I am *not!* I'll wear my hair in pigtails until I'm twenty," cried Jo, pulling off her hair net and shaking down a lengthy chestnut mane. "I hate to think I've got to grow up and be 'Miss March,' and wear gowns and always look prim and proper. If I must be a girl, I wish I had never been born."

"Hush … to say such things," whispered Beth from the darkness, her eyes wide and empty.

Frustrated, Jo picked up her yarn and needles, and shook the blue army sock till the needles rattled like castanets. Then she flung the lot of them to the other side of the room, her ball of yarn bouncing as it unspooled across the floor.

"Poor Jo," sighed Beth, shifting forward. Her body was translucent against the firelight as she reached out and tried to stroke Jo's head with a hand that even death could not make ungentle. "It's too bad, but it can't be helped. So you must try to be content with making your name sound boyish and playing brother to your sisters."

"As for you, Amy," continued Meg, "you are altogether too particular and prim. Such airs are funny when you're young, but you'll grow up soon enough to be an affected little goose if you're not careful. And your absurd use of words is as bad as Jo's boyish slang."

"If Jo is a tomboy and Amy a goose, then what am I?" asked Beth, ready to share the discussion. But not one of the sisters heard her or, if they did, not one of them bothered or had the heart to respond. After a lengthy silence, Beth whispered ever so softly, "Can anybody hear me?"

The clock struck six, and after helping Hannah sweep the hearth, Amy placed a pair of slippers on the fender to warm up for Marmee. Somehow the sight of the old shoes had a good effect upon the girls, for they knew that Marmee would be home soon, and everyone brightened to welcome her. Meg stopped lecturing and lighted the lamps while Amy got out of the easy chair without being asked.

After recovering and rewinding her ball of blue yarn, Jo forgot how tired she was and held the slippers nearer to the blaze to warm them all the quicker.

"These slippers are quite worn out," said Jo wistfully. "Marmee must have new ones for Christmas."

"I thought I'd get her a pair with my dollar," said Amy.

"I'm the oldest," began Meg, but Jo cut her off with a decided, "Well, *I'm* the man of the family while Father is away, and perhaps I shall buy the slippers. Father told me to take special care of Mother while he was gone."

"I'll tell you what we'll do," said Meg. "Let's each of us get her something for Christmas, and not get anything for ourselves."

"That's so like you, dear!" exclaimed Jo. "What shall we get?"

Everyone thought soberly for a minute until Jo announced, as if the idea was suggested by the sight of her own glove-covered hands, "I shall buy her a nice new pair of kid gloves."

"How nice," said Meg, "when you are in such need to replace your own, which are so dreadfully stained."

Jo immediately hid her gloved hands behind her back.

"She wants nothing more than to see Father," whispered Beth from the darkness, although by their reactions, one would guess that none of her sisters heard her.

"Glad to find you so merry, my darling girls," said a cheery voice at the door, and the girls all turned to welcome their Marmee. Hannah watched this exchange from the kitchen, silent and as inscrutable as always. Marmee was not elegantly dressed, but she was a noble-looking woman nonetheless, and the girls thought the gray cloak and unfashionable bonnet covered the most splendid mother in the whole world.

"Well, my dears," Marmee said. "How have you got along today? There was so much to do, getting the boxes ready to ship out tomorrow, that I didn't come home to dinner. Has anyone come by? How is your cold, Meg? And you, Jo—you look tired to death. Come and kiss me, kiss me, my babies."

While making these maternal inquiries, Mrs. March got her wet things off, her warm slippers on, and sat down in the easy chair. Amy climbed into her lap, preparing to enjoy the happiest hour of her busy day while the other girls flew about, trying to make things comfortable for Marmee, each in her own way. Meg arranged the tea table, and Jo fetched more firewood from outside. Amy gave directions, as though her two sisters were her hired servants. And Beth reached out longingly to caress her loving mother's face, but her hands passed like smoke through Marmee.

As they gathered about the table and Hannah served them, Mrs. March said, with a particularly happy face, "I've got a treat for all of you."

A quick, bright smile went round like a streak of sunshine. Jo tossed up her napkin and cried, "A letter from Father! Three cheers!"

"Yes," said Marmee, "it's a nice long letter."

"How is he faring?" asked Meg, her brow creased with dark worry.

Marmee smiled and said, "He fares well, children, and thinks he shall get through the cold season better than we feared. He sends his loving wishes for Christmas, and an especial message to you girls."

"I think it is so splendid of Father to serve as chaplain even though he was too old to be drafted, and not strong enough to be a soldier," said Meg warmly.

"Don't I wish I could go as a soldier," exclaimed Jo. "Or perhaps a nurse, if I must, just so I could be near Father and help him."

"It must be very disagreeable, to sleep in a tent and eat all sorts of foul-tasting things and drink out of a tin mug," sighed Amy.

"When will he come home, Marmee?" asked Beth, with a little quiver in her voice.

Mrs. March paused, her expression falling. The room fairly pulsed with expectation until she said, quite seriously, "Father has been ill." Small gasps of shock and concern filled the room. "Once he recovered, he wanted to stay and continue his work as long as the war lasts, but he has been discharged and is on his way home."

Squeals of delight now filled the parlor. Meg clapped her hands daintily while Jo clenched her gloved fist and thundered forth several hearty "*Huzzahs!*" while Amy fanned her face as though she were about to faint.

From her corner by the fireplace, Beth whispered something, but nobody heard her voice, drowned as it was in the cacophony of excitement at the news.

"Oh, joy!" Meg cried. "Shall we really see him soon?"

"I expect him before Christmas morning," Marmee replied as she eased herself back into her chair and, closing her eyes, soon fell asleep in the warmth of the fire and her loving family.

"Jo! Jo! Where are you?" cried Meg at the foot of the garret stairs.

"Up here!" Jo answered from above. This was followed by the sound of running feet on the narrow stairs. Jo was wrapped in a comforter on an old sofa by the window, eating an apple and reading a novel, *The Heir of Radclyffe*. Outside, the sky was overcast and threatening more snow before Christmas, which was now three days away.

The garret was Jo's favorite refuge, especially on glowering days. She loved to retire here with an apron full of apples or a piece of cheese, when the family could afford it, and a nice book, to enjoy the quiet and the society of her pet rat, Scrabble, who lived inside the attic walls. Only for Scrabble would Jo remove the linen gloves from her hands and allow him to nip her flesh with tiny, stinging bites and then lap up the trickles of blood that flowed.

When Meg appeared, breathless, in the doorway, Jo lowered her book, irritated by the interruption. Scrabble whisked back into his rat hole, his small, beady eyes glaring at Meg from the safety of the den.

Jo waited to hear the news.

"Such fun! Only see! A regular note of invitation from Mrs. Gardiner for tomorrow night!" cried Meg, waving a thin piece of parchment, and then proceeding to read from it with girlish delight. "'Mrs. Gardiner would be happy to see Miss March and Miss Josephine at a little *soirée* tomorrow evening.' A *soirée*, Jo! Just imagine! Marmee has already agreed we can go. Now, what shall we wear?"

"What's the use of asking when you know we shall wear our poplins because we haven't got anything else?" answered Jo with her mouth full of apple. A fresh spot of blood ran from the back of her left hand to her wrist.

"If I only had a silk dress," sighed Meg.

"I'm sure our poplins look like silk, and they are nice enough. Yours is as good as new, but—Oh, dear! I just remembered the burn and the tear in mine. Whatever shall I do? The burn shows badly, and I can't let any more fabric out."

"Then you must sit still all evening and keep your back to the wall. The front is all right. I shall have a new ribbon for my hair, and I'm sure Marmee will lend me her little pearl pin. My new slippers are lovely, and my gloves will have to do."

"Mine are spoiled with—" but here Jo stopped and put her hands behind her back so Meg would not see the fresh wounds. "I can't afford to buy any new ones, but I dare not go without."

"You can't ask Mother for new gloves," Meg said, frowning. "They are so expensive, and you are so careless. You have spoiled your new ones already, and she said she shouldn't get you any more this winter. Can you make do with what you have?"

"I can hold my hands behind my back so no one will know how stained my gloves are," Jo said. "That's the best I can do." She glanced at the fine white lines of scars and fresh scabs on her hands. The fresh cut tingled and was still oozing blood.

"Then I'll go without. I don't care what people say or think!" cried Jo, taking up her book again. "Now go and answer the note, and let me finish this splendid story."

So Meg went away to "accept with thanks," look over her dress, and sing blithely as she did up her one real lace frill while Jo finished her novel, her apple, and allowed Scrabble one final sip of fresh blood.

"Now is my sash right, Jo? And does my hair look nice?" asked Meg, as she turned from the mirror in Mrs. Gardiner's dressing room after a prolonged prink.

"I know I shall forget to behave myself," Jo replied. "If you see me doing anything wrong, just remind me by a wink, will you?" returned Jo, giving her collar a twitch and her head a hasty brush.

"Winking isn't ladylike. I'll lift my eyebrows if anything is wrong, and nod if you are all right. Now hold your shoulders straight, and take short steps, and don't shake hands if you are introduced to anyone." She needn't add that anyone Jo might shake hands with would notice the spots of blood on her gloves but was too polite to mention them.

"How do you learn all the proper ways? I never can."

Downstairs they went, feeling a trifle timid, for they seldom went to parties, and informal as this little gathering was, it was an event to them. Mrs. Gardiner, a stately old lady, greeted them kindly and handed them over to Sallie, the eldest of six daughters. Meg knew Sallie and was at her ease very soon, but Jo, who didn't care much for girls or silly gossip, stood about with her hands behind her back and her back carefully against the wall. She felt about as much out of place as a colt in a flower garden. Half a dozen lads were talking about skates in another part of the room, and she longed to join them, for skating was one of the joys of her life. She telegraphed her wish to Meg, but her sister's eyebrows shot up so alarmingly that she dared not stir. No one came to talk to her, and one by one, the group dwindled away until she was left quite alone.

She could not roam about and amuse herself, for the burned breadth of cloth and the stains on her gloves would show, so she stared at people rather forlornly until the dancing began. Meg was asked to dance at once, and she tripped about so briskly that none would have guessed the pain her shoes were causing her. A big red-headed youth approached Jo's corner and, fearing he meant to engage her in conversation, she slipped into a curtained recess, intending to peep out like Scrabble and enjoy herself in peace.

Unfortunately, another bashful person had chosen that same refuge. As the curtain fell behind her, she found herself face to face with the "Laurence boy."

"I didn't know anyone else was here," stammered Jo, preparing to back out as speedily as she had bounced in.

"Don't mind me," the boy said pleasantly enough, though he looked as startled as a rabbit. In the dim light of the alcove, his eyes held a curious golden glow, as if filled with flecks of metal, and his skin was unusually pale, even for mid-winter. "Stay if you like."

"Shan't I disturb you?"

"Not a bit." His teeth were wide and flat, and they glistened wetly when he smiled. Jo sensed an uncanniness about him that was both off-putting and attractive. "I don't know many people here and felt rather strange at first."

"So did I," replied Jo. "Don't go away, please, unless you'd rather."

The boy sat down again and looked at his shoes until Jo said, trying to be polite and easy, "I believe I've had the pleasure of seeing you before. You live next door to us, don't you?"

"I do," he replied as he looked at her and laughed outright, for Jo's prim manner struck him as rather funny.

That put Jo at her ease, and she laughed, too, as she said, in her heartiest way, "You arrived in town not long ago."

"Three weeks, to be exact," said the boy. "But I have already learned some things. For instance, I know you have a pet rat. Tell me, Miss March—how is he?" The boy's pale eyes shone with a peculiar intensity as if he were attempting to probe her thoughts.

"My—How do you know about my rat?" she asked, quickly shifting her blood-stained gloved hands behind her back.

The Laurence boy deigned not to reply to that, but after the awkward silence that followed, Jo continued, "He's getting along quite nicely, thank you, Mr. Laurence. But I am not Miss March. I'm only Jo."

"And I am not Mr. Laurence. I'm only Laurie."

"Laurie … Laurie Laurence. Such an odd name."

His eyes took on an amber tone which was impossible for Jo to read. Had she inadvertently insulted him?

"My first name is Theodore, but I don't like it, so I ask everyone to call me Laurie instead."

"I hate my name, too. It's so sentimental. I wish every one would say Jo instead of Josephine."

"I suspect if they don't, you could soundly thrash them," he said, a faint smile tugging at the corners of his mouth. Jo was suddenly sure that, although Laurie's shoulders were thin and slightly stooped, he had a look about him that communicated he could handily take care of himself.

"I can't thrash Aunt March, so I suppose I shall have to bear it when she calls me Josephine," said Jo with a resigned sigh.

"Do you like to dance, Jo?" asked Laurie, looking as if he thought the name suited her quite aptly.

"I like it well enough if there is plenty of room, and everyone is lively. In a place this small, I'm sure to upset something or tread on people's feet or do something positively dreadful, so I keep to myself and let Meg sail about. Do you dance?"

"Never. I recently arrived here and haven't been in people's company enough yet to know how you do things."

"Where have you been, then?" inquired Jo.

After some hesitation, Laurie said, "Abroad," but this seemed to be laden with more meaning than he was letting on.

"Abroad!" cried Jo. "Oh, do tell me about it! I love to hear people describe their travels abroad."

Laurie looked askance, his golden eyes glittering, and didn't seem to know where to begin, so Jo decided not to press the matter. She quite glowed with pleasure in this boy's presence. She decided on the spot that she liked the "Laurence boy," and she took several good looks at him so that she might describe him to the girls, for they had no brothers, very few male cousins, and boys were almost unknown creatures to them. Laurie, in particular, struck her as unique within the gender.

He had curly black hair, and pale, almost translucent skin. His large, oval-shaped eyes glittered like gold in the candlelight. His nose was handsome if narrow, and he had fine, wide teeth, though the canines appeared pointed and protruded more than usual. His hands and feet were small and slender, and he was taller than Jo and quite thin. Jo wondered how old he was, and it was on the tip of her tongue to ask, but she checked herself in time and, with unusual tact, tried to find out in a roundabout way.

"I suppose you are already pegging at college, then … I mean, studying hard." Jo blushed at her dreadful use of the word *pegging*, which had escaped her unawares.

Laurie smiled but didn't seem at all shocked. He answered with a shrug. "Not for a year or two yet. I won't go before I'm seventeen, in any event."

"Are you but fifteen, then?" asked Jo, looking at the tall lad.

"Sixteen of your years next month."

His curious use of the phrase *your years* slipped right past Jo, who commented, "How I wish I was going to college! But you don't look as if you like the prospect."

"I hate it. School is nothing but grinding or skylarking. I don't like the way fellows do either, on your pl— … in your country."

"What do you like to do, then?"

"Live and enjoy myself in my own way," replied Laurie mysteriously, "but I hope to return home soon."

Jo wanted very much to ask where "home" and what "his own way" were, but his lowering brows looked rather more threatening as he knit them together. She wanted to ask all about where he had been born and lived before coming to the States, but she changed the subject by saying, "That's a splendid polka. Why don't you go and try it?"

"Only if you will come, too," he answered with a gallant little bow.

"I can't, for I told Meg I wouldn't because …"

There Jo stopped herself and felt rather undecided whether to tell him the truth or merely to laugh it off.

"Because what?"

"Promise you won't tell?"

"I promise."

"Well, I scorched my dress quite badly, and though it's nicely mended, it still shows. Meg told me to keep still so no one would notice. You may go ahead and laugh, if you'd like. It *is* funny, I know."

But Laurie didn't laugh. He only looked down a minute, the expression on his face so puzzling that Jo began to wonder if he was having some kind of spell until he said very gently, "Never mind that, then." Then he brightened and added, "I'll tell you how we can manage. There's a long hall, and we can dance there, and no one will be the wiser."

He held his hand out to her, but she hesitated to bring her gloved hands around from behind her back. He couldn't help but see the blood stains on them.

Jo silently thanked him as he took her hand without batting an eye, and she gladly went with him, wishing she had two neat gloves like the nice pearl-colored ones he wore.

The hall was indeed empty, and they had a grand polka, for Jo danced well and quickly taught Laurie the steps, which he executed with some clumsiness she had the grace not to mention. When the music stopped, they sat down on the stairs so Jo could catch her breath. Laurie seemed unaffected by the physical activity and was just about to say something when Meg appeared. She beckoned to Jo, who reluctantly followed her sister into a side room, where she collapsed onto a sofa, holding onto her foot and looking pale and in pain.

"I've sprained my ankle dreadfully. That stupid high heel gave me a sad wrench. It aches so I can hardly stand, and I don't know how I'm ever going to get home." She rocked to and fro, wincing in pain.

"I knew you'd hurt your feet with those silly shoes," answered Jo, softly rubbing the poor ankle as she spoke. "I'm sorry, but I don't see what you can do except get a carriage or stay here for the night."

"I can't have a carriage without it costing us ever so much. I dare say I can't get one at all, for most people come in their own carriages, and it's a long way to the stable, and no one to send."

"I'll go."

"No, indeed! It's past nine, and dark as Egypt outside. I certainly can't stay here, for the house is full this evening. Sallie has some girls staying the night. I'll rest until Hannah comes, and then hobble home the best I can."

"I'll ask Laurie. He will go," said Jo, looking relieved as the idea occurred to her.

"Mercy, no! Don't ask him or anyone else. Get me my overshoes, and put these slippers with our things. I can't dance anymore, but as soon as supper is over, watch for Hannah and tell me the minute she arrives."

"They are going out to supper now. I'll stay with you. I'd rather."

"No, dear. Run along, and bring me some coffee. I'm so tired I can't stir."

So Meg reclined, and Jo went blundering away to the dining room, which she found after going into a china closet and opening the door of a room where old Mr. Gardiner was taking a little private refreshment. Making a dart at the table, she secured a cup of coffee, which she immediately spilled on her gloves.

"Oh, dear, what a blunderbuss I am!" exclaimed Jo.

"May I help?" inquired a friendly voice. And there was Laurie, with a full cup of coffee in one hand and a plate of ice in the other.

"I was getting something for Meg, who is terribly tired, and someone shook me, and here I am in a sorry state," answered Jo, glancing dismally at the coffee-colored glove. The warm fluid was scalding her hand, and she had no choice but to remove the glove, thus exposing her scarred hand and wrist.

"Oh, you poor dear," Laurie cried, taking her hand in his and touching it with a soothing caress that sent electricity through her. "You've gone and hurt yourself. Here. Come with me."

Before Jo could say a word, he whisked her along the hallway away from the crowd. When they stopped, he reached into his jacket pocket and removed a small black box. Upon closer inspection, Jo noted several small indentations on the side and a tiny green light, which Laurie directed at her hand. After he pressed a small button on the side of the box, a faint humming sound filled the air, and a cooling sensation embraced her hand and wrist like an unseen glove.

"Whatever are you doing?" Jo asked as the cool, prickling sensation ran up her hand and forearm. Ignoring her inquiry, Laurie attended to his business for a whispered count of ten, and then said simply, "That should suffice."

He replaced the small device into his jacket pocket and smiled at her.

"Your hand should feel better soon," he said, walking with her back to the dining table. "What do you say we bring a cup of coffee to your sister?"

"Oh—yes. Thank you. I would offer to take it myself, but I am sure I would get into another scrape."

Jo led the way, and as if used to waiting on ladies, Laurie drew up a little table, brought a second installment of coffee for Jo, and was so obliging that even critical

Meg pronounced him a "nice boy." Jo asked if he could use that curious device to aid her sister's twisted ankle, but he looked at her, silently scolding her as he shook his head, no.

While Meg rested her foot, they had a merry time and were in the midst of a game of *Buzz* with two or three other young people, who had strayed in, when Hannah appeared in the doorway. Meg forgot her foot and rose so quickly that she was forced to catch hold of Jo, with a brief exclamation of pain.

"Hush! Don't say anything about it," she whispered to Jo, adding aloud, "It's nothing. I turned my foot a little, that's all," and limped upstairs to put her things on.

Hannah's expression remained perfectly neutral when her eyes met Laurie's. Jo was sure something unspoken passed between their maid and her new friend, but for the life of her she couldn't tell what. Meg returned, limping, and Jo was at her wit's end until she decided to take things into her own hands. She ran out and found a servant and asked if he could provide them with a carriage. It happened to be a hired waiter who knew nothing about the neighborhood, and Jo was looking around for help when Laurie, who apparently had heard her request, came up and offered his grandfather's carriage, which had just come for him.

"It's so early. You can't mean to go yet?" began Jo.

"I always leave early. I do, truly. I find that I tire easily at such events."

Jo remembered the vigor with which he had danced and doubted the veracity of his claim, but she was pleased to let him take her sister and her home. "It's on my way," he added, "and, you know, it is supposed to snow, they say."

That settled it, and Jo gratefully accepted. Hannah hated the snow as much as a cat does, so she agreed although Jo caught another unspoken glance pass between Hannah and Laurie, which filled her with curiosity.

Once settled in the carriage, they rolled away feeling very festive and elegant. Laurie rode on the box with the driver so Meg could keep her foot up on the seat next to Hannah.

"I had a capital time. Did you?" asked Jo, rumpling up her hair and making herself comfortable.

"I did," said Meg, "until I hurt myself. Sallie's friend, Annie Moffat, took a fancy to me and asked me to spend a week with her family in Boston. She is going in the spring when the opera comes to the city. It will be perfectly splendid if Marmee will let me go."

"I saw you dancing with the red-headed man I ran away from," said Jo. "Was he nice?"

"Oh, quite. But his hair is auburn, not red, and he was very polite."

"He looked like a grasshopper having a fit. Laurie and I couldn't help but laugh. Did you hear us?"

"No, but it was very rude to laugh. What were you about all that time, hiding away there? It's unladylike."

Jo told her adventures but failed to mention the small act of healing Laurie had accomplished on her injured hand. She thrilled at the memory of his touch when he held her hand to inspect the burn. Before they knew it, they were home. With many thanks, they said good night to Laurie and crept in, hoping to disturb no one.

"What in the world are you going to do now, Jo?" asked Meg as her sister came tramping through the hall wearing heavy rubber boots, an old sack, and a hood. She had a broom in one hand and a shovel in the other.

"Going out for exercise," answered Jo with a mischievous twinkle in her eyes.

"I should think it's cold and dreary enough outside, and I advise you to stay warm and dry by the fire, as I do," said Meg with a shiver.

"Never take advice! Can't keep still all day, and not being a pussycat, I don't like to doze by the fire. I like adventures, and I'm going to find one."

With Beth watching from the shadows, Meg went back to toasting her feet and reading *Ivanhoe* while Jo went outside to dig a path in the snow with great energy. Her shovel soon cleared a path all round the garden for Amy to walk in when the sun came out. Father would be pleased to see such industry. Now, the garden separated the Marches' house from that of Mr. Laurence. Both stood in a suburb of Concord, which was still country-like, with groves and lawns, large gardens, and quiet streets. A low hedge parted the two properties. On one side was an old, brown house, looking rather bare and shabby, robbed of the grape vines that in summer covered its walls and the flowers, which surrounded it. On the other side was a stately stone mansion, plainly betokening every sort of creature comfort, from the big coach house and well-kept grounds to the conservatory and the glimpses of lovely things one caught between the rich curtains.

Yet it seemed a lonely, lifeless sort of house, thought Jo, for no children frolicked on the lawn, no motherly face smiled at the window, and few people went in and out except for the old gentleman and his grandson, Laurie.

To Jo's lively fancy, this fine house seemed an enchanted palace full of remarkable splendors and delights, which no one enjoyed. She had long wanted to behold these hidden glories and to know the Laurence boy. Talking with him at the party had only enhanced his attraction. He had only recently arrived to reside with his grandfather. The story, as Jo had heard it, was that he had studied in Europe following the death of his parents, although he had not mentioned such an event last night.

Since the party, Jo had been more eager than ever to know him, and she had planned ways of making friends with him, but she had not seen him outside today, and she began to think he may have gone away. Earlier in the day, though, she had spied a pale face in an upper window, looking wistfully down into their yard.

"That boy is suffering from a lack of society and fun," she said to herself. "He keeps himself shut up all day as if he's afraid of the sun. He needs somebody young and lively to associate with. I've a mind to go over and tell him so!"

The idea amused Jo, who liked to do daring things and was always scandalizing Meg by her peculiar performances. The plan of "going over there" was not forgotten. And when the snowy afternoon came, Jo resolved to try what could be done. She waited to see Mr. Laurence drive off, and then she sallied forth to dig her way down to the hedge, where she paused and took a survey.

All was quiet. The curtains were down at the lower windows, and the servants were out of sight. Nothing human was visible but a curly black head leaning on a thin hand in an upper window.

"Poor boy," thought Jo. "All alone on this dismal day. It's a shame. I'll toss up a snowball and make him look at me, and then say a kind word."

Up went a handful of soft snow, and the head turned at once, showing a face which lost its listless expression in an instant as the big eyes brightened and the wide mouth smiled. Jo waved, laughing as she flourished her shovel and called out—

"How do you do? Are you sick?"

Up went the window sash, and Laurie croaked out as hoarsely as a raven, "Better, thank you. I've had a bad cold since the night of the party and have been shut up."

"I'm sorry to hear that. What do you for amusement?"

"Nothing. It's as dull as tombs up here."

"Don't you read?"

"Not much. Grandfather won't let me."

"Can't somebody read to you?"

"No one will."

"Have someone come and see you, then."

"There isn't anyone I'd like to see. Boys make such a row, and my head is weak."

"Isn't there some nice girl who'd read to you? Girls are quiet and like to play nurse."

"I don't know any."

"You know me," said Jo. She started to laugh but then stopped.

"So I do," cried Laurie. "Will you come up, please?"

"I'm not quiet *or* nice, but I'll come up if Mother will allow. I'll ask. Shut the window, like a good boy. You'll catch your death. Wait until I come."

With that, Jo shouldered her shovel like a musket and marched into the house. Laurie was in a rush of excitement at the idea of having company, and he flew about to get ready, tidying up his room, which in spite of half a dozen servants was anything but neat.

Presently there came a loud ring at the door and then a decided voice, asking for "Master Laurie." A surprised-looking servant came running up to announce a young lady.

"Show her up, please. It's Miss Jo," said Laurie, going to the door of his little parlor to meet Jo, who appeared looking rosy and quite at ease with a covered dish in her gloved hands.

"Here I am, bag and baggage," she said briskly. "Mother sends her love and was glad if I could do anything for you. Meg wanted me to bring some of her blancmange. She makes it very nicely."

"That looks too pretty to eat," he said, smiling with pleasure as Jo uncovered the dish and showed the blancmange, surrounded by a garland of green leaves and the scarlet flowers of Amy's pet geranium.

"Tell the girl to put it away for your tea," said Jo. "It's so simple you can eat it and, being soft, it will slip down without hurting your sore throat. What a cozy room this is."

"It might be if it was kept nice, but the maids are so lazy, and I dare say I don't know how to make them mind."

"I'll straighten it up in two minutes, for it only needs to have the hearth brushed, and the things made straight on the mantelpiece, and the books put here, and the bottles there, and your sofa turned from the light, and the pillows plumped. Now then, you're fixed."

And so he was, for, as she talked, Jo had whisked about the room putting things into place which, when done, gave quite a different air to the room. She noticed a few objects and artifacts that struck her as unique, but she had the manners not to remark on them. One, a photograph of a lovely woman with long, black hair, seemed to be three-dimensional, to which Jo ascribed a trick of the eye. Laurie watched her in respectful silence, and when she beckoned him to his sofa, he sat down with a sigh of satisfaction.

"How kind you are," he said graciously. "Yes, that's exactly what it needed. Now, please take the big chair, and let me do something to amuse you."

"I came to amuse you," Jo said, habitually placing her gloved hands behind her back to hide the stains. "Shall I read aloud?" She looked affectionately toward some inviting books in a case nearby. Several titles, written on the spines, appeared to be in a language unfamiliar to her, perhaps Arabic or Hindoo, she thought.

"Thank you, but I've read all those, and if you don't mind, I'd rather talk," answered Laurie.

"Not a bit. I'll talk all day if you'll only set me going. Beth used to say I never know when to stop."

"The pretty one is Meg, and the curly-haired one is Amy, but I don't believe I have met or seen your sister Beth."

"Beth is—" began Jo, but she fell silent, not sure how to proceed until she ended with a feeble, "We speak very little of her."

Laurie colored up but said frankly, "Why, you see, I often hear you calling to one another, and when I'm alone upstairs, I can't help but look over at your house. You always seem to be having such grand times. I beg your pardon for being so rude, but sometimes you forget to pull the curtain at the window where the flowers are, and when the lamps are lighted, it's like looking at a living picture book to see you all gathered around with your mother. Her face looks so sweet behind the flowers. I can't help watching. I haven't got any mother, you know."

"I'm so sorry," replied Jo. "I didn't know. Do you care to tell me what happened?"

"She was from … Italy. When she died, my father, being unable to raise me on his own because his business concerns take him far and wide, sent me to Concord to live with my grandfather until I begin college."

Laurie poked at the fire to hide a slight twitching of the upper lip and a certain moistness in his eyes that he could not control.

The solitary, yearning look in his eyes went straight to Jo's heart. She had been so simply taught that there was no nonsense in her head, and at fifteen she was as innocent and frank as any child. Laurie was ill and lonely, and she was grateful for how rich she truly was in home and true happiness. She gladly wished to share it with him. Her face was very friendly, and her sharp voice unusually gentle as she said—

"We'll never draw that curtain any more, and I give you leave to look as much as you like. I just wish, though, instead of peeping, you'd come over and visit. Mother is so splendid. She'd do you heaps of good, and we'd welcome you and have jolly times. Wouldn't your grandpa let you?"

"I think he would if your mother asked," replied Laurie. "He's very kind, though he does not look so. He lets me do whatever I like, pretty much, only he's afraid I might be a bother to strangers."

"We are not strangers. We are neighbors. And you needn't worry you'd be a bother to us. We want to know you. I've been wanting to meet you ever so long. We have got acquainted with all our neighbors save you."

"Well, you see, Grandpa lives among his books and doesn't mind much what happens outside. Mr. Brooke, my tutor, doesn't live here, so I have no one to go about with me, so I just stay at home and get on as best I can until I can return."

"Return?"

"Return home," said Laurie and, like on the night of the party, Jo had the good manners not to pursue the discussion if he seemed unwilling. But even as he said this, Jo could sense the well of sadness inside him, and the thought that he felt he didn't belong anywhere or to anyone cut her deeply.

"You ought to make an effort to go visit everywhere you are asked. Then, perhaps, you'll have plenty of friends and pleasant places to go. Never mind being bashful. It won't last long."

Laurie wasn't offended by Jo's forthright manner, for there was so much goodwill in her that it was impossible not to take her blunt speeches as kindly as they were meant.

"Do you like your school?" asked the boy, changing the subject after a brief pause during which he stared at the fire, and Jo looked all around her.

"I don't go to school," she answered. "I'm a business-man … business girl, I mean. I wait on my Aunt March, and a dear, cross old soul she is, too."

Laurie opened his mouth to ask a question, but remembering just in time that it wasn't polite manners to make too many inquiries into others' affairs, shut it again, content that Jo didn't probe too deeply into his family story, either. He found her freshness and openness charming and irresistible and might lower his guard and say more than he should if he wasn't careful.

For her part, Jo liked his obvious good breeding, and she didn't mind having a laugh at Aunt March, so she gave him a lively description of the fidgety old lady, her fat poodle, the parrot that spoke Spanish, and the library where she reveled when Aunt March was napping. They got to talking about books, and to Jo's delight, she found that Laurie loved books as well as she did and had read even more than herself.

"If you like books so much, please come downstairs and see ours. Grandfather is out on business, so you needn't be afraid," said Laurie, getting up. He looked unsteady on his feet, and when he took a breath, Jo noticed a most unusual whistling sound, but she chose not to comment on it.

"I'm not afraid of anything," Jo said with a toss of the head.

"I don't believe you are," exclaimed the boy, looking at her with much admiration, though he privately thought she would have good reason to be a trifle afraid of the old gentleman if she met him when in one of his moods.

Laurie led the way from room to room, letting Jo stop to examine whatever struck her fancy. And so, at last they came to the library, where she clapped her gloved hands as she always did when especially delighted. The walls were lined with books, and there were pictures and statues, and distracting little cabinets full of strange coins and other curiosities. There were Sleepy Hollow chairs, and queer tables, and bronzes, and—best of all—a great open fireplace with Italian tiles lined all round it.

"What richness," sighed Jo, sinking into the depth of a purple velour chair and gazing about her with an air of intense satisfaction. "Theodore Laurence, you ought to be the happiest boy in the world."

"A fellow can't live on books alone," said Laurie, shaking his head as he perched on a table opposite and regarded her with his curious golden eyes. In the dimness of the room, they held a vibrant glow to which Jo found herself drawn.

Before he could say more, a bell rang, and Jo flew up, exclaiming with alarm, "Mercy me! It's your grandpa!"

"What if it is?" Laurie said. "I thought you were not afraid of anything."

"I think I am afraid of him a little bit, but I don't know why I should be. Marmee said I might come, and I don't think you're any the worse for it," Jo said, composing herself as she kept her eyes on the door.

"I'm a great deal the better for it, and ever so much obliged. I'm only afraid you are very tired of talking to me," said Laurie gratefully.

A maid appeared in the doorway and said, "The doctor to see you, sir."

"Would you mind if I left you for a minute?" said Laurie.

"Don't mind me. I'm happy as a cricket here," answered Jo, although truth to tell, she was curious to ask Laurie why he didn't use on himself the same strange healing device he had used on her parboiled hand at the party. But she let the thought slip away and watched as Laurie left the room.

While he was gone, Jo amused herself in her own way. She was standing before a fine portrait of the old gentleman when the door opened again and, without turning, she said decidedly, "I'm sure now that I should be afraid of him, for he's got cruel, dark eyes, and his mouth is altogether grim. He looks as if he has a tremendous will of his own."

"Thank you, ma'am, for that analysis," said a growling voice behind her, and there, to her great dismay, stood old Mr. Laurence. Unlike his grandson, he was squarely built, with short legs and thick, powerful arms. His eyes were as dark as ink wells.

Poor Jo blushed until she couldn't blush any redder, and her heart beat uncomfortably fast in her thin chest as she thought what she had done. Feeling terribly alone and vulnerable, she felt a wild desire to run away, but that was cowardly, so she resolved to stand her ground and get out of this as best she could. A second look showed her that the living eyes, under the bushy eyebrows, were kinder than the painted ones, and was there a sly twinkle in them. The gruff voice was gruffer than ever, as the old gentleman said after the dreadful pause, "So, you say that you're afraid of me, hey?"

"No—no, sir," Jo replied, knowing in her heart that he knew she was not telling the truth.

"And you don't think me as handsome as your grandfather?"

"Not quite, begging your pardon, sir."

"And I've got a tremendous will, have I?"

"I only said I suspect so," Jo stammered.

That final answer seemed to please the old gentleman, for he threw his head back and gave a short, barking laugh and reached out to shake hands with her. His palm, she noticed, was as rough as tree bark, which struck her as odd, seeing as it was the hand of a gentleman.

Putting his finger under her chin, he turned her face up and examined it gravely for a long time. Looking directly at him, and so close, she could see now the same golden glint in his eyes as in Laurie's. After a lengthening moment of intense scrutiny, he let her face go, saying with a nod, "You've got your grandfather's spirit, I dare say, even if you haven't got his face."

"Thank you, sir," said Jo.

"What have you been doing to this boy of mine, hey?" was the next question, sharply put.

"Only trying to be neighborly, sir."

"Neighborly, you say?"

"I wanted to cheer him up in his illness."

"His illness is no concern of yours," the old gentleman replied. "So you think he needs cheering?"

"Yes, sir. A bit, sir. He seems a bit lonely, and being around young folks would do him no end of good. We are only girls, my sisters and I, but we should be glad to help if we could," said Jo eagerly.

"Tut, tut, tut! And what news of your father?"

"We received a letter just the other day, informing us that he will be home in time for Christmas."

"What a fine Christmas present that will be," replied Mr. Laurence. "I, myself, was born on Christmas Day."

Jo had no idea how to respond to that, having heard that people who have the audacity to be born on the Savior's birthday are fated to be evil. She noticed the sudden darkness in his eyes, as if a cloud had shifted in front of the sun, blocking its warming rays.

"Hey! Why? What the dickens has come to the fellow?" said the old gentleman as Laurie came running downstairs and was brought up with a start of surprise at the astounding sight of Jo standing in front of his redoubtable grandfather.

"I didn't know you'd come home, sir," Laurie began.

"That's evident by the way you racket downstairs. Come. Behave like a gentleman." He cast a wary eye at Jo, and then added, "Perhaps young master will make the adjustment to his life here after all."

Laurie's face colored at this, and she didn't need to hear him say how much he wanted to go back home, wherever home was.

Turning to Jo, the old gentleman continued, "You're right on the money, Miss March. The lad is lonely so dreadfully far away from home. Perhaps we'll see what these little girls next door can do for him."

Jo determined it was time to go, but Laurie said he had one more thing to show her, and he took her away to the conservatory, which had been lighted for her benefit. It seemed quite fairy-like to Jo as she went up and down the walks, enjoying the blooming walls on either side, the soft light, the sweet, damp air, and the wonderful vines and trees that grew in profusion. Some of them she didn't recognize at all, and many had strange fruits on their vines and thorns on their stems. They filled the air with an intoxicatingly unearthly perfume, which hung about her while her new friend cut the finest flowers until his hands were full. Then he tied them up, saying with a happy look, "Please give these to your cherished mother, and tell her I approve of the medicine she sent to me."

"That will do. That will do, young man," said the old gentleman who was standing in the doorway of the conservatory. Jo had not heard him enter. "Too many sugarplums are not good for her. Going, Miss March? Well, I hope you will come again. Give my respects to your mother."

He bowed deeply to her, but even with his head bowed, he looked at her, and she could tell that something of a sudden had not pleased him. When they got into the hall, Jo whispered to Laurie, asking if she had said or done anything amiss. He shook his head.

"No. It was I. He doesn't like it when I enter the conservatory."

"Why not?"

"I'll tell you another day."

"Take care of yourself, then."

"I will, but will you come again, I hope?"

"Only if you promise to come and visit us, if you are well enough. Perhaps on Christmas day."

"Perhaps I shall."

"Good night, Laurie."

"And a good night to you, too, Doctor Jo."

When all the afternoon's adventures had been told, the family felt inclined to go visiting in a body, for each found something very attractive in the big house on the other side of the hedge. Mrs. March wanted to talk of her father with the old man who had known him. Meg longed to walk in the flower conservatory and see its exotic beauties, as described by Jo. Amy was eager to see the fine paintings and statues. And Beth sighed from the corner and whispered how she wished she could play the grand piano.

"Mother, what did he mean by that nice little speech he gave about the medicine Mother sent him?" asked Jo. "Did he mean the blancmange?"

"How silly you are, child," Marmee replied. "He meant you, of course."

"He did?"

And Jo opened her eyes as if it had never occurred to her.

"I never saw such a girl! You don't know a compliment when you receive one," said Meg with the air of a young lady who knew all about such matters.

"I think they are a great nonsense, and I'll thank you not to be silly and spoil my fun. Laurie's a nice boy, and I like him, and I won't have any sentimental stuff about compliments and such rubbish spoil my fun. We'll all be good to him because he hasn't got any parents, and he may come over and see us. Mayn't he, Marmee?"

"Yes, Jo. Your friend is very welcome here, and I hope Meg will remember that children should be children as long as they can."

"I don't call myself a child, and I'm not in my teens yet," observed Amy.

"And I say to be a child again would be a lovely thing … a heavenly thing," whispered Beth from her dark corner beside the fireplace. Only she noticed the way their servant Hannah was standing, unseen and silent, in the doorway, her eyes cast in deep concern.

As Christmas approached, the usual mysteries began to haunt the house, and Jo frequently convulsed the family by proposing utterly impossible or magnificently absurd ceremonies in honor of this unusually merry Christmas they faced this year with Father's promised return. She was impracticable and would have had bonfires, skyrockets, and triumphal arches, if she had her own way. After many skirmishes and snubbings, her extravagant plans were effectually quenched, and she went about with a forlorn face as she retired to the garret where she allowed Scrabble to feed on more blood than was his wont.

Snow arrived the day before Christmas and continued overnight, piling up three feet or more in the country roads and fields. Christmas Day morning dawned dark and gloomy, but the family was determined to spend their day in cozy companionship, except for Jo, who planned to spend some time with Laurie.

Perhaps because of the weather, perhaps because of her uncanny insight, Hannah felt "in her bones" that the day was going to be an unusually bad day, and she proved herself a true prophetess, for everybody and everything seemed bound to go wrong, no matter what one attempted. To begin with, Father had written more than a month ago from the Army hospital in Maryland that he expected to be home soon. Meg thought it would be exquisite if he were to arrive before they shared their holiday dinner, which Hannah took all day to prepare with help from all three girls. But with the weather choking the roads, Marmee expressed her doubts about his arrival before the New Year.

Beth felt uncommonly uneasy that morning, and with the cloudy sky casting such darkness, she shifted from her dark corner by the fireplace to the window, where she looked out with the most forlorn expression possible at the storm, which was now a raging blizzard.

On Christmas Day, the little women had outdone their best efforts to be festive, for, like elves, they had gotten up before dawn and conjured up a comical surprise. Out in the garden stood a stately snowman, crowned with Father's old top hat and bearing a sweet potato for a nose and two lumps of charred wood for eyes, and a castoff scarf wrapped around his neck. Even before the work was done, a layer of snow obscured the features, so carefully molded. After breakfast, when Marmee and Hannah looked out at it, it was nothing more or less than a shapeless hump of pure white mounted by an old beaver top hat.

Jo finally came out of her gloom when Laurie arrived in the evening after their Christmas meal, having trudged through the snow to be with them and bearing gifts. And what ridiculous speeches he made as he presented each gift to the family members.

"I'm so full of happiness," said Meg, once the presents were dispensed and the holiday treats of sugar cookies and dried fruit were consumed. As evening drew on, the storm intensified, whistling under the eaves, and each one of them had given up any hope that Father would arrive to share the blessed day in the warmth and comfort of his loving family.

"I would be truly happy if only Father were here," sighed Beth, who had returned to her corner upon the arrival of the strange boy from next door. She sensed he knew she was there, even though he never once looked directly at her. She watched with empty eyes as the festivities continued, such as they were, but by this time each and every one of the celebrants was exhausted.

"So would I," added Jo, slapping the pocket wherein reposed the long-desired edition of *The Marble Fawn* she had so wanted.

"I'm sure I am," echoed Amy, poring over the engraved copy of the Madonna and Child, which her mother had given her in a pretty frame.

"Of course I am," cried Meg, smoothing the silvery folds of her first silk dress, for Mr. Laurence had insisted on giving it to her.

"How can I be otherwise?" said Mrs. March gratefully, as her eyes went from her husband's letter to her children's smiling faces, and her hand caressed the brooch made of gray and golden, chestnut and dark brown hair, which the girls had fastened on her dress.

Now and then, however, in this workaday world, things do happen in the delightful storybook fashion, and what a comfort it is when they do. Half an hour after everyone had said they were so happy they could only hold one drop more, that drop came. Laurie had bid them all a goodnight and, wrapped in jacket and scarf, had left by the parlor door. But he was gone for no more than a minute when there came a heavy knocking on the door. Without being invited, he popped his head in very quietly. He might just as well have turned a somersault and uttered an Indian war whoop, for his face was so full of excitement and his voice so treacherously joyful that everyone jumped up, though he only said, in a queer, breathless voice, "Here's another Christmas present for the March family."

Before the words were well out of his mouth, he was whisked away somehow, and in his place stood a tall man, muffled to the eyes, who tried to say something but couldn't. His face was gaunt and gray beneath the scarf, and his eyes held a surprising glint of gold, even in the dimly lit room. Hannah, in the kitchen cleaning up after the festivities, uttered a loud gasp of surprise.

Of course, there was a general stampede, and for several minutes everybody seemed to lose their wits, for the strangest things were done, and no one said a word.

Mr. March became invisible in the embrace of three pairs of loving arms. Jo disgraced herself by nearly fainting and had to be doctored by Laurie in the hallway. Meg clasped her hands and let out a whoop of joy that was more befitting Jo, while Amy, the dignified, tumbled over a stool and, never stopping to get up, hugged and cried over her father's snow-covered boots in the most touching manner. Mrs. March was the first to recover herself. She held up her hand with a warning and said, "Hush, children! Remember Beth."

But it was too late.

The figure by the fireplace loomed closer, but then, upon making eye contact with the bundled figure, suddenly shrank back, an expression not of joy but of stark terror on her face. She uttered a low, lonely wail that mingled with the wind in the flue.

"That's not Father," she whispered, but in the ensuing chaos of Father's arrival, not one of them heard her, or, if they did, no one deigned to listen to, much less believe her.

It was not at all romantic, for Hannah was discovered standing in the kitchen doorway, her eyes wide and glistening, her face also a mask of fright that matched Beth's, which had dissolved into the darkness next to the fireplace.

"Why, what is it, dear Hannah?" asked Meg, who was the first to notice the shocked expression on their loving maid's face.

But Hannah found she could say nothing, her tongue was tied into a knot as she regarded Mr. March, all the while shaking her head from side to side and buzzing so loudly Jo was reminded of the sounds hornets might make in their hive. Her eyes narrowed with what could only have been doubt and a rising concern.

Marmee suddenly remembered that Mr. March needed rest and sustenance after what must have been a terribly grueling ordeal through the teeth of the storm, but she paused when she removed her husband's glove and took hold of his hands, squeezing them between her own.

"My Goodness, how cold you are," she said, feeling her own share of concern because she realized that her husband had not spoken a word of greeting. "Come," she said. "Sit by the fire and warm yourself."

Father looked at her with a vague, uncomprehending glance and said nothing as he walked with halting steps over to the nearest chair.

"Aren't you going to sit in your customary chair, Father?" asked Amy, indicating the old wooden rocker with the padded cushions that was placed front and center of the blazing fireplace.

Father stood in the middle of the room, looking mutely at her as though he had no understanding whatsoever of what she had just said. His gaze then wandered around the small parlor with the most mystified expression painted upon his gaunt and pale features. Mrs. March could only shudder at the thought of the ordeals he must have endured since last she had seen him. She noted now that his eyes remained clouded and uncomprehending, as though he were dazed.

All the while, Mr. March spoke not, but he forced a crooked smile when he looked at his wife, exposing wide, white teeth that, in the firelight, looked much larger than anyone remembered. After a glance at Meg, who was violently poking the fire, he looked at his wife again with an inquiring lift of the eyebrows. Mrs. March gently nodded and asked, rather abruptly, if he wouldn't like to have something to eat and drink. Jo saw and understood the look, and she stalked away to get a bottle of wine and some beef tea, muttering to herself as she closed the kitchen door behind her. There, she locked eyes with Hannah, whose expression of shock had abated not at all.

"Why, what ever is the matter, Hannah?" she asked.

Hannah did not respond. She stood immobile and shook her head from side to side and whispered softly, "Beth is right."

Meanwhile, back in the parlor, Amy, who now sat on her father's knee, whispered, "I'm glad it's over because now we've got you back."

"That's not Father," Beth repeated, unseen from the darkness in the corner. Her voice was as soft as the hush of falling snow outside.

"Rather a rough road for you to travel," Mrs. March said to her husband. "Especially the latter part of it in such weather. But you have got on bravely, and your burdens are in a fair way to tumble off very soon." She looked with motherly satisfaction at the young faces gathered around her husband and thought how the worst of their trials, too, must now be close to an end.

"Our troubles are just beginning," said Hannah, who entered from the kitchen a step ahead of Jo, who was carrying a bottle of wine and a steaming cup of beef tea.

"What do you mean?" inquired Marmee, casting a furtive glance at the maid who was moving forward, inching her way as if traversing a pit filled with snakes.

Hannah did not answer her as she cast a long, meaningful glance at Laurie, who throughout the reunion had graciously remained silent and watchful by the door.

"You see it, too, do you not, young Master Laurence?" Hannah asked, turning her full attention on the boy whose first impulse was to fade back into the darkness even if it meant going back out into the fury of the blizzard without his coat and scarf snuggly wrapped around him.

"Tell me. You see it. Don't you?" Hannah said as she took several strides toward him.

Mrs. March and the three girls watched in awe, their attention fixed on these two. Speaking up so forcefully was quite uncharacteristic of Hannah, but Laurie remained perfectly silent for a terribly long moment, his golden eyes flashing back and forth from Mrs. March to each of the girls, including Beth in the corner, and then finally at Father, sitting in his chair. Ever so slightly, he nodded and said, "He is not who I thought he was."

The expression on Hannah's face suddenly fixed with determination as she shifted her gaze again to Father and stared intently at him. Her unblinking eyes held a golden glint, like a cat's eyes in the firelight.

"He's not of our kind," Hannah said.

"Whatever are you two talking about?" inquired Meg, wringing her hands together helplessly, but Hannah said not another word. Instead, with stunning agility, she moved quickly, closing the distance between herself and the gaunt figure shivering in the chair beside the fireplace.

In other circumstances, had he not been so exhausted from his travels, Meg thought, Father would have reacted in time. But his journey home had worn him past the point of exhaustion, and his only reaction was to let out a high-pitched squealing sound as the maid came up close to him and clasped him by the shoulders with both hands. Then, with a surprising display of strength, she lifted him to his feet, spun him around, and began to push him backward, moving slowly toward the blazing fireplace.

"In Heaven's name, Hannah! What in God's name are you doing?" Marmee cried out.

She and her daughters watched, in stunned silence, unable to comprehend and certainly unable to react quickly enough to help Father. Jo dropped the bottle of wine and the cup of beef tea, which shattered on the hardwood floor, as she let out a wild cry. Everyone watched as Hannah, her face set with grim determination, struggled with Father. Faint, inhuman sounds issued from her throat as she forced him ever so slowly backward, closer to the fire. When the heel of his boot caught on a raised hearthstone, she pushed him away from her. Father tumbled backward and fell flat on his back onto the blazing logs. A bright shower of sparks corkscrewed up the chimney as the flames engulfed him with a roar.

What happened next would be the subject of great discussion for a long time afterward in the March household, but all agreed that something most unnatural occurred in their home for, indeed, it was evident that the figure they had assumed was Father was, indeed, not that personage at all. The flames quickly consumed the outer shell of the creature that had taken the shape of their loving husband and father, and writhing and thrashing about on the floor, it all the while emitted shrill, screeching sounds that reminded Jo of the cries a coyote makes in the forest on a full moon night. The skin of the being's face burned away with the hissing blue flare of a gas jet, peeling back skin to expose another visage hidden beneath, one that had scaled green skin like a frog's, large shining oval eyes the color of ebony, and three rows of needle-sharp teeth.

No one in the little parlor spoke or dared move until the figure finally stopped twitching, leaving naught but the charred bones of a most inhuman-looking skeleton. Even these soon crumbled away to a fine, gray dust. The family exchanged unspoken glances as the most noxious fumes imaginable filled the air, choking them. Marmee, in stunned stupefaction because of what she and her children had just witnessed, shook herself and commanded Laurie, who was nearest to the door, to please open the door and allow some fresh air in.

Laurie did as he was told, and in the ensuing silence, all of them could hear and not deny what Beth was saying from her dark corner by the fireplace.

"I told you that wasn't Father at the door," she whispered. "Doesn't anybody ever listen to me?"

Death Stopped for Miss Dickinson

By

Kristine Kathryn Rusch

January 26, 1863
Near Township Landing, Florida

The air smelled of pine trees, a scent Colonel Thomas Wentworth Higginson associated with home. Here, in the Florida, where dark, spindly trees rose around him like ghosts, Higginson never imagined he'd be thinking of Massachusetts, with its stately settled forests and its magnificent tamed land.

Nothing was tamed here. His boots had been damp for days, the earth mushy, even though his regiment, the First South Carolina Volunteer Infantry, had somehow found solid ground. He could hear the tramp, tramp, tramp of hundreds of feet, but his soldiers were quiet, well trained, alert.

Everything Washington, D.C., thought they would not be.

Even in the dark, after days of river travel, Higginson was proud of these men, the most disciplined he had ever worked with. He said so in his dispatches, although he doubted Union Command believed him. They had taken a risk creating an entire regiment of colored troops, mostly freed slaves, all of whom had been in a martial mood much of the month, ever since word of President Lincoln's Emancipation Proclamation reached them.

A strange clip-clop, then the whinny of a horse, and a shushing. Higginson's breath caught. His men had no horses. They traveled mostly on steamers, and hence had no need of horses, even if the Union Army had deemed such soldiers worthy of steeds—which they did not.

He whispered a command. It was all he needed to stop his troops. They halted immediately and slapped their rifles into position.

He had a fleeting thought that made him smile—a Confederate soldier's worst nightmare: to meet a black man with a gun—and then waited.

The silence was thick, the kind of silence that came only when men listened, trying to hear someone else move. Breathing hushed, each movement monitored. No one wanted to move first.

Then Higginson saw him, rising out of the trees as if made of smoke—a black-robed figure, face hidden by a hood, carrying a scythe.

Higginson's breath caught. What kind of madness was this? Some kind of farmer lurking in the woods, killing soldiers?

The figure turned toward him. In the darkness, the hood looked empty. Higginson saw no face, just a great, gaping beyond.

His heart pounded. He was forty years old, tired, overworked and over-wrought; hallucinations should not have surprised him.

But they did, *this* did.

And then the hallucination dissolved as if it had never been. One of his men cried out, and a volley of shots lit up the night, revealing nothing where the hooded figure had stood.

All around it, however, horses, men, Confederates—white faces in the strange gunlight, looking frightened and surprised. They surrounded his men, but could not believe what they saw—for a moment anyway.

Then their weapons came out, and they returned fire, and Higginson forgot the hooded figure, forgot that moment of silence, and plunged deep into the battle, his own rifle raised, bayonet out as, around him, the air filled with the stink of gunpowder, the screams of horses, the wild cries of men.

The battle raged late into the night and when it was done, rifle smoke hung in the sky, the trees nearly invisible, the wounded crying around him. Thirteen bodies—twelve of theirs, one of his—gathered nearer each other than he would have liked.

Near the spot where he had seen the hooded figure, where he had imagined smoke, in that moment of silence, before the first shot was fired and the first smoke appeared.

Forty years old and he had never been frightened—not when he attacked Boston's courthouse trying to rescue escaped slave Anthony Burns, not when he fought with the free-staters in Kansas, not when he met John Brown with an offer to fund the raid on Harper's Ferry.

No, Thomas Wentworth Higginson had never been frightened, not until he saw those bodies, scattered in a discernable pattern in the ghostly wood where a spectral figure had stood hours before, and wielded a scythe, creating a clearing where Higginson would have sworn there had not been one before.

He reassured himself: every man was allowed one moment of terror in a war. Then he resolved that he would never be frightened again.

And he was not. In the war, anyway.

But he would be frightened again, and much worse than this, in a small town in Massachusetts where he met a slight poetess, seven years later.

May 23, 1886
The Homestead
Amherst, Massachusetts

Lavinia Dickinson stood in the doorway to her sister's bedroom. It still smelled faintly of Emily—liniment and homemade lavender soap, dried leaves from the many plants she'd preserved, and of course, the sharp odor of India ink that seemed embedded in the walls.

The bed was bare, the coverings washed and to be washed again. Dr. Bigelow had initially said Emily died of apoplexy, but he had written on her death certificate that she had been a victim of Bright's Disease, which he swore had no contagion.

Vinnie had learned, in her fifty-three years, that doctors knew less than most about death and disease, but she trusted Dr. Bigelow enough to keep the sheets and Emily's favorite quilt, although she would launder them repeatedly before putting them away.

Vinnie had thought to burn them, but their mother had made that quilt, and it held precious memories. Still, Vinnie had time to change her mind. She would have a bonfire soon, before the summer dryness set in.

Emily had made her swear—had asked a solemn oath—that Vinnie would destroy her papers, *all* her papers, should Emily die first.

Vinnie had not expected Emily to die first. That bright flame seemed impossible to distinguish, even as she lay unconscious on her bed for two days, her breath coming in deep unnatural rasps.

No one expected Emily to die—least of all, Emily.

And Vinnie was uncertain how to proceed, without her stronger, smarter, older sister to guide her.

May 15, 1847
The West Street House
Amherst, Massachusetts

The moon cast an eerie silver light through Emily's bedroom window. She set down her pen and blew out the candle on her desk. The light seemed stronger than before.

She slid her chair back, the legs scraping against the polished wood floor, and paused for a moment, hoping she had not awakened Father. He would tell her she should sleep more, but of late, sleep eluded her. She felt on the cusp of something—what, she could not tell. Something life-changing, though.

Something soul-altering.

She dared not speak these thoughts aloud. When she had uttered less controversial thoughts, her mother chided her and urged her to pull out her Bible when blasphemy threatened to overtake her. Emily's father did not censure her thoughts, but he looked concerned, worrying that the books he bought her had weakened her girlish mind.

All except her father and her brother Austin recommended church, hoping the Lord would speak to her and she would become saved. She saw no difference between those who had become saved and those who had not, except, perhaps, a certain smugness. She was smug enough, she liked to tell her sister Lavinia. Vinnie would smile reluctantly, at both the truth of the statement and the sheer daring of it.

Everyone they knew waited to be saved; that her brother and father had not yet achieved this was seen as a failing in their family, not as something to be emulated. If she was not saved, she would not reunite with her family in Heaven. Indeed, she might not go to Heaven.

And, at times, such an idea did not terrify her. In fact, it often filled her with relief.

Eternity, she had once said to Vinnie, *appears dreadful to me.*

Vinnie did not understand, nor did Austin. And Emily couldn't quite convey how often she wished Eternity did not exist. The idea of living forever, in any way—*to never cease to be*, as she had said to Vinnie—disturbed her in her most quiet moments.

Like now. That silver light made her think of Eternity, perhaps because the silver made the light seem unnatural somehow.

She crept to the window, crouching before it, her hand on the sill, and peered out.

Behind their home lay Amherst's burial ground. The poor and the unshriven slept here, alongside the colored and those not raised within the confines of a Christian household. Oftimes she sat in her window and watched as families mourned or as a sexton dug a grave for a lonesome and already forgotten soul.

On this night, the graves were bathed in unnatural light. The world below looked silver, except for the darkness lurking at the edges. Something had leached all of the color from the ground, the stones, and the trees behind—yet the bleakness had a breathtaking beauty.

In the midst of it all, a young man walked, hands clasped behind him as if he were deep in thought. Although he assumed the posture of a scholar, his muscular arms and shoulders spoke of a more physical toil—farmer, perhaps, or laborer. Oddly the light did not make his shirt flare white. Instead, its well-tailored form looked as black as the darkness at the edges of the cemetery. His trousers too, although she was accustomed to black trousers. All the men in her life wore them.

He paced among the graves as if measuring the distance between them, pausing at some, and staring at the others as if he knew the soul inside.

Emily leaned forward, captivated. She had seen this man before, but in the churchyard in the midst of a funeral. He had leaned against an ornate headstone, resting on one of the cherubim encircling the stone's center.

She had expected someone to chase him off—after all, one did not lean against gravestones, particularly as the entire congregation beseeched the Lord to send a soul to its rest.

But he had for just a brief moment. Then, perhaps realizing he had been seen, he moved—vanished, she thought that day, because she did not see him among the mourners.

Although she saw him now.

As if he overheard the thought, he raised his head. He had a magnificently fine face, strong cheekbones, narrow lips, dramatic brows curving over dark eyes. Those eyes met hers, and her breath caught. She had been found out.

He smiled and extended a hand.

For a moment, she wanted nothing more than to clasp it.

But she sat until the feeling passed.

She ran to no one. She did no one's bidding, not even her father's. While she tried to be a dutiful daughter, she was not one.

And she would not run to a stranger in the burial ground, no matter how beautiful the evening.

No matter how lovely the man.

May 23, 1886
The Homestead
Amherst, Massachusetts

Piles of papers everywhere. Vinnie sat cross-legged on the rag rug no one had pulled out during spring cleaning—Emily had been too sick to have her room properly aired—and stared at the sewn booklets she had found hidden in Emily's bureau.

Once their mother had thought the bureau would house Emily's trousseau, back when the Dickinsons believed even their strange oldest daughter would marry well and bring forth children, as God commanded. But she had not, and neither had Vinnie. Austin had married well, or so it seemed at first, although he and Sue were now estranged, a condition made worse by the untimely death of their youngest child, Gib.

Vinnie wished Emily had given Austin this task. Emily lived in her words. She had better friends on paper than she had in person. She wrote letters by the bucketful, and scribbled alone late into the night. To destroy Emily's correspondence, Vinnie thought, would be like losing her sister all over again.

And yet Vinnie had been prepared to do it, until she discovered the booklets. Hand-sewn bundles of papers, with individual covers. Inside, the papers were familiar: Emily's poems. But oh, so many more than Vinnie had ever imagined.

Emily gifted family and friends with her poems, sometimes in letters, sometimes folded into a whimsical package. Her tiny careful lettering at times made the poem difficult to discern, but there, upon the page, were little moments of Emily's thoughts. Anyone who knew her could hear her voice resound off the pages:

I'm nobody, she said in her wispy childlike voice. *Who are you? Are you nobody, too?*

Vinnie could almost see her, crouching beside her window, watching the children play below. More than once, she had sent them a basket of toys from above, but had not played with them.

Instead, she preferred to watch or participate at a great distance.

But once she had been a child, with Vinnie.

Then there's a pair of us, Emily said. *Don't tell! They'd banish us, you know.*

The poems had no date, and Emily's handwriting looked the same as always. Her cautious, formal handwriting, not the scrawl of her early drafts.

These poems had meant something to her. She had sought to preserve them.

Vinnie closed the booklet, and clutched it to her bosom.

Emily lived inside these books. However, then, could Vinnie destroy them?

May 19, 1847
The West Street House
Amherst, Massachusetts

The silver light returned four nights later. It was not tied to the moon as Emily had thought because, as she headed up the stairs to her room, she noted clouds forming on the horizon.

The night had been dark until the light appeared.

Instead of peering out her window, she slipped on her shoes and hurried down the stairs. Her father read in the library. Her mother cleaned up the kitchen from the evening meal. Her older brother Austin, home from school, sat at the desk in the front parlor, composing a letter. He did not look up as she passed.

She let herself out the front, simply so that her mother would not see her.

Cicadas sang. The air smelled of spring—green leaves and fresh grass and damp ground. All familiar scents, familiar sounds. The music of her life.

The strange silver light did not touch the front of the house. Perhaps the light came from some kind of powerful lantern, one she had not seen that night.

She stole around the house, her heart pounding. She never went out at night, except when accompanied, and only when it was required. A concert, a meeting, a request to witness one of her father's legal documents.

Unmarried girls did not roam the grounds of their home, even if they were sixteen and worldly wise. She was not worldly wise, although she was cautious.

And now what she was doing felt forbidden, deliciously daring, and exciting.

She rounded the corner into the back yard. The silver light flowed over the burial ground, but did not touch the Dickinson property. The darkness began at the property line, which she found passing strange.

But as she stepped onto the grass behind her house, the silver light caught her white dress, making it flare like a beacon.

She froze, heart pounding. Revealed. Her hands shook, and she willed them to stop.

She had nothing to be afraid of, she told herself. The burial ground was empty except for the light.

She tiptoed forward, trying not to rustle the grass. She kept her breathing even and soft. She had seen deer move this way, silently through thick foliage. The grass was not thick here. The yardman kept it trim for the Dickinsons, the sexton for the burial ground.

Yet she felt as if she were being watched. The hair rose on the back of her neck, and in spite of her best efforts, her heart rate increased.

It took all of her concentration to keep her breathing steady.

To walk in a graveyard at night. What kind of ghost or demon was she trying to summon?

All of Amherst already thought her strange. Would they think her even stranger if they saw her wandering through the graves, her white dress making her seem ghostly and ethereal?

Something moved beside her. She looked over her shoulder, half expecting Austin, arms crossed, a frown on his face. *What are you doing?* he'd ask in a voice that mimicked Father's.

Only Austin wasn't there.

No one was there.

She wanted to run back to the house, but she made herself walk forward, to that small patch of ground where she had seen the man four nights before. The graves there were not fresh. One had sunken slightly. Another had flattened against the earth. A third had a stone so old that the carvings had become unreadable. The light seemed stranger here than it had from the window, leaching the color from her skin. She seemed fanciful, a phantom herself. If someone saw her, they might not think they were seeing young Miss Dickinson, but a specter instead.

Something rose behind one of the ancient tilting headstones—a column of smoke, no!, a man dressed all in black, a cowl over his head, a scythe in his hand.

Emily fled across the grass, careful to avoid sinking graves, her breath coming in great gasps. She was halfway to the house before she caught herself.

It was, she thought, a trick of the light, and nothing more. She had expected to see a phantom in the graveyard and so she had—the worst of all phantoms, that old imperator, Death.

She made herself turn. She was not frightened of anything, and she would not flee like a common schoolgirl from phantoms in the darkness.

Behind her, the sky was clear, the silver light still filling the burial ground. But there was no column of smoke, no cowled figure, no scythe.

There was, however, that handsome young man, leaning on a gravestone that looked like it might topple at any moment.

He smiled at her again, and her traitorous heart leapt in anticipation. But she knew better than to approach him—not because she was afraid of him; she wasn't—but because she knew once she spoke, this illusion of interest and attraction would fade, and he would see her as all the others had, as intense and odd and unlikable.

"Emily Elizabeth Dickinson," he said, his voice a rich baritone. "Look at you. 'She walks in beauty, like the night.'"

His use of her name startled her. That he so easily quoted Lord Byron startled her all the more. A literate man, and one not afraid of showing his knowledge of the more scandalous poets.

She straightened her shoulders so that she stood at her full height, which wasn't much at all. She knew some often mistook her for a child; she was so slight and small.

"You have me at a disadvantage, sir," she said. "You know of me, but I do not know of you."

His smile was small. "I know of many people who do not know me," he said. "In fact, I am astounded that you can see me at all."

"Tis the strange light, sir," she said. "It illuminates everything."

"That it does," he said. "You should not be able to see it, either."

He was strange, from his word choice to his conversation to his decision to lean against a gravestone. Was this how others saw her? Strange, unpredictable, something they had never encountered before?

"If by that you mean I should not be out here among the graves, you are probably right," she said. "But it is a beautiful evening, and I fancied a walk."

He laughed. "You fancied me."

She raised her chin ever so slightly. "I beg your pardon, sir."

"I did not mean that like it sounds," he said. "You saw me four nights ago, and you came to see what I was doing."

He had caught her again. "Perhaps I did, sir," she said. "What of it?"

"Aren't you going to ask me what I'm doing here?" he asked.

"Mourning, I would assume," she said. "I did not mean to intrude upon your grief."

"You're not," he said. "I am not grieving. I am just visiting my dead."

Blunt words, harsh words, but true words. He was a kindred soul. Her entire family constantly admonished her for her harsh speech. But, she said, she preferred truth to socially acceptable lies.

It seemed, however, that others did not.

She took a step toward him. His eyes twinkled, which surprised her. Before she had thought them dark and deep, unfathomable. The hint of light in them was unexpected.

"Why visit at night?" she asked. "Wouldn't it be better to come here during the day?"

"Yes, it would," he said. "But daylight is not available to me. So I bring my own."

His hand moved, as if he were indicating the silver light. But it seemed to have no obvious source. If he had command of the silver light, then he also had command of the moonlight, something no mortal could possibly have.

So she dismissed his talk as fanciful. But intriguing. Everything about him was intriguing.

He tilted his head as he looked at her. There was a power in his gaze she had never encountered before. It drew her, like it had drawn her that first night. But she was suspicious of power and charisma, much as it attracted her.

"The real question," he said, "is not why I'm here, but why you're here."

"We've already discussed that, sir. I came to investigate the light."

"Ah, yes," he said softly. "But how did you see this light?"

"Sir?" The question disturbed her, and she wasn't quite sure why. She certainly wasn't going to tell him that her bedroom overlooked the burial ground. The fact that he had seen her in her room was already an invasion of privacy no one she knew would approve of.

"This," he said, sweeping his hand again—indicating the graves instead of the light? Had she mistook the gesture?—"should all be invisible to you for another forty years."

She laughed at his naiveté. Death surrounded them always, didn't he know that?

"Death, sir," she said primly, and saw him start at the word, "is all we know of heaven. And all we need of hell."

His smile faded, and so did the light in his eye. "True enough," he said. "So. Don't I frighten you?"

He attracted her; he did not frighten her.

"I suppose you should," she said. "But you do not."

"Amazing," he said softly. "You are truly amazing."

He stood, dusted off the back of his trousers, and nodded at her, his mouth in a determined line.

"This meeting is inappropriate," he said.

She shrugged, no longer uncomfortable. "I have found that most of what I do is inappropriate," she said, wondering if she should admit such a thing to a man she had just met. "I did not mean to compromise you."

He laughed. The sound boomed across the stones. "Compromise me." He bowed slightly, honoring her. "You are a treasure, Miss Dickinson."

"And you are a mystery, sir," she said.

He nodded. "The original mystery in fact," he said. "And I think that for tonight, we shall leave it that way. Good night, Miss Dickinson."

Dismissed, then. Well, she was used to that. People could not stomach her presence long.

"Good night, sir," she said, and slowly, reluctantly, made her way back to the house.

August 16, 1870
The Homestead
Amherst, Massachusetts

Thomas Wentworth Higginson called her his partially cracked poetess. He knew, long before he traveled to the Dickinson home in Amherst, that the woman who wrote to him was different. He had many words for her—wayward, difficult, fascinating.

But none of them prepared him for what he found.

He arrived on a hot August afternoon, expecting conversation about literature and publication and poetry. He preferred literary conversation; he tried not to think about the war, although it haunted him. He dreamed of boots tramping on damp ground, of neighing horses, and startled men.

But he woke, panicked, whenever he saw the hooded figure approach, shrouded in darkness, carrying a scythe.

The Dickinson house itself was beautiful, easily the finest house in Amherst. Two vast stories, built in the Federal style, with an added cupola and a conservatory. Higginson had not expected such finery, including the extensive white fence, the broad expanse of grounds, and the steps leading up to the gate.

He felt, for the first time in years, as if he had not dressed finely enough, as if his usual suit coat and trousers, light worsted to accommodate the summer heat, was too casual for a family that could afford a house like this.

But he had known some of the greatest people in the country, and he had learned that finery did not always equal snobbery. So he rapped on the door with confidence, removing his hat as the door swung open.

A woman no longer young opened the door. Her eyes were bright, her chestnut hair pulled away from her round cheeks. She smiled welcomingly, and said, "You must be Colonel Higginson."

"At your service, ma'am," he said, bowing slightly.

She giggled, which surprised him, and said, "We do not stand on ceremony here, sir. I am Lavinia Dickinson. I'll fetch my sister for you."

She beckoned him to step inside, and so he did with a bit of relief that this clear-eyed, normal girl was not his poetess. He would have been disappointed if she had been wrapped in a predictable façade.

The entry was a wood-paneled room, dark and oppressive after the bright summer light. Lavinia Dickinson delivered him to the formal parlor dotted with lamps, marking it as a house filled with readers. He sat on the edge of the settee as Lavinia Dickinson disappeared behind a door, leaving him, hat in hand, to await instruction. He felt like a suitor rather than an accomplished man who had come to visit one of his correspondents.

Eight years of letters with Emily, as she bid him to call her. Eight years of poems and criticisms and comments. Eight years, spanning his war service and his homecoming, two moves, and changes he had never been able to imagine.

Still, her letters arrived with their tiny handwriting and their startling poems. He had looked forward to this meeting for months now, had tried to stage it for a few years. But the poetess herself rarely left Amherst and he rarely traveled there.

His hands ached slightly, and he unclenched his fingers so that he did not crush his hat.

The house unsettled him; at least, that was what he thought at first. But as the moments wore on, he realized his unease came from the whispers around him, and then something stirring in the air, like a strong rain-scented wind arriving before a storm.

The door banged open, and the storm arrived. She was tiny, with her red hair pulled into two smooth bands. Her plain white dress made her seem young—it was a girl's dress—but the blue net worsted shawl over it was an older woman's affectation. She clutched two day lilies in one fist.

He would have thought her childlike if not for her eyes. They glowed. His breath caught, and he stood a half second too late. He had seen eyes like that before, although not nearly as manic, when he sat across from the militant abolitionist John Brown, whose raid on Harper's Ferry had helped start the war.

Higginson, along with five friends, had funded that raid. He would not have done so if he hadn't believed in Brown and his extreme methods. Most people had been frightened of the man, but Higginson hadn't been. He had thought then that Brown, whom some later called crazy, had the light of God in his eyes.

Higginson did not think God existed in Emily Dickinson's eyes. An odd silver light looked through him, and even though she smiled, she did not seem warm.

She thrust the flowers at him and said, "Forgive me if I'm frightened—"

She didn't seem frightened to him. She seemed excited, like a child about to receive a treat for good behavior. She held part of herself in check, but the excitement overpowered her control, making her jitter.

"—but I hardly see strangers and I don't know what to say."

That didn't stop her. She started talking, but he had trouble listening; all he could do was focus on those eyes. Killer eyes. He had seen eyes like that in some Rebel soldiers as they bayoneted his men. He made himself breathe, made himself listen, made himself converse, but he scarcely remembered what he said.

She introduced him to her father—a colorless old man, without much humor—and invited her sister to join them, but her sister demurred.

Instead, Higginson was stuck with Emily. He felt something drain from him as she talked, a bit of his life essence, as if being around her took something from him. It took all of his considerable strength just to hold his own against her.

The comparison to a storm wasn't even apt. She wasn't a summer storm, filled with rain and thunder. She was a tornado, sweeping in and seizing all around her. Only his encounter with her did not last an instant; it lasted hours.

And when it was finally finished, he staggered out of that strange house, relieved to be gone, and thrilled that she had not touched him. It took all of his strength to hold the day lilies she had given him. The day lilies and the photograph of Elizabeth Barrett Browning's grave.

Emily had smiled at him, a strange, sad, pathetic little smile, and said she was grateful because he had saved her life.

He hadn't saved her life. He hadn't done anything except read her poetry. He had even told her not to publish it because he thought it undisciplined, like her. Or so he had initially thought.

But that evening, as he sat alone in his rented room, trying to find words to express to his wife the strangeness of the experience, he realized that Miss Emily Dickinson hadn't been undisciplined. She hadn't been undisciplined at all.

In fact, it seemed to him, she was one of the most disciplined people he had ever met, as though explosions constantly erupted inside her and she had to keep them contained.

I never was with any one who drained my nerve power so much, he finally wrote to his wife. *Without touching her, she drew from me. I am glad not to live near her.*

He couldn't write any more. He didn't dare tell Mary that he felt Emily Dickinson had taken something vital from him, that talking to her had made him feel as if he were one step closer to death.

December 18, 1854
The West Street House
Amherst, Massachusetts

Emily woke up in his arms, cradled against his chest. This man, who seemed so otherworldly, was warm and passionate. His breathing was even, regular, but try as she might, she could not hear his heart beat.

She tried not to think of that, just like she tried not to think about what she was letting him do, sneaking into her room, lying naked in her bed. Her father had never caught him here, and she used to be afraid of what her father would do.

But now she didn't have that fear. Now she was afraid of what this man would do, this man who carried silver light with him as if he held a lantern.

The light did come when he summoned it, just like he had said to her. And it fled when he asked it to leave. The darkness around him without the light was absolute. She felt same with him, in that darkness, but when he left, terror came.

And he always left before dawn.

He could not handle the light—real light. Daylight.

Her time with him would lessen as summer came, just like it always had. They lived best in winter, together.

She knew what he was. She watched him, after he left her, fading as his light faded, disappearing into the absolute darkness he created. Over time, some of his silver light spilled into her and she could see in the dark better than a cat could.

She could see him don his cowl, and pick up his scythe.

The nights he left early, the nights he arrived late, changed Amherst as well. The days after those nights she heard stories of breathing ceased, and hearts stopped, and sometimes she saw the funerals in the graveyard beneath her window, and she knew they happened because he had been there. He had touched someone.

Not like he touched her.

She was different, or so he said, had been different from the day they met. She should not have been able to see him, not until she was nearly dead herself.

But she was beginning to think she was not alive, not really, that something inside her had died long before she had found him, that her spirit had vanished, that she had no soul.

Surely, she did not feel the stirrings her family felt at revivals, and she did not feel the call of God. She understood He existed, but at a distance, not as someone who could live within her heart.

In earlier times, less enlightened times, here in Massachusetts, they would have called her a witch.

She knew this, and this man, this man who held her, he confirmed it, declaring himself lucky to have found her.

"Love," he said, "does not come to us often."

And by "us," he did not mean her and him. He meant himself and others like him, those whom everyone else called Death. She was not sure whom he worked for—the Devil? Or some unnatural demon? Or Heaven itself? For as she had said to him in their first conversation, Heaven would not exist without him.

Death had to occur before it could be overcome. And she could not die.

Or so she believed.

She pressed herself against his warm skin, losing herself in his familiarity.

To remain alive forever—to live for Eternity—to be Immortal: those things terrified her. She did not discuss them with him, because he thought them good, and she did not want to hurt him.

But he wanted her at his side forever.

And forever, to her, was much too long.

There are, he said to her once—just once—*a thousand ways to live forever. The soul must be preserved.*

Caught like a butterfly in a jar? she asked.

He shook his head, and smiled his beautiful smile at her fancy. *Recorded*, he said. *The soul must find permanence somewhere. Memory fades and eventually souls do as well. Except for a select few, kept alive in word or deed or a powerful magic.*

Have you that magic? she asked.

Sometimes, he said. *I could preserve you.*

No, she said too quickly. Then calmer, as if it didn't frighten her, *No. I prefer to sleep. I don't want Eternity.*

You are the only one then, he said.

Do you have it? she asked.

Yes, he said. *And I would like to share it with you.*

She shuddered. *Promise me you won't. When the time comes. Promise me.*

But he wouldn't promise. And that silence lay like ashes inside her heart.

May 24, 1886
The Homestead
Amherst, Massachusetts

The room had become a pile of papers. Vinnie covered every bare surface with poetry, all written by her sister. Vinnie had finally counted the sheets—counted and recounted and counted again.

Each time, she got a different number, but each time, the number staggered her. At least a thousand.

At least.

And such poems! About things Emily should not have known. Secret things. Intimate things.

Things that made Vinnie blush as she read them, hearing—despite her best intentions—Emily's voice:

You left me, sweet—Emily never called anyone sweet, and yet here it was, an endearment, casual as if she spoke it often—*two legacies. A legacy of love a Heavenly Father would content had He had the offer of....*

Emily, writing of love, the kind of love that men and women had, not love that friends or family had. Vinnie knew that, not because of the word *love*, but because of the other legacy, the one she could hear clearest in Emily's voice, the one that made her sound bitter and frightened and just a little lost:

You left me boundaries of pain, Emily said, *capacious as the sea. Between eternity and time, your consciousness and me.*

Emily was so afraid of eternity, so averse to time that she did not learn how to read a clock until she was fifteen. Time scarcely touched her, not even near the end. She always looked like a girl. Others aged, but Emily remained as youthful as she had been when they moved from the West Street House to the Homestead. She had been perhaps twenty-five or so, a young woman surely, but one trapped in amber.

Vinnie aged, going from a plump young woman to a matronly old maid. Austin had become serious, his face falling into lines that aged him prematurely.

But Emily, in her white dresses, remained the same—at least on the outside.

And who knew what had gone on inside? Clearly Vinnie hadn't. And Vinnie thought she had known her sister as a maid, not as someone who could write, *Wild nights! Wild nights! Were I with thee, wild nights should be our luxury!*

What had Vinnie missed all those years? Were the townspeople of Amherst right and Vinnie wrong? Had Emily locked herself in the house because she pined for a man who left her? Had she truly been one of those women who, like Miss Havisham of *Great Expectations*, had lost herself because of a man?

How could Vinnie have not known that? How could Vinnie have not known about the man?

She sat among her sister's papers, and tried to remember. But the poems were undated and gave her no clue—except that her sister, whom Vinnie thought she knew well, had become a mystery, one Vinnie was beginning to think she would never understand.

October 30, 1855
The West Street House
Amherst, Massachusetts

He sat on the edge of her bed, splendid in his nakedness. Was he splendid because he was immortal? Or had he been splendid in life?

Emily was afraid to ask him. She had learned that direct questions made him glare at her with those empty death-filled eyes.

Some questions she left unasked. Others she danced around, got answers to. Sometimes he just told her unbidden, told her of his extreme loneliness, and how pleased he was to have found a kindred soul.

That was what he called her. A kindred soul.

And of late, Vinnie told her that in certain light, her eyes turned silver.

Emily shuddered and pulled the blanket around her before leaning against his naked back. He bent at the waist, his hands in his thick black hair.

"You have to stop it," he said in desperation. She had never heard this tone in his voice before.

"I can't," she said. "We're moving. Father has decreed it."

He shook his head. "You have to change your father's mind."

"It's not possible," Emily said. "My grandfather built that house. He lost it. My father has waited his entire life to buy it back."

His tone frightened her; his whole demeanor frightened her. She had never been frightened of him before.

But she continued to lean against him, trying to draw strength from his warm skin.

"I can't visit you there," he said, his voice shaking. "Not until…."

"Until?" she asked.

"Not for a very long time," he said. "Unless…."

She didn't like his use of the word *unless*. But the idea made him sit up, and turn toward her, taking her face in his hands. He often did that before he kissed her, but he didn't kiss her now.

Instead, he peered into her eyes.

"I could take you now. We would be together. We could work together," he said.

And she felt something—a pulling, a change.

She wrenched her face from his grasp and looked away from him.

"No," she said.

"No?" he asked.

"No," she said. "I don't want to live like you do. I've told you that."

"But you are already half in my world," he said. "Come the rest of the way."

"No," she said.

"Then tell your father to stay here," he said.

She shook her head, resisting the urge to scramble off the bed. As long as he didn't peer at her like that again, he wouldn't be able to pull her life from her.

"You made that impossible," she said.

"Me?"

She nodded. "I am an unmarried woman. I am subject to my father's commands. I cannot influence him. So I will move with him."

And she felt—triumphant? Relieved? She wasn't sure. But not unhappy, like she might have expected. Part of her had always hoped this would end.

"You could come to the burial ground," he said.

She imagined it for a half moment—safe inside alabaster chambers, cradled in his arms—and then she shuddered. She would lose herself there. Lose herself, and lose track of time.

She didn't want to say no directly. He would get angry.

Instead, she said, "Is that why you can come here? The burial ground behind the house?"

He nodded. "I belong here."

"And I belong with my family," she said, wondering if that were indeed true. If it were true, why had she been able to see him? If it were true, why had he fallen in love with her?

"Emily, please," he said. "I won't be able to see you again, except fleeting glances at funerals."

"Or deathbeds," she said, wondering if, in some ways, that was what she sat on. A deathbed.

"Or deathbeds," he whispered.

She closed her eyes, not willing to see his anguish. And when she opened them, just a moment later, he was gone.

So was the strange silver light.

And something else—a part of her. A part she had not realized she'd had.

She went to the window and looked out. He was walking among the graves, like he had the first night she had seen him, his robe over his arm, his scythe carried casually in his left hand.

Walking away.

She wondered when she would see him again. How many years? How much time?

Would he again sit on her bed and tell her he loved her? Or would he be angry?

She wasn't sure she ever wanted to find out.

May 24, 1886
The Homestead
Amherst, Massachusetts

Vinnie clutched a pile of poems in one hand. So many about death. Perhaps those were even more shocking than those about love. And the death poems—they weren't typical reminiscences. They were odd, like Emily had been odd, and a bit unfathomable.

Vinnie had even heard Emily speak some of them aloud. Only Vinnie had not realized they were poems at the time.

Like this one, which Emily had spoken late one night, almost unbidden. She looked up from her scratching pen, and smiled sadly at Vinnie. Emily didn't speak the poem exactly as written. She added a bit to make it conversational. But Vinnie remembered it as if it had happened just a week before instead of decades ago.

"Sometimes I think a death-blow is a life-blow to some," Emily said, "who, until they died, did not become alive."

Vinnie had stopped walking by, looked at Emily oddly, and then shrugged, wondering what had provoked that outburst. She still did not know.

Had someone died recently? Had Emily been reacting to something? Or had she simply felt an inspiration?

Except that it felt true, as if something provoked it. Emily often broke into strangely structured speech when provoked, and now Vinnie knew why.

She had been reciting her own poems.

Vinnie wished she could go back, wished she could recapture memories of all of those recitations. Maybe she was; maybe that was why she heard Emily's voice whenever she read a poem. Maybe Emily had spoken them all.

Vinnie clutched the poems against her chest. How could she burn them? They had bits of her sister in them, clinging to them, as if she had not yet died.

March 8, 1860
The Homestead
Amherst, Massachusetts

They were calling her crazy and maybe she was, maybe she was. Certainly she felt wild-eyed and broken, her thoughts swirling in her head. Emily had taken to writing them down, capturing them in bits of paper, and then sewing them into bound booklets like she had done her herbs just a few years before.

At the West Street House, when she used to roam the garden, when she wandered the burial ground.

Emily buried her face in her hands. Her room here in the Homestead was larger than her room in the West Street House. She had a conservatory and a better kitchen. She should have liked it here, in the best house in Amherst.

She should have liked it.

But she didn't.

Her room here overlooked the street. The house was far enough back so that street sounds seemed faint, but through the trees, she could see the horses, watch the carriages, see the *life*.

She let her hands fall. Then she grabbed a sheet of paper, its smoothness soothing to her fingertips. She stared for a moment at the windows, then grabbed her pen and dipped it in ink.

She hadn't thought she would miss him.

I cannot live with you, she wrote. *It would be life, and life is over there behind the shelf the sexton keeps the key to....*

She paused, sighed, and held the pen away from the paper so it wouldn't blot.

She wasn't alive without him. He had taken something from her. Everyone noticed it. They had always thought her strange, but now they feared her, and she wasn't quite sure why.

She hid away from them, mostly because she didn't want to see the fear in their eyes.

She wrote, *I could not die with you.*

Was she writing him a letter? And if so, where would she leave it? Did she truly want him to find it, to know she missed him?

Nor could I rise with you, because your face would put out Jesus's....

Her hand trembled as she wrote.

They'd judge us—how? For you served Heaven, you know, or sought to. I could not.

No one dared see these. Not him, not anyone. Think of what they would say. Think of what they would do to her, even in this enlightened time.

She shuddered, feeling the temptation to go to him. But she could not. She dared not.

So we must keep apart, she wrote to him. She *was* writing to him now. She had known that, but she finally acknowledged it. *You there, I here, with just the door ajar....*

The door ajar. That was what the others felt. She straddled the world between, half her life there, half here. She hadn't fled him quickly enough.

She hadn't known what he would cost her, what she had chosen. Then, five years ago, she had tried to go back to a normal life, not realizing it was too late.

So she lived in this strange half-world, neither here nor there, not willing to cross the threshold into his life—and Eternity, not able to fully live in hers.

She hadn't expected this, and she had no idea how to live with it.

Except to scrawl the maddening thoughts. Except to try to quell the feeling of panic, always rising inside.

Her pen, her paper. Her silence. She had nothing else left.

April 20, 1862
Worcester, Massachusetts

The envelope itself looked a bit odd, the handwriting tiny, the edges a bit too thick. That Higginson noticed it was odd too, considering the volume of mail he got lately. He had published an essay titled "A Letter to a Young Contributor" in the *Atlantic Monthly*, hoping to slow down the volume of unsolicited submissions the magazine got as the war got underway. Instead, his essay increased them. And worse, they were all addressed to him.

Only the most select made it to his study in Worcester. Later he would say he added the thick envelope because he had known it carried something marvelous, but at the time, he had taken it only because it struck him as unusual.

He sat in his leather-backed chair, a mound of manuscripts on one side, and his own writing paper on the other. Books surrounded him. He didn't keep newspapers in his study, preferring they remain in the parlor. The news since Lincoln's inaugural a year before had been ugly at best, and Higginson wanted to keep horror out of his study.

He had a hunch it would enter his life all too soon.

He slit the envelope with his letter opener, careful not to disturb the papers inside. A second envelope tumbled out, followed by five sheets of paper—four poems and an unsigned letter. He opened that envelope first, only to find a card inside with the name Emily Dickinson printed upon it in pencil. The five pages had been written in pen.

Intrigued, he started with the letter:

Mr Higginson,

Are you too deeply occupied to say if my Verse is alive?
The Mind is so near itself—it cannot see, distinctly—and I have none to ask—
Should you think it breathed—and had you the leisure to tell me, I should feel quick gratitude—
If I make the mistake—that you dared to tell me—would give me sincerer honor—toward you—
I enclose my name—asking you, if you please—Sir—to tell me what is true?
That you will not betray me—it is needless to ask—since Honor is its own pawn—

The breathless style startled him and it carried over to the poems, all untitled. Of course the verse lived; he had never seen such life in poetry, and he had read a lot. An untamed life, that reflected the writer more than any other poems he had ever read, as if the writer put herself on the page without regard to convention, or even to a reader.

He reread all of the documents before answering Miss Dickinson. Her verse was alive, her words breathed. But the grammatical errors grated on him. He tapped the tip of his pen against his teeth. He had somehow to tell her that she wasn't yet ready for publication without destroying the spirit that crackled out of the poetry.

Finally he decided he would operate on the poems himself, and she would be able to learn from his surgery. He meticulously copied what she had done, then set about to repair it.

October 5, 1883
The Evergreens
Amherst, Massachusetts

It was a mistake, Emily knew it was a mistake, but she couldn't stop herself, she didn't dare stop herself, didn't dare *think* about any of it as she clung to Vinnie's arm and stepped outside the house. The fresh evening air seemed a mockery—next door, right next door, little Gilbert was dying, didn't the Gods know that?

Of course they did; they had ordered it, and because they had ordered it, she cursed them for reveling in the death of children.

She adored Gib, her brother's youngest child, born late. Witty and funny and oh, so alive, he made her feel like a child again. Certainly she hadn't laughed so hard in the years before he learned to speak—maybe she hadn't laughed at all.

She loved him, her heart's child, and now typhoid was taking him, and she couldn't stay away, even though she knew she should, even though she tried.

She had picked the right moment to flee her own mother's bedside, and her father's too. Vinnie had to tend the dying, because Emily could not, frightened as she was of ever seeing *him* again.

But she could not flee Gib's bedside and forgive herself. Sometimes love made harsh demands, and this was one.

She walked across the yard into a house as outwardly familiar as her own. Huge, built in the style of an Italian villa, the Evergreens housed the other Dickinsons, the ones who ran her life—her brother Austin, his wife Sue, and their three beautiful children.

That Austin had all but abandoned Sue few knew except Emily. She didn't approve of Austin's mistress, Mabel Loomis Todd, but Emily didn't dare disapprove either, not after the way she had lost herself all those years ago. Austin was here tonight, but Miss Todd was not, and Emily was grateful for that. Even though she knew Miss Todd frequented Emily's home, Emily had not seen her and preferred to pretend that Miss Todd herself was little more than a ghost.

Vinnie put a hand over Emily's as they walked up the steps into the Evergreens. Emily had not been inside in fifteen years, seeing it only from the windows of the Homestead. Her heart pounded as if she had walked a thousand miles, and the smell—the smell nearly turned her stomach.

It was a sick house, reeking of camphor and vomit and despair.

But she continued forward, leaning on Vinnie a bit too much, walking up the stairs to Gib's bedchamber, the smells growing stronger, harsher, more insistent.

Vinnie, bless her, did not say a word. When they reached the door, Emily let out a sigh of relief. *He* was not there. Gib would not die this night.

The boy looked small in his bed, too thin for an eight-year-old, too frail to be the vital child Emily so adored. Sue—grown matronly in middle age—saw Emily and hugged her so tightly that Emily couldn't catch her breath. Austin peered at her from his post near the bureau.

"You're too frail," Austin said. "We don't need you ill as well."

Emily glared at him, and Austin looked away, as everyone did when she gave them her gimlet eye. Then she sat beside Gib and took his hand.

His eyes opened for a brief moment and he saw her. "Aunt Emily," he breathed, his voice raspy and congested.

"Gib," she said, unable to find words for the first time in her life.

His skin was too hot, his eyes glistened with fever. He turned away from her, but kept his hand clamped around hers. Sue placed wet cloths on his forehead, and Austin fretted about feeding the child.

But Emily simply held his dry little hand, hoping he would look at her again. He did not.

Instead, there was an emptiness in the room. She looked up, the hair on the back of her neck rising. She and Gib were momentarily alone. Sue had gone for more cloths, Austin for water or perhaps just to escape, Vinnie to find camphor to ease Gib's increasingly labored breathing.

The light suddenly turned silver, and Emily inwardly cursed. She had not made her escape.

He had come, and he would see her, an old woman, losing a child of her heart.

She didn't look up. Instead she wrapped her free hand around Gib's.

"Don't take him," she said. "Please don't take him."

"You know I can't do that." His voice was as she remembered, only more musical, deep and filled with warmth. "I have missed you, Emily, more than I could ever express."

"Don't." She brought her head up, and her gaze met his.

Damnation, he was still beautiful. His cowl was down, his scythe against the wall. He looked like he had moved in, and despite that, despite the horror of it, she felt his pull even now. He reached out to touch her and she leaned away.

"This is about Gib, not me," she said. "Don't take him."

"I must," he said. He didn't sound sorrowful. He didn't know Gib. She did.

"Take me instead," she said. "My life for his."

He shook his head. "You're already half mine, Emily," he said. "It's not a fair trade. Is there another life you would give for his?"

Her heart chilled. He would have her trade someone else's life for Gib's? What kind of bargain was that?

"Take me, *please*," she said. "You have always wanted me."

He nodded. "And I still do. I love you, Emily."

She knew that; she also knew that she had loved him once, and feared him too. She didn't fear him now. All she feared was his power.

"So you have what you want," she said. "Leave Gib. Let him grow up."

He looked at his hands as if they were not his. Then he sighed. "I cannot, Emily. His soul is incandescent. Pure."

She knew his next words, but she didn't want to hear him say them. "And mine is not."

"I'm sorry," he whispered. "But you can come with us."

"No," she said. "*No.*"

He touched Gib, and Gib froze—froze!—the heat leaving his body.

"*No,*" she said again. "No!"

And then they were both gone—he and Gib, the scythe, everything—leaving only a frail shell behind.

Everyone came back into the room as if they had been summoned, Sue leading, tears on her dear familiar face, Austin looking ancient and horrible, and Vinnie, Vinnie, hands clasped to her chest.

They crowded the body and Emily staggered away, mouth tasting of paper, eyes dry, head aching.

"Take me home," she said to Vinnie. "Please."

Emily had to go home now, taking her fragile, ragged, worthless little soul. If she hadn't had a fruitless romance with *him*, if she hadn't wasted all of that time, she still would have seen him here, and she could have bargained with him, she could have given him her soul in place of Gib's and it would not have been worthless. Gib would have lived, and so would she.

But *he* had cheated her of that. He had known, and he had cheated her, because he claimed he loved her.

Could one such as that love?

She didn't know. She didn't want to think of it. Not now, and maybe not ever.

May 24, 1886
The Homestead
Amherst, Massachusetts

Twilight was falling as Vinnie picked up the last pile of poems. She had just lit Emily's favorite lamp, giving the room a brief scent of kerosene and burned wick.

Vinnie's hands shook. She was exhausted, but unwilling to quit. The poems— ah, the poems—they were Emily, and more than Emily. They were about her life too.

There's been a death in the opposite house, began one, and Vinnie set it aside. She could not read that. It was about Gib. There were a number about Gib, some even calling him by name.

Gib's death had destroyed Emily. From that moment forward, she had been ill, although most did not know it. She continued her letters and, clearly, her poetry, but little else, her eyes hollow, her expression always a little lost.

Not with a club the heart is broken, Emily whispered, *nor with a stone. A whip so small you could not see it….*

Like a poem, Vinnie thought. Like a poem.

"I can't do it, Em," she whispered as if her sister were still here. For all she knew, her sister was alive in the poetry, haunting the room like a restless ghost. "I can't do it."

Burning the poems would be like losing Emily all over again. And storing them would be wrong too, because Austin or his daughter Mattie might burn them, following Emily's wishes.

Vinnie would burn the papers, burn the letters. She would do that much. But the poems were alive, like her sister had been, and she could not destroy them.

Finally, Emily had to step out of her room and let the world see her as Vinnie had seen her, all those years ago—vibrant and witty and filled with an astonishing love.

May 15, 1886
The Homestead
Amherst, Massachusetts

He came like she knew he would, his face filled with triumph. Emily was too weak to fight him. She couldn't get out of bed, she couldn't even open her eyes, yet she could see him, sitting on the edge of the bed, his hand gripping hers.

"Are you ready to join me, Emily?" he asked, not trying to disguise the joy in his voice.

"No," she said. "I will never join you."

"You have no choice," he said. "I take everyone."

"But you do not keep them," she said. "You taught me all those years ago how to defeat you. When the memory is gone, the soul goes too. After Vinnie, after Austin, after Mattie, no one will remember me."

"Except me," he said.

"And you do not count," she said, "because you remember everyone you touched."

His eyes widened just a little. "You hate me, Em?"

"For Gib," she said. "I'll never forgive you for Gib."

"Never is a long time," he said.

"But do not fear," she said. "I have escaped Eternity."

"Would it be so bad, Emily, spending forever with me?" he asked.

"Yes," she said. "It would."

"You do not mean it," he said as he took what was left of her soul. She felt a momentary relief, a respite from pain she hadn't realized she had, and then a brief incandescent sense of joy.

Only a few more years and they would go quickly. Vinnie would see to it. Nothing of Emily would remain, nothing except a name carved into a stone above an old and sunken grave—and someday, not even that.

She had won. God help her, she had finally won.

May 15, 1892
Cambridge, Massachusetts

Higginson had the dream again. He used to dream of that clearing in Florida, filled with bodies laid out symmetrically. But ever since he turned in his edited version of *The Poems of Emily Dickinson* to the publisher, this dream had supplanted the other.

Emily, as he had first seen her, red hair parted, white dress, beseeching him not to betray her. *Honor me*, she would say, her eyes silver and terrifying. *Honor me.*

And he would say, *I am. I am making your work known.*

Then she would raise her arms, like a banshee from Irish lore, and screech, and as she screeched, the hooded figure would rise behind her and clasp his arms around her, dragging her to the clearing and all those dead men....

And Higginson would wake, heart pounding, breath coming in rapid gasps.

This morning, after the dream, he threw on his dressing gown and made his way to his study. He knew why he had had the dream this time. Another volume of *The Poems by Emily Dickinson* had arrived with a note that this was the seventh edition.

Seven. And more to come. He and Mabel Loomis Todd had barely touched the thousand manuscripts Miss Dickinson had left. He admitted to no one how surprised he was; he had thought her words too strange for the reading public, her gift too rare.

But they adored it, some, he thought, in part to the surgery he had felt it necessary to perform, ridding it of her excessive dashes and her breathless punctuation. But still, the essence of her lived.

Are you too deeply occupied to say if my Verse is alive? she had written him in that very first letter.

And now he could answer her truthfully: her verse was more alive than ever. *She* was more alive than ever.

So why had the first sight of the seventh edition filled him with such horror?

He picked it up and thumbed through it—stopping suddenly at unfamiliar words. He did not recall editing this poem.

He eased into his favorite chair, book in hand, and read:

> *Because I could not stop for Death,*
> *He kindly stopped for me;*
> *The carriage held but just ourselves*
> *And Immortality.*

There was no despair mentioned in the poem, and yet he felt it, like he felt that banshee scream.

What had she written to him once, when she mentioned his books about the War?

My wars are laid away in books.

Yes. Yes they were.

He closed the volume, determined to never open it again.

Twilight of the Gods

By

Chris Ryall

"Lie to a liar, for lies are his coin; Steal from a thief, for that is easy; lay a trap for a trickster and catch him at first attempt, but beware of an honest (wo)man"

Arab proverb

PREFACE

I'd never given much thought to how I would die ... because I never had to. My fate was written by any number of foolish scribes who put pig's blood to parchment to tell of the coming of Ragnarok that we gods will soon face.

For those of you mortals who haven't yet sat around a campfire and heard those tales, *Ragnarok* means "the twilight of the gods." As in, the day the sun ceases to shine on us and you humans are forced to find some other—lesser—group of deities upon whom to cast your prayers.

That said, it tends to make you rethink what you know about your impending fate when you unexpectedly find yourself staring down the business end of a sword, as I now was.

She pulled me close, her blade poking a bloody kiss into the underside of my jaw. She stared at me with those cold eyes of hers. It appeared likely to me now that my time would come sooner than was written. I suppose, all things considered, it's better at this point in my life to perish in the arms of a passionate woman than it is to do so in the flaming conflagration those annoying poets go on about.

Still, had I known then what I know now, I never would've come here to Jotunheim in the first place.

Oh, who am I kidding? I always knew it would go down exactly this way. I made *sure* of it, in fact. Your dreams are what you make of them, after all, and my foolish dream of finding love was always going to lead me to this.

The huntress drew back her sword, its perfectly honed blade reflecting a silvery line across its intended target—my neck. I suppressed a yawn so as not to embarrass her. Death can be so tedious. And not much is worse in the eyes of Loki than tedium.

1. THIRD WINTER

Before I get to that sordid business, let me back up a bit. My father offered to drive me there in his chariot. It wasn't so much that he wanted to personally escort me out of town as much as he just needed me to leave Asgard proper under my own power while that was still an option.

It was to the frigid wasteland of Jotunheim that I was now being exiled—an action that he assumed brought with it feelings of great horror for me.

I loved the golden spires of Asgard, but my presence here was no longer working for me, or for the general populace. They wished me politely removed for a time, as my father explained.

"Loki," my father said to me, "I must spirit you away from Asgard in the darkness of nightfall. For if brave, all-hearing Heimdall becomes aware that you still reside within these walls, he will pull your entrails from your body, tie them to my ravens' wings and send them a-soar. And I shan't blame him in the least."

That was why my father was the leader of all Asgard—his ability to put a positive spin on dire events.

My father stared at me. His one remaining eye was likely looking me up and down, filled with its usual mix of pity and remorse-tinged loathing. This time, I didn't notice, because it was the ocular cavity where his other eye used to occupy space that was truly troubling me. My father once plucked out that offending eye in what I consider to be a misguided quest for knowledge. After all, I venture to say that the knowledge he received upon removing the orb was something along the lines of "don't pull your own eye out, fool; it hurts like hell!"

My one-eyed father had his other son, my half-brother, constantly by his side, so what need had he for me now? We don't look alike, my father and I, and not just because I have two good eyes with which to see. We're not blood relations, he and I. Heimdall, the miserable oaf, Asgard's sentry, liked to spread vile stories that I am actually descended from two malicious frost giants, and ended up in Odin's care after he slew my real parents in battle.

In addition to Heimdall, who seems to have taken it upon himself to report my misdeeds to my father, my lunkheaded step-brother Thor also seeks to curry favor with Odin. And since he *is* the fruit of my father's well-traveled loins—I have been feeling like naught but an unwanted burden.

My dear father, king of the gods tho' he may be, likes to feel needed, and it's Thor who truly needs the supervision and help. Thor would likely forget to eat were not my father there to provide sustenance. This is not a smart lad I'm speaking of. Whereas I am an entity unto myself, dependent on no man or god. But still....

"I've been wanting to leave for a while, father." I had practiced this speech since the recent incident that really turned opinion against me, and I was starting to believe it myself. "It's my *dog* who raises my concern—I don't want to leave him here. He needs me, that pup. Can I—"

"It is no longer a question of your *wants*, child. Remaining within these walls will result in your immediate death and dismemberment, and I'd prefer that not happen under my auspices."

"Dismemberment, *too*? Why is everyone so mad, father?"

"My son, need you ask? The *brightest* of us has been extinguished through your misdeeds."

My father had a way of cutting to the quick.

"You must go. But I will watch over you from afar," he said. "Be it as a hawk, or a bear or—"

"Or a rutting pig, my father? Or ... no, I forget myself, mother is doing her dutiful best to finally curb your rutting, isn't she?"

I could suddenly see enough distaste for me in his one eye to be glad that its mate was no longer perched on the other side of his nose.

We departed that evening. Forgoing his sky-chariot, my father chose instead to spirit me away in the guise of a snow owl, and he clutched me, now transfigured into a common rat (not *my* choice of animal, mind you), in his talons. (Also, this was not my preferred way to travel, let me tell you.)

As we traversed the night sky, my father remained silent. I noticed the temperature dropping considerably. In the sky, I mean. My father's own temperature was already matching the frigid air before we even took flight.

"Father, might we stop for some warmth? My teeth are chattering, and this rat-body isn't equipped for...?"

"Your teeth chatter like the rodent you have become, my son. Now remain quiet."

Quiet wasn't in my nature whether I was rat or god, however.

"Father? The cold ... it persists beyond the norm, doesn't it? We should be basking in a warm spring evening for this flight, should we not?"

"Aye, Loki, that we should." He squeezed my rat-form a little tighter. Perhaps unconsciously. But likely not. "It would indeed be a renewed spring world for us all, had your machinations not led us to this point.

"You, my son, have brought on Fimbul Winter. Ragnarok cannot be far away now."

Fimbul Winter. That is, winter lasting for three seasons in a row, without break. Winter so cold, it threatens to crack the nine worlds in half. The ever-winter. The end-storm. The—

"Loki, are you listening?"

"Of course, father. Cold, snow, Armageddon. Got it." I think he kept talking but really, with the cold numbing my tiny ears and still more talk of our pre-ordained fates, who could be expected to properly listen?

"I was saying, Loki, that if you gaze across the horizon, you will see the world-tree, Yggdrasil. Its branches extend into the heavens and across this world, as well as others. Perhaps soon you will sit under its all-encompassing coverage and reflect upon what you have done. Perhaps there, you will learn what I seem unable to teach you."

"Possibly, father. Or perhaps I will instead become a beaver and eat through its braaaaaanches—!"

My father released me from his talons suddenly, his wings never beating any slower as he did so. I dropped down in the night sky, the heavy clouds through which I fell coating me with a layer of ice that only helped increase my speed.

My father the one-eyed owl was already out of sight when I struck the ground, and hit it hard, I did. But at least the impact jarred loose all the ice and soot stuck to my ratty fur.

Before changing back to now-bruised human form, I lay on the ground, letting my bones and muscles stitch themselves back together. My flattened lungs gasped for deep breaths of air. I was a rat, I was bruised and dirty, and I was alone in the cold, dark night.

So it was that Loki the trickster-god came to Jotunheim. Just in time for the new school year to begin.

This frozen area of the eternal realm was where I was now stuck—an action that I took to with equal parts horror and anticipation.

I enjoyed living in Asgard, the grandeur and pomposity of it all. I was enamored with the extreme seriousness with which most of my godly cohorts went about their day. I loved deflating those pompous balloons. But I also felt alone inside its stately walls.

"Loki," my father spoke to me through one of his ravens, which now took perch upon my shoulder—abandoned by him though I had been, he couldn't just sever the golden string entirely and loose me on snowy Jotunheim without parting words—"though you be not born of my blood, still are you my son. Still will I care for you from afar."

"Still will you use your bird to make sure I don't pull a fast one and leave this frozen wasteland, father. I know well how you work."

"Dearest Loki," the raven said again in its best bird-like approximation of my father's stentorian tones, "I helped you avoid the reckoning that you were due. But the forces you have set in motion cloud the mood here every day, even as the doom-clouds gather in the sky."

"Yes, yes." Now he had birds trying to make me feel guilty?

"You misunderstand. My message is two-tiered. The first thing I want to impart is that I need the time you spend in Jotunheim's school system to be productive; you need to learn humility, honor, and respect."

"I hope those classes are offered here, All-Father."

"And the second thing I need you to know is that there may not be an Asgard for you to return to when your lessons are done."

Well, this was an interesting tactic to take. "Packing up and moving where I can't cause any more mischief, father?"

Have you ever heard a raven emit an exasperated sigh? I just did. "The forces in fiery Muspelheim are gathering, Loki. Fimbul Winter is but the beginning."

"From there, I'd expect the cold of this never-ending winter to dampen even the spirits of Muspelheim fire-demons, my father."

"Always levity from you when gravity is needed. I could no longer protect you from retribution were you to remain in Asgard, and now, I must devote my energy toward preventing the impending conflagration. In short, I cannot keep watch over you. You will be alone, my son."

We said our goodbyes. The bird resisted my attempts to kiss it on its lips, in part perhaps because it possessed no such lips. As it flew off, my father's bird-words rang in my head—I was alone. Again, as it ever was.

Well, my dog would join me soon. Hopefully under nicer transport from Asgard than I had myself.

I took refuge in a nearby barn and pondered my situation. The surrounding meadow and its wild horses grazing nearby would suit my dog just fine once he was sent along to me.

Removed as I was from Asgard now, away from the familiar faces and regular opportunities to scheme against those windbags, I began to feel more alone than I ever had before. And one never wants to enter a new school fully alone, not even the great trickster-god himself.

Jotunheim High School had a total of three hundred and thirty-six—now thirty-seven—students; the number of Asgardian schoolchildren upon whom I could visit my many pranks had numbered into the thousands. Also, I knew those children; I knew their parents. I likely out-schemed generations of the same family. Here, however, I knew not what to expect. I would be the outsider to these students. If I was lucky, that is. Worse still would be for my reputation—and my recent misdeed, which so many in Asgard found unforgivable—to follow me here.

I knew from my earliest days of consciousness that I would never fit in amongst the Asgardians. Physically, I could alter my form to adopt the typically bulky form of your average god-son. But mentally, it was apparent I'd never be one of them. Instead, I took comfort in the goat-meadows; as a fish in the lakes and streams; in my time soaring the heavens and excreting upon the heads of the self-important gods in my midst. But among others my age who dwelled within the realm eternal—I always felt removed from them. I certainly never befriended anyone there.

Walking around my new surroundings, I happened upon a frozen patch that reflected my own haunted visage back to me. I looked sallow, pale. So no problems there, anyway. But my heart—the very organ that many ... okay, most ... accuse me of not possessing—beat with a certain ache I'd not noticed before.

Add to that the nagging feeling in my head that the idea of an outsider such as me ever knowing true love was nothing but folly, and it becomes clear why a single tear escaped my eye that night, rolled down my cheek, and froze there (damned Fimbul Winter). The hollow ache in my heart persisted all night.

And the pain was just beginning.

I arrived at the school early the next morning. This is because the hours I keep are my own, and I refuse to be told when to arrive anywhere. Which occasionally leads to awkward moments where I arrive too early, or even worse, on time, without aiming to do so.

I went to the school's administration office, where a heavyset woman with a braid the thickness of my forearm looked me up and down.

"I don't recognize you. New one, then, yah?"

"Yes, yes," I said, taking sudden interest in my boots as I felt her eyes looking me up and down.

She handed my class assignments to me and I walked off, paying no heed to her parting platitudes and empty words about how I should do my best to fit in. Were I not trying to keep away the attention of the Asgardians who wanted my head, I might well have fit my sword in her back. Had I been able to keep my sword, that is. She confiscated it from me before I headed off, telling me that weaponry was allowed only in the hands of the teaching staff, not the students. Already this school's rules were proving tough to take. Perhaps I would have been better served to follow my original plan of disguising myself as a fish and swimming in streams to avoid the vengeful eyes of Heimdall and his ilk back home.

My first class was Olde English. The teacher spat out my name with distrust as she read it upon my class assignment. "Loki Odinson." I felt all eyes from the other students on me. O, for the ability to use my magicks so that I might transform their eyes to stones, that I might then cast each and every one into the river.

Our reading assignments in the class were handed out. As I exited the class, I assumed that the minor trickery required for me to turn it to smoldering ash in my palm would raise no suspicions.

A voice surprised me as I brushed the ashes from my hand. "Hey, the teacher called you 'Loki Odinson,' right? Hi, Loki Odinson, I'm Eilif!"

Gods help me. Upon turning to face this intrusive wretch, I saw that he had to be a departed soul who resided in Valhalla, the land where dead warriors were welcomed upon their passing. Eilif was obviously here as part of the school's exchange-student program. His face and hands were disfigured from burns he no doubt suffered in his final battle upon this plane. In Valhalla, such a visage would appear healed, for the warrior's shade was returned to its most beautiful upon acceptance into the hall of the dead. But here, in this school, his appearance was distracting and rather repulsive.

"Just 'Loki,'" I said, doing my best to avert my eyes from his scarred countenance. "Although I'd prefer you not only not call me by name but also forget my name and countenance altogether."

"Hah! Good one. Anyway, I'm Eilif!"

"Yes, so it would seem, you are."

"They sometimes call me Eilif the Lost, but I'm not that bad with directions. I mean, the fire I walked into seemed like it sprung up out of nowhere. Lots of fires have sprung up lately. Seems like ever since beautiful Balder the Brave was killed by recent treachery that fire and pain have been around every corner. Well, maybe not fire here, since it's so cold and snowy and cloudy but still, wow, yeah."

If Eilif's previous utterance were to be transcribed, let me just tell you that there is no way a scribe could portray the speed with which one word followed another. Eilif needed to earn his nickname and get lost ere I pluck his tongue from his charred face and feed it to a toad of nondiscriminating palette.

The droning timber of his voice quickly became naught but an unintelligible buzzing in my head as it soon was apparent that he required neither response nor acknowledgment in order to keep merrily prattling on.

Eilif and I shared another class, and his incessant talking continued throughout. Following that, we headed in separate directions and I thought I was through with him. But unfortunately, as I later made way to the many spits where fire-roasted lunch awaited us, he approached me once again.

It had been a long day already and not yet half-done, and the constant feeling of scorn from teachers and students alike had been mentally exhausting. I craved neither food nor the companionship of Eilif, who was as interested in explaining to me the breed of goat we were to consume as I was in trying to tune out his voice.

It was then that my aches, my hunger, my loathing for both myself and all others … all of these discomforts left my body in a flash, for it was there in the lunchroom at that moment that I first noticed *them*. A group of mysterious strangers across the lunching area. The rest of the world seemed to turn insubstantial and gray in comparison to what I now saw.

There were four students all hunched together, keeping their distance from everyone else. Every one of them possessed a near-translucent skin tone, as pale as anyone yet to be spirited away to Valhalla's halls. Their hair colors and body types varied greatly, yet there was something about them that made them all seem the same. I couldn't quite put my finger on it. Had I been able to, I would've saved myself the grief to come.

The smallest of them all stood a foot taller than anyone else within sight. They all had dark eyes, with deep shadows under those ebony eyes. I was nigh mesmerized by what I saw, but it wasn't because of their overall appearance.

No, I stared because their icy faces were inhumanly beautiful, like visions glimpsed in an oracle's reflecting pools. One in particular, a female. They all bore the visage of godlike beings. Yet I was myself a northern god, and familiar with the surrounding pantheons. Which begged the question …

"Who *are* they?" I said in a breathless tone.

By this time, Eilif and I had been joined by other students he knew. One of them was a female fire-demon named Surty, another a lowly Viking child. They ignored my query; instead, Surty spoke at length about being here in Jotunheim as part of the advance scout for some invasion or other. If I had a gold coin for every time I heard someone talk about their intent to invade somewhere, I could swim in a pond-full of gold. Besides, I could not be bothered to listen to her when there was a much more captivating scene displayed in front of me.

Surty changed her tactic, moving from talk of impending war to a subject that actually interested me—the answer to my question of just who was the bedeviling creature in front of me. She said, "They're the Geirrods. Those blondes are Grid and Griep, the thin one is Porr, and that brunette," she paused for effect, "is Gjalpa."

I ran the name through my head. *Gjalpa.*

"They all live together with Geirrodr and his wife in the northern shadow of Yggdrasil."

"They don't look related," I said.

"Oh, they're not." Surty had clearly grown bored with this conversation, and she absentmindedly melted the leftover chicken bones in her grasp as she spoke. "Some say they moved here years ago. Some say they've always been here. Geirrodr adopted all of them, wherever they're from."

As we spoke, I glanced again at the group of over-tall strangers. From across the room, Gjalpa appeared to turn her head and stare at me. Not just look in my direction, but into mine own eyes. Is that ... is that even possible, that she should notice an outcast such as I?

Well, let me correct that—of course it's possible that she would notice me. For am I not still Loki? But regardless of my opinion of myself, I quickly turned away. When I looked back a moment later, she and her group were gone.

"Time to get going," Surty said. "Got to study. Schoolwork before making war." She wandered off with her friends, leaving me alone with my thoughts. And Eilif.

"Where you headed next, lemme see!" He grabbed my class schedule from my hand. "Ahh, you've got Metallurgy next, same with me. C'mon, I can walk you there. I'll show my nickname isn't accurate any more! Eilif the *Found*, I am!"

I prayed that Heimdall didn't hear the sound of my eyes rolling from here to Asgard, but it wasn't out of the question.

In the Metallurgy class, my luck improved when Eilif drifted away to sit with others he knew. For an anonymous and disfigured dead Viking on loan to the school from Valhalla, he certainly seemed to know a vast array of people. He took a seat in the back of the room, his endless prattle wafting away from my ears as I headed toward the one remaining open seat. It was then that I noticed the person occupying the seat next to where I was headed—*Gjalpa Geirrod.*

I took my seat next to her. As I sat, I turned to look at her. At her shoulder, anyway—her actual head sat at least another head's length above mine. These were not small people, the Geirrods.

She turned away from me, and her frosty demeanor was palpable.

As the teacher, a hideous dwarf who I could scarcely stand to lay eyes on, began his lesson, I noted that Gjalpa's hand was frozen in a fist. The waves of coldness continued to emanate from her. Had I somehow so wronged her with my furtive glances earlier that she was filled with cold loathing for me? Or was this normal behavior for her? My reputation, my recent misdeed in Asgard ... those could not have followed me here so quickly, could they?

I dared not speak to her until she relaxed her fist.

This continued on for the duration of the class. The disgusting dwarf spoke much, danced around animatedly as he spoke of smelting steel, and did his level best to keep the class engaged. I paid his foul self no attention whatsoever. Despite the perceptible chill I felt, sweat escaped my brow in a trickle and I prayed to my mother that Gjalpa not notice my discomfort.

Finally, the clang releasing us from our lessons sounded. Better to have poisonous venom dripped on my face for all eternity than to have to experience that awkwardness again. Gjalpa arose before the bell could finish chiming and quickly exited the class.

"Loki." It was Eilif, already at my side. These people moved quickly. "Wow, did you pierce Gjalpa's heart with a mistletoe arrow or what?"

"What?! Of—of course not, why would you ask such a thing? And with such a choice of weapon? I ... whatever do you mean?"

"Hey, take it easy," he said. "I've just never seen her act like that before, that's all."

So this was not her normal behavior. I carried home that small comfort.

The night was a long one for me. My dog had yet to be sent to me, and I missed his company. But I became even more dismayed when I replayed Gjalpa's bizarre behavior over and over in my head. She didn't know me well enough to behave in such a manner.

I was also troubled by the fact that this bothered me. I have e'er been alone but not lonely. Until now. Loki, the One, the ever-present, the independent trickster-god, could not escape the pangs of loneliness that washed over him. Er, me. The barn floor was especially uncomfortable this night, and sleep was long in coming.

The next day was better ... and worse. All night, I dreaded Gjalpa's angry glances to come the next day. I longed to confront her and demand to know what her problem was. It seemed somehow important to know.

It turned out that my sleepless night was for naught, as she wasn't in school at all. None of the Geirrods were. It was especially disheartening to realize this since the sun broke through a bit, making the day rather pleasant, for a land in the throes of a year-long third winter, that is.

Gjalpa and her adopted family didn't attend school the rest of the week.

The following week, walking across the meadow to my Armament class, I noticed the Geirrods gathered around the chariot parking area, feeding their horses. They joked and laughed with one another. In short, they looked like normal kids. Taller by far than the others, yes, but lighter of spirit than I saw upon my first introduction to them. I wondered if my great sense of loneliness was what caused me to project such strange personality traits on Gjalpa upon meeting her.

Gjalpa turned suddenly, again staring across the field and, seemingly, directly into my eyes.

Even worse, she suddenly began walking this way.

I hesitated for a moment, turning this way and that, pondering which way to go just long enough for her to appear in front of me, cutting off any escape option. Giantesses can cover a lot of ground very quickly, I noted mentally.

"Hello," she said. Her voice was like the beating of a snow owl's wings across a crisp winter's night. Unsure of myself in her presence, I said nothing.

"Hello," she repeated, not acknowledging my awkwardness. "My name is Gjalpa Geirrod. I didn't have a chance to introduce myself before. You must be ... Loki."

"H-how do you know my name? I mean, why did you call me Loki?"

"Well, in class when you sat by me, the professor called you that name. "

"Ahh, right. That vile, disgusting dwarf."

She smiled. "Yes, the teacher. You raised your hand when he referred to you as 'Loki,' so it seemed reasonable to assume that that was indeed your name."

"In-indeed." Stupid stupid stupid. I brought my gaze up to her face, an action which required me to crane my neck nearly to its breaking point. It was then I noticed her eyes.

"Did you ... did you go sleepless last night?" As soon as I asked the question, I regretted it. Stupid stupid stupid.

"No," she said. Her eyes were blazing red right now, a contrast to the deep black the first day I saw her. I noticed she clenched her hand into a fist again. But despite that implied threat of violence upon my person, or perhaps because of it, I felt a sense of calm around Gjalpa. Calm like I had rarely known in all my days.

We spoke not again of her changing eye color—really, for one such as I who could alter his physical appearance into any living creature, what difference did variable eye color make? Our conversation continued on.

"It's good news about the snow, isn't it?"

"Not really," I said.

"You don't like the cold? You'd think that nearly a full calendar's turn of the same weather might have acclimated you."

"It's ... not my favorite," I said. I wanted to be more forthcoming with this person. I wanted to tell her how I felt a connection with her already, but I dared not say more. Yet.

"Perhaps the amassing fire demons will bring a more temperate clime," she said. I only think she was joking. "You must find Jotunheim a difficult place to live."

"You have no idea. However, an unpleasant life is still preferable to the alternative back home. Things there were ... complicated."

"Why did you come here? You can tell me."

"I …" I hesitated. Were my secret to get out, the rending of my limbs could be soon to follow. And I was rather attached to my limbs, and they to me. However, there was something in her plaintive manner that appealed to me. I let down my guard and told her who I was. I told her everything. Only later would I realize what a mistake this was.

"… and so, it was really nothing more than a prank gone wrong. Grear Balder used to boast of his impervious nature, how only the mistletoe plant could gravely harm him. Am I truly to be faulted for putting that boast to the test? Yes, Balder was the most beloved of all the northern gods, and yes, he was slain by a mistletoe arrow that did indeed pierce his heart. Some could argue that I was directly responsible for this death."

"*Some*?" She smiled again, eyes blazing red but possessing no judgment in them.

"Okay, well, *all*. But really, he must share some blame for making that kind of boast. It felt like a direct challenge to one such as me."

Was I saying too much? I kept the story as truthful as possible, although I did not mention the fact that I would indeed have slain that preening fool myself had I thought I could get away with it. Instead, I armed the blind god Höðr with an arrow carved from mistletoe. But how could I have known that the unseeing fool would strike a killing blow?

"The one thing I hear of mistletoe," she said smiling, "is that the plant has other, more ... mutually *beneficial* ... uses than just mayhem."

And with that, Loki's own heart suddenly felt pierced. We spoke no more. She looked down into my eyes. I stared up at her, her head looming large in my vision, a source of brightness amidst the storm clouds that had again gathered overhead.

I know not how long we spoke, for time stopped moving during our conversation. However, when it did restart, it did so in a hurry. As we stood in the field, a carriage led by two large horses started to take flight in the distance behind us. But as I would learn later, the foolish coachmen only had with him one large carrot, and neither horse was willing to share with the other. The piebald horse slammed his head into the other horse in an attempt to snatch the carrot away. This sent the carriage careening wildly out of control. Right for us!

The coachman was helpless to stop this as the horses battled, themselves oblivious to anyone in their path. The carriage slid recklessly out of control across the ground, with us in its path. As much as the fates like to predict our end, they are often wrong, and I assumed that my time of demise was only seconds away.

Suddenly, Gjalpa leapt in front of me, crouching down and touching the ground with both hands, palms pressed flat against the hard-packed dirt.

The horses and the carriage suddenly slid to either side of us, as though they struck patches of ice that did not exist moments before. The carriage slammed hard into the wall to the left of us, although I did not see this—I had shut tight my eyes, preparing for the crushing impact.

I opened my eyes and saw Gjalpa looking into them. The redness I saw in her eyes before was gone, her eyes again beautiful black pools. "Loki—Loki, are you all right?!"

"I-I'm fine," I said. I cast my eyes to the carriage. The horses were damaged, perhaps unable to ever fly again, but still living. The coachman was less fortunate. Which mattered not, since had he not perished in this collision, he would have met Loki later this evening and learned a valuable—and final—lesson in driving care. As it was, I made a mental note to revisit the two horses at midnight and impart the same lesson. My puppy, being sent to me this afternoon, would be in need of a good snack.

"Gjalpa, how ... how did you turn the carriage so? It appeared to strike twin patches of ice, but the ground...."

"The ground on which we stand has no such ice, Loki. I was right next to you. The horses luckily veered off at the last instant."

As she helped me off the ground, I doubted my senses, and I doubted her story more. Magic was not exactly an unknown commodity in my life, and I was sure

I saw something magical today. "No, you were ... in front of me. But you touched the ground, and then they slid away...."

"No, no."

"Yes, I saw you, Gjalpa."

"No. Please, Loki, *trust me.*"

I wanted to trust her. I did. But fooling the eyes of a trickster-god is easier said than done. Still, I felt a bond with her that was new and surprising to me, and not so easily discarded. So I chose not to press the issue. The important fact of the situation—that Loki yet lived—was the only tangibly important detail anyway, and so I let the matter drop.

"I—thank you, Gjalpa. For, um, talking to me, I mean. I am—I should go. I'm a bit shaken up, and I must prepare my barn for the arrival of my dog. He is being sent to me, and he'll be hungry. I must prepare for him a nice *supper.*" I looked at the two injured horses as I said this.

We parted. She went back to rejoin her adopted family, and the crowd that had gathered similarly departed. No one wanted to be present when the foolish coachman was spirited away to the halls of the dead lest his guides decide he needed additional company on that particular journey.

Yet I stayed. I bent down to touch the ground in front of me. While all the hard-packed soil was cold to the touch—nothing in this endless winter town was anything but cold—I could have sworn that I felt icy patches that dissipated under the warmth of my touch. Nothing was visible to the eye, and so I had no proof.

I considered what this meant, and tried to make sense of the jumbled thoughts running around through my head. I felt like I was close to puzzling out what I was thinking, for I felt a familiarity with Gjalpa, a kinship unlike any I'd known before. I might well have avoided the anguish to come had I not been interrupted, but a crackling in the sky jolted me from my reverie.

2. THIRD WHEEL

I'd been told many things about the Valkyries from my father and the elder gods. Those death-obsessed riders of winged horses, those shield-maiden choosers of the slain, those vengeful spirit-warriors who would not only take departed souls to the death-land of Valhalla but also, occasionally and capriciously, grab those still living and take them there as well. These horrid creatures were said to be monstrous in appearance, horrible of manner and blackened of soul.

"You only ever want to meet the Valkyries *once* in your life," my father told me as a child. "And even then, many souls wither in their presence before ever being able to complete the journey to Valhalla's fabled halls."

It seems my father never met hyperbole he didn't love. For the Valkyries who appeared now in front of me through an electrified hole in the sky possessed one other trait my father neglected to mention, or perhaps never knew for himself (after all, with only one eye, it's difficult to see things clearly)—they were impossibly, inarguably gorgeous.

As the three riders entered the school grounds on winged horses so white in color that they fairly glowed with brilliant light, the shield-maidens themselves nearly burned my eyes, so great was their beauty.

One in particular especially caught my eye. Never before today had the eyes of Loki been so ensnared so easily, but for the second time in recent memory, I was seized by feelings new and unexplored.

The third Valkyrie to exit the rift in the air was also the youngest. She appeared roughly my age, while the other two were visibly older and battle-hardened.

The other two administered to the needs of the deceased coachmen, but the smaller one approached me. "Who are you, o man, that you stand in the presence of the Valkyries with gaze that withers not?"

Formal types, these Valkyries. "I am Loki," I said.

"Brynhilda, I," she said. Her hair was the finest gold, woven into lustrous, thick braids. Her silver battle armor seemed to be protecting a very pleasant figure.

"And who are ... you know, your friends?"

"Friends we are not, godling. We are Valkyries one and all. My companions Geirdriful and Geiravör are both known for their prowess with the spear, as well as their caring touch in bringing the einherjar to Valhalla's hallowed halls."

"'Einherjar'? Surely a reckless fool who ran himself into a wall, nearly striking my person while doing so, doesn't qualify as a valiant warrior worthy of Valhalla?"

As Brynhilda started to answer, her shrewish companions cast their gaze in our direction. "Brynhilda! Leave the mortal alone and help us administer to this dead soul!"

She scoffed in their general direction. "Surely two such capable Valkyries as you are capable of preparing one mortal without young Brynhilda getting in your way!"

I whispered to her, suppressing my smile at her sharp tongue. "Can you also tell them that Loki is no mortal but a god most strong?"

They shouted back at her. "Foolish girl! Dost you not know that you talk to Loki the viper, Loki the snake, Loki the Balder-killer?"

Such was my lot when my reputation preceded me. There was no hiding anything from Valkyries.

"That was *you*?!" Brynhilda smiled largely enough to reveal to me all of her perfect teeth. "Pay them no mind, Loki Odinson! Valhalla's halls are better for having the great Balder in it. And to have orchestrated the death of one so fair and beloved, heedless of the consequences to come, well, that is ... that's just *cool*!"

Her stoic Valkyrie demeanor disappeared and she was a girl again. A girl with a battle-sharpened sword and fitted armor of the finest metals, but a girl in Loki's presence nonetheless. It appeared that even Valkyries who whiled away their days taking away departed warriors preferred the company of "bad boy" gods like myself. Would that I had known before that my machinations would prove so appealing to the fair sex.

"Fair Brynhilda, when you mentioned before that my actions against Balder had great consequences, what did you mean?"

"Oh, never mind that now, Loki. Come, let us take a flight and talk a while." She reached down from her perch upon her steed, offering her hand so that I might join her on the back of her horse. Only, her horse was having none of that. Flaring flames from its nostrils, the horrid creature whipped its head around at me and would have snapped my hand off in its powerful jaws had Brynhilda not intervened. "Er, that is, come, Loki, let us instead take a walk. My horse will wait here for us."

It appears none but Valkyries may sit upon their horses. Which suited me just fine. Perhaps my fair pup could use a meal of *three* such animals tonight, instead of just the two I already planned....

Upset were Brynhilda's traveling companions, but even they admitted that the wretch they were carting away did not require the aid of three Valkyries. They allowed her pass, commenting that they appreciated the constant business I sent their way, and also looked forward to seeing me very soon. Which sounded on the surface to be a polite thing to say, but their wicked smiles told me there was deeper and more disconcerting meaning behind their words.

At the moment, I cared not about such things. I was entranced by Brynhilda as we walked. Partly because she seemed entranced with me, and any girl who admired Loki deserved in turn my admiration for their strikingly good taste.

"That coachman your Valkyrie-sisters spirited away—why did he gain admittance to a hall of warriors, anyway? Have the qualifications for Valhalla lapsed?"

Brynhilda, who also stood nearly a head's length taller than me, considered this even as she used her sword as a walking stick, absentmindedly carving lines in the ground with its tip as we walked. "No. He was, as you say, a fool. But the coming conflagration—an event that will be forever marked as starting with your plot against fair Balder—will fill Valhalla's halls with warriors, and our need for servants to suit their needs has grown."

"*My* actions, you say?"

"Why, yes, Loki. Twilight is approaching. Fair Balder's passing has ignited the flames of war, and the fire-demons from the depths have amassed an army of considerable enough size to finally—"

I cut her off with another question. "Never mind that now," I said. "Since you Valkyries seem to know so much about, well, everything, what do you know of the Geirrods? Are they normal?"

"The Geirrods? The girl who helped the demise of yon coachmen? The other shield-maidens said that she is one of the cold ones."

"The cold ones?"

She stopped and looked directly into my eyes. "Yes. The Jotun. Your people call them *frost giants*. According to legend," she continued, noting the shock in my eyes, "they are the bane of the gods and the natural enemy of us Valkyries."

"But ... why? They seem ... well, they seem nice."

"Nice they are not, Loki. For, you see, their abilities are not only far beyond those of mortals, but their way of dealing with threats benefits not Valhalla. They tend to freeze their enemies, encasing them in glacier-thick blocks. This leaves them incapacitated, forever removed from the field of battle, but still living. And as such, off-limits to us Valkyries and denied rightful admittance to Valhalla."

"But," I countered, "if they are not claiming the lives of warriors, this makes them not dangerous to be around, right? These Geirrods, they're not like the frost giants of eons past, are they?"

"No," she said, getting gravely serious. "They're not *like* those horrible frost giants from days of yore.

"They are the *same* ones."

My slumber that evening was again long in coming. Brynhilda eventually took her leave, returning to Valhalla in an acrid burst of smoke and lightning. She told me she would have difficulty returning to see me without just cause, said cause being another dead soul to cart away to the great hall. I told her that I could see to that on a regular enough basis should she decide that she would like to see me again. She said she would, and she leaned in and kissed me on the cheek, sending a jolt of electricity through me.

I instantly began plotting out who I could trick into dying so that I might see her again.

At school the next day, I made it through the rest of my studies in a daze. In part because there was nothing to be learned about life from repulsive dwarves and the other moronic persons presented to me as educators. Better that Loki should educate them about the ways of the world by cleaving their heads from their shoulders. But I digress.

I had much to ponder. Loki the loveless, Loki the forlorn, Loki the ever-detested ... this is who I was in Asgard. This is how I saw myself. And suddenly, to be given a different perspective twice in the course of one day was worth heavy consideration.

I did feel a kinship with Gjalpa that was hard to explain, although made easier by the suggestion of her origin, considering the rumors of my own frost-giant lineage.

Then again, perhaps the frost-giant rumor was just Brynhilda looking to undercut the competition. After all, if she knew upon arrival that I was the Loki who was responsible for filling her hall with saps like Balder, then could she not also peer into my heart and see that I was smitten with Gjalpa?

Similarly, did Brynhilda realize that her very nature drew me to her as well? A shield maiden who proved to be so much more alluring than I was ever led to believe was an intriguing prospect indeed.

Was this what it had come to so suddenly? Choosing between Team Gjalpa or Team Brynhilda?

Perhaps I could seek to date both of these enchanting creatures? After all, was I not Loki, the great trickster? If I could not maintain the deception of becoming embroiled in relationships with both of these delights, was I any more worthy of my nickname than Eilif was of his?

I feel that loyalty is for lesser men. Or for bramble-headed louts like my half-brother Thor, who had not the brainpower to consider loving more than one other at a time. But I was not cut from that same simple sackcloth. Rather, if gods like my own father Odin had shown me anything, it was that all options are viable, and all outlets are to be pursued simultaneously. Great Loki the unloved deserved to make up for lost time. And besides, if Brynhilda could only come see me while also collecting the dead, I could just schedule those visits carefully around any other engagements I might have. *This could work.*

But first, the question of Gjalpa's origin needed to be answered.

It was yet another dreary, cloudy day, the air growing ever more frigid. Fimbul Winter was seriously unpleasant the longer it persisted. Had I been informed that my machinations against Balder would result in such a terrible climate, I might well have chosen another god against whom to focus my ire.

I saw Surty upon arriving on the school grounds. She was speaking conspiratorially with two other fire demons, neither of whom were familiar to me.

"Good morn to you, Loki. Enjoying the cold weather? For now?" She winked at the other two.

"Yes, well, a good morning would be one that does not freeze the air in my lungs, Surty," I said. The two fire demons with her chuckled at that, though I knew not why.

"Coming right up," she said. Again, the other two laughed. I kept walking, paying no heed to that foolish girl or her flaming compatriots. In another day, I might well have set rock vipers against their flaming ankles as payment for their folly, but today, I was too anticipatory over the idea of seeing Gjalpa again and had no time to listen to their prattling.

I saw her standing with her other "family" members, and once again, she seemed preternaturally aware of my presence and turned to look at me. Only this time, her eyes blazed and I could read them clearly, even from a distance: "Stay away."

This girl was demonstrating considerable mastery at sending mixed signals. But I acquiesced, and went to class.

She took her seat next to me some time after the lessons had started. Her eyes were the color of deepest black.

"Gjalpa, I...."

"Shh, Loki. Not here."

"Not here? But we only sit and listen to a detestable dwarf. I will never take lessons from such a monster, I will—"

"Loki, *please*. I know you have questions."

How could she know that?

"After school. Meet me under the branches of Yggdrasil."

"Er, Gjalpa, if you're not aware, the great world-tree's branches extend out across the nine realms. One could spend several lifetimes searching under those limbs and never find what he was looking for."

"Silly. Under the *big* branch, I mean. The one that blocks all of the sun's rays from reaching Jotunheim."

Silly. She called me silly. Whereas before, Loki would have plucked out the tongue of any who dared refer to me in such a way, when she said it, it made me warm inside. And in this terrible winter-world in which we all now lived, I would take the warmth where it came. *Silly*. This girl was utterly charming.

If she told me then that she possessed the power to read minds, I would not have doubted it, for she suddenly turned and looked at me with a smile that set my heart soaring into Yggdrasil's great branches already.

After our lessons were complete—lessons that had me plotting out the demise of someone who would allow me to see Brynhilda soon (the dwarf was my leading candidate)—I briskly made my way to great Yggdrasil.

It is difficult for the mortal mind to fathom Yggdrasil's size. Its mammoth trunk out of which its world-encompassing branches grew was thick enough at the base to require seven lifetimes to walk a circle around it. Its branches spanned galaxies, extending across all horizons of possibilities. But even amongst that unfathomable largeness, there was one limb that stood out. Fortunately, its location was near enough to Jotunheim that I reached it in a reasonable amount of time. Under this branch, the sun has never shown through—not even a sliver of its rays could penetrate the canopy above. It was there that I waited for Gjalpa. I did not have to wait long.

"I'm sorry about earlier today," she said upon arrival, her appearance next to me surprising me despite the fact that I was always at the ready for anything. Her speed belied her size. "My ... brothers and sisters, they are wary of me getting too close to outsiders."

"Outsiders? Then let me *in*, Gjalpa. I have no wish to remain on the outside. I feel ... a connection with you. A closeness I wish to nurture. I just ... I need to know some things before I can fully surrender to the feelings I have now."

"Loki, these words you tell me, they should scare me away. I am not so quickly drawn to others. I don't easily let down my guard, but something about you ... it make me think that I could see myself spending all day with you. Every day."

All day? *Every* day? "Gjalpa, I-I think I know why your eye color changes as it does."

"Oh, is that so," she said, arching an eyebrow under which sat an ebony eyeball.

"Yes, when I first saw you, your eyes were black as a dwarf's heart, curse that hated race. But then, another time, they flamed red."

"Is my eye color really what you have questions about, gentle Loki?"

Gentle? Me?

"In truth, Gjalpa, no. It was ... when the carriage nearly struck me, it slid out of the way on patches of ice. Patches *you* created."

She dropped her eyes. But was that still a small smile pursing her lips? "This, again? How would I even do something like that, Loki? I am no goddess of the type you knew back in Asgard. I am a simple, humble—"

"—frost giantess," I finished.

She looked up at me. "Oh, that is ... what—why would you say such a thing?"

"It makes sense, Gjalpa. The ice patches. Your immense size. Your eye color changing from black to red when your temperature warms. Besides, I was talking to the Valkyrie and she said—"

"*Which* Valkyrie? When were you talking to a Valkyrie? And *why*?" She demanded, eyes blazing cold black fire. I saw her hands ball up into fists, and this time, so tight did she clench that particles of ice formed on the outside of her knuckles.

"Um, yesterday, when they collected the body, I stayed and talked to one of them, Brynhilda. She was ... she was nice." I said that last part in barely more than a whisper.

"*Nice*?! Valkyries are not nice! They steal the souls from men, which they then trap inside a placid hall, far away from the battlefield! That is torture for warriors born! And it seems they also use their evil ways to spread foul and deceitful rumors about others."

Now, typically, when I have had conversations with women about affairs of the heart, it has ended with me either deceiving them into making a decision that they ultimately regret, or perhaps just transforming them into field mice to be eaten by crows. So my reaction to Gjalpa's anger was surprising to me. I reached for her hand.

My palm made contact with her knuckles and stuck, so icily dry was her hand, so teeth-chatteringly cold. But I didn't care.

"Gjalpa, fair Gjalpa. I know not the truth of my own origins; I only know the rumors and hearsay that the children of Asgard whisper about me. So I am not one to sit in judgment over another in this regard. Besides, I have only heard tell of how proud are the frost giants. They battle against the gods, knowing full well that the gods are more powerful but never acquiescing. Why, my own doltish brother alone has slain many a frost gi— er, I mean, they have my respect. As would you. If that was indeed your true nature."

"My true nature, as you put it, Loki, necessitates that I hide who I am. It's not so easy. Why do you think I am absent on some days?"

"I ... I only know that on those days, my heart feels diminished."

She smiled a sad smile at me, and then stood, drawing herself up to her full, considerable height.

"Then perhaps I should demonstrate what would happen were I to show up at school on days when the sun does break through. Loki, if you will. The great limb of the world-tree that blots out the sun over Jotunheim—pull it back that the sun's rays might finally peek through. Even in this Fimbul Winter, it's a rather temperate day, and the sun will be eager to break through a spot it has never had a chance to caress before."

I did as she asked. I quickly wove a lasso out of discarded leaves and branches and, turning into an eagle to allow me to fly it up high, circled the branch. We gods have tricks that mortals cannot even guess. I returned to my human form and pulled the loop taught, and yanked. The great limb creaked and groaned, but could not deny my godly power (well, once Gjalpa added her own considerable strength to the pulling, that is).

The branch bent and bowed downward, opening a hole in the canopy. Above it, the sun, so eager to reach this virgin spot of land upon which it had never been, cast sunny rays of warmth down, down.

The solar rays caressed Gjalpa. They didn't touch me, for Loki ever dwells in the shadows, but they did embrace the girl next to me, anyway. Her eyes softened and again changed from deepest black to darkest red. But even more surprising was the effect it had on her skin.

Her face and hands began to appear luminescent, sparkling as though her body were covered with thousands of tiny diamonds. Her skin's brilliance was stunning to behold. I was awestruck. Never have I seen a more beautiful, captivating sight. Her sparkling, bejeweled skin cast a glow of utter brilliance across the forest floor.

I was so taken aback by this that I saw great teardrops fall from my eyes and land at my feet. Only, it was then that I noticed that my eyes were in fact dry, and the falling drops of dew were coming from fair Gjalpa herself. Tears of her own? No—the drops were emitting from her cheeks, from her hands and wrists, her very fingertips seeming to melt, turning first to slush and then quickly to water.

"Um, Loki ... the branch—"

"Ahh! Right away, my sweet." We released the rope, the great branch snapping back into place, the sun once again denied access to this land.

Her skin quickly returned to its normal icy appearance. It was perhaps fortuitous that I brought on Fimbul Winter since, other than the fact that it is said to be the precursor to the gods' demise, its frigid temperatures quickly restored her to normal.

We sat under the branch a while, her hands in mine. "So, a little sunlight...."

"You see our dilemma. We quickly go from sparkling like jewels to puddling like dew drops. But Loki, thanks to you, and this tree, the sun need never reach me now. You give me hope of a shared existence. We could travel beyond the frigid wastelands of my homeland and see all there is to see. Every day, we could be together!"

"Every day? Well, now, see, Gjalpa, I do crave the idea of sharing my time with another, but maybe not *all* my time, if that makes any sense? I have much that I do, and some of that time requires it be spent away from the accompaniment of others."

She placed her other hand on top of mine. And squeezed. I could feel my very marrow drop by degrees as she did so.

"Now, Loki, it is not the way of the frost giant to have dalliances. We keep to our own kind out of an effort to protect one another from hostiles. So the only way for me to bring an outsider—especially a god who has admitted his own brother has slain my kind—is for us to form an ever-lasting and impenetrable bond with one another. This is what I require of you, Loki. This is what must be, if *we* are to be."

I did my best to mask the look of growing horror in my eyes. Spend every minute with another, even someone I had started to care about? Be showered with affection all day long, without end? How could anyone of independent mind and means truly want such a thing?

I was quickly leaning toward Team Brynhilda, when all of a sudden, the branches suddenly exploded around us. Fragments of wood and leaf peppered across our faces and arms. I was momentarily blinded by the maelstrom, but unfortunately, my other senses were not similarly dulled. My nose still worked, and it detected a familiar scent of electricity. Brynhilda was *here*.

She flew into the clearing, leaping from her steed before it had even set foot on the ground. She drew her sword and walked toward us, her heavy bootfalls making deep impressions in the soft ground. The swaying of her sword back and forth made a deep impression upon me.

"Loki! What is the meaning of this? What are you doing here with ... *her*?!"

"Er, hello, Brynhilda. Who died and made you, uh, work?"

"Never mind that! Well, if you must know, an oafish Valhallain exchange student named Eilif got himself lost and ended up getting the other half of his face burned off in an Advanced Smelting class. That drew me back to Jotunheim, only to find you absent from school and cavorting under Yggdrasil's fair branches with a lowly *frost giant*!"

"Eilif? Poor Eilif met an untoward end again?"

"Loki, what does that bovine mean, 'lowly frost giant'?!"

"Loki! What does *she* mean by 'bovine'?!"

Things were quickly spiraling out of control. I had to get control over this situation before things became so untenable as to alert Heimdall or the other Asgardians as to my location. As it was, entirely too many people in Jotunheim had learned my true nature.

"Girls! Can we all just calm down—and keep our voices down? There is no need for such enmity."

They both turned as one and glared at me, cowing me into silence, until I thought of what Brynhilda had said.

"Did you, fair Brynhilda, really say that the name of the recent departed was Eilif?"

"I did. His dwarvish teacher miscalculated a lesson and Eilif suffered as a result. But his suffering is like nothing compared to the suffering you will undergo, should you chose the company of that vile frost giant over that of my own."

Well, now I had even more reason to escape this predicament, so I might pay back that horrible dwarf for his folly. It seemed my dog would soon eat well all week, assuming I was still mobile and had all limbs attached with which to feed him.

"We were ... just talking, Brynhilda," I started.

"Just talking! Loki, you were professing your undying love to me," said Gjalpa, ruining the moment I was trying to create.

"Undying, eh? We shall see about that!" And with that, Brynhilda reached down with one hand and plucked me from where I stood, throwing me into the clearing and advancing on me. She poked her sword into the underside of my jaw, and we were suddenly full circle with where this tale began.

"Loki, before I separate your lying head from your bony shoulders, I give you one more chance—be true to your word and offer *me* your heart forever, that you may accompany me on my tasks and serve my needs. I am a Valkyrie and cannot shirk my duties, so this is what is required that we might be together."

Well. That didn't sound much fun at all. Suddenly, the option of her removing my head from its shoulders didn't sound like the worst option presented before me.

Brynhilda's blade was knocked away by a ball of ice. It was followed quickly by two more ice-balls, hurled at great velocity by Gjalpa.

"Hands off, shield-witch! Loki is *mine*!"

Brynhilda blocked the second ball of ice with her metal wrist guards, but the first struck her squarely in the face. She spit out ice and epithets with equal rancor. "Foul, frigid snow-pig! Loki is *mine*, heart and soul! Especially soul! You cold-hearted monsters don't know the first thing about how to properly love another!"

"Oh, but I suppose *you* do, you carrion-carrier!"

This was getting interesting. Gjalpa ran forward and grappled with Brynhilda, knocking her sword from her grasp. It landed near my feet. As the fighting devolved into thuggery, I rapidly weighed my options.

Clearly, the idea of dating both women would avail me not. And after hearing the words that came out of both mouths during the heated arguing, it had me suddenly wondering if I should instead remain a solo player. Perhaps Team Loki had no room for such controlling types after all. Loneliness was a state with which I was well accustomed, and it was obvious that I would not willingly give up my independence in trade for fealty and servitude. My heart, which had always operated independently of others, had tricked me into thinking it needed companionship.

Trickery. Of course. Was I not, despite my recent foray into romantic ineptitude, still Loki? A solution—the only true solution—presented itself to me.

I picked up Brynhilda's sword (only with great effort. I managed to choose two of the strongest women I have ever come in contact with, another good reminder that I would be wise to find my way out of this double-sided predicament).

As my two potential consorts fought on, I swung her sword around twice, spinning my body to build up momentum. I then released the blade upward with all my might. The sword spun end over end into the sky, finally striking the great branch I had earlier pulled back. The sword's honed edge cleaved through the giant limb without effort. The branch, separated from the trunk, started to move and sway. Finally, the weight of it pulled it loose, and the great branch fell.

It plunged down, down, and the whistling sound of its descent was great enough to stop the two warrior-women from the battles.

"Loki—" they said in unison, but only one of the two uttered my name with any confidence.

As the branch traveled downward, so too did the sun's rays. Once again they bathed Gjalpa, and Brynhilda as well. Frankly, the two women looked utterly gorgeous inside the funnel of warm light.

Then Gjalpa's skin took on its bejeweled tone again, although it began melting at the same time. The concentration of the sun's rays, with no canopy with which to slow it, accelerated its effect on her. And this time, there *were* tears intermingling with the drops of water emitting from her skin—both hers and mine.

As Gjalpa began puddling across the forest floor, she looked at me for the last time. Her legs had melted away enough that she was now my height and looking me directly in the eyes for a moment, before continuing her moist downward trajectory.

"I am undone, Loki," she gurgled, "may you forever burn in fiiiiiiiire...." She trailed off. Liquefied lips can't easily utter words, it seems.

I felt a tinge of sadness, but fought it off when I reminded myself that Loki was never meant to be simple husband to anyone. Now, on to the second part of my quickly thrown-together scheme. I spun around to look at the Valkyrie.

Brynhilda was grinning from ear to ear. She pulled loose her sword, which had also fallen back to earth and embedded itself up to its hilt, and stepped toward me.

"Loki! I knew from the moment I met you that you had sharp senses! You knew that frigid behemoth wasn't right for you, and you knew I was! Oh, Loki!"

She rushed toward me, planning to embrace me. I grasped her shoulders and held her away, at arm's length. "Aren't you forgetting something, fair Valkyrie?" I motioned to the puddle on the ground.

"Oh, I will never forget what you have done! You have chosen a life with me, my lord. We should get to work at once, making plans and sharing our lives!"

"Well, one of us should get to work anyway, only it is not wise Loki."

"What are you—" The reality of the situation began to settle in, if the look in her eyes was any indication.

"You, my Brynhilda, are a *Valkyrie*. While a life of acquiescing to your demands and carrying your helmet while you work might hold appeal to some, it holds absolutely none for Loki. But my lack of interest in your profession does not negate the fact that you are required to see those labors through now."

As I spoke, Gjalpa's spirit arose from the moist ground. "The giantess perished in battle, and is awaiting its final ride to Valhalla's halls. You cannot deny your responsibilities, Brynhilda. You are a Valkyrie first, as you reminded me. Gjalpa has earned her seat inside the hall. Best be off with you, then, before your maiden-sisters become aware of you shirking your duties. I do not imagine that would sit well."

She stared at me with death in her eyes. But maybe it was just a trick of the light. No, it was probably death. Pulling her sword and waving it in my direction, she screamed, "Perhaps I should take *two* recently departed souls with me to Valhalla, deceitful snake!"

"Ahh, Brynhilda," I sighed, picking an errant branch shard out of my teeth. "Would that the Valkyries were understanding enough for you to set aside responsibilities in order to carry out your petty grievances and keep poor, departed souls waiting. But I do not believe they are. Best be off now. Alas, our love just cannot work around such requirements. Would that it were not so."

I turned away, lest my growing smile turn into outright laughter. She knew she had no recourse. To betray the trusted duties of a Valkyrie was to renounce one's heritage and be kicked out of Valhalla for all time. I was counting on her hate for me not being quite great enough to supercede her desire to remain within those hallowed halls. I was right, but barely.

As Brynhilda saw to her labors, I looked at the two one last time. Gjalpa's shade was now in the Valkyrie's grasp and being prepared for her trip to Valhalla. If looks could kill, well, my own twilight would be upon me sooner than was written.

"Farewell, my ladies fair. Would that things could have been different. But, as the expression goes, Loki dost not need any clinging vines. Farewell."

"Loki," I heard Brynhilda say. I looked at her. Gjalpa's soul sat perched on the winged horse behind Bryn. She refused to turn her head toward me. But Brynhilda did, and her eyes blazed with red-hot anger so great that I wondered if she too was part frost giant. "The Twilight of the Gods is upon the land. Your death is foretold, and is imminent. So don't think we will be separated for long. For when your corpse settles onto the ground during the coming battle, I will be there personally to see that you are taken to Valhalla, where we may spend all eternity together.

"And Loki," she paused. "Once inside the great hall, the only kisses I plan to shower you with shall be made of tempered steel."

She dug her heels into her horse, and the beast at once began flapping its great wings, until she and Gjalpa rose off into the sky and out of sight.

Again with this talk about a coming battle and Loki's imminent demise. My current dating situation resolved, it was now time I did something about that as well.

3. MATCH-MAKING

As I exited the forest and was free of Yggdrasil's shade, I noticed that the problem with the cloudy and frozen sky had begun to resolve itself, in the form of great flames that licked across the horizon. It seems that our Twilight was upon us. The gods were destined to fall.

On the long and thankfully lonely walk out of the forest, I began thinking about the various things people had said when speaking of the coming battle. Surty and her flame-demon friends had definitely talked about things I chose not to hear because I was too taken with affairs of the heart. Which was yet another reason to remain so unencumbered. One can only properly see to one's own survival without the blinders of love.

The gist of what everyone said about the imminent end of everything is that it all began with Balder's death. Would that I had known ... well, I would not have changed a thing. That prig needed to be taken down. But this meant that if I was responsible for starting this process, I should similarly be able to stop it, at least where my own personal doom was concerned. All of Asgard could go hang for all I cared. If enabling Balder to die also helped bring about the doom of Thor, Heimdall and the others, well, that was a better chain reaction than I could have hoped. But the loss of Loki would be too great indeed, at least to me. Still, we all had a part to play, and I would play mine. At least to a point.

It was not fated that Loki would meet his end during our coming Twilight—it was *written*. That makes a world of difference. The Fates are rarely wrong about their castings, but the men who write things down and pass them off as fact are prone to mortal error.

As I returned home and found my dog at last waiting for me, I thought about the end of the gods. Many of them deserved to fade away into the twilight, or to be locked away in Valhalla's musty halls. After all, the gods as I knew them were capricious creatures, driven as much by emotion and lust as by reason and need. But I, up until my most recent escapade, was not. I was and am fueled by a much stronger thing—the desire to make mischief and to do wrong unto others. And it was precisely those things that made me realize I needed to live beyond our foretold ending. Loki is necessary in the world to come, whereas the other gods are not.

"Here, pup! Here, boy!" My beloved pooch ran to me, licking hunger across his lips.

"Good boy! Are you hungry, pup? Well, let us be off, then, my little *Fenris*. It's finally time for you to sup. I spotted a full moon peeking out from behind a cloud on my walk back here. Perhaps that planetoid would make a good first morsel for you. But save a bit of room, for I've a nice dwarf-snack in mind for you, too."

As my dog, Fenris the Wolf, leapt into the heavens, prepared to devour sun, moon, and gods alike, I wondered what the fire-demoness Surty was doing right now. It occurred to me that I should call on her. Her team was leading the charge against the gods and she was positioned to know victory in the coming battle. Plus, she was cute enough. She could likely use a good consort to accompany her through.

And if that potentially star-crossed romance didn't survive the terrible battle to come, perhaps upon my return in the next world, I should try my luck dating a vampire. I heard they are rather easy to manipulate.

Pokky Man

A Film by Vernor Hertzwig

By

Marc Laidlaw

VERNOR HERTZWIG

FILMMAKER

In 2004 I was contacted by Digito of America to review some film footage they had acquired in litigation with the estate of a young Pokkypet Master named Hemlock Pyne. While I have occasionally played board games such as Parchesi, and various pen-and-paper role-playing games involving dwarves and wizards, in vain hopes of escaping the nightmare ordeals that infest my soul, I was hardly the target audience for the global phenomenon of Pokkypets. I knew only the bare lineaments of the young man's story—namely that he had been at one time considered the greatest captor of Pokkypets the world had ever known. Few of these rare yet paradoxically ubiquitous creatures had escaped being added to his collection. But he had turned against his fellow Trainers, who now hurled at him the sort of venom and resentment usually reserved for race traitors. The childish, even cartoonish aspects of the story were far from appealing to me, especially as spending time on a hundred or so hours of Pokkypet footage would mean delaying my then-unfunded cinematic paean to those dedicated paleoanthropologists who study human coprolites or fossil feces. But there was an element of treachery and tragedy that lured me to look more carefully at the life and last days of Hemlock Pyne, as well as the amount of money Digito was offering. I found the combination irresistible.

HEMLOCK PYNE
POKKY MASTER
To be a Pokky Captor was for me the highest calling—the highest calling! I never dreamed of wanting anything else. All through my childhood, I trained for it. It was a kind of warrior celebration ... a pokkybration, you might say, of the warrior spirit. I lived, ate, breathed, drank, even pooped the Pokky spirit. Yes, pooped. Because there is dignity in everything they do. When it comes to Pokkypets, there is no room for shame—not even in pooping. In a sense, I was no different from many, many other children who dream of being Pokky Captors. The only difference between me and you, children like you who might be watching this, is that I didn't give up on my dream. Maybe it's because I was such a loser in every other part of my life—yeah, imagine that, I know it's difficult, right?—but I managed to pull myself free of all those other bonds and throw myself completely into the world of Pokkypets. And I don't care who you are or where you are, but that is still possible today.

VERNOR HERTZWIG
Hemlock Pyne's natural enthusiasm connected him ineluctably with the childish world of Pokkypets—the world he never really escaped. The more I studied his footage, the more I saw a boy trapped inside a gawky man-child's body. It was no wonder to me that he had such difficulty relating to the demands of the adult world. In cleaving to his prejuvenile addictions, it was clear that Pyne hoped to escape his own decay, and for this reason threw himself completely into a world that seems on its face eternal and unchanging. The irony is that in pursuing a childish wonderland, he penetrated the barrier that protects our fragile grasp on sanity by keeping us from seeing too much of the void that underlines the lurid cartoons of corporate consumer culture, as they caper in a crazed dumbshow above the abyss.

PITER YALP
ACTOR
I think we knew, and assumed Hemlock knew, where was this was probably heading. And it's hard to see a person you care for, a friend of many years, make the

sorts of decisions he made that put him ever deeper into danger. It didn't really help to know that it was all he cared for, that all this danger was justified in a way by passion, by love. And when you saw him light up from talking about it, it was hard to argue. He'd never had anything like that in his life. I mean, he'd been through a lot. Coming back to Pokkypets, sure it seemed childish at first, but he was so disconnected from everything anyway, we had to root for him, you know? But we still feared for him. He never did anything halfway, you know? Whenever he started anything, you always knew he was going to push it past any extreme you could imagine. So it was only sort of ... sort of a shock, but more of a dreaded confirmation, when we heard the news. I remember I was in the kitchen nuking some popcorn for dinner, and the kids were watching Pokkypets on, you know, the Pokkypets network ... and then our youngest said, "Look, it's Uncle Hemlock!" Which seemed weird at first because why would he be on their cartoon? But then I saw it was the Pokkypets Evening News, and even though the sound was turned up full, I found I couldn't hear what the anchorman was saying. I just stared at the picture of Hemlock they'd put up there ... the most famous shot of him, crouched in the Pokkymaze, letting an injured Chickapork out of a Poachyball ... and from the way the camera slowly zoomed back from the photo, I knew right then ... he wouldn't be coming back to us this time.

AUGUSTINE "GUST" MASTERS
SEAPLANE PILOT

I was friends with Hem for years and years, used to fly him out here to the Pokky-maze in midsummer, come and collect him before fall settled in; I'd check in from time to time to see how he was doing, and drop off the occasional supply. He was a special sort of guy, and there won't never be another like him. For one thing, he was fearless, as you can imagine you'd have to be to try living right here like he did. From where we're standing, you can watch the migratory routes of about 150 different types of Pokkypets; everything from the super common Pecksniffs, to the Gold-n-Silver Specials, to the uniques like Abyssoid, who comes up out of this here lake once a year for about thirty seconds at 8:37 a.m. on September 9, and only if the 9th happens to fall on a Tuesday. Really it's a Captor's dream, or would be if it wasn't a preserve. Hem came out here every year, and never once tried to capture or collect a single one of the Pokkys ... in fact they were more likely to collect him. He got adopted by Chickapork to the extent you couldn't tell who belonged to who. Anyway ... he made it a point of pride that he never carried a Poachyball, that he was here to protect the Pokkypets, to prevent them from being collected. When he was young he was a heck of a Captor, but once he put that aside, that was it. He didn't try charming them with flutes or putting them to sleep;

he didn't freeze or paralyze them with any of Professor Sequoia's Dust Infusion, or Thunderwhack a single one. He came out empty-handed, and tried to make a Pokky out of himself, I guess. If I had to pick one thing, I guess I'd say that right there was his undoing. That and Surlymon.

VERNOR HERTZWIG

What others saw as evidence of everything from low self-image to schizophrenia, was to Hemlock Pyne nothing more than a kind of dramatic stage lighting, necessary to cast an imposing shadow over a world that considered him but a small-time actor in a community theater production. It did not matter to the rest of the world that in this tawdry play, Hemlock Pyne had the leading role; but to Pyne himself, nothing else mattered. He had cast himself in the part of the renegade Captor who would give himself completely to his beloved Pets. That it was to be a tragic role, I suspect would not have stopped him. And while he seems to have had premonitions of his fate, he could have asked any number of those who spent their lives working in and around the Pokky Range, and have heard many predictions that would end up remarkably close to the eventual outcome.

AUGUSTINE "GUST" MASTERS

Right here is where I came in for my usual rendezvous, at the appointed time, ready to take him out of here. At first I thought maybe I had the day wrong, because usually I'd expect to see him with all his gear packed up and waiting here on the shore. It was later in the year than he'd ever stayed, not our usual date, so I thought it was my mistake, and I went hollering up the hillside trail here toward his camp, figuring maybe he could use a hand packing up his stuff. But halfway up the trail here I got a really funny feeling ... not a nice feeling at all. I never travel here without a few extra Poachyballs, and some Coma Flakes—I mean, I'm no Hemlock, I come prepared for anything. And I was just freeing up a Poachyball in case I had to make an emergency capture, when I heard this grumbling in the brush off to the side of the trail, and very clearly I could hear a big old Pokkypet crawling around in there, just saying its name over and over again so there was no mistaking what I was up against. Going, "Surly ... Surly ..." Like that. Just a nasty old Pokky, saying its name like a warning ... that one bad note over and over again.

Well, I don't mind saying it scared me, and forgot about trying to catch it, since that's a tough one to collect even if you're fully prepared. I didn't have any Pokkypets of my own to back me up. So I hightailed it back to the plane, and took off, just cold and sweatin', my guts full of ice water, you know. I tried to get Hemlock on his radio a couple times, but no answer there, and I was starting to believe we weren't going to get any more answers at all. I brought the plane in low over the maze, low as I could, and the way Hem would hide his tent in the trees I knew it would be hard to get a clear picture of what was going on there—but as I was flying over, the wind swept over pretty hard. Banked me a bit just as it was parting the trees around his campsite, and I got one clear look that I'll never forget. Right below me, the tent had been flattened so that the poles were sticking up out of it. Gear was scattered everywhere—clothes, camera equipment, pots and pans. And Hemlock was scattered everywhere too, in and around the tent. I hardly knew what I was seeing. His head staring up at me, on the other side of the site from his chest; an arm here, a leg there. I couldn't tell if his eyes were open, but I didn't see how they could be. I figured he had to be sleeping after an attack like that. I knew I'd need help getting him out of there, so I banked into the wind and headed back to town.

HEMLOCK PYNE
10 DAYS BEFORE THE END
This is Surlymon. He's a very old Pokkypet, and we're just getting to know each other. I'm not usually here in the Pokkymaze this late in the year, but I had a little upset at the airport and decided I was not ready to leave my Pokky friends just yet to return to all the ... all the bullpoop and the hassle of ... of poopy humans back in the so-called real world. Just wasn't ready. So here I am, and some of my old friends seem to have moved on, and some new Pokkys have moved in. It's the migratory time, you see ... all a completely natural part of the Pokkypet cycle, and pretty exciting to see it in action. Not to say that there isn't danger here—there's plenty of it. But that's what keeps me going. Nobody else could do what I do ... give themselves to the protection of the Pokkypets the way I do. And they respect me for it. They know that I have the best of intentions ... that I'd be one of them if I could. But in the meantime, I'm getting to know Surlymon here ... getting to earn his trust. Isn't that right, Surlymon? We're getting to know each other. Yes we are! Yes we are! Now ... hey ... HEY! Watch it! Back off! That is not cool, Surlymon. Not cool. Good, Pokky. Okay, good old Pokky. Yes, you're a good old boy, I know, I know. I love you. I love you. I'm sorry I had to snap at you like that. I'm Hemlock, okay? Hemlock! Hemlock! Hemlock! I love you. Hemlock loves you. Hemlock. Hemlock. ... Hemlock.

AUGUSTUS "JUSTICE" PEACE
HELICOPTER PILOT
I've known Gust for years, and through him I knew Hemlock Pyne, though we weren't what you'd call close. That day he came back with news about Hemlock's troubles, I could tell he'd seen something that nobody should see. Well, we called

the Pokky Park Service, which is basically every other person around here, and we got three Captors together and I took us out in the chopper. We landed on Baldymon Hill, which overlooks the Pokkymaze, and they went on down there while I kept an eye on the chopper, ready to light out at a moment's notice. I could hear them when they caught up with the Surlymon. They had some pretty tough pets with 'em, but that sonofabitch was tough. It took all three Captors in full Pokkybattle, and each one of them used at least three Poachyballs, setting their own pets on the Surlymon. It took eight—eight!—Pokkypets to wear down that Surlymon. I think the final attack was a full-on Typhon-Crash-Mastery move, and then the Surlymon finally went into slumber. It was only then that the thing was vulnerable and they could poach it. I heard all this, mind; I didn't see any of it ... but I'll tell you, every time I heard that thing giving out its call, my blood ran cold. "Surly! Surly!" Well, I can't do it. It was a horrible sound, though. When they finally came crashing through the underbrush dragging the Poachyball, with their own poor little pets limping along behind, the Captors looked like they'd been involved in the struggle themselves ... and I don't mean psychically.

But then it was over to me and Gust. He led me back down the hill and into the maze, to the campsite, and there was Hemlock Pyne in a dozen pieces. It was weird and awful. Gust called his name a few times, trying to wake him up, because we didn't really realize the extent of it yet.... It was a sleep like nothing we'd ever seen. I had some Sudden Stir powder with me and I sprinkled it in his eyes, but it didn't do a thing. And I've never seen a Pokkypet or Captor yet who could sleep through that stuff. After a while we decided we'd best get him into town to the Pokky Clinic, so we gathered up the pieces. Filled four Poachyballs with the parts. That was all we had to carry him in.

MADRONA SEQUOIA
FRIEND, POKKYOLOGIST
What Hemlock wanted was a way to mutate into a Pokkypet himself. He was very, very uncomfortable being in his own skin, especially when it meant he was a Captor or Master of Pokkypets. He wanted to merge with the Pokkys ... become one of them, share in their alchemic process. Hemlock sensed a transformative power in them, and he wanted this for himself. When he was studying with me, we went through the triadic life cycle of the typical healthy Pokkypet, following its course in many, many creatures. When he first went out into the Pokky Range with the idea of studying and protecting the pets, you know, he placed himself in the habitat of the Pigletta. It was a good fit for him, since they are such friendly creatures, but his ulterior motive was to bond so closely with one that it would

allow him to stay with it through all its transformations. Of course, everyone who adopts a Pigletta feels that theirs is special, and that they have a unique friendship ... but in Hemlock's case I think there is a real argument for this. After all, he had stopped collecting at that point; he never stunned his Pokkypet or trapped it even briefly in a Poachyball to subdue it. He made friends with it as if he were another of its kind, and in his second summer back there, he was witness to its first transition into Chickapork. I know how much Hemlock wanted to see the final change to Boarax ... which, sadly, took place in the autumn immediately after Surlymon, so he missed it. This, as I say, was a spiritual quest for him, and he welcomed its transformative intensity from the first, even though in the eyes of other Pokkypet Captors he immediately went from role model to traitor. This was when people started saying he was crazy, sending nasty letters, even making threats. This is when the Missile Kids stepped up their attacks on his character. It got harder and harder for me to bear, but Hemlock said to pay it no mind. It didn't bother him. The only thing that bothered him anymore was any sort of threat to his beloved Pokkypets.

VERNOR HERTZWIG
At the same time that Hemlock Pyne was alienating his former worshippers, he was winning for himself a new audience that would one day be captivated by his insights and his breathtaking cinematic records of his life among the Pokkypets ... a life that few have ever attempted, let alone accomplished. Going through his films, I found him to have possessed an innate genius—not only for capturing Pokkypets, but for capturing moments of pure cinema. Here, we see Pyne in his early summer campsite, a spot he pitched between the dens of burrowing Chickaporks, so that he could live among the frolicking Piglettas.

HEMLOCK PYNE
This is Chickapork. My Chickapork. We're longtime buddies, aren't we, yes we are. Chickapork is my most beloved Pokkypet, and it's really important to understand that we are mutual friends. I do not own him. I did not capture him. I have never imprisoned him in a Poachyball. So you see, it is possible for us to have a harmonious relationship with these beautiful creatures without havinge to ... Hey! This ... this is Pigletta ... this is one of Chickapork's offspring or little sibs, I'm not sure exactly—hey, where are you going with my cap? Come back with that cap, Pigletta! That is a very important cap! That was a gift from Professor Manzanita! Oh ... oh god, oh no.... A lot depends on that cap, Pigletta! Get ... give me back my cap! WHERE'S MY FUCKING POKKYMASTER CAP?

PROFESSOR MANZANITA
POKKYPET EXPERT

In the field, it was obvious that he wanted nothing more than to be a Pokkypet. He would act just like them. The simple continual act of stating his identity with such clarity, this thing the Pokkypets do incessantly, Hemlock adopted this behavior. If you weant out to visit him in the field, or if you were an unsuspecting Captor who came across him, Hem would act as if human language and human behavior were completely unknown to him. He would just say his name at you, over and over, like a Pokkypet. His mantra, his act of affirmation: Hemlock. Hemlock. Hemlock. He saw the Pokky world as a rare and simplified place, everything streamlined and stripped down to this one act of self-naming. That world had a siren's allure for him. But that world ... simply did not exist. The truth was far more complex.

TAIGA MOSS
CURATOR, POKKY NATIONAL WILDERNESS MUSEUM

Well, I'm afraid although Hemlock Pyne might be a hero to some people, to us he seems simply deluded. Our relationship with the Pokkypets goes back tens of thousands of years, to when we believe the Pokkys and people shared this land. We treated each other with respect, and we have done so throughout our history. We created the original Poachyballs, and we captured and collected the first Pokkypets to be captured and collected. We held the first Pokky battles; those rituals are very ancient, the result of the relationship between man and Pokkypet. So there is a very long tradition of understanding between our people and the Pokky people. I would say that what Hemlock did was the ultimate disrespect. In living among the Pokky, in treating them as cute cartoon characters, he crossed a boundary and paid the price. The ultimate price. There is a reason he will not wake up, and honestly, we don't expect him to. I think a lot of people are in denial about the sort of trouble he caused for himself ... and really for all of us, because I don't know if it will stop with Hemlock. There has always been this barrier from time long past ... and he damaged it. Irretrievably. It's plain to see if you'll just look at him. Truly look at him for once.

DR. JASPER CHRYSOLITE
POKKY CLINIC

We are here, in cold storage, at the Pokky Clinic, because quite simply this is the only place we have been able to arrest the very strange and terrible processes that have Hemlock Pyne in their grip. In those steel drawers behind me, if I were to open them, you would see Hemlock Pyne much as he was when they brought him in to me for revival. As you already know, I was unable to wake him, even with the finest waking compounds at my disposal. I say "much as he was" because Hemlock did not stay as he was in those first hours. The separate parts of him lost their normal color ... some began to swell, others to wither ... and there was a terrible odor associated with him, which I would rather not go into. Whatever this process is, some sort of Pokky contagion he caught from Surlymon or elsewhere in the Pokkymaze, I had a sort of hunch that extreme cold might arrest it. And so we arranged for some cold storage, which has indeed seemed to do the trick. We will of course keep trying to wake him as time permits, and if we can devise some other approach to his condition. We also have that Surlymon captive and under observation, in hopes of understanding better what happened ... but for all we can tell, it is simply a Surlymon like every other Surlymon. There is nothing special about it. Which makes us think that whatever strange thing happened to Hemlock Pyne, it was purely a result of his peculiar make-up, his particular situation. It behooves us therefore to try and understand Hemlock himself a little better. Really, what else can we do?

CRYSTAL BURL

Would I say I was his girlfriend? Why, yes, yes I would. I mean, not always, but ... but we were always friends. We founded Pokky People together. We were insepa-rable. We met when we were both working at Mistress Masham's in the Mall, and Hem was in charge of the Pokky performance. They had a little routine they did where the Pokkys would come out and dance on your table—I mean, various small Pokkys. Nothing large or unhygienic. All the food at Mistress Mashams was served under silver covers, and the Pokkypets would whisk these away with a big flourish. Hem would come out with a half dozen Poachyballs, open them up, and set the Pokkys going. I thought it was pathetic, and I told him so ... and he confided in me that he was only in there as a saboteur. I thought he was kidding, trying to im-press me, but no ... one night right after we really got to talking, he went into his usual routine, but everything was different this time. He'd packed a bunch of wild Pokkys into the balls, and he let them loose in the middle of a little kid's birthday party. The Pokkys went crazy—eating up the food, tearing into presents, getting underfoot. And out of nowhere Hem kept producing more and more Poachyballs, opening them up, setting them free. He was laughing, we were both howling, and the more freaked out everybody got, the more delighted Hem was. It seemed to feed the Pokkys' frenzy. They were swinging from the light fixtures, smashing win-dows, breaking out into the streets ... oh, it was on the news that night and for days, and it was really the beginning of Hem's mystery ... because right after that he disappeared. I didn't see him myself for months and months. It turned out he had made his first visit to the Pokky Range.

VERNOR HERTZWIG

Alone in the wild, Hemlock began to craft his own legend—fashioning himself into a creature as strange and colorful as the Pokkypets he adored. Against a backdrop of untouched wilderness, he portrayed himself an uncivilized man, fearless and ferocious yet as sweet as the creatures he refused to capture. It was as if in liberating the Pokkypets wherever he found them, he was setting free some caged part of himself.

HEMLOCK PYNE

I used to just dabble in Pokkypets. I captured and trained them like everyone else. I saw nothing but what was right in front of me. I never looked any deeper. And I was troubled. Our world, the world of people, is so shallow ... it's just a thin coat of paint, right on the surface, and that's enough for most people. The Pokkys are colorful and cute and uncomplicated, and that's all they need to know. But this wasn't the truth, and without truth I just ... I wasn't making it. I needed the truth that was under all that. I did drugs. I drank. I lived a crazy, crazy life. Nobody knew me. I didn't know myself. I was drinking so much, doing so many drugs, it was destroying my mind. All the colors started to blur together. I couldn't tell Chickapork from Leomonk from Swirlet. It was like when you mix all the colors of paint together and you just get a grayish brownish gunk. And then one day a Flutterflute, I was drinking on the beach, out of my skull, and a Flutterflute landed on the bottle just as I was about to take a swallow. Who knows ... it might have been my last swallow. I might have drained that bottle and thrown it aside and walked out into the waves and that would have been the end. But I watched that Flutterflute there, getting in the way of my drink, and it looked at me and said, "Flutterflute!" That's all, that's what they do. So simple. Just that beautiful simple statement: "Flutterflute." And something in me ... I felt something emerge, as if from a chrysalis, bright and clear and strong, and I said, "Hemlock Pyne." Everything in my life was as simple as that. "Hemlock Pyne." That is what I was, and it was enough. It was deep. And what that meant was everything else was deep. Bottomless. And everything changed for me right then, right that very moment, saying myself back to that Flutterflute. I say it a lot now. It saves me every day: "Hemlock Pyne."

VERNOR HERTZWIG WITH CRYSTAL BURL

VH: Now please explain to the viewers, Crystal, what it is you have here.

CB: What I have here, Vernor, is Hemlock's last recording ... recovered from his campsite ... the recording of the Surlymon.

VH: Now I understand there is some uncertainty whether the recorder was running already or whether it was turned on during the Surlymon's attack, and if so whether it was Hemlock himself or the Surlymon that switched it on. But that doesn't really matter, does it? What matters is the contents of the tape, which you, I believe, have never listened to, is that correct?

CB: That is correct. Dr. Chrysolite said I had probably better not.

VH: Dr. Chrysolite is a wise man and you do well to listen to him, but his prohibition does not apply to me, so I am going to listen to the recording now. The lens cap was never removed during the battle, I am just going to listen to the recording if I have your permission to do so.

CB: I give it, yes.

VH: If you will, please, to start the ... there now, I hear wind, very loud, and something like a ripping sound ... perhaps the tent's zipper. Actually, yes, it sounds as if the Surlymon is coming in range. I can hear it quite clearly saying its name over and over again: Surlymon ... Surlymon.... And now clearly I hear Hemlock, much closer. Of course we know he had no Poachyballs, and no other Pokkys with him at the time. He is really alone against this creature. The Surlymon is saying again, "Surlymon. Surlymon." And occasionally just "Surly," as if it is too excited to say its full name.

CB: They do that sometimes when they're excited ... even add extra syllables....

VH: And now Pyne is ... he seems to have hit on a desperate strategy ... he is saying his own name several times to the creature. It is almost as if they are having a conversation, like so: Surly ... Surlymon ... and Hemlock says Hemlock. Hemlock Pyne. Hemlock. He's saying it again. And the Surlymon seems to be having none of it. Surlymon. Hemlock Pyne. Surlymon. Surlymon. Hemlock Pyne. Hemlock Pyne. Hemlock. Surlymon. And now a terrible, terrible sound. You ... you must never listen to this recording, Crystal.

CB: That's what Dr. Chrysolite recommended as well, Vernor.

VH: Hemlock Pyne. Hemlock Pyne. Hemlock ... Surlymon. And now I hear nothing but Surlymon. You must destroy this tape, Crystal. I think that is the only course of action.

CB: I will, Vernor. I will.

VH: Surly. Surlymon. Surlymon. Surly.

HEMLOCK PYNE

We are here at the edge of the Pokkypet Arena, deep in the Pokkymaze. The Pokkys have never allowed me this close before, but I think it is a sign of their acceptance—a sign of how far I've come—that they are allowing me to set up my camera here overlooking the arena and film their battles in progress. Remember, these are entirely natural and unstaged ... these are not like the Coliseum battles that human captors arrange, which go against the will and the inherent nature of the Pokkypets. What you are seeing here is the source of humanity's watered-down commercially driven arena battles. This, my friends, is the real shit.

Now it looks like a Scanary is going into the arena, setting the first challenge.... Scanaries have three attacks: Wing Blast, Chirplosion, and Tauntalon. This is a fairly good combination unless your Pokkynemesis happens to have natural resistance to more than one of these. Let's keep our fingers crossed. And now ... it looks like ... yes, it's a Pyrovulp. Oh, this is going to be intense! Pyrovulps are extremely vulnerable to Tauntalon—extremely. But if the little guy can get past the Scanary's first attack, then things could get interesting. And it looks like ... Scanary is rearing back, puffing up a little bit ... just look at those gorgeous chest feathers ... could be Tauntalon coming in first.... But no! Wings going out, we've got a blast coming in, and Pyrovulp has got its head flame forward. This was a very bad move on Scanary's part, and I think it's going to regret.... Would you look at that! Wing Blast has fed Pyrovulp's headflame. The whole Pokky is on fire, just burning up ... this lets Pyrovulp bypass an entire part of its normal attack and go straight to Auraflame! The only risk, and I'm not sure he knows it, is that Auraflame can easily feed into Scanary's own ... oh my god oh my god.... Auraflame, incredibly powerful and hot, has triggered Scanary's innate Chirplosion. I am moving away from the Arena, friends, because when this happens, the blast can spread far outside the—WHOA!

VERNOR HERTZWIG

In his records, Hemlock speaks less and less of the human world; civilization and its pleasures recede into the distant past, remembered only for its discontents. At the same time, the brilliant, colorful struggles of the Pokkypets, seeming so much simpler, become more and more a symbol for the conflict of his soul. Deeply torn, it is as if he battled himself in an arena of his own devising. But no longer a Captor or a Trainer, without Pokkypets to do his fighting for him, every injury cut deep into his psyche.

LARCHMONT AND GLADIOLUS PYNE
HEMLOCK'S PARENTS

LP: This is Hem's Pokkypet collection, much as he left it when he moved away from home. I'm afraid we encouraged him more than we should have, since he was a somewhat lonely boy, and he got such pleasure from them. His first Pokkypet was a gift from my mother, who had an affinity herself with the little things—

GP: I thought he won it at a state fair, throwing dimes in Collymoddle bowls, or a prize he won at school.

LP: —no, it was from my mother. I think he's still got the card in his room somewhere pinned up on a bulletin board. We knew there wasn't much of a future in it, but that's not the sort of thing you can worry about when you just want your boy to be happy ... but as he got older and we saw he wasn't moving on to other things, wasn't progressing if you will, then we started to get a bit worried. But somehow Hemlock found a way to make a living at it early on, doing his shows and trainings and whatnot; and although we were disappointed that he felt he had to move all the way to the other side of the country to pursue his interests, we did support him in it. It seemed like his Pokky career was really taking him somewhere. Then, well, I don't know how much truth there is in this, but he tried out for the part of Burny, the Pokky Trainer in Chirrs, and according to him he was first in line for the part, but then Woody Harrelson tried out for the role and they gave it to him. Well, really, that was the beginning of the end for our boy.

GP: He just sort of spiralled out of control.

LP: I held it against Woody for a long time, but ... well....

GP: It's hard to keep a grudge against Woody Harrelson. He's a fine young man.

CRYSTAL BURL

We used to go to the Pokkypet stores in the mall, and Hem would get really upset looking at them in captivity, and he always talked about starting a Pokkypet Liberation Front—but that's not what Pokky People is about or ever was about. Pokky People allowed him to channel his frustration into something positive. You have to understand, the frustration turned so easily into anger. He could be the happiest most joyful person you'd ever met, but the flipside of that was ... was also there. He could be very dark at times. I know he felt that if he didn't have Pokkys, he'd have gone to some very bad places with some very bad people. The Missile Kids, for instance—they tried to recruit him for a while, and I think he was attracted. They could be very seductive. You know, Minny was a real minx, and Sal was sarcastic and cutting, but I know Hem respected them as Trainers ... and then that weird Pokky they had with them all the time, Feelion. In the way that Hem could almost convince the Pokkys that he was one of them, Feelion had a bunch of us convinced that he was one of us. But though Hem flirted with the Missile Kids, he eventually came to believe they were on a bad path—I mean, certainly in terms of drugs they were doing crazy things ... I think even their Pokky was on amphetamines.

HEMLOCK PYNE

If people knew, truly knew what wonderful creatures these Pokkypets are ... they would consider, as I do, that to capture them, to try and train them, to force them through their tri-stage transformations at an accelerated pace—that all this goes against nature. Look at little Chickapork here ... just look at her. She is my hero. So sweet, so loving, so intelligent ... truly a hero. And to think that people want to put her in a ball and give her performance drugs and and and just dump her out in the coliseum to battle against other Pokkys that humans—fucking humans!— have declared her enemies ... it's just sick! And it makes me so angry. Because she's perfect. The lifestyle they live out here in the wild, it's perfect. I have learned so much from these creatures, but it's hardly the beginning of what we could all be learning from them. Our lives ... there's something missing from them that these Pokkys have mastered effortlessly. We need that thing. We don't even know what we're missing ... but I'll tell you ... it's something fucking huge. And without it, we're so far short of perfection it's not funny. That's why nobody's laughing, isn't that right, little Chickapork?

VERNOR HERTZWIG

As his differences with reality widened into a schism, Hemlock Pyne fought reality with tooth and claw. If it did not fit his idealized view of nature, it was reality that must be bent and even broken to fit. His insistence that Pokkypets held a deeper meaning does not stand up to scrutiny. Where Hemlock looked at the colorful characters and saw inscrutable depths, I see only crisp lines, primary colors, two-dimensional expressions. Even in this Rhinophantom, which Pyne in his writings calls a juggernaut of disaster, evokes in me no such premonition. It is just a cute, cuddly pet, that has undergone completely ordinary metamorphoses into a brute that is dumb and awkward, yes, but completely without malice.

HEMLOCK PYNE

...What I found in the bushes here, by the side of the river, is something new to the Pokkymaze. I would like you to study it with me. This is something we have to understand, but I'm not convinced we can. We are so good at missing the point! I discovered this earlier today, just after dawn, and I haven't touched the scene ... I've just been waiting for it to get light enough to record. Now, in the night there was the sound of a Pokkybattle. This is rare enough, but not unheard of in mid-summer. What is unusual is that it took place far from the Arena, and quite near my tent. Just a very weird sound of two Pokkys calling back and forth to one another in solitary combat. I couldn't hear them clearly, but you can see now that they both cast exhausting spells on one another, and, well, here they are. They show no signs of waking or getting along with their day. You can see the Porphyrops has been trampled down into the mud, and the Glumster is just lying with its eyes open, which is a strange position for an incapacitated Pokky. I don't want to intrude in their natural cycle, but I've made some very gentle sounds and I've been getting progressively louder, trying to see if I can wake them gradually. But so far no luck. I have to say, I feel very privileged to see this. To my knowledge no Pokky Captor or Trainer has ever observed this sort of behavior. I am the first. These are the sort of secret revelations the Pokkys have granted me now that I have become such a part of their pattern of life. And these are exactly the things that I need to protect from the rest of the world.

AUGUSTUS "JUSTICE" PEACE

There were really no poachers in this area. The one exception might be the Missile Kids, Sal and Minny, and their Pokky mascot Feelion. But I don't believe they went up there to poach anyhow. The couple times we were concerned and apprehended them, there was no sign they'd been up to any actual Pokkypoaching. What they did do, I'm pretty certain, was show up to bother Hemlock Pyne. Tease him. They made a lot out of being his rivals, you know. And I'm sure it drove him nuts.

HEMLOCK PYNE

I'm here at the shore, this is so upsetting, here at the shore watching those fuckers ... those goddamn poachers ... Sal and Minny. I know what they're up to. They're rubbing my nose in it, that's what they're doing. They've come in to poach—look at that boat full of Poachyballs! There's just no question ... they know I'm watching even though I'm well hidden here. What kills me, fucking KILLS me, is that they have the full support of the Pokky Park Service. It's criminal. It's so corrupt! You just ... the lesson here is that you just pay off the right people and you can come in and capture all the Pokkypets you want. Well, I'm not letting them get away with it. They think they can ... what's that?

"Feeeeee-lion!"

Do you you hear that? They've turned their Feelion loose.

"FEEEEE-LION!"

This is just sick, it's perverted. They've trained their Pokkypet to turn against its kind. This poor Feelion doesn't realize they're using it to lure in unsuspecting Pokkypets ... to pull them in where the Missile Kids can capture them. Well, we're not going to let them get away with that. No fucking way.

"Can you Feeeeel me, Pyne? Can you Feeeeeeeelion me?"

Did you hear that? So much for them calling me paranoid. There's no mistaking that for ... for a threat!

"Feeeeee-lion!"

The cruel thing is, I can't even report them. Because I know they are here with the full knowledge of the Park Service. I can't believe I get grief for coming out here to protect these poor creatures, while Minny and Sal just waltz in, pack their Poachyballs full of innocent, defenseless Pokkys.... To think the rangers would actually try to stop me from getting close to the pets, while these guys ... I'm sorry, I can't talk. This is making me too upset. I'm in tears over this!

VERNOR HERTZWIG
Pyne's disgruntlement became so great that he finally turned against the people who had given him the opportunity to work in the Pokkymaze in the first place. His associates became, in his mind, implacable enemies. There is a sense in his final days of rage that he no longer saw anything beyond the picket of Pokkys, among whom he counted himself, except an homogenous foe.

HEMLOCK PYNE
Oh, I know who they are, all right ... I know they set me up for this those ... those goddamn fucking motherfuckers. You know who you are, you fucking shithead mothercockingfucksuckfuckers! I'm out here trying to help these beautiful creatures, while you're just swimming in corruption ... you don't care a thing about preserving their environment. You people who have sworn to protect it, you've become the thing we have to protect it against! Motherfuck! This ... it's just not right. It's fucked. So very, very, very, very fucked.

CRYSTAL BURL, AUGUSTUS "GUST" MASTERS, PITER YALP
We've come here today to honor Hem, and to pray for him to wake up real

soon. We don't understand what happened to him—what was different this time that he refuses to wake up. We were thinking that maybe if we came out here, to a place that was dear to him, we'd have some insight ... we'd get a glimpse of Hem's thinking.

This right here is his favorite camping spot, where he'd come and spend the first part of the summer at the foot of the Pokky Range before heading north into the Maze. He chose this spot because it was right between two Chickapork dens. There's footage of him playing with the Piglettas, and then of course when one of them made its second-stage transformation into Chickapork, Hem and that Pokky bonded real hard. It's been a year now, and those original Pokkys have gone on and become Peccanaries and Boaraxes; the ones grazing out there in the meadow, one of them might have been Hem's own Chickapork.

I wonder if they miss him. I sure do.

VERNOR HERTZWIG

The irony of Hemlock's last trip is not lost on anyone who looked at his life. As the days of fall grew shorter, he left the maze as he always did, with no desire to return to civilization, but knowing he could not make himself comfortable among the hibernating and overwintering Pokkys. However, an encounter with an airport Pokkypet vending machine, in which Hemlock tried to buy the freedom of every captive Pokkypet but soon ran out of quarters, sent him rebounding from the crass commercial exploitation of his beloved Pokkys, straight back into the wilderness. Returning to the maze later than ever before, he found his familiar environment had been altered by advancing chill; and his familiar Pokky friends had moved on their migratory routes, while new creatures moved into the maze to overwinter there. Creatures such as the Surlymon.

HEMLOCK PYNE

I am back, friends. I didn't know I would be doing this, obviously, and I would not recommend it to anyone else ... but frankly, I find it exhilarating. I am overjoyed to be back here. The longer I can put off dealing with the fucking human world, the happier I'll be. And you know what? This is a part of the Pokky life cycle I have never seen. This is a learning moment! I have never been here in the winter ... and though I won't be staying for the whole season, I will certainly see more of it than any person ever has. Because no other person—Trainer, Captor, or civilian—has stayed even this long. Who knows what I'll learn, what wonders await?

VERNOR HERTZWIG

Toward the end of the process of compiling this account, we received access to Pyne's final recordings. Here we see him with a large grouchy Pokkypet that almost certainly is the Surlymon that finished him off. Of most interest in these studies is that this Pokky appears to have changed radically sometime between the date this footage was taken, and the time of its capture by the Pokky Rangers. Experience gained in a battle is the usual mode by which Pokkys gain sufficient energy to transform into their morpheme. And it is hard not to conclude that it was the battle with Hemlock Pyne that caused this Surlymon to undergo its third transformation. Most confusing to Pokkyologists is that while its form changed dramatically, its name and its song remained the same: Surlymon....

Here, Hemlock records the untransformed Surlymon stalking the maze in an endless search for amusement. He seems to be searching this simple creature for a deeper meaning, but whatever it is eludes him, as it eludes us.

HEMLOCK PYNE

I don't know what this Pokky wants. Superficially, it seems to be looking for food and interested in nothing else. But there is something the Pokkys have, something innate in them, which draws me. I feel sometimes so close to them, I almost have a name for it—one I could express to myself, but which might be impossible to communicate to others. There is something ... something there.

VERNOR HERTZWIG

But here I must disagree with Hemlock Pyne. The cute cartoon features, so simplistic and round and bright, need evoke nothing beyond the simplest emotional connotations associated with their coloration. He looks for depth where none exists. The Pokkys have no secrets, and nothing to teach us. If anything, this is their entire lesson: They mean nothing, and nothing about their relationship with us is real.

DR. JASPER CHRYSOLITE

If I open this door and pull out the tray, you can see the desperate effort we have undertaken to keep Hemlock comfortable in spite of the bizarre process that seems to be having its way with him. Here you see his head, the eyes still closed in an attitude of sleep that for all intents and purposes seems permanent. Here, his hand, somewhat distressed after its short stay in Surlymon's mouth. The torso, on which the head hardly fits at this point. Part of a leg. The other parts, all gathered from the maze, do not quite add up completely. But this still seems the sort

of risk Hemlock stated repeatedly he was willing to take to be one with these creatures, to learn the lessons they carried with them. Lessons, perhaps, that may one
day apply to us, as we share their natural world?

HEMLOCK PYNE
I know I have felt something like this before, but the shortness of the season
sharpens this sense of giving. I have the words now. They have given them to me.
I owe the Pokkypets everything I have. Everything. And I owe them completely.
I would die for these creatures. I would die for these creatures. I would die for
these creatures.

VERNOR HERTZWIG
We still have no idea what he means.

Vicious

By

Mark Morris

There was this bird. John said she was bad news. But then John thinks everyone's bad news. He's just fucking paranoid.

Not as bad as Malcolm, though. Malcolm thinks the CIA and the FBI and fuck knows who else is following us. He thinks they're waiting for the chance to blow us all away. Wipe the Sex Pistols off the face of the earth.

Well, ha fucking ha. They won't get me. I'm Sid Vicious. I'm fucking indestructible. I'm gonna live forever.

This bird, though. Came on to me after the gig. These American birds love me. "Sid, Sid, fuck me." "Yeah, alright, darlin'. Anything to oblige."

John says I'm disgusting. He says I'm turning into a Rolling Stone. But he's just uptight and jealous. He ain't as pretty as me. Ain't got no anarchy in his soul no more. I'm the only one with any anarchy left. Steve and Paul. What a couple of cunts. They're just the backing band. After the gig tonight Steve went mental. Said I was out of control. Said I was dragging them all down.

"We're *supposed* to be out of control, you fucker," I told him. "We're the Sex Pistols."

He told me if I didn't sort myself out I'd be out of the band.

"You can't throw me out," I said. "You'd be nothing without me. People don't come to see you. They come to see me."

"Yeah," said John. He was sitting in the corner on his own, with a can of beer in his hand like an old man in a pub. "But that's 'cos most of the morons who go to the circus prefer the clowns to the artistes."

He don't know what he's talking about. He's so full of shit. He's a miserable bastard. They're all miserable bastards. Not me, though. I'm having a great time. I ain't got no gear, and that's fucking killing me, but at least I'm making an effort.

Thing is, I hurt all over from not having any stuff, and I can't sleep, and every time I eat something I throw it back up. And I fucking itch. Itch, itch, itch. All over. My arm, where I cut myself, and my chest, where I carved Gimme A Fix (and I don't even remember doing that), and my fucking bollocks. My bollocks most of all.

I thought I had some disease. I thought I was dying. Our tour manager, Noel Monk. He's a fucking hippie, with a moustache like a fucking faggot cowboy, but he's all right.

"Noel," I said. "There's something wrong with me. I fucked some bitch before I come here and I fucking itch like crazy."

He laughed. "Don't worry, Sid. You got crabs, that's all," he said.

So yeah. I hurt and I itch and I'm sick and I need some stuff so bad and I'm missing Nancy, but that don't stop me enjoying myself. Fucking America. It's great.

So this bird. She come up and she wanted to fuck me. We were hanging out after the show. We're in this place. Baton Rouge. Louisiana. The Kingfish Club.

I was feeling all right. I was drinking peppermint schnapps 'cos it stops the hurting, and Noel had given me some of his valiums, and I was floating. Everything soft and mellow. And this bird said, "Sid, you're beautiful. I want to fuck you."

And so we fucked. Right there on the bar. Animal magnetism. People were watching and taking photos, but I didn't care. Let 'em. It's their problem if they wanna be perverts, not mine.

She was going down on me, and I was lying back, thinking of England (ha ha ha) and then there was all this shouting, and I opened my eyes, and there was Noel and Glen, one of the security blokes, and some other geezers, and everyone was going apeshit. Glen was trying to grab someone's camera and Noel was pulling the bird off me, and so I took a swing at him with my bottle, but I missed.

"What the fuck are you doing, Noel?" I said. "You said I could shag who I wanted."

It's true. He wouldn't get me no smack, but he said any time I saw a bird I liked he'd bring her to me.

"And so you can, Sid," he said. "But not here. Here is a bit too ... public."

I saw John out of the corner of my eye. He curled his lip and sneered at me. He looked disgusted.

"Where then?" I said.

"We'll find somewhere. Come on."

They took us away. Me and the bird. It was like being arrested. Surrounded by all these bodies. Big guys. Like a fucking moving wall. I saw faces through the wall. A blur of faces, looking at me. I spat at them. "Fuck off." They were like demons. Grinning. Eyes shining. "Fuck off, fuck off." I wanted to slash them all open.

We didn't have a hotel. When the equipment was packed we were all getting back on the bus and driving through the snow and the dark and the shit. Endless fucking black roads. Driving and driving.

I don't mind the driving, to be honest. It's a bit boring, but it's all right. I like that we stop at roadside diners. Steak and eggs. I love my steak and eggs. Steak rare, eggs runny. But I can never keep it down. Eat it all up, yum yum, lovely. But then my guts cramp and I have to run for the bog and throw it back up again. All over the wall. In the sink. Everywhere. Blood and puke all over America. Sid was here.

"Oi, Glen," I said.

Glen looked at me. He's a big fucking guy. Big fucking beard. I told him only hippies and arseholes have beards, but he's all right. Glen's tough.

"Yeah, Sid?"

"Where we going tonight?"

"When we've finished here, you mean?"

"Yeah."

"We're going to Dallas, Sid."

"Oh yeah," I said.

Dallas. That's where that President got shot. I remember my mum telling me about that when I was a kid. Big deal. Big news. Maybe we'll get shot in Dallas too. Maybe we'll be as famous as that President.

"Dallas," I said. "Yeah, brilliant."

Noel and Glen found us this place backstage. Fucking broom cupboard. Sink in the corner.

"We'll be right outside, Sid," Noel said, "so don't get any smart ideas about running out on us."

"I won't, Noel. No way."

He shut the door. It was fucking dark in there, but me and the bird fucked on the floor. I was knackered. I felt sick. I puked in the sink. My head was pounding.

"You okay, Sid?" the bird asked. She tried to touch me, but my skin was sore. Her touch was like needles. I shrugged her off.

"Don't fucking touch me," I said.

"Jeez," she said. "What's your problem?"

"You," I said. "You're my fucking problem."

She went all whiny. "What have I done wrong, Sid? Tell me what I've done wrong and I'll put it right."

"I need smack," I said. "You got any smack?"

"No," she said.

"Then you're no fucking good to me," I said. "Why don't you fuck off?"

She started to cry. Black lines trickling down her face. I felt bad. "Fucking hell," I said. "Don't cry."

"I can't help it. You're mad at me."

"No, I'm not," I said. "I'm not mad at you. I just need some stuff. Noel and that lot, they won't let me out. They won't let me go anywhere. They think if I go off somewhere I'll end up killing myself."

"And will you?" said the bird. Little squeaky voice.

I laughed. I was hurting again. Sweats and chills. Body cramps. "Yeah, probably," I said. "Or some fucking cowboy will shoot me. They hate us here. Fucking America hates the Sex Pistols."

"I don't," said the bird. "I love the Sex Pistols."

"Yeah, well, you're one of the smart ones," I said. "Most people are scared of us. They think we're gonna destroy America."

"You should," said the bird. "You should destroy America. It's a dump. I hate it."

"Yeah," I said. "It's a fucking dump."

"Maybe I'll come to England," the bird said.

"Don't bother," I said. "It's a dump there too."

I didn't wanna talk no more. I finished the Schnapps and curled up on the floor and closed my eyes. I hurt all over. I just wanted everything to go black.

"Do you want me to go?" the bird asked.

"I'm not bothered," I said. "Stay or go. I don't care."

I went to sleep. I had these dreams. Bad dreams. Faces looking at me. All these fucking faces. Shouting and laughing. Twisting out of shape. Turning into something bad. I was trying to push them away, but I was trapped. I couldn't get out. I couldn't breathe. I was a kid again. I was crying for my mum. I was cutting myself. Slash slash, across my arms, across my chest. I wanted the pain and the blood. But there was no pain, no blood. I couldn't make myself bleed. I couldn't feel anything. I cried out, but I couldn't make any noise.

"Shh, mon petit."

The voice was in my head. It went through me like a cold breeze on a hot day. It blew all the shit and fear away. Made me feel calm.

I opened my eyes. Big brown eyes looking down at me.

"Who are you?" I said.

This wasn't the bird I'd fucked earlier. This was someone different. Light brown skin. Smooth, like toffee. Big brown eyes and big red lips. Black hair in little twisty dreads. She was fucking beautiful. She was so beautiful I couldn't breathe.

"You want to be saved?" she said.

I was shivering. My leather jacket was over me like a blanket, but the floor was cold underneath me and I felt like there was nothing left of me but bones.

"Saved from what?" I said.

"From yourself."

"Dunno what you mean."

I tried to sit up. I felt so weak. She had to help me. She jangled when she moved. She was wearing all these bracelets and necklaces. She smelled like flowers and spice and dark forests.

"How did you get in here?" I asked her.

"I go where I please," she said.

She put her hand under the tap in the sink and turned it on. She held her dripping fingers over my face. I opened my mouth and the water ran over my lips and tongue and down my throat. It tasted sweet, made me feel like a kid again. Everything new and bright.

"You want to be saved?" she asked again.

I shrugged. "I dunno. Are you one of those Jesus nutjobs?"

She laughed. "I believe in spirits, mon petit. Do *you* believe in spirits?"

"Yeah," I said. "Whisky and vodka."

She didn't laugh this time. She reached out and touched a badge on my jacket. "Is this true?"

"What?"

"'I'm A Mess.' Is it true, mon petit? *Are* you a mess?"

I looked into her big brown eyes. They held me. They were fucking hypnotic. It was like just by looking at me she was clearing all the shit out of my brain. I wanted to cry. I felt it all rushing up through me like puke. I nodded, but I couldn't speak.

"Tell me," she said.

I still wanted to cry, but I swallowed it back down again. "I'm a junkie," I said. "I'm fucked up. I don't wanna be, but I can't help it. People offer me stuff and I can't say no. But I'm gonna get straight. I am. I'm gonna get straight and pull this band back together. I'll be a better bassist than that art school cunt, Matlock. We'll conquer the fucking world. We're the best fucking band there's ever been."

I stopped. It sounded like someone else talking. After a minute I said, "My head is fucked up. I don't know what's true and what isn't anymore. I don't know who I am."

"Who do you *think* you are?" she said. "Tell me everything. Let it all out."

"I'm Sid Vicious," I told her. "I'm a Sex Pistol. I'm a fucking star. I'm the bass player who can't play. I'm a joke. A pathetic junkie. I'm gonna live forever. I'm gonna be dead before I'm twenty-five. I fucking love Nancy. I can't live without her. She's fucked up my life. She's the worst thing that ever happened to me. John's my best mate. He looks out for me. I hate him and he hates me. He's got no future. I want him to fuck off. I love him. I don't wanna lose him. Everything's falling apart. Everything's turning to shit. We're gonna rule the fucking world. We're gonna be heroes. We're gonna destroy America. Malcolm's a fucking genius. Malcolm's a cunt who doesn't care about us. I'm gonna be a legend. I'm gonna be forgotten."

I couldn't stop. It was like cutting my arm and watching the blood spurt. I put a hand over my mouth to stop it pouring out of me. What I was saying was all true and all lies. It was everything and nothing, the good and the bad, the dream and the nightmare. They were different, but they were the same. It was all happening together, all at once, and I was stuck in the middle.

"You are at the crossroads, mon petit," the girl said.

"The crossroads, yeah," I said.

"Which way do you go from here?"

"I dunno."

She was staring at me, like she could see the thoughts fighting in my head. What was I? The bassist in the best fucking band in the world? Or a walking fucking cliché, press fodder, Malcolm's fucking puppet? If I cleaned myself up, got myself together, we could be fucking huge, we could go down in fucking history as the band that changed music forever. But did I really want that? Did I wanna be a legend? Did I wanna be Elvis Presley twenty years from now, fat and ugly and useless, dying of a heart attack on a fucking toilet? Did I wanna be a dinosaur, like Led Zep and Pink Floyd and all that hippie shit? Did I wanna be a fucking *rock* star?

Fuck that. Fuck it all. I'd never be fucking *establishment*. But I'd find a way. My way.

The girl was still staring. Her eyes were glittering. At that moment she could've been an angel or a demon.

"It is your decision," she said.

"Is it?"

"Of course. If you want it to be."

"Can you help me?" I asked her.

Instead of answering, she stood up and held out her hand. "Come with me."

"Where we going?"

"To get you what you need."

I took her hand and she pulled me up like I weighed nothing.

"Noel and Glen are outside," I said. "They won't let me go."

She smiled. "Like I say, mon petit, I go where I please."

She pushed open the door and led me outside. Noel and Glen were sitting in the corridor playing cards. They didn't even look at us.

"Come," she said, and she gave me a little tug. I kept thinking that any second Noel would look up and say, "Where do you think you're going, Sid?"

But he didn't. Him and Glen just kept playing cards.

"What's wrong with 'em?" I whispered.

"They cannot see us," she said. "To them we are like the wind."

"Yeah?" I said. I walked right up and leaned over them. "Oi," I said. They ignored me.

I laughed. It was like being a fucking superhero. The fucking invisible man. Noel had a can of beer on the floor by his chair. I picked it up and spat in it. He didn't respond.

"Oi, Noel," I said. "You're a fucking cunt."

He kept on playing cards.

I laughed again. And then suddenly I felt scared. I looked at the girl.

"Am I dead," I said. "Am I a ghost?"

She smiled. "No, mon petit."

"But no one can see me," I said. "I don't like it that no one can see me. I don't wanna be ignored."

The girl was still holding my hand. She leaned in and whispered in my ear, like it was a secret. "Trust me, mon petit."

I felt calm again. "Yeah," I said, "all right."

"Come," she said.

We went down the corridor and out through the stage door, into the main hall. There were still a lot of people around. Roadies, journalists, some fucking groupies and fans. I thought they'd turn round and look at us, but no one did. It was weird. It was good not being hassled, but I like it when people look at me. I like seeing their faces when they recognise me. Specially the birds.

There was no sign of Steve and Paul and Malcolm. I knew Steve and Paul were sick of all the driving, and earlier Steve had said he was gonna tell Malcolm that from now on he and Paul wanted to fly to the gigs like proper fucking pop stars, otherwise he'd fuck off home, so maybe that's what had happened.

John was still there, though. Still hunched over in the same place with his can of beer and his fag. He was surrounded by cunts hanging on his every fucking word, but as usual he looked bored and pissed off. He always took the piss out of me for being a "Daily Mirror punk," but he was just as bad. He was all right on the bus, then soon as he went out in public he turned into a moody, hostile cunt. Johnny Rotten, the punk rock star.

I was glad he was there, though. Glad he'd decided to stay with me and not fuck off with the others. Maybe it'd be easier with the others gone. Maybe we could be mates again. I hope so. Me and him, we're the real Sex Pistols. The others are just fucking wankers.

Me and the bird walked right across the room and no one even looked at us. We walked out of the room and out of the door and into the night.

It was fucking cold. Raining. Downtown Baton Rouge was a dump. The whole of America was a fucking dump. That bird had been right.

"Where we going?" I said. "I'm not fucking walking nowhere."

"Didn't I tell you to trust me?" the girl said, and she tugged on my hand again. "Come."

I don't like being told what to do, but with this girl it was all right. I didn't even wanna fuck her. Well, I did, but it would've been wrong. It would've been like fucking an angel or something.

She had a pick-up truck parked round the side of the club. An angel with a knackered fucking shitmobile of a pick-up truck. Ha fucking ha.

She opened the passenger door and told me to get in. I did. I was cold, shivering. She started the engine. It sounded like an old man coughing his guts up. I put the heater on, but I was still cold. But at least I didn't feel sick anymore. At least I didn't have stomach cramps. At least I wasn't itching.

"What's that smell?" I said.

"Crawfish. My brother is a fisherman. He supplies restaurants here in town and out in the bayou."

There was a fucked-up music system with a tape hanging out of it. I pushed the tape in and turned it on.

"What's this music?" I said.

"It's zydeco."

"Zydeco? What the fuck's that?"

"Roots music. You like it?"

"Yeah," I said. "It's good. It's like reggae, but faster."

"It's the music of the land," she said. "The music of the blood and the soul."

"Like the Sex Pistols," I said.

She smiled. "You think your Sex Pistols will play zydeco music?"

I grinned. "Yeah," I said. "Why fucking not?"

We drove out of town. It was just traffic lights and rain. The world looked like it was melting. The roads turned to dirt tracks. The truck bounced in and out of pot holes. Trees and swamps all round us. Shacks at the side of the road.

Then there weren't even any shacks. Just trees tangled together. Bent over and covered in slime. No stars, no moon, just darkness. I didn't know where we were and I didn't care.

The girl pulled over at the side of the track and turned off the engine. When the engine stopped the music did too. That's when I knew the sound of rusty violins weren't part of the music. They were insects screaming in the darkness.

She looked at me. Big brown eyes glowing.

"We're here," she said.

"Where?"

"At the crossroads."

"So where do we go now?"

"That's your decision, mon petit."

I got out of the truck. It had stopped raining. The trees dripped. The world still looked like it was melting. There was a smell of something old and rotting. I liked it here. It was dead, but it was away from the madness. Away from everything.

Something slithered in the darkness nearby and splashed into the water. I thought of the mayhem behind me. The blood and puke and shit and fights. The first sweet rush of smack through my veins and into my brain. I thought of all the people and the noise. The faces crowding me. Demon eyes and hungry mouths. Sucking my life away. Feeding on my corpse.

"I wanna stay here forever," I said.

"Which way, mon petit?" said the girl.

I turned round. Round and round on the spot. I didn't know what I was looking for, but then I saw it. A light through the trees. An orange glow. Like the moon had fallen out of the sky and was sinking into the swamp.

"There," I said. "Let's go there."

We walked towards the light. Insects made a noise like a thousand rusty doors creaking all at once. Things moved around us. I remembered Glen telling me on the bus about the animals they get here. Alligators and snakes and poisonous spiders. He told me hoping it would scare me. So I wouldn't run off to find some smack.

Well, fuck you. I'm Sid Vicious. I ain't gonna get eaten by no fucking alligator. I ain't scared of nothing. I'm the most dangerous fucking animal in America.

The light was farther away than it looked. We walked for ages, my boots splatting through mud and water. The girl walked next to me. She seemed to blend in, like she was part of the land. She moved silently, like she was floating.

The track got narrow. Water lapped on both sides of us. Things moved in the trees. Things splashed in the water. I thought of thousands of demon eyes watching us. Thousands of grinning mouths full of sharp teeth. I had no smack, no booze, nothing to keep the pain away. But I felt all right. The girl was my drug. My fucking angel.

Then the track widened into a clearing. In front of us was a wooden shack. It was raised up off the ground with a porch at the front. Orange light was shining out the front windows. Something flapped on the roof. Tarpaulin or plastic. When we got closer I saw the windows were covered in wire mesh. Big fucking moths were bouncing off them, desperate to get to the light.

I looked at the girl. The light was shining in her eyes, making them glow in the dark. She looked like a cat. A fucking leopard walking on two legs.

"Where are we?" I said. "Who lives here?"

"Why don't you find out, mon petit?"

I walked up the steps and knocked on the door. There was a sound from inside. A rusty old creak that might have been a voice. I pushed the door open. "Hello?"

The place was gloomy. Candles burning. Flickering shadows. Ratty old furniture. Wooden floor. It smelled old. Like old people. Dead and stale. There was no one here.

"Hello?" I shouted again. "Anyone home?"

There was a doorway at the back of the room. A big black opening. The shadows made it move and sway. It made me think of a mouth. An old man's mouth. No teeth. Yawning, struggling for breath. A voice came out of the mouth. Small and tired and creaky. It said something in a foreign language. French or something, I dunno.

I walked across to the door. Boots clomping on the wooden floor. I stuck my head through the opening, looked into the room. Couldn't see a fucking thing. Pitch black. I heard something moving, rustling.

"Who's there?" I said.

The scrape of a match. A flame. Behind the flame a yellow face, hanging in the darkness. The flame moved across, lit a candle. Light jumped into the room, surrounded by black moving shadows. The light was orangey-brown. There was a big bed and an old woman lying on it. She was fat and saggy. The light made her brown skin look shiny, like polished wood. She had bulging eyes. A big fuzz of black hair. The candle-light made the ends of her hair twitch like snakes.

"Hello," I said and grinned at her. "Who the fuck are you then?"

She said something else in a foreign language. I didn't know if it was her name or what.

"I ain't got a fucking clue what you're talking about," I said.

The girl spoke. I didn't even know she was behind me until I heard her voice. She said something foreign to the old woman and the old woman said something back. They spoke quickly. Jabba jabba jabba.

"What's she say?" I said.

"Her name is Madame Picou," said the girl. "She says she will help you."

"Madame what?" I said.

The girl spelled the old lady's name for me.

"Hello, Mrs. Picou," I said to the old lady. "I'm Sid."

The old lady said something. I shrugged.

"Madame Picou says take a seat," said the girl.

"All right, thanks," I said. There was a wooden chair under an old dressing table against the wall. I went over to it, and just for a second, when I looked in the mirror, I saw a skull looking back at me. I jumped and looked again. It was just me. In the candle-light my skin was white and my eyes were full of black shadows. I noticed things hanging off the sides of the mirror. Beads. Snake skins. I dragged the chair over to the bed and sat down.

The old lady jabbered again. She leaned towards me. She was so fat that she grunted like a pig as she rolled on to her side. A big fucking fart ripped out of her. I nearly pissed myself laughing. I was still laughing when she took my hands and looked at them, turning them over. Suddenly she shoved up the sleeves of my leather jacket and ran her fat thumbs up the insides of my arms.

I stopped laughing when I felt her stab something into my arm. Right into the fucking vein near my elbow. I was used to needles, but I wasn't expecting it and it made me jump.

"Ow!" I shouted and pulled my arm back. "What did you do that for, you cunt?"

I was angry. I wanted to smash something. Her face or her fucking furniture. I stood up and then I felt a hand on my shoulder, warm breath that smelt of spice and perfume against the side of my face.

"Hush, mon petit."

"She fucking stabbed me," I said.

"It is nothing," the girl said. "Relax."

My anger went away. Just like that. I sat down again. Suddenly I felt tired. Really tired. I couldn't move. I felt so relaxed that I couldn't even lift my hand from my leg.

"What's going on?" I said.

"It is nothing, mon petit," said the girl. "You are fine."

"I can't fucking move," I said.

"Madame Picou has paralysed you. But it is only temporary. Do not worry."

"What's she paralysed me for?"

"It is necessary."

"Why?"

Instead of answering me, the girl and the old bird jabbered at each other again. It seemed like the girl was asking questions and the old bird was giving her instructions, waving her arms about.

The girl went away. The old bird stared at me. Her face didn't move. She didn't blink.

"What you staring at?" I said.

She didn't answer.

Then the girl came back. She had some stuff in her hands. She put it on the bed.

There was a little doll made of string and cloth and twigs. A pair of scissors. A pin cushion. A little cloth bag. A bottle with some sort of liquid in it.

"What's going on?" I said.

The old bird put her finger to her lips and hissed at me.

"Shush yourself, you cunt," I said. "What's that? A fucking voodoo doll? You gonna put a curse on me or something?"

"It is a gris-gris," said the girl.

"What the fuck's that then?"

"It is to bind us together," she said.

"What do you mean?"

The girl took my hands and knelt in front of me. Usually when she touched me she made me feel calm. But I was getting scared and that made me angry. I'm a Sex Pistol. I ain't supposed to be scared of nothing.

"I need you, mon petit," the girl said. "I need you to save me."

"I thought *you* were gonna save *me*," I said.

"I would if I could, mon petit," said the girl. "But you are beyond redemption. I am sorry."

"Fuck off," I said. If I could've moved I would've smacked her one. But I couldn't, so I spat on her instead. My gob hit the side of her face. A big greeny. She just stayed where she was. Looked at me sadly and let it trickle down. Then she stood up.

She and the old bird jabbered some more. The old bird was waving her arms about, telling her what to do. The girl picked up the little doll. She got something out of her pocket and showed it to me. It was a picture of me, cut out of a newspaper. I was up on stage playing my bass. The girl pinned the picture of me to the little doll and gave it to the old woman. Then she picked up the scissors from the bed and came towards me.

"Fuck off," I said. "Get away from me." I spat at her again. It hit the front of her dress, but she ignored it.

I tried to move, but I was still fucking paralysed.

"You cut me and I'll fucking kill you," I said.

She reached out towards me. She made a sound through her teeth like she was trying to calm a fucking wild animal. When her hand got close enough I tried to bite it, but she was too quick. Her hand shot up and grabbed my hair.

"Fucking get off," I said.

She brought up the other hand with the scissors and cut a bit of my hair off.

"*Fuck off!*" I screamed at her. "*I'll fucking kill you, you bitch!*"

She held up the tuft of black hairs. Like she was showing me I didn't need to worry 'cos she'd only cut off a few. The old bird held up the doll, and the girl stuck the hairs to it. There was so much Vaseline on them that she didn't need glue or nothing. The old woman put the doll down on the bed and then picked up the little cloth bag and opened it. There was some sort of powder in it. I wasn't sure what it was, but it looked like smack. The old bird sprinkled some of the powder over the doll and started to jabber something in a foreign language. She closed her eyes and started to sway from side to side.

"What the fuck's she doing?" I said.

"Offering your image to the spirit," said the girl.

"What for?"

"So that we can seal the bond."

I shook my head. "What is this fucking bond? What are you doing to me? I ain't done nothing to you."

The girl looked at me. "I was like you, mon petit," she said.

"What do you mean?"

She pointed at the badge on my jacket. "I was a mess. I was ..." She mimed injecting a syringe into her arm.

"A junkie?"

She nodded. Behind her the old bird was still swaying and jabbering.

"And now you're clean?" I said.

The girl pulled a weird face. Like: not really. "You will *keep* me clean," she said.

"Oh yeah?" I said. "And how am I gonna do that?"

"By accepting my desire as your own."

I asked her what she meant, but she just smiled and turned round and went into the other room.

"Oi!" I shouted. "Don't fucking walk away from me! Come back here, you cunt!"

But she was gone. The old bird was still swaying and muttering. I could see her bulging eyes moving under her eyelids.

"And you can shut the fuck up as well," I said.

But she didn't. She just kept on and on. Jabba jabba jabba.

A few minutes later the girl came back. She'd taken all her clothes off. She was naked. Gorgeous. The most beautiful girl I had ever seen.

"Fuck," I said. "Are we gonna shag? Is that part of this voodoo shit?"

The girl smiled, but she didn't say anything. She came towards me. The light slid across her naked flesh. It was like she was made of golden oil. I didn't think it was possible for anyone to be so beautiful. I loved Nancy, but this girl made Nancy look like a skanky old slag. I didn't know whether I had a hard-on 'cos I couldn't feel anything from the neck down. But in my brain I had a hard-on. The biggest fucking hard-on in the world.

I sat there staring at her with my mouth open as the girl came over. My eyes couldn't get enough of her. I wanted to touch her so bad. Fuck all that angel stuff from before.

I was staring at her tits and cunt, so I didn't notice the tattoo at first. It was only when she started to pull my leather jacket off that I saw she had a tattoo of a thin black snake around her right arm.

"What's that?" I said.

"Le Grand Zombi," she replied.

"You what?"

"It is the serpent. It protects me from harm."

"Bollocks," I said. "Oi, what you doing with my jacket?"

She had my jacket off me now. She threw it on the bed at the old bird's fat ugly feet and looked at my arms.

"So many scratches, so many bruises," she said. She sounded sad. "Why do you hate yourself, mon petit?"

"I don't hate myself," I said. "I fucking love myself. I'm fucking brilliant, me."

I grinned at her, but she just looked sad. She turned away from me. Beautiful arse.

She picked up the little bottle and pulled the cork out of it. Then she started to shake out the liquid inside, spraying drops of it over the old bird and the voodoo doll.

The old bird didn't seem to mind. Didn't even notice.

The girl closed her eyes and started to jabber like the old woman. She started to dance too, her body rippling like a snake, her tits jiggling. She really got into it, went into a kind of trance. She shook more of the liquid over herself. Poured it over the snake tattoo on her arm, making it shine. Then she sprinkled the liquid over me, over *my* arm, the one I'd cut open. The wound had gone septic, but I couldn't feel it, not now. I looked at the arm as the liquid splashed over it, but only for a second. Looking at the girl's jiggling tits was much more fun.

Both of the fucking women were totally out of it now. Jiggling and jabbering.

All that ju-ju voodoo bollocks. The girl kept splashing liquid round. All over me, over her, over the old bird holding the doll.

"I'm fucking bored of this," I said loudly, but neither of them heard me.

The girl kept splashing water until the bottle was empty. Then she threw the bottle away.

The jabbering changed. It was creepy. It was like the two of them were linked together or something. Suddenly their voices got deeper. Slower. They started saying the same words. The old bird held out the doll and the girl grabbed it. They both clung to it like a couple of kids fighting over a toy. The girl reached out with her other arm and grabbed my hand. I couldn't do nothing about it. We were like a human chain. The old bird and the girl still swaying and jiggling like nutters.

"What is this? Ring a ring of fucking roses?" I said.

Then the snake tattoo on the girl's arm started to move. I thought it was just the light at first, or my eyes, or that fucking stuff the old bird had injected into me fucking up my head.

"Fucking hell," I said. I squeezed my eyes shut, then opened them again. The snake tattoo was still moving. The thin black snake was curling down the girl's arm like a stripe on a fucking barber's pole. Down towards her wrist. Towards her hand. Towards *my* hand.

I tried to break free, but I couldn't move. I shouted and spat at her, but it made no difference.

The snake tattoo wasn't a tattoo no more. It was a real snake. It made a rustling sound when it moved. Its tongue flickered in and out. Its little yellow eyes fucking stared at me.

I yelled out when it moved from the girl's hand on to my hand. Then it was coiling up my arm. Taking its time. I couldn't feel it, but I could see it. I moved my head back as far as I could, terrified it was going to come all the way up my arm and bite me in the neck like a fucking vampire. Maybe it'd eat my eyes. Or crawl down my fucking throat and choke me. Maybe it'd go inside me and lay eggs and loads of baby snakes would hatch out and eat their way out of my stomach. I screamed at them to get the fucking thing off me, but they were still out of it, jiggling and chanting.

The snake moved up my arm to just above my elbow. Then it stopped. It gathered in its coils, bunched up. Now it looked like the belt I wrapped round my arm when I wanted to find a vein. The snake tightened round my arm until a big blue vein popped up in my elbow. I could see the vein pulsing away. Slowly the snake lifted its head. Then it struck. It opened its mouth wide and sank its fucking fangs right into the vein.

I screamed. I couldn't feel nothing, but I screamed.

"Get it off, you bitches! Get this fucking thing off me!"

My voice sounded weird in my own head. Rough and echoing. Like it was someone else's voice shouting from down the end of a long metal tunnel. My body was still paralysed, but my arm felt hot. I thought of the snake's venom mixing with my blood. Rushing through my body, travelling to my heart and my brain. I wondered if I was gonna die. The thought of dying didn't seem too bad. If I died on tour I'd get in the papers. I'd be on the front page. Yeah, that'd be all right.

My thoughts were falling apart. The room pulsed in and out, getting small then big, bright then dim. I didn't know the two birds had stopped their voodoo bollocks until the girl knelt in front of me. She took my hands. She smiled at me. Face shiny with sweat. Big brown eyes glowing. Even now she was beautiful. She'd fucking killed me, but she was beautiful.

"The snake is my desire, mon petit," she said. "You must feed my desire as well as your own. This way only one of us will die."

I could hardly keep my eyes open. My head was like a heavy rock. I tried to speak. I heard the words in my head, but I don't know if she did.

"Fuck you," I said.

Then it all went black. When I woke up it was dark and I was shivering. There was a hammering sound. Voices.

"Sid! Sid!"

I didn't realise I could move until I sat up. I felt like shit. Body aching, full of cramps. Covered in cold sweat. Arm, chest, and bollocks itching like crazy.

I looked around. My head felt full of broken glass. I was in the broom cupboard in the Kingfish Club. The cupboard where I'd shagged the bird. The cupboard where the girl had come to me.

There was no one here now. Just me.

"Sid! Sid!"

"What?" I shouted.

The door opened. It was Noel.

"We're all packed up, Sid. Ready to move on."

"Where we fucking going?" I said.

"Dallas, Sid. We're going to Dallas. Come on, man. You want a hand?"

Noel came into the room and helped me up. I rushed over to the sink and puked my guts out.

"You okay, Sid," Noel said.

"No, I feel fucking terrible," I said. "I need some stuff, Noel. I need it now."

"No stuff, Sid. You know that. Soon as we get on the bus you can have some valium. How's that sound?"

I wasn't listening. I remembered what the girl had said. "You must feed my desire as well as your own."

I took my leather jacket off. Curled around my arm was the little black snake. It lifted its head and flicked its tongue at me. I screamed.

"Jesus, Sid," Noel said. "What's wrong?"

"*Get it off me, Noel!*" I yelled. "*Fucking get it off me!*"

"Get what off you, Sid?" Noel asked.

I held my arm out. "*The snake! Get the fucking snake off!*"

Noel looked at my arm. "There's no snake, Sid," he said. "You're hallucinating, man. Come on."

He walked out of the room. I looked at the snake wrapped around my arm. The snake only I could see. I looked at the blue vein pulsing in the crook of my elbow, and in that second I knew.

I was lost. Lost for good. There was no way back.

Feed the snake, I thought. *Feed the fucking snake.*

I put my leather jacket on and followed Noel out of the room.

From Hell's Heart

By

Nancy A. Collins

I am hesitant to relate the tale I am about to tell, largely because it does nothing to bolster my claims of sanity. But if I am to convince others of my innocence in this matter, I have no choice but to recount the singular events that have lead me to this cold cell.

I am first-generation Canadian, my parents having migrated from their native Scotland to this wild and boundless land. I have long harbored a deep fascination with the rough-and-tumble lifestyle of the French-Canadian *couriers de bois*, those rugged pioneers who helped shape our fledgling nation. Because of this, I left my home in Toronto for the wilds of what, until recently, was known as Rupert's Land, with the intention of becoming a trapper. However, my enthusiasm proved far greater than my woodscraft, and I found it all I could do to survive the first heavy snowfall.

As luck would have it, while on a visit to a trading post, I made the acquaintance of a certain Dick Buchan and Ben Martin. They, too, were new to the trapping game and having a hard time of it. We agreed that it was a lonesome and difficult business, especially during the long winter months, and decided to pool our resources and become partners, running our traplines from a home shanty near the vast shores of God's Lake.

Of the three who comprised our rustic enterprise, I was the youngest. Buchan was, at the ripe old age of twenty-seven, the eldest of our group. He was a tall, well-developed specimen with copper-red hair and a beard to match, and claimed to have a wife and child in Winnipeg. Martin was a year or so his junior, and as stout and strong as an oak barrel, with dark brown hair and a feisty sense of humor.

Come the thaw, my partners and I transported our bundles of fur to the trading post at God's Lake. From there they were loaded onto boats and ferried the two hundred miles to the York Factory on the southwestern shore of Hudson Bay.

After dividing our profits three ways, we discovered we had done far better together than we ever could have alone. We had done so well, in fact, we were able to hire on a Cree Indian, who went by the name of Jack, to cook for us and keep an eye on the home shanty while we were off tending our traplines.

As far as I could tell, Jack was older than any of us, and claimed to be the son of an *ogimaa*, which is a cross between a chief and a shaman, to hear him tell it. I don't know about any of that, but I do know he could play a mean fiddle, which he often did to pass the time on those long winter nights.

I am not going to lie and say that we went without arguments or differences of opinion. But for the most part, despite being brought together by happenstance and necessity, the four of us found one another's company agreeable. This I attribute to the fact three of us shared similar backgrounds and had each, as a boy, worshipped the hardy voyageurs and colorful Mountain Men who loomed so large in our newborn nation's identity, while Jack knew little English, although he did speak French passing well.

Summer is short in this part of the world, full of mosquitoes and dragonflies, and Fall is shorter still. The first snows came early, turning the towering pines and hemlocks white by the third week of October. The next day Jack frowned at the sky and muttered something about not liking something on the wind, but I did not pay him much heed. Although we cursed the cold and having to trudge about on snow shoes, we knew this meant the beaver, fox, and rabbit would be changing into their prized winter coats all the sooner.

Our humble home shanty was the hub for traplines that extended for twenty miles each in various directions, like spokes on a wheel. Some followed the borders of the lake and the streams that fed into it, and caught mostly beaver, otter, muskrat, and mink. Others extended inland, and brought us raccoons, foxes, lynx, coyote, and the occasional bear. Along these routes were a series of tilts—squat ten-by-six structures with sharply angled roofs, fashioned from notched spruce logs trimmed by hand to fit tightly together without a single iron nail—that served both as supply depots and shelter. During the trapping season, I and my companions would set out along one of these "spokes," checking and resetting our traps along the way, until we reached the end of our territory, then we would head back via an adjacent line.

The snow was already six inches deep, even more where the wind had driven it into drifts, when we set out to check the lines. Martin headed west, while Buchan and I headed northeast, leaving Jack to tend the fires at the home shanty. Each of us was outfitted with an Indian sledge, which we towed behind us, and enough provisions to withstand a fortnight in the bush. The sled dogs were to remain with Jack, to be held in reserve for swift traveling and transporting heavy loads to and from the trading post.

As I said, Buchan and I set out together. The plan was for me to follow him to the first tilt on the line, then he and I would go our separate ways. I would head north in the direction of Red Cross Lake, while he would head east, toward Edmund Lake.

We set out just after dawn and arrived at our destination just after noon. We spent the remaining hours of daylight left to us weatherproofing our shelter by gathering moss and alder twigs, which we used to line the walls and roof, while throwing out the rotted remains of the previous season's insulation.

As the sun set, we crawled through the two-foot square opening at the tilt's gable end, tacking off the entrance with a piece of elk hide. In the far corner of the shelter was a portable stove fashioned from a long, rectangular hard-tack tin affixed to a short pipe that vented through the roof. We lost no time in putting the makeshift fireplace to good use, and soon the interior was quite warm. It was a snug fit for two grown men, but comfortable enough. As I bedded down for the night, I could hear the wind whistling mournfully about the eaves of the shelter. Every now and again the gusts would rattle the hide that served as our door, as if something outside was desperately trying to find its way in. However, I was too tired to entertain such fancies for long, and soon fell asleep.

At some point later that night I was shaken from a sound slumber to find Buchan's urgent voice in my ear. I opened my eyes to darkness so black I could not see my companion's face, though I knew from the heat of his breath that it had to be inches from my own. Although I had no way of knowing what time it was, I instinctively knew it was midnight.

"What's the matter?" I mumbled.

"Do you hear that?" Buchan whispered.

I focused my senses, still blurred by sleep, but all I heard was the howling of the wind.

"There's nothing out there," I replied tersely. "Go back to sleep."

"Are you sure?" Buchan asked, his unseen fingers digging into my shoulder.

I listened again, and this time I became aware of a weird noise off in the distance: half-roar, half-wail. "It's probably something in one of the traps," I said. "A wolf, perhaps, or maybe a lynx. They can make a hellacious racket when they're caught."

"You're probably right," he said, apparently mollified by my explanation. With that, Buchan rolled over and went back to sleep.

I lay there for a long moment, listening to the cry laced within the wind, trying to identify it, but the noise soon fell silent. I told myself that whatever was responsible for making it had died or moved on, and returned to my slumber. However, the dreams that filled the remainder of my night were fitful, providing little in the way of rest.

The next day I rose with the sun, only to find my companion already up and about. As I relieved myself against a nearby tree, I spotted Buchan kneeling in the snow roughly fifty yards from the tilt, checking one of his traps. Without warning he suddenly cut loose with a string of particularly virulent curses.

"What's the matter?" I called out.

"You were right about that noise last night," he shouted back. "There's something in the trap!"

"What did you catch?" I asked.

"You tell me," Buchan replied, an odd look on his face.

The creature in the trap was unlike anything I have ever seen, alive or dead. There seemed to be something of every animal in it, yet not enough of one to identify the whole. It had the teeth of a rodent, the claws of a lynx, a tail like an opossum's, the build of a fox, a snout like a bear's, and the wide, flat skull of a badger, with deep-set eyes that glowed bright red. Stranger than the creature being slat thin was it being completely devoid of fur. Its naked flesh was ashen and covered with suppurating sores, which stank like rotting meat. Judging from its smell and contorted position, it was clear to the naked eye that the animal was dead. Yet although its left foreleg was firmly clamped within the jaws of the cunningly concealed fox trap, I did not notice any signs of blood, either fresh or frozen, in the fresh layer of snow.

"Sweet mother of God—what is that thing?" I gasped.

"I'll be deviled if I know," Buchan replied, eyeing the wretched beast with open distaste. "Perhaps a freakish wolverine, or a raccoon eat-up with the mange. In any case, it's of no use to me or the Hudson Bay Company."

However, as Buchan moved to free the carcass from the trap, the supposedly dead animal miraculously came back to life and, with a vicious snarl, sank its yellowed fangs between the trapper's thumb and forefinger.

"Son of a whore!" Buchan bellowed. Without a moment's hesitation he pulled the skinning knife from his belt and plunged it into the foul beast's right eye, killing it once and for all.

"Are you alright, Dick?" I asked, staring at the bright red blood that now stained the white snow.

"I'm fine," he replied stoically, wrapping his wound with a length of cloth from his coat pocket. "It's not the first time I got bit by something I caught." He picked up the empty trap and slung it over his shoulder. "I'm going to move a hundred yards up the line, just in case there are any more like that bastard nosing about."

As I trudged after my friend, I glanced back at the strange creature, only to see its gaunt and hairless body sinking into the snow, as if the very land was conspiring to obliterate all traces of its existence.

After a breakfast of pemmican and black coffee, I shouldered my pack and, after bidding Buchan farewell and good hunting, headed east, dragging my sledge behind me. I quickly put the strange, hairless creature out of my mind. Obviously it was some kind of diseased freak of nature. What else could it have been? In any case, the beast's days had been numbered, even before it wandered into Buchan's trap. How much longer could it have continued to survive the winter?

I spent a fortnight in the wilderness along the line, checking, emptying, and resetting my traps, living off the land as well as my provisions, thanks to my trusty rifle. The work was hard and the weather unaccommodating, but nearly every night I enjoyed a meal of fricassee rabbit or roasted spruce grouse, and slept in comparative warmth and comfort. There are many who toil in the factories of Toronto and Winnipeg who cannot make such a claim.

As I arrived back at the home shanty, my sledge groaning under the weight of the early winter bounty, I saw was my other partner, Ben Martin, chopping wood in the dooryard. He had returned the day before with an impressive number of beaver and mink to his credit. That night we sat in front of the camp stove and exchanged tales of our foray into the bush while enjoying Jack's venison cutlets.

I related the tale of the strange, hairless beast Buchan caught, and we had a good laugh at our partner's expense. Rather, I should say Martin and I found it humorous, as the story seemed to unsettle Jack. As I turned in that night, I fully expected to see Buchan trudge into camp within the next day or so, cursing a blue streak, as was his habit, and bellowing for hot coffee and a plate of beans.

However, two days passed without Buchan's return. And then another. Come the evening of the fourth day, Martin and I decided to go looking for him. Buchan could have fallen victim to a bear or a mountain lion, perhaps even wolves. But he could have just as easily—and far more likely—run afoul of poachers, most of which would not think twice about killing an unwary trapper for his furs.

The next day we harnessed up the dogs and set out into the vast Manitoban wilderness, with Martin acting as musher and me riding in the sledge's basket, my rifle cocked and ready in case of trouble.

Thanks to the dogs, we reached the first tilt on the eastern spoke within an hour. Upon arrival, we were surprised to see what looked to be Buchan's sledge parked beside the shelter, buried underneath a heavy shroud of snow. Martin and I exchanged worried looks. Whatever fate had befallen our friend, it had happened shortly after his arrival, over two weeks ago.

I knelt down and lifted the hide that served as the makeshift door of the tilt, only to recoil from the smell that came from inside. I was instantly reminded of the diseased creature that had bitten Buchan, and I wondered—somewhat belatedly—if the beast might have suffered from leprosy or some other communicable illness. After my eyes adjusted from the bright glare of the snow to the dim interior of the shelter, I could make out a figure huddled on the floor, wrapped in filthy blankets.

"Buchan—is that you?" I asked warily, poking the lump with my rifle.

Whatever was inside the mass stirred feebly and issued a groan so anguished it set the hairs on the back of my neck on end. I put aside my gun and motioned for Martin to help me pull Buchan free of the tilt. As our friend emerged from the rank darkness, I was shocked to see his strapping frame reduced to little more than skin and bones. If not for his moaning and a feeble stirring of his limbs, I would have thought him dead.

"Merciful God, Buchan. What happened to you?" Martin exclaimed.

The best our partner could do by way of a response was to lift his right hand, which was swollen to three times its normal size and black with infection. It was from this putrid wound that the smell of rotting meat came. Buchan's eyes were sunken deep into his skull and seemed as capable of sight as billiard balls.

Martin and I wrapped him in the bear skin we had brought with us, but as we drew near the sled, the dogs began growling and barking, and a couple even lunged as if to attack. Martin had to take the whip to the wretched beasts, cursing them at the top of his lungs, in order to get them back in line.

I sat in the basket of the sled, holding Buchan tightly in my arms, while Martin drove the dogs. A mile or two out from our base camp, a snow storm started up. As it grew stronger I thought I heard something that sounded like wailing hidden within the wind. Buchan, who had lain as still as a dead man until this point, suddenly began to tremble and twitch, as if taken by a fit. I shouted to Martin to get us home as fast as possible.

By the time we reached the home shanty, the snowstorm had become a blizzard, blasting us with sleet that stung like millions of tiny icy knives. Jack hurried to greet us, only to halt upon catching sight of Buchan, whom we dragged between us as if escorting a drunken friend home from a bar. The look on the Cree's face was one of utter fear.

"Don't stand there gawking!" Martin snapped. "Get the dogs out of harness and feed them!"

Jack nodded his understanding and moved out of the way, giving us a wide berth. Martin and I entered the cabin, placing Buchan on his own bunk. As he lay there, I was struck by the peculiar sensation that what lay before me was not, in fact, the man I'd lived and worked alongside for the better part of a year, but an *approximation*. I instantly realized how absurd a fancy it was, yet I could not help but feel that someone—or *some thing*—had hollowed out Buchan and climbed inside, and was now looking out at me through stolen eyes.

Buchan's moaning became a groan and he began to writhe underneath his blankets, as if something was gnawing on him. His eyes opened and he licked his chapped and bleeding lips with a pinkish-gray tongue. It was clear from the look in his eyes that he wanted desperately to communicate something to us.

"What is it, Dick?" Martin asked, leaning close so as to hear.

Buchan's voice was as dry and brittle as kindling, but there was no mistaking what he said: *"Hungry...."*

"Rest easy, chum," Martin said reassuringly. "You're safe now. I'll have Jack fix you some soup."

This seemed to placate Buchan, and he lapsed back into unconsciousness. Martin took me aside and spoke in a low voice so he would not be overheard. He had been a barber-surgeon before coming to Manitoba, and as such served as the camp physician when necessary.

"He's got a raging fever," he said grimly. "He's got to lose that hand if he wants to survive, no question about it. But I'm going to need laudanum from the trading post if I'm to amputate."

"I'll go fetch it."

"Are you sure you want to risk it? That's a pretty bad storm out there, and it'll be getting dark soon...."

"Buchan would do the same for either of us," I replied. "Besides, the dogs know the way there and back by instinct, storm or no. You and Jack try to keep him alive while I'm gone."

"Speaking of which—where'd that red devil get off to?" Martin frowned. "It doesn't take *that* long to feed dogs."

I threw my parka back on and went outside, shouting for Jack to get the harness and gang lines back out. As I went behind the cabin to where the dogs were penned, I looked around for some sign of the camp cook, but he was nowhere to be found. Then I realized two things at the exact same time: the smaller of the two dogsleds was gone, and half the dogs were missing.

Martin was kneeling beside Buchan's cot, wrapping the ailing man's hand in bandages soaked in hot water in order to draw the infection out. He looked up at the sound of my cursing, which preceded my arrival by a good thirty seconds.

"That son of a bitch Jack has run off, and he's taken most of the dogs!"

"When this damned storm has blown over and Buchan is on the mend, I'm going to make it a point of tracking that heathen bastard down and skinning him like a beaver!" Martin growled.

"He was always an odd duck, if you ask me," I replied. "When he saw us carrying Buchan, you would have thought he'd seen the devil himself. Something scared him. I'll be damned if I know what."

I lost no time hitching up the three remaining dogs to what was now our only sled and striking out for the trading post, which was twenty-five miles from the camp. Normally it would take two-and-half hours to get there, but that was in good weather. With the storm as bad as it was, I had to trust in the dogs' instincts and sense of direction, as the trail that lead through the forest was all but obliterated by the wind.

After an hour or so, the storm suddenly dissipated and the dogs were able to pick up the pace. Just as the sun was about to set, I was rewarded by the sight of the fort-like walls of the God's Lake trading post. My team glided through the front gates just as they were preparing to close them for the night.

Inside the trading post were several buildings, including a kennel for visiting trappers to house their sled teams. I paid the old Indian who hobbled out to greet me a few shillings to feed and water my dogs. Taking the bundle of furs I'd brought with me from the sled, I then headed into the store to do my trading.

The interior of the Hudson Bay Company store was not that different from the average mercantile in Winnipeg. Inside the large log building a counter ran along the right side of the room, with a glass case on the end, displaying such items as horn-handled buck knives and six-shooters. The shelves along the wall behind the counter were stocked with bolts of cloth and other merchandise. Several items of clothing, such as flannel shirts and heavy jackets, hung from the ceiling. Opposite the counter, standing in the very middle of the room, was a large metal stove, about which were gathered several wooden chairs.

The clerk behind the counter was a dark-haired Welshman, whom I had had dealings with before and was friendly with. He lifted an eyebrow as I dropped my bundle of furs before him.

"You're here late," he commented as he sorted through what I'd brought him. "Will you be putting up for the night, then?"

"Not tonight," I replied with a shake of my head. "I've got to get back to camp. Buchan's down sick. Martin sent me in to trade for laudanum and rubbing alcohol. I also need a couple of dogs to replace some stolen from me."

"Buchan, eh? That's odd. The gentleman over there was just asking about him earlier."

"What gentleman?"

"The one warming himself by the stove."

I turned to look in the direction the clerk pointed, and spotted a figure sitting hunched in one of the chairs drawn close to the stove, puffing on a pipe. He was dressed all in black and sitting so still I had not noticed him when I first entered the room. At least, that is the only reason for why I could have overlooked such a distinctive individual.

Judging from the gray in his hair and mustache-less beard, the man was in his fifties, with a physique seasoned by sun and hard work. Indeed, his skin was tanned so deep a brown he looked to have been cast of bronze. As I dropped my gaze, I saw that his right leg was missing just below the knee, beneath which he wore an artificial one made of ivory.

Although unusual as his prosthesis might have been, it was nothing compared to his manner of dress, which was not only woefully inappropriate for the harsh climate of Manitoba, but also strangely anachronistic, seeming to be at least twenty-five years or more out of date. It consisted of a black wool mariner's jacket, a dark-colored cravat, and an odd-looking wide-brimmed black felt hat with a buckled ribbon band.

"Where did *he* come from?" I exclaimed. The sight of a sailor at the trading post was not that unusual, for the merchant marines aboard the ships that ferried the Hudson Bay Company's stockpile of furs to England often came ashore, but that was during the spring, after the thaw had melted the ice.

"I'll be damned if I know," the clerk replied with a shrug. "The old Indian who sees to the gate said he simply walked up out of the snow, just as you see him here. Mighty queer business all around, if you ask me, what with all those *thees* and *thous* of his."

As the clerk went about tallying up the furs I brought in for trade, I decided to see what this strange, solitary figure wanted with Buchan.

"Excuse me, mister—?"

As the sailor turned toward me, I realized my attention had been so focused on his peg-leg and clothes I had somehow failed to notice the slender, livid white scar that started in the hairline above his brow and ran down his face, disappearing behind the cravat knotted about his neck. Whether it was a birthmark or evidence of some horrific wounding, I could not tell.

The one-legged man glanced at my outstretched hand, but did not move to take it. Instead, he removed the pipe from his mouth and slightly bowed his head in acknowledgment. "I was once called captain," he intoned in a rich, deep voice. "But thou may call me Ahab."

"I'm told you've been looking for Dick Buchan."

"Aye, that I am, lad," Ahab said, nodding his head once again. "Dost thou know where I might find him?"

"He's one of my partners," I explained. "Are you a friend of his?"

Ahab shook his head as he returned the pipe to his mouth. "I have never met the gentleman. All the same, I have business of the utmost importance with him."

"Might I inquire as to the nature of that business?" I asked.

"My own," Ahab replied curtly. The dark look the older man gave me was enough to stop me from pressing the matter.

"I'm sorry if my question offended you, sir. Do you mind if I sit and warm myself?" I asked, pointing to the pot-bellied stove as I drew up a chair.

The man called Ahab nodded and silently gestured with his pipe for me to join him. As I sat beside him, I fought the desire to stare at the strange mark about the older man's neck, and instead focused my attention on the same thing as he: the glowing embers and flickering flames on view through the vents in the stove's hinged door.

After a couple of minutes I grew equal parts bored and bold and decided to resume my questioning. "I take it from your clothes that you are a sailor?"

Ahab nodded and said with a small, humorless laugh, "Though now I am dry-docked, I once spent forty of my fifty-three years at sea."

"Did your ship come into the Bay before it froze?"

The darkness that had previously filled Ahab's eyes now threatened to reappear. He shook his head and returned his gaze to the stove. "No—I came a different way."

"Do not take my question wrongly, sir; but your manner of speech is most unusual—where do you hail from?"

"I am a Nantucket Quaker, good sir," Ahab replied, not without a touch of pride. "A Yankee, if thee will."

"You are very far from home, then."

"Farther than thee can imagine," the old sailor said, his voice melancholy. He took the pipe from his mouth and gave it a sharp rap against his peg-leg, knocking the ashes onto the floor. "Enjoying a good smoke is one of the few solaces those such as me and thee—men who make our living on the knife-edge of the world—can count on," he said, waxing philosophical. "Yet once, in a fit of pique, I threw my pipe in the ocean because it could not soothe me. But now all is forgiven between us, and it provides me comfort once again."

I was about to ask Ahab how he could possibly be smoking the same pipe he had hurled into the sea, when the clerk called out that he'd finished his accounting. I excused myself from the old salt's company and returned to the counter.

"I can trade you the laudanum and rubbing alcohol, but not the dogs," the clerk said, pointing to the bottle of Dr. Rabbitfoot's Tincture of Opium.

"Can't you extend us credit? You know we're good for it. The dogs I got now aren't enough to last the winter. If one or two go lame or die on me, I'll be on foot until spring."

"I wish I could help you out, but the Company don't allow credit," the clerk said with a shrug of his shoulders. "Cash on the barrelhead or trade only—them's the rules."

A sun-darkened hand suddenly slapped down onto the clerk's open ledger, placing a gold coin atop the page.

"I'll buy thee the dogs thou needest, my friend," Ahab said. "Granted I ride with thee to thy camp."

The clerk picked up the gold piece and turned it over in his hands, giving out a low whistle of admiration. The coin was a doubloon, the border of which was stamped *Republica del Ecuador: Quito.* On the face were three mountains: on top the first was a flame, the second a tower, while atop the third was a crowing rooster. Above the three mountains was a portion of the zodiac, with the sun entering the equinox under the sign of Libra. The coin seemed to glow in the dim light of the trading post, as if it possessed a life of its own.

"What say thee, clerk?" Ahab said. "Is that coin enough to buy his dogs?"

"But there's a hole in the middle of it ..." the clerk pointed out weakly.

"It is *gold*, is it not?" Ahab said sternly, in a voice that could be heard through a hurricane. "Now give the man his dogs!"

The clerk cringed as if he'd been struck with a cat o' nine tails. "Yes, sir," he replied obsequiously. "As you wish, sir."

As the clerk wrapped the supplies I'd come for in a bundle of rags to protect them from breaking, I turned back to face the man called Ahab.

"I appreciate your generosity, sir. And you are welcome to ride with me back to our camp. But I warn you, Buchan is extremely ill. In fact, I came to the post to trade for medicine in hopes it will save his life. There is a very good chance that he will be dead by the time we get back."

"All the more important that we leave as soon as possible," Ahab said grimly.

As I headed for the door, the sea captain fell in step behind me. There was a line of pegs on the wall just inside the door, upon which were hung several different outer garments, including my own. As I pulled on my gear, I was surprised to see Ahab reach, not for a coat, but for a harpoon that stood propped up against the doorjamb.

It stood taller than the man himself, with a shaft fashioned from a hickory pole still bearing strips of bark. The socket of the harpoon was braided with the spread yarns of a towline, which lay coiled on the floor like a Hindoo fakir's rope. The lower end of the rope was drawn halfway along the pole's length, and tightly secured with woven twine, so that pole, iron, and rope remained inseparable. The harpoon's barb shone like a butcher's knife-edge in the dim light. It was indeed a fearsome weapon, made all the more intimidating by its incongruity.

"Where is your coat, sir?" I exclaimed, when I realized that my new companion planned to step outside dressed exactly as he was. "It's below freezing outside!"

"Do not concern thyself for my comfort," Ahab said calmly. "I have been in far more inhospitable climes of late."

"Why do you carry a harpoon on dry land?" I asked, shaking my head in disbelief.

"Where a shepherd has his crook, and the cowboy his lariat, this is the instrument of my profession," the old mariner said matter-of-factly. "Wherever I go, it follows with me."

As we approached the kennel to fetch my team, the dogs set up an awful racket. However, it was not the snarling expected from sled dogs jockeying amongst themselves for dominance within the pack, but growling born of genuine fear. The lead dog, his nape bristling and ears flat against his skull, snapped at me as I moved to harness him. If I had not jerked my hand back when I did, I most certainly would have lost some fingers.

Before I could unfurl my dog-whip, Ahab stepped forward and planted the butt of the harpoon in the frozen mud of the kennel yard, glowering at the wildly barking huskies with those strange eyes of his. One by one, the dogs fell silent and lowered their heads, skulking away, tails tucked between their legs, without the old sea captain having to utter a single word.

"How did you do that?" I asked, amazed by what I had just seen.

"I have stared down my share of mutineers in my day," Ahab replied. "There is not much difference between a dog and a deckhand; if they smell the slightest whiff of fear, they will tear thee limb from limb."

I added the three new dogs Ahab had staked me to my existing team and harnessed them to my sled. I served as musher, while Ahab sat in the basket. With an old horse blanket draped about his shoulders for warmth, and his harpoon held across his lap, the dour sea captain looked like some grim Norse king preparing for his final battle.

As we exited through the trading post's gates, I looked up at the night sky to find it filled with the shifting radiance of the Aurora Borealis. It was by this light that we made our way back to camp.

Once we were off, Ahab did not utter a single word, but instead stared into the darkness, lost in whatever thoughts he kept locked inside his head. As a man who turned his back on the predictability of city life in favor of a wilderness as isolated and unknown as the uncharted ocean, I felt a certain kinship toward the taciturn Quaker who had forsaken the certainty of solid ground for a pitching deck and the vast horizon of the open sea, despite his strange demeanor.

The weather for the return trip was cold but otherwise clear until a mile or so out from our destination. Suddenly the wind picked up and quickly grew to gale-force, accompanied by increasing snowfall. Once more, I heard the eerie wailing within the storm, which grew stronger the closer we got. I could not escape the sensation that somehow the blizzard sensed our approach, and was not at all pleased by the intrusion.

The snow was so heavy I could barely discern the outline of the cabin. Despite my heavy boots and fur-lined gloves, my hands and feet felt like blocks of ice. I was looking forward to warming myself by the fireplace, the humble chimney of which jutted from the roof of the shanty like the bowl of a giant's pipe. Given my own chilliness, I could only imagine the discomfort Ahab was experiencing. He'd said that he'd lost one leg to a whale, which I had no reason to doubt, and now I feared he might lose the other to frostbite, as well as some fingers. My concern proved to be ill placed, however, for he climbed out of the basket as easily as if he was stepping out of a carriage. Using his harpoon as a walking stick, Ahab made his way toward the darkened cabin without so much as a backward glance.

"Come back here!" I shouted over the howling wind. "I need help putting up the dogs!"

If the sailor heard me, he made no show of it, but continued his beeline to the front door. I grabbed the lantern from the sled and hurried after him, cursing loudly the whole way. I knew Martin well enough to easily envision what his first reaction would be to the sight of an unannounced stranger armed with what looked like a spear entering his abode in the middle of the night. I caught up with the Quaker before he could put his shoulder to the door.

"Are you daft?" I growled. "If you go barging into a trapper's cabin like that, you're apt to get shot for an Indian or a poacher! And I am in no hurry to clean your brains off my walls!"

"Forgive me, friend," Ahab said, stepping aside so I might go ahead of him. "The prospect of concluding my business has made me ... incautious."

Holding up the lantern so that its light would illuminate my face as well as the darkness, I pushed open the door of the shanty. The interior of the cabin was as dark as a well digger's snuffbox.

"Martin! Hold your fire and sheath your knife! It's me!" I called out. "And I have brought a visitor."

I expected to hear my partner's voice in return, telling me to close the damned door before I let in a polar bear, but there was no reply. I crossed the threshold into the darkness, Ahab's ivory peg-leg tapping against the rough-hewn planks of the cabin floor close behind.

I hadn't taken more than a couple of steps before I collided with a piece of furniture. I lowered the lantern so I could see where I was going and was shocked to find the interior of the cabin in utter chaos. The table on which my companions and I ate our meals had been reduced to kindling, along with its accompanying chairs, as if demolished in a brawl. My heart sank at the sight of several sacks of flour and sugar—provisions for the entire winter—dumped amidst scattered traps, furs, cookware, and clothes. The fire in the stone hearth had gone out, its ashes kicked out into the middle of the room, and the cabin was nearly as cold as the wilderness beyond its walls.

"Martin! Buchan! Where are you?" I cried, swinging the lantern about in hopes of it illuminating some sign of my friends. My mind rushed about in circles, as if caught in one of my traps. Had poachers broken into the cabin, looking for furs to steal? Or was this the result of an Indian attack? Perhaps Jack had returned, and he and Martin got into a fight?

I fell silent, hoping I might detect a response. Instead, all I heard was a low, grunting noise, like that of a rooting hog, coming from the back of the cabin, where the shadows were the darkest. Lifting high the lantern, I moved to investigate the sound.

I found Buchan—or rather, what had become of him—crouching in the corner. His back was turned toward me and I could see not only that he was completely naked, but every vertebrae along his spine as well.

"Buchan—what happened? Where's Martin?"

In response, Buchan spun around to face me, growling like a cornered dog. Save that he was covered in skin, which was by now ash-gray and fairly bursting with weeping sores, he was little more than a skeleton. He was so gaunt the ribs in his chest stood out like the staves of barrel, and his diseased flesh was pulled so tautly across his pelvis it looked as if it was wrapped in leather. But the worst of it was that Buchan's face was smeared with gore and saliva, and in his bony, claw-like hands he clutched the half-devoured remains of a raw liver. I was so shocked by his wretched condition, I did not at first realize that Martin lay sprawled at Buchan's feet, split open from anus to throat, his guts scooped out and piled beside him like those of a field-dressed deer.

Suddenly, strong, iron-hard fingers dug into my shoulder. It was Ahab. I had been so horrified I had forgotten he was there.

"Stand aside, friend," the sea captain said grimly. "For this is the business I must attend to." Ahab hoisted the harpoon, his voice booming in the close confines of the cabin like ocean waves breaking against the shore. "*Wendigo! Cannibal Spirit of the North! I am Ahab, hunter of fiends! And in the Devil's name, I have come to claim you!*"

I do not know if the light from the lantern held in my trembling hand played tricks on me, or if what I saw was what indeed happened; but as Ahab hurled the harpoon, the thing I knew as Dick Buchan seemed to grow, like a shadow cast upon a wall, becoming taller and even thinner than before. He then turned sideways, seeming to disappear, causing the razor-sharp harpoon to sail past harmlessly and imbed itself into the wall of the cabin.

Buchan reappeared just as suddenly as he had disappeared, but now he was standing in front of the hearth of the fireplace. With a terrible shriek, more like that of a wounded elk than a man, he raised his arms above his head, causing his body to elongate yet again, and shot straight up the fireplace chimney. I was so dumbfounded I at first did not believe my own eyes—until I heard the sound of footsteps on the roof overhead, followed by a wild, maniacal laughter.

Ahab snatched the harpoon free and hurried for the door, moving as fast as his missing leg allowed. He charged out into the snowstorm, bellowing curses in seven different languages with the heedless bravery peculiar to those who have hunted down and slain creatures a thousand times their size. The dogs—still in harness and attached to their gang line—frantically barked at whatever it was that was stamping back and forth across the roof over their heads.

As I crossed the threshold to join my companion, I felt something snag the hood of my parka. I looked up and, to my horror, saw a long, bony arm reaching down from the eaves above. I tried to tear myself free of whatever had hold of me, but was unable to break its grip. The thing on the roof gave a single tug, as if testing the strength of its hold, and I found that my boots no longer touched the ground.

As I was dragged upwards to whatever awaited me on the roof, my mind flashed back to Martin's fate, and I began to kick and scream as hard as I could. Suddenly Ahab was there beside me, jabbing at the thing on the roof with his harpoon.

"Leave him be, wendigo!" he shouted angrily. "Thou hast feasted enough for one night!"

The creature cried out in pain and released its hold, sending me tumbling into a snowdrift. As I got to my feet I saw it squatting on the roof like a living gargoyle. It no longer bore any resemblance to Buchan, save that it was roughly the shape of a man. Its arms and legs were as long as barge poles, and the horns of an elk grew from its skull. Its eyes were pushed so far back in their orbits they at first seemed to be missing—until I caught a flicker of reddish light in each socket, like those of a wild animal skulking beyond a campfire. Its lips were tattered and peeled back from its gums, revealing long, curving tusks the color of ivory. Even from where I stood, I could smell its stink—that of death and decay, just like the horrid freak that had bitten poor Buchan.

"Laugh all thee like, monster!" Ahab shouted at the ghastly apparition. "Thou shalt not escape! I did not drown thirty good men to be bested by the likes of thee!"

As if in reply, the creature shrieked like a wild cat, its voice melding with the whistling north wind. It got to its feet and jumped from the roof of the cabin to a nearby pine tree, clearing a distance of thirty feet as easily as a child playing hop-scotch. As I watched in amazement, the creature darted to the very top of the towering pine, which swayed wildly back and forth in the wind, climbing with the agility of an ape.

Ahab drew back his arm and hurled his harpoon at the abomination a second time. It shot forth as if fired from a cannon, the towline flapping behind it like a pennant, only to fall short of its target. Apparently unfazed, the beast leapt into the uppermost crown of the tree beside it, and then the one after that. Within seconds it had disappeared from sight, its scream of triumph fading into the distance.

"Come inside," I said. "The thing is gone. It's over."

Ahab shook his head in disgust as he trudged back into the cabin, his harpoon slung over one shoulder like a Viking's spear. "It will not wander far—not while there is still meat on our bones."

I did not argue with the man, but instead busied myself with releasing the dogs from their gang line. As I returned them to the kennel, I decided it would be wise to keep them in their harnesses, as I foresaw a need to leave camp in a hurry.

Upon returning inside the cabin, I found a fire set in the hearth and saw that Ahab had draped a length of canvas over Martin's savaged corpse. The old sailor sat on a stool that was still in one piece in front of the fireplace, sharpening his harpoon with a piece of whetstone.

"You owe me an explanation, old man," I said sternly. "Whatever your business with Buchan, it now concerns me."

"Fair enough," Ahab replied. "Ask me what thou wilt, and I will answer thee true. But I warn thee, friend—thou might find this truth unbecoming to reason."

"You seem to know what that thing is—you called it *wendigo*. What is it?"

"It is a spirit, of sorts. The Indians of the North—the Cree, the Inuit, the Ojibwa—know it well," he explained, pausing to light his pipe. "It comes with the winter storms and is driven by a horrible hunger for human flesh. Some say it overtakes those who stay too long alone in the wilderness, while others claim it possesses only those driven to cannibalism. Of the last I have my doubts, for I have known many a cannibal in my travels, some of whom were men of good character, if not Christian disposition."

I stared at Ahab for a long moment, trying to determine if he truly believed what he had just told me. Under normal circumstances I would have laughed and called him a lunatic. But things were far from normal, as evidenced by poor Martin, lying there under his makeshift shroud.

"How is it you knew poor Buchan was afflicted by the wendigo?"

"My friend, are thee sure of thine desire for knowledge?" Seeing the steadfastness in my gaze, the old sailor gave a heavy sigh. "Very well, I shall answer thee, as promised. It is my business to know the unknowable, for I have been set a task unlike any since the labors of Hercules. Where once I hunted the great beasts of the ocean, now I stalk the fiends of Hell."

I could no longer hide my incredulity, and responded to this declaration with a rude laugh. "Have you lost your mind?"

"I was once mad, but no more," Ahab said sadly. "Would that I had the balm of insanity to allay my suffering; for I am just as sane as thee, my friend, if infinitely more damned."

"What are you babbling about?" I snapped, my patience finally worn thin.

"Once, decades ago, I bragged of being immortal on land and on sea. Now I find I must bear the burden of that boast for all eternity."

As I listened to the old sailor's rant, the hairs on my neck stood erect. The dark fire deep in Ahab's eyes frightened me in a way the wendigo's did not. It was one thing to be stalked by a fiendish creature, quite another to be trapped with a lunatic.

"Ah, I see the look in thine eyes," Ahab said with a grim smile. "Thou hadst seen what thou hath seen, and yet thee still deem me mad? What of *this*, then?" He pulled aside the cravat about his throat, revealing the marks of a noose no man could have survived. "Aye, I am dead. I have been such since long before your birth. I was once a righteous, God-fearing man, but I was made wicked by my pride and blasphemous by my wrath. I was determined to avenge myself on the whale that took my leg, and offered up my immortal soul in exchange for its annihilation.

"It did not matter to me that I had a child-bride and an infant son awaiting me in Nantucket. Nor did it matter that thirty men, brave and true, had placed their lives and livelihoods in my care. There was a fire in my bosom that burned day and night, and naught would extinguish it, save the blood of the whale that maimed me. Now my child-bride is a withered crone, my infant son dead on the end of a Confederate's bayonet, and my brave crew, save for one, sleeps at the bottom of the sea.

"I chased the accursed beast halfway across the world, and sank my harpoon into its damned hide, only to run afoul of the line. A flying turn of rope wrapped itself about my neck, yanking me below the waves, drowning me within seconds. Yet, to my horror, though I knew myself dead, I was still aware of all that transpired about me. I was helpless witness to the destruction of my ship and the deaths of my men by the whale I had pursued across three seas and two oceans.

"And when it was over, the hated whale pulled me down, down, down—past sunken galleons, past the lairs of slumbering leviathans, past the drowned towers of long-lost kingdoms—down to the very floor of the ocean. With dead man's eyes I beheld a great chasm, from which boiled dreadful beasts with the bodies of men and heads like that of jellyfish. These abominations freed me of my tether and escorted me down into the rift, which lead into the very belly of the world, Hell itself. There I swam not through a mere lake of fire, but an entire ocean, until I came at last to a great throne.

"The throne was fashioned of horn and upon it sat the King of the Fallen, the Devil himself. The Lord of the Damned resembled nothing so much as a gigantic shadow in the shape of a man, with wings of flame and eyes that shone like burnished shields. The Devil spoke unto me, and though he had no mouth, his voice rang like a gong, shaking me to my marrow.

"'Ahab', he said, 'Thou promised me thine soul in exchange for the life of the whale. Yet here you stand before me, and the fish still swims! Let it not be said that I do not honor my covenants. I have within my kingdom a park unlike any seen on Earth, with trees of bone and rivers of blood. I would populate it with monsters for the pleasure of my sport. Bring me as many fiends as men you led to death, and I shall return thy soul, to do with as thou wish.'"

Although I did not want to believe the outrageous tale the old sailor had just told me, my curiosity got the better of me. "How many men died under your command?"

"Nine and twenty," he replied solemnly.

"And how many monsters have you hunted?"

"This will be the second," he admitted. "There. I have told thee what thou asked, nothing more, nothing less. I have come to this place on the Devil's business, and I cannot leave until it is finished. It is as simple as that."

"I have had enough of this lunacy!" I exclaimed, hoping the anger in my voice would hide the fear in my heart. "You are welcome to the cabin, but I am taking the dogs and returning to the trading post!"

"The wendigo will be upon thee within minutes of setting forth," Ahab cautioned.

"I have my rifle and my axe," I countered. "I won't be as easy to kill as Martin."

"Mortal weapons are of no use against that thing."

"It seemed to let go of me quickly enough when you jabbed it with that over-glorified pig-sticker of yours," I pointed out.

"This is no mere harpoon," Ahab said, nodding to the spear lying across his lap. "It was forged from the hardest iron there is: the nail-stubs of steel horse-shoes—the ones that racehorses wear. I myself hammered together the twelve rods for its shank, winding them together like the yarns of a rope. The barbs were cast from my own shaving razors—the finest, sharpest steel to ever touch human skin. But, most important of all, it was tempered not in water, but the blood of three pagan hunters, who, at my bidding, opened their veins so that the instrument of my revenge might partake of their strength. Thus I baptized it not in the name of the Father, but the Devil himself. *That* is why the wendigo feared it."

"All that may very well be true, but I am not a man prone to fancy. If I can see a thing, and hear a thing, and most certainly *smell* a thing, then to my mind it is of this world, not the next. And that means I can *kill* it. And if it gets in my way, I will do just that, Devil's menagerie or no!"

"I have no claim on thee," Ahab said quietly as he returned to his whetstone. "Escape if thee can."

I had no idea if Ahab was mad, damned, or a liar, and I had no desire to find which was the truth. Lantern in hand, I left the cabin and hurried to the pen where the dogs were kept. However, before I was halfway there I heard an unholy cacophony of yelps and barks. I quickened my pace, trying not to lose my footing in the knee-high snow and ice, and arrived at the dog-pen just in time to see the wendigo attack the last of the team.

The wendigo, now easily twice the size of man, held the hapless animal by the tail and lowered it, head-first, into its gaping mouth, the jaws of which were dislocated like those of a serpent. The fiend's belly was hideously dis-tended, far beyond human limits, and I could clearly see the outlines of the other dogs squirming underneath its ash-gray skin as they were digested alive. The wendigo's jaws snapped shut like a trap, severing the tail of the last dog, which fell to the snow in a gout of crimson.

I had been so horrified by the scene before me, I was rooted to the spot. But the sight of the dog's blood snapped me out of my petrified state, and I turned and fled back to the safety of the cabin. I did not dare turn and look behind me, for fear of what I might see in pursuit.

As I burst into the cabin, I found Ahab where I had left him, patiently applying the whetstone to his harpoon. "The dogs are dead!" I shouted. "It ate all of them!"

Ahab nodded as if this was something to be expected. "The wendigo is hunger incarnate. No matter how much it eats, its belly is never full; it exists in a perpetual state of starvation. The more it eats, the larger it grows; the larger it grows, the hungrier it gets. There is no end to it."

My mind was still reeling from the fresh horror I had just witnessed, and was only just realizing I was trapped. While I might have been able to flee the wendigo using the sled, there was no way I could possibly escape the camp on foot. It was then I surrendered my disbelief and embraced Ahab's reality as my own.

"How can we fight against this monster?"

If Ahab had an answer I did not hear it, for, at that exact moment, the window in front of which I stood abruptly shattered inward. I turned to see an emaciated arm as long as I am tall reach through the broken sash. I screamed in terror as the wendigo's fingers, the tips black from frostbite, closed about my leg, dragging me inexorably toward whatever stood on the other side.

Ahab was on his feet as quick as lightning, his harpoon at the ready. Without hesitation he dashed forward and plunged the spear into the wendigo's arm. The monster screamed in agony and anger as it let go of me, the absurdly long extremity withdrawing like a snake fleeing a fire.

"I have cost it an arm, if I'm lucky!" the old sailor said excitedly, pointing to a foul-smelling, tar-like substance splashed across the floor. "That bastard won't escape me by climbing the rigging *this* time!"

Harpoon in hand, Ahab rushed out of the cabin and into the snowy night. I followed close behind, for fear the creature might return while he was gone. I saw Ahab standing in the door-yard beside the sled that was to have been my escape, surveying his surroundings with eyes accustomed to scanning the open ocean for the fleeting flash of a fluke or the spume of a distant whale.

"Thar she blows!" Ahab sang out, pointing to a shambling shape moving off in the distance. I could barely make out the gray silhouette framed against the darkness, but it was obvious that the wendigo's right arm hung uselessly at its side.

Ahab hurled his harpoon after the fleeing figure. Because it had its back to us, the creature was unable to play its trick of turning sideways and disappearing, and this time the harpoon found its target, striking the creature between the shoulder blades.

The wendigo roared in angry pain and instantly took flight, running faster than any creature on two legs ever could. Ahab quickly grabbed the towline attached to the end of the harpoon and secured it to the brush bow of the sled.

"Fare thee well, friend," Ahab said as he took his place behind the handlebars. "Lord willing, we shall never meet again, in this world or the next!" And with that the sled sped away, shooting across the snow-covered landscape like a longboat dragged by a stricken whale.

As the Devil's huntsman and his monstrous quarry disappeared from sight, I could hear Ahab's shouted curses carried on the wind, mixed with the unholy wail of the wendigo, until they became one and the same.

So exhausted was I by the terrors I had undergone, I returned to the cabin, where I immediately collapsed into a deep sleep. When I awoke the next day, it was to find the blizzard abated and a gun in my face.

I discovered that a posse had been sent out from the trading post in search of me on account of my stealing three dogs. I insisted that I was innocent of the charges—that the dogs had been paid for, cash on the barrelhead. But even if they had been willing to believe me in regard to the dogs, there was still the matter of the mutilated corpse that lay twenty feet from where I slept.

I was promptly arrested for the murder of Ben Martin—as well as Dick Buchan, even though his body was never found—and taken back to the trading post and locked up in the stockade. And here I sit, awaiting the thaw, when I will be taken down to Winnipeg and put on trial.

I tried to explain about Ahab, and how he had bought the dogs for me, but the clerk who had waited on me and took the doubloon in payment claims no such person was ever in his store, nor is there any coin in the trading post's coffers matching the description I gave.

My only hope is that Jack will reappear and vouch for what he saw in Buchan's gaunt, sunken eyes. For now, too late, I realize the reason for the Indian abandoning the camp. If he does not come forward, then I will either be hung as a murderer or imprisoned as a madman.

Sometimes, late at night, when the frigid wind blows out of the north and whistles cruelly through the bars of my cell, I still hear Ahab's voice as he is dragged across the vast, uncharted wilderness by his captured fiend: *"Run! Run! Run to thy infernal master! To the last I grapple with thee; from Hell's heart, I stab at thee!"*

Frankenbilly

By

John Shirley

O kay ... recording. I'm going to splice this with Henry's story, and make a whole presentation. I'm not sure if I can go ahead with my plans on it, though. I got a kind of warning today.

This recording is made on August 7, 1981. It's been, what now, about fifteen years since Henry came riding onto Corriganville, out in east Ventura County. What I'm going to remember for you now happened in 1966.

Now let me set the scene. It's the summer of '66, the day the rider comes, and we're shooting *Billy the Kid Versus Dracula* on the Corrigan Ranch. Me, I'm the soundman, hoping this is the last shot of the day. It's a damned hot day, even in late afternoon with the wind blowing in from the Mojave. My head throbs and my sweaty shirt rasps on my back as I adjust the boom mic over John Carradine and Harry Carey, Jr. Wishing I wasn't there at all. Getting paid barely enough money to make it worth showing up. But it's the only job I can get. Hell, the only job any of us could get.

Harry's playing a wagonmaster, Carradine is a vampire, and both are in cos-
tume, standing by a covered wagon, trying to catch some of its shade. "John,"
Harry says, "Why the hell are we in this crap picture?" Not much trying to keep
his voice down.

Carradine just laughs affably, says in that voice that seems too deep for his
skinny little body, "Because if we didn't we'd have to pursue honest labor, Harry."

Harry starts to answer back but then he shades his eyes with his hand and
squints up at the hills over the movie ranch. "Looks like a rider up there, on top
of that hill. Damn hot day to be riding out in the sticks."

Sounds like a line from a movie—a better one. I turn to look and yeah, there's
a guy on a black-and-white pony up there raising some dust, moving his horse
slow, watching us. I'm thinking it's one of the wranglers, probably, then get a funny
feeling seeing him up there. The stranger's a long ways off. I can't make out his
face, but I can feel him looking right at me.

Then the director shouts at me to get the goddamn duct tape slapped on the
boom mic and get out of the way for the take.

Two and a half hours later the ordeal's over for now. No night shoot today.
So I'm sitting at a card table set up by my little silver Airstream trailer, a hundred yards up-slope from the set, on the little dirt road that passes behind the
"town." It's dusk, half an hour after we stopped shooting, trying to get the
damned Revox reel-to-reel to stop jittering. Of course, we mainly did sound-
to-film recording, but I'd been collecting some wild sound and atmosphere
stuff for the foley editor to use later. And I'm listening to the crickets as the
sun goes down, and fumbling with the reel-to-reel's switches—screwing up,
because, to be honest, I'm drinking, right? More than usual, I mean. Been getting worse all year.

My wife ran off to Las Vegas with a broken-down stuntman, about a year before, took my savings with her. I'm forty-five years old and working on Poverty
Row junk like this. My daughter hasn't spoken to me in almost a year, and I got
fired off the last shoot for drinking.

Tequila. Maybe that's why Henry picked me. Or maybe he saw the stamp of
destiny.

So I'm sitting in front of my Airstream, nursing my Cuervo, when I hear a
clopping and catch this funny smell—not so funny, more like strange and sick. I
look up from the recorder set up on the card table, and there's this leathery snag-
gletoothed rider squinting down at me from his horse. He's skinny, got jug ears
and long gray hair. The sunset is in his eyes—blue eyes under heavy dark eyebrows. On his worn-out old saddle is a rifle holster, with what I assume is a prop
Winchester in it.

I glance past him, see a trail of dust still hanging in the crotch between the scrubby hills. I figure this is the rider Harry spotted, the one watching us this afternoon. He's ridden down out of the eastern Santa Susana foothills around Corriganville. Old Crash Corrigan bought the ranch land back in the '30s and turned it into a low-budget movie set, mostly for Westerns and serials, but they made all kinds of pictures here, and parts of pictures. Even some Tarzan, and television, later.

But this rider, he's coming from the mountains—and on the other side of those mountains is the Mojave Desert. I figure he can't have come that far. Must be an extra fooling about with one of our rented horses, all afternoon. "If Mr. Beaudine sees you took one of our horses out for a joy ride," I advise him, "he's liable to fire your ass off the shoot."

"Don't know a Mr. Beaudine," he says to me. He had a voice that went from squeaky to gravelly in a few syllables. "Anyway, this here is my own damn horse. Pedro's his name."

"*Beaudine*'s his name—the director of the goddamn movie," I say. I remember trying to figure out how old the rider was—couldn't guess. Might be old or just weather-beaten, premature gray. I've never seen such leathery skin. Like it was stripped off, run through a tannery, and put back on. His hodgepodge outfit doesn't look like it belongs to the standard western costuming they put the cast in. He's wearing an antique military jacket—khaki, a few brass buttons left, yellow collar—like something one of the Rough Riders would have worn going up San Juan Hill. He has big dusty clodhopper boots on, dungarees, and a stained, dust-coated sombrero. There is a red bandana around his neck, though. That's the only bit of costumery on him that seems to go with the production.

He sits there, on one of those black-and-white Indian ponies, a grimy Pinto stallion who snorts and lowers his head to the ground, looking for something to crop up, but there's nothing but sage.

Music plays from one of the other trailers, a song by the Beatles. "Drive My Car." The rider looks toward the sound. "Now that's a queer song," he says. "'Beep beep beep,' they say." He sticks the tip of his tongue out to catch it between crooked buck teeth, as if to keep from laughing.

"That's the Beatles," I say.

"Sounds more like birds peepin' away," he says. "Say there, bub ..." And he leans over pommel of the most worn-out old saddle I've ever seen, to look real hard at the bottle of Cuervo sitting on the table. "That ta-keeler there?"

It takes me a moment to figure out he meant tequila. "Sure. Climb down and have a slug, bro." Anything to take my mind off my life....

He steps down off the horse, doesn't bother to tie it up. The Indian pony wanders off, and the rider doesn't seem worried about it. He limps energetically toward

the other camp chair, sits with a grunt, slapping the dust off his dungarees. He ac-
cepts the bottle from me. "You ain't got a glass? I'm not barrel boarder. I'll have a
glass if they is one."

"Sure...." I go into the trailer, find a second glass, and when I come out I see
him poking at my tape recorder.

"Now don't touch that!" I tell him, sharply. "Not cool, man!"

He draws his hand back, sits up straight, shrugging, adjusting his bandana.
"You use that machine to make a movie picture?"

"Just for certain kinds of sound effects. Here ..." I pour him the tequila.

He takes the tumbler and raises it to me. "Here's how!" He knocks back half a
glass like nothing. He's real quiet for a minute, his face shaded by that dirty sombrero. "That's good ta-keeler," he says, at last. "Didn't drink much till ... after.
What's your name, bub?"

"Jack," I tell him. "You?"

"Gone back to my own given name. Henry. Well, it was William Henry
McCarty but I liked Henry."

I sit next to him. "You changed your name at some point, huh? Police trouble?"

"You could say. Started out, I went by Antrim, after my stepfather. He was a
right son of a bitch. Never knew my real Pap. Later, when I got in some trouble
for shooting that pig-snout Cahill, I went by Bonney. William H. Bonney." He
smiles ruefully. "Alias Billy the Kid."

When he says that, I'm thinking, *Oh Jesus, we got a live one here. A grade-A
liar or a grade-B lunatic.*

It's cooling off now, and he pushes his sombrero back so it hangs off his neck
by the chin string. His hair's all tangled together. He goes on, "Got a cabin in
southeast California, by the border now—and about twelve mile from my cabin,
they got one of those places with the movie screens up so high. Folks drive their
jalopies up to them, watch 'em outside. I can't get me a jalopy because I got no
identity papers. So I take Pedro out and they let me sit on the ground by my horse
and watch the pictures. They give me a little work, now and then. Pedro, I had
him five years ... where's he gone to?" He looks around for the horse. "There he
is. Don't wander off too far, Pedro.... What was we talking about?"

I'm guessing this is his idea of an audition. All "method" like, living the part. I
pour myself a drink. "So you want to play Billy the Kid in this picture? They've
cast that part already, Henry."

"Me? No, I'm too old to play ... the Kid." He grins, showing his crooked buckteeth. I'm thinking I've seen that face before, in a photo. He goes on, "But I expect
I can be a help. Heard that Wyatt Earp got paid for talking about things." He spits
in the dirt. "He advised on some Tom Mix movie picture. If that head-busting

Kansas cow-fucker could get the do-re-mi, why not me? I need some money for Doc Vic. Got to have some chemistry supplies."

"You want to be a consultant, you mean? Oh that's right … you used to be William Bonney, alias Billy the Kid." I smirk and pour him another. Then it occurs to me that even though he left the Winchester on his horse, I ought to glance at him to see if he has a gun or knife or something, seeing as he's either half or whole cracked. I don't see a weapon, but one could be tucked under that old military coat. "Were you in the military?"

"No, I took this coat off a fella. He didn't need it no more. I just like the buttons."

He takes the refill in as dirty a hand as I've ever been around. And while I'm noticing this, I see a pale zigzag of scars all around his right wrist. Sewing marks, sutures, all laced up. There's something else odd about his hands but it takes me a bit to work it out. Then I get it: his right hand is larger and a bit darker than his left. His left is small as a boy's of maybe fourteen.

"You are looking at my sewin' scars," he says, frowning at me.

"Um—car accident?"

"Nope. Now, I heard that this here movie picture—" He pointed toward the production set, just visible between the old-timey false-front buildings of Main Street. "—is about Frankenstein and Jesse James. Now I didn't know Jessie but I know all about that German doctor. Much as a man can know about that one— he was not a man who showed his insides … oh, here's how." He drains the rest of the tequila in his glass, *boom*, just like that.

"Wrong show," I tell him. "We'll be shooting *Jesse James Meets Frankenstein's Daughter* pretty soon, but this is *Billy the Kid Versus Dracula*."

"It's what? Guess I heard wrong then. I come too soon. This here's Corrigan Ranch?"

"This is it. And the picture we're doing now is *you* … versus Dracula."

"Dracula, you say. I saw an old movie about him, back before pictures could talk. But he ain't real. Frankenstein, now, he was real—only that doctor's name's not Frankenstein. Howsomeever, I read that Miss Shelley's book. There's people say I cain't read. It ain't—it's not true. My Ma taught me, before the consumption took her. I read that *Ivanhoe* once. Most of it, anyway."

Henry seemed to be talking more to the setting sun than to me. He was staring unblinking right into it, over the top of the fake saloons on the dusty street Corrigan Ranch used for its cheap oaters.

"So Frankenstein was real, huh?" I said, sipping tequila, wanting to hear more of this fantasy. "That's far out." It'd make a great story to tell around the set, anyhow.

"That name Frankenstein was a lie Miss Shelley made up. A *book alias*, you might say. His name was Doctor Victor Von Gluckheim. Doc Vic, that's how I think of him—he knew that Miss Shelley and her friends, had 'em out to his castle in Austria. She was young, real young, then, no more'n eighteen. He showed her some things he was working on. Made a dead frog and a rabbit come alive, right in front of her. Showed her a dead man he bought, fella died in a lunatic house. Working on sewing that onto another fella, trying to revive 'em. He was in a struggle with death, don't you see. Was Doctor Vic told me this. Now, Doctor Vic was pretty old when I met him. 1881—more'n ninety years old. But he looked maybe sixty. He come over to this country back in 1816, running from trouble back home. Graverobbing charges, as you might expect. So he come out to hide in the territory where he could do his work in peace. I met him two days before Pat Garrett shot me."

I'm listening to him and sometimes I'm trying not to laugh and other times I stare at those mismatched hands and I wonder. My nephew George, in those days, worked for *Confidential* magazine. It occurs to me then that maybe there's some way I can get a story to sell him for *Confidential*. Something like, "'Billy the Krazed' Raids Movie Set." I'm testing the recorder anyway, so why not? "Billy the Kid—In His Own Words." Hell, I'd read it.

"Tell you what," I say. "You tell me how you met Frankenstein, or whatever he called himself, and I'll try to get you the consulting job. If you do get it, it won't pay much. Maybe we can do something with your story, anyhow. I could record it on this machine...."

Damn if his story couldn't be a movie itself. I think so now and I thought so even then.

Henry thinks about it and then he says real slow, "Maybe you're the one I saw in the dream."

"Which dream is that?"

"I had a dream that a fella would tell my story, my true story, but I had to ride the mountains to find him. Since my time with the doctor I've learned to take advice from dreams." He looks at me and says, real slow, "My story's been percolatin' in me many a year and it could be the time has come. I'll do 'er. One thing though—you got anything to eat, maybe some pork and beans? I like those canned pork and beans...."

"Got some canned chili. I'll get you some, but don't touch that machine."

So he eats some chili out of the can with a spoon, cold, really relishing it, his yellow teeth chewing with his mouth open. He seems to have some trouble swallowing, and drinks a lot of my jugged water to get it down. When he's done he asks, "You got a truck I see to tote this here modern trailer. I expect there's a battery in that truck? One of those big car batteries?"

"Sure. Why?" Is he thinking of stealing my truck battery? Maybe he's got a broken-down truck in the hills somewhere.

"I'll show you, by and by. Got a smoke, there, bub?"

Does he mean grass? "Lucky Strikes, if that's what you mean...."

"Now that's a name I like. Did some prospecting. Never had a lucky strike that wasn't a smoke."

I give him the pack and matches. He puffs the cigarette and drinks tequila and I switch on the tape recorder. What's coming up now is his voice, spliced in after my voice: Mr. William Henry McCarty aka Henry Antrim aka William H. Bonney— alias Billy the Kid.

There is a lot of lies told about me. One is that I'm left-handed. You can see I am no lefty. Another is that I was some kind of full-time cow thief. I threw a wide loop in my time but I'm no cow thief, or hardly ever. I was a good hand for Mr. Tunstall. It's true I did start out as a horse thief with ol' Johnny Mackie. Another lie is that I killed a man for each year of my life. Here's the truth on the Holy Book: I killed but nine fellas, before Pat shot me. After that, well....

See, bub, I was in Fort Sumner, in New Mexico Territory, visiting my girl Paulita. Her brother Pete was keeping a close watch on her. He didn't like a wanted man dating his sister.

We was to meet up in the cantina. I was playing cards that warm night, my back to the wall, watching the door for her, and for law dogs. I was a dozen hands into a game with a couple of vaqueros up from Old Mexico. I pretended to drink more ta-keeler than I was, letting them get good and drunk so they make all the wrong calls. Then into the cantina came this nervous, quick-walking old man with a big bush of white hair 'round his head and a beak of a nose. He wore a funny old gray suit and knickerbockers and he chewed a crooked cheroot. He spoke the Español to the bartender. Spoke it with a funny accent. "What the hell kinda Spanish that old duffer's talkin'?" I said it out loud in English, not thinking he'd understand me.

But he did. He turned, with his Spanish wine in his hand, and looked at me real close, raising one of those old spectacles on a stick to do it with; and he said in English, "I have learned my Spanish in Spain, young man. But me, I hail from Germany." He said it like, *Chermany.* "But I know many languages," says he. "Even some Comanche, I know." He looked me up and down and says, "I have not seen you here before...."

"You want to play some cards, old horse?" I ask him. "I'll take German gold same as any other."

When he smiled, there were only a few teeth in there. "No, I think not. You are an interesting young man. You have the stamp of destiny on you. Such I have learned to see."

That's how he talked. *"Such I have learned to see."* Struck me as real entertaining. A man sure gets tired of vaqueros and blacksmiths and cowpunchers for company. Here was a man who'd traveled to Europe. My Ma, she was born in Ireland, and I was born in New York, and I hankered to see more of the world. Especially when my neck was like to be fitted for a rope halter in New Mexico.

"The stamp of destiny," I repeated. "I like that."

He nodded and drank his wine, staring at me the whole time, then he gave me a little bow, from the waist, and walked out of the cantina.

"Well, I'll be goddamned," I said, and the bartender laughed.

"The doctor, Señor Victor, he has a silver mine," said the bartender. "But with no silver in it."

He told me the doctor had a cabin at an old silver mine that was all played out, some miles from town. He had some way to make ice down in that mine, where it was cool, and sometimes he sold it to the town. He did some doctoring on 'em too but most were scared of him.

"But he always smiles, and speaks softly to me." There was a priest, there, in the cantina, as drunk as any one of us, hearing me and the bartender talking, and he spoke up. He said, in Español, "The devil always wears a smile, and speaks with a soft voice."

I put it out of my mind and set to playing stud. That ricket-legged little Mexican dealing had given me three aces down. He was grinning, thinking he had me with his two pair, and his tall, drunken partner with the pitted face was trying to look all cucumber-cool so I knew he had a hand too. So I said, "Boys, let's bet it all out there, and see what happens."

They went for it and when the next cards were dealt I had me a full house, aces full of tens. When we turned those cards over I never saw two sicker-looking vaqueros. I scooped up the double eagles, except for one to buy 'em enough a drink or two, gave 'em a wink to go with it, and walked out. I was tired of waiting for Paulita—I was going to take the bull by the horns and find her.

I went out to my mare and was leading her out through another alley to the street, thinking about where I'd look for Paulita, when I heard a scuffling behind me. I knew right away what it was—the drunk vaqueros wanting their money back. I jerked my single-action and turned. Sure enough, they were coming out into the moonlight, side by side, the tall one unlimbering an embossed-silver shotgun while Mr. Rickety-legs was aiming his pistol. The pock-faced bastard fired and missed so wide I never even heard the bullet pass. Hell, he didn't even hit my horse. I couldn't hardly miss him from eight paces, and my first round caught him right in the middle of the chest, knocked him back off his feet. The other vaquero would have done for me with that shotgun but the damn fool hadn't cocked it. He was working on that, cussin' to himself as he realized it wasn't set, when I shot him through the throat, just above the collarbone—that'd be right there on you, bub. And over he goes, crying out "Madre Mia" and then spitting blood. He rolled over, tried to crawl away. I spent two more bullets making sure of them—and then I knew someone was watching. I could feel it.

I looked around to see a shadow shaped like a man out on the street, standing by a buckboard. There was a big halo, like, of white around its head. Then I worked out it was that German doctor with the light from the whorehouse behind him. He said to me, "Ach, hold your fire! The law will be here, chure—but if you help me load these men on my wagon, I'll tell them you were not here. And I will pay you for your help. You have already helped me much tonight."

He held up a little leather sack and jingled it. What did he mean, I'd helped him? Then I remembered that doctors liked to cut open dead folks to see what made 'em tick—and what made 'em stop ticking. And this man, something about him seemed like a kindly old uncle. Never had me a kindly old nobody. So I said, "You can keep your gold, I'm flush now. Come ahead."

We dragged the bodies to the buckboard, heaved them on. I heard some shouting, someone asking for the constabulary, the voices of the whores talking in Spanish nearby, so as soon as he got up on the buckboard I slapped his horse's rump and it pulled him off into the night.

Pretty sharp after that I rode off to Paulita's cabin, out on the edge of Pete Maxwell's ranchland. We were shacked up for true, hardly going out, for two days.

Well sir, we were drinking and lovin' up in that shack on a hot July night, not so different from this one, bub. But hotter, it was, hotter'n a whorehouse on nickel night. We got hungry, as you do. I thought I'd go to her brother Pete's house, cut some beef from his stores like he'd offered, maybe have a drink and talk to him about Paulita. Clear the air. We used to be friends.

I had no shirt on that night, just some jeans. No gun, because I didn't want to spook Pete. Just a knife in my hand for cutting some steak for me and Paulita. I rode over, barefoot and bare-chested, singing to myself. I was a pretty good tenor, you know. Hard to believe, hearing me now.

I was drunk but able to sit a horse, still remember that the air felt good on my skin as I rode. I reined in when I saw some strangers on the porch of Pete's place. I was wanted for shotgunning Bob Olinger and shooting one or two others, so I was nervous. I skirted around to the back, dismounted, and went in the back way, carrying that knife. Went to Pete's room to ask him who those fellas were on the front porch—couple of deputies, is who they were, I found out later—and then I see someone in there, just the shape of him in the dark. Doesn't look like Pete to me. So I say, "Quien es?" and *boom*, the fella shoots me. When his six gun goes off, that flash showed his face. Pat Garrett. I'll never forget it. Fella I'd ridden with, turned sheriff. He looked scared as a deer in a ring of wolves, even though he was facing a man without a gun.

He fired twice. One round went through my right hand, changed direction when it smashed a bone, passed through and smacked into my left leg right above the kneecap. Second shot cut into my chest. I guess it nicked an artery, and spilled a mess of blood into my lungs. Getting shot like that felt like being kicked by the meanest mule ever was.

Then I was flat on my back, trying to breathe, and Pat was yelling to his men, "I shot Billy, by God!" And there were a lot of voices, including Pete's. Then I thought: I expect I'm dying. Everything went black.

Next thing I remember is a stroke of lightning against the blackness. The blaze of the thunderbolt seemed to linger there, not going away like lightning usually does.

Second thing I remember is a voice speaking in foreign, like a man muttering to himself. I tried to open my eyes but they were too heavy. "Mr. Bonney, you are stirring, I see," he said to me. "Das ist gut. But now, sleep...."

After that, I remember the pain of sitting up. It never hurt so much to sit up, bub. The light hurt my eyes at first, too. Even though it was just a railroad lantern, down in a dark hole in the ground. Doc Vic had him a little operating room way down in that played-out silver mine of his. There was what looked like telegraph wires on the ceiling, nailed to the rafters, and there was a machine, big as a pedal sewing machine, 'cept it had a crank on it. Doctor Vic was turning the crank, faster and faster, and I felt right then like someone poured pure grain alcohol in my veins and lit it on fire. Soon after I went under again.

Next time I woke I felt some better. Just kind of funny. Like part of my body was missing, or half missing.

Something else was missing. I couldn't remember my name. Or who I was. Took me a long time to get that back. Years. It was in there somewhere, but locked away. Doc Vic said it was something to do with my poor brain losing breathing-air when Pat killed me.

Pat Garrett did kill me, too. The doc told me he bribed the Mexican fellas watching my body, replaced it in the coffin with one of the vaqueros I shot, or part of him. The doc drug my body back to his mine, covered in sawdust and laying on blocks of ice. He took it down deep underground, patched it up and he put the life back in it. He says my spirit was hanging around my body, like they do for a time after dying. When he called down the lightning for me it's like my spirit rode that lightning down—like a bronc-buster riding a thunderbolt. Rode it right back into ... up here. My brain.

I realized, when I woke up, that I was nekkid as a jaybird. This did not sit well with me. I was cold, and felt like a man with his back to the door on a night when his enemy is looking for him. But what bothered me more was all that sewing. My right wrist was sewed up. And my hand looked all wrong. That's because it wasn't my hand—Pat Garrett fair destroyed that hand—and this one belonged to that pock-marked vaquero I killed. You can see it's too big for me. My left leg from the thigh down belonged to that other hombre. It's crooked and fat, but I make do with it. Now, some of my inner parts is theirs too. I got my own heart, thank God, but my lungs belongs to the tall vaquero. Later I got me a new liver— a young priest died from falling off a horse, and the doc sent me to dig up the body. Hadn't been embalmed—liver was still good, he said. It was in winter, too, that helped keep it fresh.

Doctor wouldn't take body parts from people who died of disease on account of they was tainted. He liked to get the bodies of folks been killed from falls or hangings—or from being murdered, long as it wasn't poison. That's why he kept watch on me that night. Said he knew I was a killer the minute he laid eyes on me. Knew I'd tangle with those Mexicans. He saw the stamp of destiny on me, and he saw their destinies too—short.

How'd he do that? He spoke of the power of lightning and "animal magnetism." That thunderbolt power he put in me—he put it in himself. Not quite the same. He takes his different, in something he calls a charged tonic. He says that's because he never died. But me, I got to have it right in the old nerves. Now I got what he calls a feeder, right here in the back of my neck, just under my collar.

Me and him, though, we had one thing in common. The thunderbolt, it changed us both somehow. It makes a man live longer. Real long. And it makes him sense things, like a rattler sensing your footstep a ways off with his tongue on the rock.

When I woke up in that mine, he called me Billy and that sounded right. I had a few memories of my mother coughing her life away in a bed; of pulling hand-cuffs off my hands, seeing as the cuffs was too big for them; of seeing a pal gunned down. But I couldn't connect none of it. Seemed like it all happened to someone else. And when Doc Vic saw I couldn't remember much, he said he'd take care of me. "In essence," said he, "I am your father."

Now that made me feel good. I couldn't remember much of my past but there was something in me longing for a father. I guess it had always been there. So I went right along with that.

And I served that man for more than twenty-five years. That's right. For twenty-five years I never ventured far in daytime. Only at night.

One hot day, a diamondback twice as long as your arm came into the mine and reared up, hissing and rattling. That thunderbolt the doc put in me came flashing up so I was faster than the rattlesnake. It struck at me but I caught it right under its jaws—caught him a whisper away from my neck. I could feel his tongue tasting the skin on my throat. I held him out at arm's length and sent that lightning through my hands to him and that ol' snake just went rigid as a pine branch and started smoking. I burned his golden eyes right out of his head. We ate cooked rattler that night—cooked then and there.

Most of the time we stayed up north, out east of Fort Sumner, at the mine where Doc Vic poked and prodded me and made notes. He had a feud with Old Mister Death himself, so he kept on with his work to build other fellas up out of nothing but spare parts, like in that Mary Shelley book. He got one of them up and moving too, but that patchwork fella was an imbecile and mostly drooled and played with his private parts. One day he just keeled over dead.

I did errands and I dug in the mine and gave the silver to Doc Vic. It was mostly played out but there was a little silver to be found. And we still sold ice to the town, now and then. Time passed full queer for me in those days, and years went by like weeks.

One time an outsider came snooping around, knowing the old doctor had gold. This poor excuse for a road agent was a red-headed son of a whore with a scraggly beard and an eye-patch. I smelled him before I saw him—my senses was that acute, and Lord knows he smelled high. I came out of the mine, sniffing the air, that evening and then seen him ride up on a bent-backed hammerhead roan, and I said, "Smelled you coming, bub. What you want here?"

Gingerhead cleared his throat and he said back, "Your money or your life." He waved a rusty old pistol I doubt would have fired anyhow. "Bring that old fool out and I better see his gold. I've got a short-fused stick of dynamite in my saddlebag and I'll set it burnin' an' chuck 'er in the mine unless I see gold fair quick. Silver'll do, too."

"Sure, bub!" I said, grinning like I was simpleminded. "I'll do that!" And as I said it I walked up to his horse. "Let me just help you down, there, you can come and get the gold."

I knew he wouldn't go for that but it confused him a moment or two, and that gave me time to step close. I grabbed his belt and dragged him down off his horse, and threw him on the ground. To me he was light as a half-empty feed sack. I stepped on his gun hand, and while he was blinkin' his good eye and cursing, I took the gun and tossed it in the brush. Then I knelt down, put my hand on his neck and let go some of the thunderbolt, sent it burning into him, just like that rattler. Boom, he went stiff, his remaining eye popping halfway out. I started in to choking him and he couldn't fight, being all stiff with the electricity.

I killed him quick and good, drug him off to the mine, where the doctor praised me, and chopped him up for parts.

Now, you notice I don't carry a gun. That vaquero couldn't shoot straight and I got his hand. I can manage a Winchester if I have time to aim, is all. And anyway I don't need a gun so much now, with the thunderbolt in me.

Now at that time, more than twenty years after Pat shot me, my brain was finally mending. Killing this gingerheaded fella seemed to wake something up in me. Made me want to go sniffing around the world.

So the next night, when the doc was resting, I came out of the mine—and I smelled something in the air. It was perfume, wafting from the town though it was some miles off. It seemed to call to me. So I lit out, not even understanding what I was doing, headed into Fort Sumner. It was a full moon, like the night I met the doc, and I heard the sound of a piano from the cantina. I was starting to remember cantinas, and a few other things, like the women you find in them. I had my charge that morning, and still felt strong from it. If a man doesn't exert himself too much, why, a charge'll last a good three days—but it's when you first get it that you feel like you could take on an Army and laugh.

When I got near the cantina out comes a young fella dressed like a Spanish rancher, and walking like he's had too much ta-keeler. I stared and stared at him. I thought for a moment that it was me.

He looked a hell of a lot like I did when I was young. The young fella took no notice, just kind of weaving off down the street.

In a doorway next to the cantina there was an old barefoot peon in a sombrero, a gent we sometimes bought grub from. I asked him in Español, "Who's that fella?"

Said he, "That's Señor Telesfor Jaramillo." I asked him who this Telesfor's mama was. I didn't know why I asked—but somewhere in me, I was starting to remember things.

He tells me, "His mother was Paulita Jaramillo. She married Señor Jaramillo and this child came soon after." He grinned in a way that told me it was too soon after. Then he came over all solemn. "But she has died now...."

I felt struck by lightning of a different kind then. Paulita dead, and a child born to her—a grown child who looked like me. All of a sudden I had a fierce headache, and I had to sit down, right there on the road, because of what was coming back to me. I was hammered down by a hailstorm of pictures in my mind.

Telesfor Jaramillo. He had to be my son with Paulita. And then I remembered who Telesfor's father truly was—remembered all about myself. William Henry McCarty. Alias William Bonney. Alias Billy the Kid.

Now, I had no real fear anyone in town would recognize me. It was more than twenty years, and I looked a helluva lot different anyhow. My skin—well you can see for yourself. The doc had dipped me in some kind of preserving tonic when he first brought me to the mine, and it still shows.

I thought of going after that young man, telling him who I was—but I could not tell him *what* I was.

He believed he was the son of this Señor Jaramillo. It was better he went on believing that. Because I was a kind of half man, and half corpse. I could not bear for him to know what I was—and I could not lie to him.

Bub, I felt like my heart had been dropped down a deep cold well.

I determined to leave Fort Sumner. I could not be so close to my son and never speak to him.

I am ashamed to say I scarcely gave a thought to old Doc Victor. He had plenty of his charged tonic to hand—but I should have stayed with him, for he'd been poorly. I just stood up, there in the street, and walked to the livery stable. I had some gold on me, which the doctor give me for emergencies. I would make my way. I would be weaker without the thunderbolt cranker—but surely I could live without it....

I found an old man working at the livery and bought him tequila to get some questions answered. I found out there was no use going after Pete Maxwell, who betrayed me to the law—he died in 1898, and was beyond my reach.

But I could get to Pat Garrett, for he was known to be alive and well.

I bought a horse and saddle and I rode out to find Pat.

Everyone knew about Sheriff Garrett; they all knew he had killed Billy the Kid and was damned proud of it. Crowed about it in a book.

Ol' Pat was still in New Mexico—had him a ranch in the San Andres Mountains. I set to finding his place, asked around in those hills, saying I wanted work with him. Couple of cowpunchers pointed me to his place.

When I got close, I climbed a bluff that looked down on Pat's layout, spying it out. I was laying there, flattened down and admiring his herd of quarterhorses, trying to decide how I'd kill him—when I started to feel real weak. I ate some jerky and the food helped, but not enough.

Then I knew—it was the thunderbolt. It seemed I needed it to live on, after all. Maybe it was a kind of addiction. I'd never been so long away from the cranker, and hadn't counted on the exertion. Seemed three days was all a charge was good for.

I had to ride hard to get back home. Killed my horse just getting there. I made it into the mine, staggering by the time I got to the cranker and got my thunderbolt into me.

I reckon I had come back looking sickly, but Doc Vic didn't look much better than me. He was laid out flat on his back in the lowest chamber of the mine. He had been slowing down some—age finally catching up. He didn't say so, but I worked out that my being gone for three days had kind of knocked his pins out from under him. Doc was powerful attached to me. The son he never had, is what I was. I knew just how he felt, for I had to let go of my own son.

Laying there on his cot, he took my hand, smiling real sad, and said that he needed to go to sleep and kind of die, for a while—but he wouldn't be thorough-going dead. He would build himself up, from inside, only it would take time, a long time.

He closed his eyes, and asked me to lay him out on the ice we kept in the mine. He'd go into the long sleep there, and it'd take care of him.

I will tell you straight, bub, it made me weep like a woman when he said that. He was the only father I'd ever known. I was to be alone in the world again. And I'd run out and left him to fend for himself when he was feeling low.

So I gave him the tonic he kept ready for this long sleep, and he drank it right down—and went stiff as a board. But I could feel through the "animal magnetism" and all—he was still there. Every so often, his heart beat, just one little thump ... and a little while later, another.

I wrapped him up good, like he told me, in some medicine-soaked bandages. Then I went about my business. I had some of Doc's gold and silver—and I had the buckboard and a couple of horses. I put the cranking thunderbolt machine in the buckboard, then I rode out.

I thought about shooting down old Pat on my own, face to face. Wouldn't that have given him a turn, seeing me a short breath before he died? But there was a long memory in New Mexico about Billy the Kid. It concerned me. I had a horror of having people look at me and laugh at the patchwork Billy I was now. Then too, the habits of staying hid had gotten strong with me. I was Billy, but I was also a man who'd spent most of twenty-five years in an old silver mine. No, I had to do for Pat Garrett from a good distance. Keep Billy the Kid out of it.

So I played the harmless old saddletramp, and asked around about Pat's doings. I found that folks around about there had no great affection for him and his bad temper, especially a onetime cowboy turned goat rancher, a hardbitten red-faced young fella name of Jesse Wayne Brazel. Pat was always shouting at Brazel to keep his goddamn goats off his land.

I went to Brazel, and played some cards with him—and made sure I lost. This will sometimes make a foolish man trust you. Then we talked about his troubles with the old sheriff—and I allowed as how I had a reason to hate Garrett too. I told him real quiet that if he'd kill Pat, I'd pay him for it—and I'd pay some "witnesses" to lie and say it was self-defense.

Brazel said he knew a notorious killer name of Jim Miller who might do it. I said I'd pay him, or Miller—whoever did it. And I'd bribe up some witnesses. Jesse Wayne Brazel agreed.

I kept watch on the road betwixt Brazel's land and Pat's, from up in the hills. I had a spyglass and everything. It was cold up there, at my little camp in the boulders, just fifty yards over that road. Hell, it was February. But I didn't feel the cold so much—maybe if you've been dead, you're too well acquainted with the cold to be offended by it. The wind was singing a song and nipping my ears when two days later, I spotted Jesse Brazel, on the red dirt road down below, riding along one way, with his friend Print Rhode, and they come across Pat riding along in a buggy the other way, off to town. Pat was riding with a man named Adamson. Brazel stopped him and they argued, probably about those goats eating up all the grass Pat wanted for his quarterhorses.

I watched close, grinning to myself, that spyglass pressed hard to my eye. I saw it all.

I saw Pat Garrett get out of the buggy to relieve himself, pissing off the trail, steam rising up from the puddle. He was still talking, real loud and sharp, the whole time he was peeing—I could make out a word or two about property lines.

Pat was half turned away and Brazel and Rhode saw their chance. Brazel nudged Print Rhode, who stepped up to Pat, pulled a pistol, and shot him in the head. Pat fell dead in midstream, wetting himself on the trail. I was sorry I couldn't be there for him to see who done it to him. But I felt the satisfaction of it all the same, better'n a good meal after a hard ride. I had finished Pat Garret—and got it done safely.

Later, with me spreading around the gold, it was fixed up that it was self-defense, that Pat was going for the shotgun in his buggy. A fine lie it was too, and it protected me from being found out. No one knew Billy the Kid was still alive, and that he'd worked it to have Pat Garrett killed—for killing Billy the Kid.

But that feeling of satisfaction dried up quick as a waterhole in the August sun. A few days later, I watched from afar as the pallbearers put Pat in the ground—and soon's they were gone from Boot Hill, and the colored fella with the shovel had finished and gone home, down I went to the cemetery. I was all charged up with thunderbolt, and dug Pat right up. I pried open the coffin, hunkered down, put my hand on his chest, and shot the thunderbolt right into him. It made his eyes snap open so the coins flew off. His eyes kinda swiveled about in their sockets—he almost seemed to see me. 'Course, his brains was shot through and he was decayed some, but there was a spark hanging around him and I felt like he knew me, for a moment. "I just wanted to say howdy to you, Pat," I told him. "Wondering if you're enjoying your new digs. I put you here myself, Pat. It was me! I sure hope you can hear me." His mouth opened a little, and a worm crawled out and I could see the worm was glowing from the thunderbolt. Pat made a rattling sound, like he was trying to talk—and his eyes looked in two different directions. One of those eyes was smoking—and it sizzled away to nothing. I tried to jolt him awake again ... but he was gone. Still—that's what I call shaking the last drop from the bottle. I filled in the grave, hoping he could feel it, and made my way from there, back to the buckboard, feeling more revenged.

The bribes I paid the witnesses cost me the last of my gold. I went back to the mine, and checked on Doc Victor. He was the same as before, half dead and half asleep, all wrapped up on the ice. I toted him out, and a load of ice, and then I sealed the mine behind us, blowing up the entrance.

Traveling by night I took ol' Doc Vic and the thunderbolt cranker in the buckboard, cooled with ice.

I was set on seeing California. I had time.

Time's mostly all I've had since, bub. I found a spot to rest myself in the Mojave, out in the brush, and mostly I've been out there since. I put Doc Vic down in another old mine close by my cabin.

By day I do odd jobs. Sometimes I crank up my machine. I keep it in repair. And I find other ways to get a charge. Which reminds me....

That is the end of Billy's recording. But I'll tell you what happens next.

It's getting dark, as the tape runs out. Billy clears his throat, spits, drinks some tequila, then suddenly stands up and limps toward my truck, on the other side of the trailer. I follow after him, wondering what he's up to. He doesn't even ask my permission—singing "Buffalo Gals" to himself, he lifts up the hood of the truck. Propping up the hood, he turns to me and says, "I expect you think all this I told you is the biggest goddamn lie you ever heard. And maybe my hand was sewn up on the wrist by a regular surgeon. Well, have a look at this."

Then he takes off that red bandana and turns his back to the truck. That's when I can see a copper wire sticking out the back of his neck, at the top of his spine. It's a bit blackened and slightly melty, but solid enough. He takes a coil of wire from his pocket, twists it onto that piece of metal sticking out of his neck and fixes the other end on the truck battery. He fiddles with it—and then *crack!*, there's a spurt of electricity. I jump back, startled. I smell ozone and burnt flesh and I see him go rigid, grinning real horribly, standing there shaking like a preacher with his pants down.

Then it stops. The battery is drained. He's panting. He jerks the wire loose, and shakes himself, shivering and grinning. He coils up the extra wire, his eyes real bright. A wisp of smoke rises up from the back of his neck. It's getting darker out there by the second—but I can see him clearly, because there's some shine coming off him. His buckteeth are glowing and the whites of his eyes are sparkling with energy.

"I come a ways from my thunderbolt cranker," he says, his voice rough and strong. "I needed that jolt." I don't like the way he's looking at me. He goes on, "I'm thinking about your voice machine—that's the one got me worried. I put my story on there. I come here because I need some money. But there won't be any money, not real soon, ain't that right?"

"Would take a while, yeah. Maybe I can sell this story of yours or ..."

"No, no, you can't do that. I changed my mind on it. When I ponder it—why, it's not safe for me. It's not what was in my dream. I'll find some other way to get the money I need. I got to buy supplies, to help Doc. He's coming back to life, but he's still mighty weak. That recording thing won't be of any help any time soon." He paused, and rubbed a thumb and forefinger together thoughtfully, watching the sparks that crackled between them. "Howsomeever, it's good I set it down, for my story's told on there—and that's enough. Someday I'll give it to folks, but not yet.... Anyhow, bub, I'm going to take that roll of talk with me."

"The hell you are," I say sharply. "That tape belongs to me!"

He's still got that charged-up bucktoothed wolf grin on him. It's making me sick to look at it. He steps toward me. "I was afraid I'd have to kill you. And here we is...."

Billy reaches out his hand toward my neck. Electricity crackles blue and yellow between his fingers.

But the Corriganville security guard, Carlos, is coming along behind the buildings below us, flashlight in his hand. "Carlos!" I yell, backing away from Billy. "Need help up here! Intruder's trying to rob me!"

Carlos comes waddling up the slope, shouting, pulling his gun. He's a fat man and doesn't move too fast. But Billy doesn't like the look of that uniform and pistol. He hesitates now, eyeing Carlos—and I take that chance to run back to the Revox. I pull the tape reel off the machine and toss it into the back of the trailer. Then I lock the Airstream up and I toss the key far away into the darkness. Figure I'll get a locksmith later, or just bust down the door myself.

I turn around—and there is Billy, faintly glowing against the dimness. His eyes are sparking with anger and he's reaching for me—and there's a flash.

Then I am shaking on the ground. I'm not hurt too bad—mostly just stunned. Billy stands over me like he's going to finish me.

But Carlos fires a warning shot as he gets to the road and Billy is slipping around the other side of the trailer. I hear him whistling for Pedro and then I hear hoofbeats—and Billy the Kid is riding away.

I leave the area, soon as I get my truck battery charged. I head up to Northern California. Scared, but not ready to give up that tape. Might have done something with it, too, like write that screenplay—but I slide right into the bottle and mostly forget about the tape. I lose my house and my truck to drink.

I hit a bottom, deep down.

Then I find my way to AA—and I'm six years sober now. Working for a cable company, still living alone in my old Airstream. Thinking about that screenplay I'm not writing.

But this morning, I see a strange young woman standing out by my mailbox. She's wearing a camouflage-type military tee shirt and jeans. She's got almost no chin to her; she's tanned real dark and has her hair tied back in a dirty ponytail. I step out of the trailer, and she says to me, "Billy sent us to tell you, you're to give up the tape. His mind has found you, Jack, and you cannot hide now. He said to tell you and now you've been told. You get the tape ready, in a box, and we will come for it."

Then she gets in a dusty old Chevrolet, and it rumbles off.

That makes me remember a newspaper article from about two months ago. I saved it, pretty sure who they were talking about....

So I go into the Airstream and dig the clipping out of a junk drawer and read it again. And now I'm thinking that when I'm done with this recording, I'm going to go to the newspaper reporter who wrote this, and play this recording for him. I'll sell it all to him. Someone needs to know. Okay—I'll read that clipping out loud now:

> (Mojave Desert News) Reports that an unusual clan of religious devotees has taken root in the Southeastern Mojave have been confirmed by the Caliente Sheriff's Department. A number of complaints have been registered with the sheriff about the group, which is called "Children of the Thunderbolt." Residents in the area complain of late-night intrusions onto private land. There have been allegations the group has raided graves of the recently interred. Sheriff LeCoste has said the organization seems to be a "cult" that centers on the worship of a very old man, who is in a coma underground. The cult is directed by a man who is "the old man's Messiah," one Henry "Billy" Billson,

claimed to be ageless and magically powerful. The sect is said
to be comprised of about thirty-five young people, many of
them armed and dangerous....

I figure I better go down to the bus station with the tape and get the hell out of
town so I can sell the story to the press. And I mean right now.

I'm signing off. This recording is now—

*Hey there, bub. It's been a long time. You'd best turn that off. I wouldn't want to
burn up the machine when the lightning comes. And the lightning's come to you,
bub. Time to climb up, and ride the thunderbolt....*

The Green Menace

By

Thomas Tessier

I was weeding one of the flower beds out front when the black Cadillac came up the gravel drive and stopped just a few feet away from me. With its hooded headlights and the two huge chrome bullets mounted on the wide grille, it looked like some giant mechanical land shark. At the time—this was in May of 1955—I thought it was one of the most beautiful cars I'd ever seen.

The man who got out of the Caddy dropped a cigarette to the ground and crushed it with his shoe. He was wearing a plaid flannel shirt, not tucked in, and khaki slacks. He didn't look like someone who spent a lot of time outdoors. The skin on his face was chalky and I could see that he had office hands. It was still the middle of the afternoon and he already had a shadow filling in along both sides of his jaw.

"Hey, kid," he said to me. "Give me a hand here."

I dropped the hoe I was working with and followed him around to the back of the car. He opened the trunk. There were two suitcases inside, one a little smaller than the other, as well as a black briefcase. He immediately grabbed the smaller suitcase and took that one himself.

"Get those other two for me, would you."

"Sure. How long are you staying?"

He ignored that, slammed the trunk shut, and stomped up the wooden steps to the veranda and through the front door, like he knew the place. Which he didn't; I was sure he'd never been to Sommerwynd before. Though I do remember thinking there was something vaguely familiar about him, like maybe I had seen his face on a baseball card a while back—not one of the keepsies.

My father was at the desk and quickly fell into conversation with the man as he signed in. I wasn't really paying attention, just standing there, waiting to find out which room he was given. But then my mother came out of the office, followed by my grandfather, and I saw the adoring look on their faces as my father introduced them. And then my father gestured toward me.

"And you have already met Kurt, our son. Kurt, this is our distinguished guest, Senator Joe McCarthy."

So that was why he looked familiar. I'd seen his face in a newspaper or on the television. But I was still a couple of months shy of sixteen at the time and had no interest at all in politics. The only thing I knew about him then was that he was a Commie-hunter and was loved for it by a lot of people, especially in our home state of Wisconsin. I nodded and mumbled something incoherent when McCarthy glanced at me and shook my hand. He had a so-so grip and cool, dry skin.

"Kurt," my father continued, "anything the Senator needs or wants while he is our guest, please see to it at once, or tell me or your mother."

"One thing," McCarthy said, raising a hand, his index finger extended. "I am here to get away from Washington and all that for a little while. So, I'd appreciate it if all of you would skip the 'Senator' stuff and just call me Joe." He looked at me again and gave a thin smile. "That includes you, kid—Kurt."

He was in room number 6, the best of the nine guest rooms at the lodge. It had the widest view of the lake, its own little balcony, and the largest bathroom. He kind of exhaled when he stepped inside and looked around, like he was not impressed. I heard an odd clunk when he set down the smaller suitcase he carried. He reached into his pants pocket, pulled out a money clip, and peeled off a dollar bill. He handed it to me.

"When you get a chance," he said, pointing to the coffee table in the sitting area, specifically to the clamshell ashtray on the table, "I'll need a bigger ashtray. And a bucket of ice."

"Yes, sir."

Knotty pine. He was surrounded by knotty pine, floor to ceiling on every wall, and it made him feel kind of edgy. Joe was fifteen minutes into his escape-from-the-rest-of-the-world, as he thought of it, and he was already wondering if he had made a mistake. Just one more in a long list of them, ha ha.

He was at Sommerwynd, a small fishing lodge on a small lake in a remote corner of northwestern Wisconsin. It didn't have a telephone, and the nearest town was twenty-odd miles away. It was the perfect place to go to ground for a while, to relax, recharge his batteries, and think about what he wanted to do next, to plan his next moves. If there were any. Billy O'Brien knew the Wirth family, who ran Sommerwynd. Billy had made the arrangements for Joe. Billy was a friend who stayed a friend—he didn't drift away, like so many others had. But now Billy had landed Joe out in the back of beyond, and Joe was not sure it was such a great idea after all. Still, give it a go. He could always leave whenever he felt like it.

Joe reached both hands behind him and up under his loose shirt to unhook the holster and the .22 clipped to his pants belt. He set them down on the bedside table. Then he pulled his left pant-leg up and unbuckled the holster and the snub-nosed .38 he wore above his ankle. He put them on the table next to the big arm-chair on the other side of the room. He'd never had to use either gun—yet. But Joe knew he had millions of enemies out there and he was not about to go down without a fight if any of them decided to come hunting for him.

He pulled the smaller suitcase close to the writing table, where he was sitting. He flipped the latches and carefully opened it on the floor. Inside, securely wrapped in cloth hand towels, were eight bottles of Jim Beam, along with Joe's favorite Waterford crystal whiskey tumbler. He put the drinking glass and one bottle of the bourbon on the desk, closed the suitcase, and set it down on the floor, right next to the night table beside the bed. He cracked open the bottle, poured a couple of fingers, and took a good sip. That helped. He lit a cigarette, then took another gulp of the whiskey, savoring the mixed flavors of bourbon and tobacco in his mouth. That's more like it, he thought, feeling a little better already.

I fetched a heavy glass ashtray from the supply cupboard and then went to the ice house, where I chipped off enough small chunks of ice to fill a large thermos. I wasn't expecting another tip, and didn't get one. He took the ice and the ashtray from me at the door of his room, muttered thanks and kicked the door shut with his foot.

I saw him again that first evening when he came down to the dining room for supper. The season at Sommerwynd didn't really start until after the Memorial Day weekend, so the only other guests were an older couple, the Gaults, who visited every year. McCarthy nodded politely to them when he entered the room, and then sat as far away from them as he could. He looked like a man with a lot on his mind—more than once I saw him wipe his hand down across his face and give a slight shake of the head, as if he were trying to change the subject of his thoughts.

My mother explained to me how McCarthy had been a kind of national hero, rousting out Reds who had infiltrated the American government, leading the fight to preserve the American way of life and protect our country from the threat within. But his enemies struck back and somehow managed to get the U.S. Senate to censure McCarthy in a vote the previous December. So that was what he had come to Sommerwynd to get away from.

At the time, I didn't understand much of it and I wasn't curious to learn more. I just nodded as my mother went on about what a good man McCarthy was and my father chimed in to say how gutless, shameful, and treasonous the Senate was in their action against him. I remember trying to translate it into baseball terms. He was like a pitcher who made it to the big leagues, a rising star, but then his opponents figured out how to hit him, and beat him. Guys like that— if they don't learn a new pitch or change their delivery, they don't often make it back to the top.

It was a nice evening to sit out on the front veranda or back patio, or for a stroll down to the boat dock, but McCarthy finished his meal, skipped dessert and coffee, and went back upstairs to his room. I did catch a glimpse of him a little while later, about the time when the frogs start up their chorus. I was taking the day's food scraps out to the compost heap near the vegetable beds. On my way back to the house, I saw him sitting at the table on the small balcony off his room. McCarthy didn't appear to notice me; he was probably just staring off at the view across the lake and the rising moon. I saw a curl of smoke in the dusk light, and a sudden glow from his cigarette as he inhaled.

The frogs were having a party, somewhere down the right shoreline some distance from the lodge. They began croaking and thrumming away even before the sun's descent reached the high tree line on the far side of the lake. At first, Joe didn't mind listening to them. It was the kind of nature sound you would expect to hear in a place like Sommerwynd—frogs croaking, owls hooting, bats flapping in the night air, a fish jumping and slapping back into the water. Sounds that felt right.

But after an hour and a half of it, Joe began to wish they would just shut up. "Come on, give it a rest, guys," he muttered as he poured another drink.

It amazed him how loud they were. The frogs didn't appear to be close to the lodge, their ribbity croaking seemed to come from a fair distance away—and yet, the volume they produced was quite strong. And the numbers of them. It didn't sound like a group of six or eight frogs, more like dozens and dozens of them. As darkness settled in for the night, their noise and numbers actually appeared to increase. Maybe the sound just carried very well in the deep stillness of the location, with the lake surrounded on all sides by forest.

Joe finally had enough of it and went inside, shutting the door to the balcony. He could still hear the frogs, but their sound was greatly diminished. He fixed another drink and pulled out *Triumph and Tragedy,* the final volume of Winston Churchill's history of the Second World War. He knew he would need something to occupy time like this at Sommerwynd, and he figured that Churchill was a good man to read when you were in a tough spot. He had already tried the radio in his room, but the only station he could pick up faded in and out of static—he caught a bit of a song that sounded like Patti Page being electrocuted.

Joe read for a while, then set the book aside. It was one of those moments—occurring more frequently of late—when he felt he had little or no patience left for anything. Not the book he was reading, not the room he was sitting in, not the building or place he was in, nobody he knew or encountered, not the weather, the season, the time of day or night. Nothing, not even himself.

He picked up one of his pistols and toyed idly with it in his hands. There was a certain comfort to be found in the kind of inanimate object that is simple in design and serves its purpose, and needs no other reason to be. A spoon, a fork, a knife, a shovel, a clay tile, a garden hose. A gun. Like this one. There had been moments in the past year when he was almost tempted to go that route. But his enemies would have loved it if he did, and he would never give them the satisfaction.

He could still hear the frogs. Jesus Christ, didn't they ever stop? It was a low throbbing sound, boombadaboombadaboom in an endless beat. Fat, slimy creatures rumbling in the muck. Joe undressed, crawled into bed, and turned off the table lamp. He quickly fell asleep, but drifted back up very close to consciousness some while later, again dimly aware of the frogs—still going at it.

Croak—you're croaked.

Croak—you're croaked.

Joe didn't turn on the light. In the darkness, he got out of bed, got a hold of his tumbler and the bottle of Jim Beam, poured one more large one, fumbled for a cigarette and the matches, and eased himself into the armchair. He did all this without opening his eyes, because to do so would make him more awake, and the whole point of getting up was to maintain this state of semi-consciousness, drifting along the edge of the one and the other, not quite awake or asleep. He knew without forming the thought that it would take two cigarettes to finish this drink. Then he would transport himself back to bed, and sleep would come again, and then it would finally hold.

Croak—you're croaked.

Joe made a kind of sighing, humming noise, not much more than a low, droning murmur within himself. It didn't sound like anything, but he knew what he meant by it. He meant: *Fuck you. Fuck all of you.*

McCarthy didn't come downstairs for breakfast the next morning. He did just make it in time for lunch, but all he wanted was coffee, and a lot of it. Mom brewed up a fresh pot for him and he drank most of it while sitting on the front veranda, one cup after another, each with its own cigarette.

I was nearby, working again on the flowerbeds, but I didn't say anything to him. It seemed pretty clear that he wanted to be left alone. He looked as washed-out and beat-down as anybody I'd ever seen. I tried not to keep glancing up at him, but it wasn't easy. Just knowing he was somebody important, or had been.

When he'd had enough coffee, McCarthy went back inside and I didn't see him for almost an hour. Then he came on the veranda again, this time with a little bounce in his step. He clattered down the front stairs and came over to me.

"Tell me something, kid," he said. "What's with those frogs?"

"You mean their croaking at night?"

"That's exactly what I mean. They kept me up all night."

He said it almost as if it was my fault, and his blue eyes bored into me like I knew something I wasn't telling him. Which I didn't.

"It's the time of year when they do that," I replied with a shrug. "It can be annoying at first, but you get used to it and don't even notice after a while."

"If they make that kind of racket every night, I won't be here long enough to get used to it." McCarthy started to step away, but then he turned back to me. "I'm going to go for a walk. Are there any good trails here, so I don't get lost?"

"Sure. There's one that goes all the way up to the top of that ridge," I said, pointing off to the rising tree line to the east, "There's a nice view at the top, and then the path circles down and around, back here to the lodge."

"Uphill," McCarthy said. "That sounds kind of strenuous."

"There's another trail that goes all the way around the lake," I told him. "It sticks pretty close to the water and it's mostly level ground."

"That sounds better."

I gave him directions to find the path—out behind the house, beyond the generator building, the boat dock, and my grandfather's workshop. McCarthy nodded his head and set off on his hike.

A little less than an hour later, I heard the gunshots.

Joe took note of his surroundings as he walked. It was an odd kind of place, Sommerwynd. The lodge itself was nice enough. The lake was small but picture-perfect, and had no other development on it. According to Billy, some well-connected and well-off people visited Sommerwynd from June through September, valuing it for its remoteness and natural setting. Free use of a canoe or rowboat, fishing, swimming, hiking. There was supposed to be a tennis court, though Joe hadn't seen it yet, and would not be interested anyhow. Still, he wondered how the Wirth family managed it all, with just the four of them there at present. But then he figured that they probably just hired a few temporary workers to help out in the busy months.

He passed the first cinderblock building, which had four large propane tanks attached, and he could hear the generator humming inside, providing the electricity that kept the lodge going. A little farther on, he found the second cinderblock building, also painted white. It had no windows. The kid had referred to it as his grandfather's workshop. In other words, Joe thought, that's where Grandpa goes to get away from his family for a while. Have a drink in peace, flip through the few issues of *Playboy* he had smuggled in, and remember what it was like back when.

He soon found the trail, and before long it swung in with the shoreline of the lake, so that the trees behind him cut off any view of the lodge, and he was alone in the woods. A fly or a bug of some kind buzzed him for a couple of seconds—he swatted at it and kept walking, and it went away. Joe thought, not for the first time in his life, that Nature is overrated.

The path hugged the water for a good stretch, and there were a couple of times when Joe spotted small fish in the shallows. That was nice. Then, maybe a half hour into his hike, he came to a spot where the trail swung to the right, away from the lake and into the woods. He stood on a large flat rock that sat at the edge of the water and he studied the scene for a moment. He figured it out. A stream entered the lake here, but over time enough silt had accumulated to back up some of the flow, which created a small, swampy lagoon. The path went inland to get around this obstacle.

Joe was about to continue his walk, but then didn't. The lagoon itself was kind of pretty. It was too early for lily pads, but the glassy black water was already laced with duckweed. The rock he was standing on was in the shade, making this a good spot to take a break. He pulled the hip flask out of his back pocket and sat down on the rock, his feet dangling a few inches off the ground. A sip, a cigarette. There was a cool breeze coming off the lake, and he sat facing into it, enjoying the way it felt on his skin, the way it rippled the water. Yeah, Nature was overrated, but it did have its moments.

Part of him wanted to go back to DC and resume the battle. Or restart it, more accurately. But another part of him said that the battle was over, finished, and that he had lost it. Forget it, move on. But move on to what? What was left? For a while, it was as if the whole world watched him and listened to him—how do you get that back? Because now, he was invisible.

An odd sensation crept over him, that he was not alone. He turned around, wondering if someone from the lodge had come with a message, but there was no one on the trail. Then Joe looked at the lagoon—and he saw a pair of eyes in the water. Dozens of pairs of eyes, just breaking the surface, looking at him. It startled him, but he quickly realized that this lagoon was where those noisy frogs lived, and there they were, looking at him. The lagoon was full of them, more than he could count.

Joe stood up, flicked his cigarette into the water, and stepped down off the rock. A few feet away, a frog crawled forward, partly out of the water. It was huge, the size of a watermelon. *Jesus.* Joe looked around, spotted a pebble, picked it up and flung it into the lagoon. It splashed close to one frog, but the creature didn't move. A couple of frogs had emerged from the lagoon and were now crawl-hopping toward him. Joe pulled his right foot back and kicked one of them back into the water. The frog was so heavy that Joe felt the strain in his ankle muscles. The frog flopped backward, just a couple of yards away, righted itself, and began to move forward again. The other frog, now on the ground, jumped and caught Joe's ankle in its mouth. Teeth, the damned thing had teeth! Joe tried to shake it off, but the frog held on. Joe raised his other foot and slammed it as hard as he could down on the frog's head.

Nothing—that was what he got for wearing sneakers in the woods. And that was when he noticed that the frog had whiskers around its mouth, which shot out like small blades, one of them piercing Joe's calf. What kind of frogs were these, that had teeth and sharp barbels like a catfish?

Think about that later. The pain began to hit him. Joe reached behind his back, got his .22 out, held it to the side of the frog's head and squeezed the trigger. Blood and flesh flew, and the frog at last dropped off his ankle. But Joe was astonished to see that other frogs were coming forward, at him. Calmly, he aimed the pistol and shot them in the head or face, until the gun was empty. He had a couple of boxes of bullets back at the lodge. He reached down to get the .38 from his good ankle, and proceeded to empty that into another bunch of frogs as they got closer to him.

Then, he knew it was time to leave. Joe grabbed one of the dead frogs by the leg and hurried away with it, back to the lodge.

Well, we'd seen these frogs, of course, and thought nothing of them. They never bothered us and we never bothered them. My grandfather, Klaus Wirth, claimed to have refined some of their unusual features through cross-breeding. He was a biologist, a great admirer of Luther Burbank. He had returned to Germany in the 1920s to continue his research work. He was not a Nazi, but after Hitler came to power he was not allowed to leave the country, and was pressed into government scientific service. In my family, none of us ever seemed to know quite what that meant. In any event, my grandfather returned to Wisconsin after the war, refused to seek work at any university, and declared himself in retirement. Still, he conducted what he called "research." He and my father converted the old chicken coop into what became my grandfather's workshop. We knew that he had scientific equipment, and animals imported—even that he had obtained frogs from Africa, with teeth. Still, whenever my grandfather hinted at a "breakthrough," my mother and father rolled their eyes.

Now we had Senator Joseph McCarthy sitting on the patio, one bare foot propped up on a chair, my mother carefully wiping his wounds with disinfectant, me and my father standing nearby, not knowing what to say. My grandfather hung back a couple of yards from the rest of us, looking as if he hoped that this would all blow over and he wouldn't have to move to Argentina.

And on the flagstone, a dead frog. With half of its head blown off. With nasty-looking teeth and whiskers. I'd seen them, but never one close up. It was very big, green and black, and it looked heavy, although I didn't try to lift it. The animal was so slimy and ugly, I wanted nothing to do with it.

My parents were endlessly apologetic, but McCarthy kept going on and on, asking questions they couldn't answer, suggesting that there was some actual plot or plan in place—yes, there, in the middle of nowhere in northern Wisconsin—to somehow create a vicious creature that would eventually wreak havoc on the land.

"This is the goddamn *uber*-frog," McCarthy shouted.

At that point I actually reached down and ran my fingers along the teeth in the open mouth of the dead frog. They were not large, but felt very sharp. I stood up and backed away, wiping my fingers on my pants. My grandfather gave me a little nod of the head and I stepped back to see what he wanted. He whispered in my ear.

"They eat fish and bugs, nothing more, that I know of." Then he added, "They grow too quickly, this new stage."

My mother had McCarthy's leg all cleaned and wrapped by then, and he did seem to be a little more composed. Still, he glanced at my grandfather and said, "I'd like to take a look at that workshop of yours, Pops."

My grandfather suddenly turned icy—something I cannot remember ever seeing until that moment. His eyes narrowed and he spoke quietly through a slight smile.

"I do not believe you have security clearance for that."

McCarthy did a little double-take at that, but before he could come up with a response, a woman screamed. I knew right away it was Mrs. Gault, since she and her husband were the only two people not on the patio. Sure enough, the Gaults came around one of the hedges screening off the generator building, Mrs. Gault limping, sobbing, and assisted by her husband.

"She's been attacked," he said. "By a frog!"

"They're coming," Mrs. Gault wailed.

"Masses of them," her husband added.

I took off while he was rambling on. I ran down across the lawn, around the line of hemlocks, past the generator building, and then I saw them. They hadn't reached my grandfather's workshop yet, but they were closing in. Hundreds of huge frogs, hopping fitfully through the tall grass—toward the lodge, us. I turned around, ran back to the patio, and told my father what I'd seen. He just kind of went into a distant stare for a few moments.

My mother, who was already wiping and dressing Mrs. Gault's ankle-bite, said, "Perhaps we should all go inside."

"Or just leave," Mr. Gault snarled.

That was when McCarthy raised his hand and wagged his fingers at me. I went over to him. He pulled a key out his pocket and handed it to me.

"In my room, in the large suitcase, there's a couple of boxes of bullets. Go get them for me. Quick!"

Looking back, I was caught up in it. I flew.

The lodgekeeper, Karl Wirth, looked frozen, but Joe knew what had to be done. They could run like rats, or they could stop this in its tracks. It wasn't really a choice.

"Do you have any guns?" Joe asked.

"A rifle, a shotgun," Wirth replied.

"That's it?"

"Yes."

"I thought this was a hunting lodge."

"Fishing, swimming, boating," Wirth said. "A bit of hunting in season, but that's for the guests. They bring their own rifles. I'm not a hunter myself."

"Get them," Joe ordered. "And all the ammo you've got."

Wirth hurried away obediently. Joe told Mrs. Wirth and the Gaults to go inside the lodge. He walked out on the lawn, toward the lake. His leg throbbed, but the pain was not unbearable. He was a little past the generator building when he spotted them, a black and green wave surging forward. Ugly bastards. Oh yes, he'd put a stir in them, no doubt about it. But it was inevitable. These people, the Wirths, were living in a dream—oh, we don't bother them, they don't bother us. Just drifting along, until the time came when it was too late, and the moment became one of *their* choosing, not yours.

The kid was back, with the bullets. "Ever use one of these?" Joe asked, handing Kurt the .22.

"I did target shooting a couple of times."

"Good enough. Load up, and aim for the ones in front. Take your time, they're not exactly fast on the ground."

Joe led the way and when they got to the old man's workshop, they began plunking frogs along the advancing front line. It shook him, how many there were of the beasts. He knew then that they didn't have nearly enough bullets. At some point, they would have no alternative but to run for their cars and flee. But Joe noticed that as he and the kid moved laterally, so did the frogs. Vicious, but very dumb creatures. Where could he lead them?

I admit, I was into it. Maybe because it didn't seem to be that dangerous a threat, really. We always had the option of leaving, and coming back later with some kind of professional or state help to eradicate the frogs—or whatever would be done with them. But I got a kick out of picking them off, one at a time, seeing their fat bodies pop in blood and pus. It was like, suddenly you're in a movie, and you're playing this part, and it's more fun than what you'd normally be doing at that time of day.

Unfortunately, we ran out of bullets fast, and there were *a lot* of frogs still coming. My father arrived then, with his rifle and shotgun and a couple of boxes of cartridges. McCarthy grabbed the rifle and started snapping in shells. He moved us away from the direction of the house, and the frogs followed, coming after us—I thought that was so smart of him, but I didn't know what good it would do. McCarthy directed my father's fire, a shotgun blast here, there, almost as if he were steering the flow of the frogs as they came at us. Whenever one edge of the wave appeared to be moving closer, McCarthy fired a couple of shots himself, picking off frogs that he took to be leaders in the throng.

We got to the generator building, and the frogs had come around both sides of my grandfather's workshop. My father and I stood there, waiting for McCarthy to say or do something, but he was standing there, letting the frogs get closer and closer. Finally, he turned to me.

"You run that way around the building, back to the lodge," he said. "If they start getting close, pack everybody in the cars and get out." He turned to my father and said the same thing, except that he pointed my father in the other direction around the building. He slapped us both on the back. "Go!"

"Wait," I said. "What are you going to do?"

"Just gonna let them get a little closer and make sure they're coming on both sides, then I'll be right behind you."

Except that he wasn't right behind us. My father and I met up on the patio, and moved out into the driveway area on the other side of the hedges so that we could see what was happening. We saw the frogs closing in on the generator building, and then McCarthy scrambled out on the side away from the house, running toward the edge of the woods. He was limping, but made good time. The frogs were coming around both sides of the generator building, toward the house. Some peeled off, to go after McCarthy. He dived into the brush at the edge of the tree line, and a moment later, rifle shots rang out. I was slow when it came to following his line of thought, but it became clear a few seconds later when he hit one of the propane tanks, and it went off, and the others followed almost immediately. *Whoomph! Whoomph-whoom-whoom-whoomph!*

It took me years to decipher the visual images I have in my head. Yes, the fireball dominated, but eventually I began to see that a flat sheet of flame also spread out at the same time. Lower to the ground. It was lost for a time—I kept seeing sheet metal fly off the roof, cinderblocks blasted into chunks. We stood there for a long time while the smoke and dust and debris settled. Then we could see a lot of scorched frogs, dead on the ground, and I spotted a few others still alive, retreating toward the lagoon.

Son of a bitch, it worked. Joe stood up and walked toward the house. He looked all around, but couldn't see a live frog that wasn't heading the other way. It would do for now, but the problem remained, and would have to be dealt with.

He found the kid and his father on the patio, both looking shell-shocked, though the kid had a smile lurking on the edges of his mouth. Joe liked that, and slapped the kid on the back.

"You did good."

"Thanks!"

Joe turned to the father, was it Karl or Klaus? He wasn't sure, but it didn't matter. The guy was just standing there, hoping that normal life would somehow be restored to him. Joe smiled reassuringly.

"You've got insurance, right?"

It took a few seconds, but then the man nodded.

"Ah, good, you'll be fine then."

Joe went inside, packed his things, came downstairs, and tried to check out. Mrs. Wirth wouldn't let him pay a cent. She was very apologetic, as was Joe. The lodge had no electricity now, so everyone was preparing to move out until repair work could be arranged and carried out.

"Just a thought," Joe said before he left. "I wouldn't try to explain this in too much detail. An accidental explosion is an accidental explosion."

Tell her husband the same thing, and he probably wouldn't get it, but Mrs. Wirth nodded immediately. When Joe was turning away from the front desk, he saw the kid crossing the other side of the lobby.

"Kurt, would you grab a couple of these bags for me?"

We got over it. We spent a few days at our winter house 40 miles away while Dad got the insurance and repair stuff taken care of, and the investigation went the usual path of least resistance. An accident is an accident, there was no question of gain in the case. And we went back, and had a good season. The new generator was a beauty and actually saved money.

My grandfather never went back to his workshop. When he died a couple of years later, some people came in and took away his equipment, and my parents just let the empty building rot. As was always the case in my family, when there was no need to talk about something, we didn't.

I've learned a lot about McCarthy since then, and it's hard to find anything in it that I like. I think he grew up at a time and in a place where he learned that if you didn't beat up the other guy, he'd beat up you, and he lived accordingly. I know what it's like to grow up feeling alone. When I heard a year or so later that McCarthy had died in a hospital, that he was an alcoholic and had struggled with all kinds of health issues, I thought it was a very sad end to an important life. Later, after I got to know more about him, I came to think that it was just a sad end to a life. He was not a likeable man, but I have to say that I kind of liked him at the time.

My father died of a heart attack a few years later. My mother had to sell Sommerwynd. For a long time nothing much happened out there, but there are a lot of very expensive summer homes on that lake now.

The frogs? The state killed them off, as an invasive species. At least, I think they killed them all off. I don't live there anymore. I'm in sales, in Madison. No wife, no kids, not sure how I ended up here. But I'm doing okay.

Still a long drive ahead. Joe decided to kill it now. He pulled into a place called The Valley Inn while the sun was still visible in the sky. A string of bungalows in the middle of nowhere, on the road to nowhere. Let's say nothing about the room, but that it had a television and got two snowy channels. He poured a couple of fingers of Jim Beam into a plastic cup, and lit a Pall Mall.

Might as well have done this in the first place.

Quoth the Rock Star

By

Rio Youers

The Lyric Theater, Baltimore, MD.
Friday October 13, 1967.

They described him as electrifying and passionate—a rock shaman charged with a dark, sexual energy that left the audience breathless. They used adjectives and superlatives that, while approbative, meant nothing to Jim. He slithered across the stage, trapped in the lights like a lizard in the sun, and vocalized from the depths of his soul. He looked at their faces and heard them calling—*screaming*—his name. They held out their hands, as pale as flowers. They threw their energy at him, and he held it, and cast it back in crashing black waves.

Electrifying.

Passionate.

Rock shaman.

He wrote lyrics—splashed his soul to music—to entertain their intellect, and to offer glimpses of his mind. He was a poet, through and through. The performances were recitations; dark verse married to melody. A war raged in Vietnam and every other band clapped their hands and placed flowers in their hair. His band rode the snake. They sermonized from a barely imagined rim where the day destroyed the night. They sang about fire and death ... The End. They were a four-man orchestra, bleeding dark colors. They created symphonies of psychedelia and challenged their audience to break on through. But for the most part, all they saw—this audience, with their pale-flower hands and flashing cameras—all they saw was a drummer, a guitarist, a keyboardist, and a charismatic, enigmatic lead singer with a pretty face.

They saw nothing.

Jim Morrison sprawled on the stage of the Lyric Theater, motionless, held in the moment like something painted. A fallen leaf, perhaps, curled and brown. Or a still river: deep, uncertain waters. The crowd chanted his name and he looked at them from his prone position, but saw little through the stage lights' glare. He had dropped acid before the show and he could feel it biting the corners of his consciousness. There was a black, velvet curtain in front of him and beyond it the audience roared. Not individuals, but a singular entity: a massive mouth gushing nonsense, filled with teeth. The stage vibrated with the band's extemporization. He could feel it through his cheekbone and ribcage, and in the delicate plates of his skull. He closed his eyes and felt the music. Ray's fingers blurred across the keys: tiny demons filled with fire. Robby twisted his guitar and women-shaped melodies snaked from the speakers. John smashed his drums like a child smashing glass.

You don't know me, Jim thought. *You think you do, but—*

His left hand flexed, clutching the trembling stage. He closed his eyes and his mind buckled. Cold blood ran through his body. His back arched and he imagined a thick tail swishing behind him. The crowd roared like an ocean, his blue eyes snapped open (glowing yellow in his mind), and for one heartbeat the backs of his hands appeared covered with hard scales.

See me CHANGE, Jim thought. A trick of the stage lights, maybe. An effect of the acid, almost certainly. Either way, he licked his lips with a forked tongue and sprang to his feet. The band emerged seamlessly from their improvisation and, half-human/half-lizard, he slithered to the mic stand. Grasping it, he stood in the spotlight, clad in tight leather pants and Cuban-heeled boots, while the crowd's singular mouth rumbled. They cast their affection at him, and he reciprocated with his soul. He purred into the mic and his voice formed bridges. His eyes fluttered, blue again. Cool sweat glimmered on his throat. Jim sang the final verse and chorus of "The End," and then sank through their applause like a man wrapped in chains.

ᴡ   ᴡ

Midway through the encore—"When the Music's Over"—Jim noticed the raven. It circled above the crowd, sometimes swooping low, mostly riding the thermals of their energy. He should not have been able to see it: a black and heavy bird amid such darkness, but its silky feathers caught the glow of the stage lights, allowing him to discern it with ease. Indeed, it appeared to shimmer preternaturally, finding light where there was none. As Jim recited the poetry section of the song, he heard the raven caw—a discordant, brilliant sound that punctuated every verse. He followed its flight around the theater, thinking it should soon disappear (it wasn't real, after all, but surely another lysergic twist), but the raven proved pertinacious. Before the song's end it glided over Jim's head and alighted atop Ray's keyboard bass. The bird shook its dark feathers and looked at the singer. It cocked its head and blinked bright eyes. Ray continued to play, oblivious.

I need that bird, Jim thought. *I need to feel its feathers ... know that it's real.*

Distracted, Jim finished the number. The music ended and the lights went out. The raven shimmered and watched him.

Camera flashes and questions, hands touching him, too many people calling his name. The whole world was backstage. Reporters, VIPs, groupies, friends of friends, industry people, hangers-on, lackeys, and dogs. He was pulled in too many different directions, but went to none of them. At times like these Jim floated away:

Part-fantasy, part-memory. All-refuge. A highway in the desert, a tangle of metal, and a scatter of bleeding Indians. An accident ... he didn't know what had happened. He stood in the middle of the road and absorbed the chaos, listened to the screams. He turned his gaze to a dying man thrown to the side of the road, broken and bleeding. Jim's fragile heart drummed. The Indian looked at him....

"Jim ... Jim."

"What is 'The End' really about?"

"Your appearance last month on *The Ed Sullivan Show* caused—"

"What's your stand on the war in Vietnam?"

Jim watched the Indian die—saw the life flutter from his eyes. Fascinated, he stepped a little closer, and then witnessed something amazing: the Indian's soul, slithering from his broken body. It shimmered, moon-bright and lizard-shaped, and crawled toward the boy....

"Jim ... come on. Come with me, baby."

He recognized Pamela's voice and opened his eyes. She stood before him, protecting him from the barrage of senseless attention. His cosmic mate. His love. Her red hair burned and he touched it, and felt her in his fingertips.

"Hey, baby," he said.

She smiled. "Come with me, Jim."

He started to go with her, but paused. Beyond Pamela—beyond the swarm of people—the raven swooped and landed on a rail. It pecked its glowing feathers for a moment, and then looked at him.

I know what you are, Jim thought. *You flew from a broken body. You're someone's soul.*

"Are you okay, baby?" Pamela touched his face.

The raven cawed. It rapped on the rail with its bony beak.

"Gonna fly tonight," Jim said, speaking to Pamela but looking at the bird. "Real high. I may never come down."

She kissed the underside of his jaw. "Don't leave me, Jim," she said.

But he did leave; twenty-five minutes later he was walking the streets of Baltimore, having escaped the backstage madness. He told the guys that he was stepping outside for some fresh air—didn't mention that he was, in fact, following the raven.

An unusual fog draped across the city, in places so thick that Jim could hardly see an arm's length in front of him, and then it would dissipate and hang in smoky ribbons, coiled like snakes around the streetlights, whispering across his skin as he walked. The raven flew just ahead of him, moving from fencepost to trashcan to the hood of a parked car, and as Jim drew close it would ruffle its feathers and take wing again, leading him deeper into the night. He drew his collar tight and followed with his head down, eyes up. Cars hissed by, too close, too loud. Their headlights bullied the fog, revealing its seams.

Maybe none of this is real, Jim thought. *The raven, the fog, the cars. Maybe I'm still on stage, trapped in my haze while the band plays.*

It was cold, too, and the fog was heavy with moisture. It tasted like camphor. The city's light gave it a burned hue, and within it the raven shimmered, just like it had in the theater. There was no chance of him losing sight of it, even when the mist thickened; it glimmered, like the Indian's soul.

My soul, Jim thought, weaving slightly. His boot heels clicked rhythmically off the sidewalk. He heard car horns sounding, a train shuddering along the Northeast Corridor, and the raven's bruised cry, teasing him along.

He spared little thought for Pamela or the guys. They'd all be looking for him, no doubt checking the restrooms and darkened backstage areas, expecting to find him entertaining one of the many female partisans who had crashed the after-show parade. They would give up soon enough, if they hadn't already, conceding that he had gone AWOL, and not for the first time.

"Not for the last," Jim said. He smiled. The raven worked its wings and carried him away. He walked, listening to his boot heels, watching the raven. He had no idea where he was. Down alleyways and beneath trembling overpasses, across silent streets and through neighborhoods of old brick and faceless glass. He had lived in many cities across the United States—an unsettled upbringing; the eldest child of a Navy Admiral—and they all started to feel the same after a while. Climatically different, sure. Demographically diverse, certainly. But they shared a similar *feel*, he thought: just grids upon grids, filled with buildings and stoplights and authority, sustained by people who worked and ate and prayed and copulated: the great American prison. No wonder he continued to move around ... to slip through the bars and fly.

But this place, this town ... it felt different. Maybe it was the—

acid

—camphor-taste of the fog, or the kinked streets and heavy, ancient brickwork. Jim wasn't sure, but he knew he had never been any place like this before.

Where am I?

In reply, the raven uttered an abrasive cry, circling in the mist to alight upon a street sign. It was archaic in design: wrought iron, with gilded letters on a sooty background. Jim smiled when he read the sign.

"Yeah, pretty neat," he said, nodding. "Now I know this isn't real."

The raven snapped its fat wings and tapped its beak against the sign.

It read: Night's Plutonian Shore.

Strings of fog curled around the elaborate ironwork, and with a burst of angry sound the raven took flight, leaving a spray of black feathers that swayed to the damp sidewalk like burned leaves. The bird cawed, flickering in the mist, and then swept down, beneath a rustic archway and into a narrow alleyway. It flew ahead ... a glowing apparition in the distance.

Jim followed, boot heels clicking.

And the sound of his heels was soon enveloped by another sound, not dissimilar: the ticking of a clock, only it was loud—*too* loud, booming from within the confining alleyway, making the fog tremble and the old bricks shake in their joints. Jim covered his ears but, like the music when he had been lying on the stage, he could feel the thunderous ticking vibrate through the plates of his skull. He screamed, but could not match the sound.

The raven swooped and glittered ahead of him.

Death, Jim thought. *I can hear you. Tick-tock, my pretty child, my sweet one.*

He screamed again.

It grew darker, colder, narrower, as he stepped deeper into the alleyway. Soon all he could see was the fog and the raven, and he had to put his arms out to his sides to make sure that the walls were still there. The bricks were slick beneath his fingertips, like snakeskin, and they continued to quiver as the ticking sound crashed around him.

"What do you want?" Jim asked the raven. "Do you want my death? My broken body?"

He received no reply from the bird, which soared and, for a moment, flickered from view. Jim stopped and waited. Moisture gleamed on his brow and he drew his arms close to his body. He had never felt so alone. Five long seconds. A drifter on Night's Plutonian Shore. And then the raven reappeared with an almost musical swish of wings and Jim sighed, drawn toward it, walking quickly.

He could hear his boot heels again; the ticking had subdued to normal volume. Not that *any* aspect of this night could be considered normal.

I don't know what's going on, Jim thought. *But I have to see it through. I have—*

Something touched him in the darkness. It felt like fingertips brushing over his cheek. He cried out and stepped back, and a steely hand clasped his upper arm from somewhere else. Jim shook it loose, staggering slightly—felt someone else touch his face, and yet another hand reached out and grabbed the lapel of his leather jacket. He slapped it away, crying out again, shuffling down the alleyway as yet more hands poured from the darkness, each seeking some small part of him. He could hear voices, too, melding with the clip of his heels and that constant ticking: *Jim ... over here, Jim ... Jim ... look this way ... over here....* A sudden burst of light that he recognized as a camera flash. Jim shielded his eyes, but not before he saw what the alleyway had become: a jungle of hungry arms, bursting from the walls, hands snatching. *Jim ... right here, just one shot ... this way, Jim ... look....* Another camera flash. Hands grasped at him, fingernails raking down his leather pants, clawing his jacket. He could feel them in his hair, on his throat. He started to run, pushing the arms away as he hastened down the alleyway. His heart clamored in his chest and for the first time he felt afraid. He closed his eyes and the camera flashed again, urging its harsh glare against his eyelids. The silhouette of the raven—wings spread—was printed against the shocked membrane of skin.

Jim crouched, eyes closed, head down, and went to his refuge:

This memory/fantasy ... looking at the Indian's soul: a lizard-shaped thing of light, slithering across the blacktop. Jim watched it all the way, its tail swishing heavily, its spines fully erect. He could hear, from amidst the chaos, a baby crying, and a young man screaming. Blood ran across the highway and the morning sun painted every-thing bronze.

Another camera flash, lighting the alleyway like fire. The hands continued to grab at him, but softer now, and fewer of them.

"And all my days are trances," a soft voice spoke from somewhere in the alley-way. "And all my nightly dreams/are where thy dark eye glances/and where thy footstep gleams."

Jim's heart ran harder, but he wasn't afraid. It was adrenaline, icy and crys-talline—a sense that something life-altering was about to happen. He watched as the soul-lizard crawled steadily toward him, its claws clacking and scratching on the road. Would it simply disappear ... to the place where souls float freely? Jim shook his head; he knew what was going to happen. The soul-lizard stopped a short distance in front of him, lifted itself to its rear legs, and suddenly sprang. A cool flash of light, and Jim felt it penetrate his vulnerable body. He held out his arms and stared at the scrubbed blue sky.

CHANGE.

CHANGELING.

I am the Lizard King.

Jim stood and opened his eyes. No cameras, no grasping hands. It was, once again, an alleyway of old brickwork, flooded with lambent fog. The raven had disappeared, but ahead of him—not twenty feet away—glimmered a streetlight. Like the sign, it was archaic in design, emitting a plush yet tasteless glow. It was not, however, the streetlight that demanded Jim's attention, but rather the indi-vidual standing beneath it.

Jim blinked sweat from his eyes, took a deep breath, and started toward him.

"There is a gentleman," the individual said, "rather the worse for wear."

"I guess I was born that way," Jim said, drawing nearer.

The man laughed—a dry sound, like splitting wood. He was of slight build, with a wave of black hair and a full mustache. His eyes were dark, yet penetrative, sparkling beneath a well-formed brow, and his clothes were as old-fashioned as the streetlight he stood beneath. Jim—a disciple of the written word—knew exactly who he was.

"How shall the burial rite be read?" the slight man inquired. He pulled a watch from a pocket in his vest and flipped it open. The ticking sound grew loud again. Not booming, like before, but loud enough.

"The solemn song be sung?" Jim added.

The man nodded approvingly. "The requiem for the loveliest dead/that ever died so young?"

Jim took another step forward. "This is the craziest trip yet, man."

The man smiled and glanced at his watch. "A trip, you say?"

"Yeah ... I say."

"Do you know who I am?"

Jim laughed. His chest ached with the force of it. "Yeah, I know. You're the Acid Man, the King of Trips. Nothing more than a long, prolonged derangement of the senses, inviting me—as ever—to obtain the unknown."

"Am I real?"

"You're real in my head," Jim replied at once. "So yeah ... that makes you real."

"And if I were to inform you that I am real *outside* your head?"

"You're Edgar Allan Poe," Jim said, smiling. "You died in eighteen forty-something."

"Nine," Poe said.

"Yeah ... nine. You *can't* be real outside my head."

"But if I am?"

Jim smiled again, but his eyes dulled with uncertainty. "Then I would say that on this occasion ... I really *have* obtained the unknown."

"The unknown," Edgar Allan Poe said, and his dark eyes danced. "Welcome to my world, James."

"Oh the bells, bells, bells/what a tale their terror tells/of despair." Poe let the watch swing, pendulum-like, from its chain. "How they clash, and clang, and roar/what a horror they outpour...."

Jim cocked his head, listening to the watch's infinitesimal cogs strike unnatural sounds in the musty air. It sounded more like a heartbeat, he thought. His own, perhaps, thumping life into this esoteric body. He shuffled forward, standing now in the stale glow of the streetlight. A single glance upward, looking for the raven, expecting to see its ghostly radiance high above, like the moon behind cloud. But there was nothing. It was just him and the man.

Poe.

"Time is running slight," he said, snapping the watch closed and dropping it back into his vest pocket.

"Same for everyone," Jim said.

"But it ticks so loud for you," Poe said. "Jangling and wrangling. So close."

Jim raised one eyebrow. "Should I be afraid, Mr. Poe?"

"What is there to fear?"

"You tell me," Jim replied. "Your watch stopped ticking over a hundred years ago; I would expect you to have all the answers."

Poe nodded. He leaned against the streetlight, casting no shadow.

"We are very alike, James," he said. "Both of us flexing—raging—from our dark, internal corridors, largely condemned and misunderstood. We are children of arcane verse ... American poets."

"Why did you bring me here?"

Poe held out his hands. "You brought yourself."

"I followed your bird. Your soul."

"Drawn by the unknown ... testing reality."

"Why?"

"Because, like me, you're curious. You seek truths in untoward places." Poe pushed away from the streetlight. He took two silent steps toward Jim. The fog swirled around him—odd, dancing shapes. "I understand you, James, like no one else. I know how your mind works, and what you desire. We're quite the same, you see."

"Really?"

"Indeed. Like you, I'll always wander this dark path. I'll always be a word man."

"Better than a bird man," Jim said.

The fog curled and waned, and Jim could see, behind Poe, a wooden door. His mind continued its trickery; the door was not part of any building, or built into any wall, but stood alone, rather plain, appearing to hover in the thinning fog as if some divine brush had painted it into existence. Jim took a step toward it, half-smiling.

"What is this?" he asked.

Poe looked from Jim to the door, and then back to Jim. The watch thumped in his pocket, and Jim's heart kept time.

"The Door of Perception," Poe replied.

"I would think, Mr. Poe," Jim started, "that you could be more original."

"I may surprise you yet."

A legend had been inscribed upon the door—neat little letters. Jim had to step closer to read them:

> Who entereth herein, a conqueror hath bin;
> Who slayeth the dragon; the shield he shall win.

Jim felt a runnel of sweat trickle from his hairline, into the hollow of his cheek. He looked at Poe, searching his eyes for some suggestion of unreality— a frailty in the seams, perhaps, where imagination had hurriedly put him together. But Poe showed no such weaknesses; he appeared as real as anything Jim had seen.

I need to come down, Jim thought. *I need to escape.* He reached out and touched Poe, then turned and touched the door. Both solid. Both *there.*

The ticking sound continued to make the air shudder. Jim was no longer sure if it was the man's watch, or his heartbeat.

He touched the door again. "Where does it lead?"

"The Other Side," Poe said, smiling.

"Naturally."

"Time is running slight, James." Poe touched the door and with a childlike cry it swung inward. Jim's gaze was dragged to the opening: a rectangular rift in the fog. He could see nothing of the Other Side, only darkness: a bed of black fuel waiting to be ignited.

"It's a grave," Jim said. He tried to inch away but could not. "If I step through that doorway, all of this becomes real. I'll never wake up."

Poe raised his eyebrows. "How much of the unknown do you truly wish to obtain?"

"I'm not afraid." But his heartbeat suggested otherwise. Like the watch, it clashed and clanged and roared. Disorientation swept over him and he staggered either forward or backward, his legs buckling, the fog whirling in his brain. He remembered the arms that had thrust from the alleyway walls, and wished that he could feel them now. They would grab and scratch and make him bleed, but they would hold him upright and keep him from falling into that terrible doorway.

"Come, James," Poe said, stepping toward the darkness.

"I think I'll stay here," Jim said, trying to back away, but the doorway inched toward him. He turned around, his breath catching in his throat, and then the doorway shifted—to the side, and then in front of him again.

"Truths and answers abound." Poe's eyes glistened like the raven's feathers.

"I think I'll just wake up now."

"Come ..." And with a single step Poe disappeared into the darkness, leaving nothing but his voice, spiraling in the air, as thin as candle smoke: "Come ... follow me down."

Jim tried to—

WAKE UP

—convince himself that none of this was happening, and with the same mindspace he fought/thought to resist the doorway. But it *pulled* him, tempting, like a drug he had already taken. The more he struggled, the closer he got ... until finally, with his heart crashing and a terrible moan rising from his chest, he succumbed.

Darkness: a thousand nights crammed into one tiny space.

The door slammed closed.

❦   ❦

Ladies and gentlemen ... from Los Angeles, California ... The Doors.

He heard the band's driving intro to "Break On Through" and stepped into the spotlight. The crowd erupted; he could feel the air trembling. Adoration, like a warm sheet falling over his cold body. *A pall,* he thought, trying to gaze beyond the stage lights, hoping to see their faces. They rippled and flapped and created such a frenzy of sound, but he could see only darkness. He slithered to the mic stand, as he always did, listing slightly, and prepared to sing the opening verse. The lyrics were ingrained in his mind, but the words that came from his mouth were all wrong: a deviant, broken, criss-cross of mad language. Nobody appeared to notice, however; the band continued to play, and the crowd kept cheering.

"The darkness in my temps âme/mort in le desert...."

Where's my head, man? This is wrong, all wrong—

He could hear ticking, thumping ... beyond the applause, the wild, flapping crowd.

"Beautreillis dreaming/L'enfant cries/le corbeau comes to eat my eyes...."

Jim screamed into the mic: a blistering torrent of bruised sound. It felt like he was chained to some crazy carnival ride, spinning and flashing while a calliope played. *Get me off this thing,* he thought. He tried to tilt out of the spotlight, but it followed him across the stage, as close as a tattoo. *Get me OFF.* The audience flapped their devotion, like the rumble following a thunderclap, and the band played on. Jim turned to them, confounded ... only to see a grotesquery so spectacular that all the strength deserted his legs. He fell to his knees—wanted to cry.

They played their instruments with notable gusto, with normal hands and bodies, but from the collars of their normal clothes sprouted oily, ravens' heads. Their beaks were long and black, and their round eyes glimmered in the stage lights.

I'm still tripping, Jim thought, getting slowly to his feet. *I didn't wake up, I'm still—*He turned again to the crowd and at that moment the house lights came on. The theater blazed and Jim could see everything: the main floor and balcony, the doors and walls and catwalks. And, of course, he could see his audience ... a million thunderous fans.

Not human—not even close.

Ravens packed the auditorium. The air was almost solid with them, bursting from their seats, scattering feathers, without room to fully work their wings, sinking down and bursting up again. They cawed and flapped, creating dissonance that sounded like riotous applause. And beyond this sound, beyond the music, he could still hear that ticking; that heartbeat.

Clash and clang and roar.

Jim held out his arms, shrieked, and ran to the edge of the stage. He threw himself off, and for a—

heartbeat

—moment thought he would fly, but then he was plummeting ... through feathers and beaks and claws. The theater floor opened up and he fell for too long. *So this is the Other Side,* he thought. *No one here gets out alive.* Laughter touched the edges of his scream, and just as he began to believe that he would fall forever, he landed in a twisted room of Poe's design, where the sound of his heartbeat shook the wooden floorboards, and where the raven was waiting.

"Four days prior to my death," the raven said, "I was found on a street here in Baltimore, in a most disheveled state. I was incoherent ... bewildered, having been missing for a number of days. Many questions were asked, not least of them how I came to be wearing somebody else's clothes. I was hastened to Washington College Hospital, where I regained consciousness only long enough to declare, 'Lord help my poor soul,' and then I passed into this otherworld ... Night's Plutonian Shore."

"Yeah, I remember reading about it," Jim said. "So much mystery surrounding your death. That's some way to go, man."

The raven nodded. It was perched upon a crooked tower of ancient books, among them Swedenborg's *Heaven and Hell,* Machiavelli's *Belphegor,* and Sir Launcelot Canning's *The Mad Trist.* Dust puffed rhythmically from between the dry pages as Jim's heartbeat rolled through the floorboards.

"My wife, Virginia, died," the raven said, "and my world turned to darkness. No—an unimaginable blackness. Take a knife to darkness, cut it, and it would bleed the stuff of my world. Of course I turned to the demon drink—prolonged my senses to obtain the unknown. I believed in a between-world wherein Virginia lay as pale as cloud, her eyes open, her sweet heart moving. I strived to reach this world by way of alcohol ... and sometimes I did; I held my dearest Virginia, in reverie, and my tears fell into her open eyes. Such ardor affects one's state of mind, and mine deteriorated quickly. My life was in pieces, and so I sought, in my delusion, to obtain another."

The raven flapped its wings. The tower of books creaked, and with a little snap of sound the bird hit the air, to alight, moments later, upon a bust of Pallas. Jim followed its short flight with glazed eyes. He sat against a stone wall and waited for this to be over.

Was there a quicker way out? Jim glanced around Poe's room. It was a grand space, confined by the detritus of creativity: the books and the bust, of course, along with crates and coffins that spewed exoticisms: an angel of the odd; the musings of Thingum Bob, Esq.; an oblong box; a loss of breath. The crates were stacked to the vaulted ceiling. There were window ledges, but no windows, only the shapes of windows carved into the stone. Likewise there was no door. The wooden floor ticked and thumped, and oval portraits (depicting yet more oddities) trembled on the walls.

No way out.

The raven rapped and tapped upon the bust, demanding Jim's attention.

"Thought I," it said, "that a man whose coat is worn and frayed will simply acquire a new one. Could the same not be done with a man's life ... to cast aside the cracked shell and inhabit one of fortitude? My diminished mind certainly believed so, and thus began my peculiar endeavor."

Jim looked at the shapes of the windows, seeking some seam of light, something he could rift. There was nothing. He studied the gaps between the floorboards, which sighed with every frantic crash of his heart.

Rap-tap upon the bust again.

The raven ruffled its feathers. "It was a desperate period for me—seeking a new body, one not so forlorn, so broken. For the simplest transition, I sought an individual not unlike myself, slightly younger, perhaps, but ablaze with the fire of creativity. In time I made the acquaintance of a brilliant young poet named Christopher Reynolds, and through wile, device, and dementia attempted to possess his physical form."

Jim looked at the raven. He imagined souls floating in the breeze, a glowing menagerie, seeking some warm place to land.

"You have to remember," said the raven, "that I was very sick ... confused."

"That's what happens when you crawl back in your brain," Jim said.

"For several days we struggled, clawing and biting. I assumed his clothing, but nothing more; Reynolds's soul was lion-shaped and it bested me. He threw me—shattered and delirious, still dressed in his clothes—to the cold streets. The fight was over; I had lost. My life was finished. In the passages of delirium before my final breath, I realized my mistake, and vowed that it would be different next time. 'Lord help my poor soul,' I uttered, and turned then to my raven form. And for these last one hundred and eighteen years I have flown Night's Plutonian Shore—an ancient lunatic—waiting for the right soul ... the right *poet* ... so that I might swoop and live again, young and beautiful, infinite with creativity, as dark as sin."

Jim tilted his head and blinked. His heart thumped harder.

"And here you are," the raven said.

"Except none of this is real," Jim said.

"If that's true, you have nothing to fear." The raven bristled, its feathers so slick they looked wet. "I'm taking your life, James. That's why you're here."

Jim got to his feet. He pushed away from the wall and took two sideways, unsteady steps. "You're just a dream. Or some freight train of hallucination barreling through my consciousness. I can't believe this is happening."

"Think of me as an angel," the raven said, "with wings where I had shoulders ..." It held up one talon. "... as smooth as these claws."

"I want to wake up now," Jim muttered.

The raven cawed and, once again, rapped its hooked beak upon the bust. Cracks appeared in Pallas's smooth white eyes. "I'll not make the same mistake again, James. The eyes, you see ... the eyes are the windows to the soul. This time I know the way in."

Jim shook his head and screamed.

WAKE UP!

"Be not afraid," the raven said, and Jim heard its wings snap at the air. "You don't want your life, anyway. Your audience—your world—is full of scavengers, tearing you to pieces. They don't understand you. *Nobody* understands you."

Jim remembered the grabbing arms and camera flashes. His heart slammed like an earthquake and he saw, in his mind's eye, his audience: a million frenzied birds, ready to claw.

"No," he said. His voice seemed far away.

Even the band ... different creatures.

I'm alone, he thought, and closed his eyes.

"From the thunder and the storm," the raven said. "And the cloud that took the form/(when the rest of Heaven was blue)/of a demon in my view."
Its wings made thunder, and all Jim saw was darkness.

Follow me down.

Dawn sun. A blind red eye, unblinking in the east. The smell of oil and sand and the sound of weeping ... of hurting. Jim stood among the chaos, naked, violated. Blood dried in the dead Indian's hair. His brown hands touched nothing. A breeze rippled his clothes. Jim felt the soul-lizard inside him, twisting like a child. He embraced it and kept it warm. NOW YOU'RE MINE AND I AM YOURS. *He felt the stroke of its tongue, the flick of its tail. The chaos made crazy shadows. Jim looked at his. It slithered and pulsed and Jim thought,* SEE ME CHANGE.

Time is running slight.
I understand you, James.

We're quite the same, you see.
Follow me down.

CHANGE.
CHANGELING.
It opened its eyes.
I am the Lizard King.

The lizard's blood ran cold and slick and angry. Its scales flushed with fresh color, and it squatted close to the trembling floor. The raven swept low and dragged its talons across the lizard's rigid back. The lizard hissed and flicked its tongue. It struck with one claw, but the raven was out of reach. It flapped its wings and ascended to the top of the book tower.

"I'll destroy your soul," said the bird. "I'll leave your body empty and gasping, and then I'll simply glide inside."

"And if my body dies?" the lizard said.

"It is young and strong," the raven replied. "And not ready for death."

"You should know I'm not afraid."

"The foolhardiness of youth." The raven shook its feathers. "You think you know darkness; you write songs about 'The End' ... but you know nothing. When you have lost the one thing you truly loved ... when the eye of madness glares long and hard upon you ... when shadows touch your every waking moment and fill your mind with screams ... only then will you know darkness. But you, lizard, are yet a shimmer; and I shall fill that beautiful body, and take it to incredible places."

With a passionate cry the raven took wing, rising from its perch and soaring toward the lizard. It extended its claws, screeching, wanting to strip its thorny skin. But the lizard flexed its spines and lashed forward with snapping jaws. They collided with harsh cries and an explosion of black feathers. The lizard felt its tough skin tear, its cold blood drip. It raked its claws across the raven's wing, shedding yet more feathers, and then the bird was rising again, to the lip of a crate, where it squawked and dragged its wounded wing.

The lizard showed its forked tongue. "You're going to have to do better than that."

The raven rapped and tapped in anger. "As will you, lizard."

And so began the clash of souls. No way to tell how long it lasted; no sense of night or day about the room—only the thud of Jim's heartbeat, running alternately fast and slow, connected to his soul as it fought, and then rested.

They attacked in spells, coming together in a mad and angry tangle. The lizard would clamp its jaws on the raven's wing, and the raven would gouge and peck, finding the soft flesh between its scales. They formed a new shape, a new monster: a lizard with wings; a raven with scales. This twisted creature would roll and scramble across the dusty floor, swishing its tail and spraying feathers, until—too exhausted to fight—it would separate to its component parts, blood-streaked and hurting, needing time to catch breath.

"You can't beat me, raven," the lizard said. Its yellow eyes flashed.

"Give me time." The raven's feathers dripped red. Its beak was notched and dull, like an old spearhead.

"You've had your time."

Another clash, squawking and crying. The raven covered the lizard's eyes with one wing and pecked at its unprotected stomach. The lizard twisted and whipped its tail, spines smashing against the bird's body. They rolled across the floor, scattering fragments of Poe's mind. The tower of books crumpled with a monstrous groan, old pages tearing loose and splashing across the floor. Crates toppled, spilling their arcane contents. Portraits were punched from the walls, and sagged in their cracked frames.

Puddles of blood. Two bruised, torn souls. The raven flapped with wounded wings to the lid of a split coffin. The lizard slithered into the shadow of an overturned crate and licked its broken scales.

"Almost over," the raven said. "Time is running slight."

The lizard trembled. How long had it been here, trapped in this fog-covered nightmare—this unforgiving trip? Days? Months? Its life before seemed like a long-ago thing. It recalled the baked earth of authority, and the cool nights of love. It recalled crawling into the public eye and seeing its blindness. Verses and choruses tumbled across its memory, as thin as matchsticks. Pamela's hair, smelling like smoke and honey, and the touch of her lips. Sleeping on rooftops and in the backs of cars. Mescaline and acid and the cold, constant drip of liquor. What was real? Could it be that the life it thought it had been living— the rock star, the poet, the Lizard King—had been an elaborate dream all along?

Had this dream stopped?

Jim's heartbeat drummed through the floorboards, but it was slower now. Weaker. *That's my body*, the lizard thought. *Slowly dying*. And with this realization came the knowledge that the heartbeat was the doorway. It was the *only* real thing. The only way out.

My heart. The lizard shifted its bleeding body. *My life*.

Beating slowly ... slowly.

The raven attacked again (motivated, also, by the rock star's dying body). It swooped with heavy black weight and sent the lizard spinning into one corner. It followed with its talons and beak, tearing the lizard's hard skin.

"His body is mine," the raven cried, blood dripping from its claws.

The lizard blinked its yellow eyes, puffed out its spines, and fought. Another long and wearing clash, entangled for hours, biting and scratching, lurching through the scattered ruins of Poe's mind. There came a final, fatigued flash of anger, and then the souls separated. The raven limped to its refuge and hid beneath one fractured wing, while the lizard pulled itself to the center of the room.

My heart, it thought.

The sound, now, was all too slow.

My life.

It was beneath the floorboards. Beneath this place of dark invention.

The only way out.

While the raven cowered and bled, the lizard gathered its remaining strength and, with claws flashing and tail slapping, assailed the trembling floor. It sought—as had been the case all night—the merest seam of unreality, and eventually found one: a crack in the floorboards, which with one hard lash of the tail became a split, and then a rift. The heartbeat grew louder, and cool blue light fanned from the wide seam. The lizard worked furiously, smashing and clawing great chunks of the floor away. The closer it got to—

life

—escape, the brighter the light became, the louder the heartbeat.

The raven fluttered from its perch and limped toward the lizard, dragging both wings. It screeched and showed its talons, defiant, but powerless. Its eyes were dull black stones and its feathers were crumpled. The lizard spared it a single glance, and then struck with its tail, connecting hard with the bird and flinging it across the room. It thudded against the wall, a broken thing. Blood-mottled feathers settled around it, as thick as oil.

The lizard roared—more lion than reptile—and clawed away a jagged section of floor. The light that erupted was geyser-like, rushing to the high ceiling, filling the room like music. The lizard had to turn away, momentarily blinded, and when it was able to look again it could see the source of that brilliant light.

His heartbeat. His life.

A door.

It shook in its frame as the life it knew—rock star, poet, and lover—pounded on the other side. And as the lizard crawled into the light and through the doorway, it heard two things clearly. The first was the raven:

"This is just the beginning," it squawked from its shattered place. "I will get you soon ... *soon* ... *SOOOOOOOOOOOOON.*"

The second sound was softer, kinder. The lizard clung to it as it fell through the doorway and into the light. Pamela's voice, like rain on piano strings.

"*Don't leave me, Jim,*" she said, and the lizard closed its eyes—could feel her hair, and the sweet touch of her breath. "*Don't leave me.*"

He opened his eyes and looked, immediately, for the raven, but all he could see, blessedly, was Pamela's face. Her crystal eyes and freckled skin. She kissed him. One of her tears fell on his upper lip. He smiled and licked it away—thought for one moment that his tongue was forked.

"All right, all right," he said. "Pretty neat, pretty good."

Beyond Pamela, the Baltimore night was glittering black, skimmed with cloud. No fog. No raven. Jim sat up and Pamela kissed him again.

"We thought we'd lost you," she said. "We came out here looking for you, but you were nowhere to be found. We looked everywhere, and when we came out again ... there you were."

"I guess I was in the shadows," Jim said. He got to his feet, brushing grit from his leather pants. The rest of the Doors were there, clustered around the backstage entrance. They looked concerned ... frightened, even.

"One of these days, man," Ray said. "You're not going to wake up."

"I'll always wake up," Jim said. "I just don't know where."

He stepped away from them, leaning slightly to one side, his heels tapping on the ground. He could feel the lizard inside him, healing.

"Where are you going, man?"

Jim didn't answer. He kept walking.

Rue Beautreillis, Paris, France.
Saturday July 3, 1971.

The city slept, lights flickering like candles, with just a hint of violet dawn burning the horizon.

The raven alighted upon the balcony of the fourth-floor apartment, shook its slick black feathers, and waited.

The End, Beautiful Friend

The Happiest Hell on Earth

By

John Skipp & Cody Goodfellow

May 5, 1972
To: Spec. Agent R. Stanley
Federal Bureau of Investigation

As you probably know, Prisoner #0003 has died, after 37 years in solitary confinement for his role in the Animal Wars. He was the last and longest-held of the original conspirators, the rest having either been executed or paroled to their new homeland in Florida when Nixon and Governor Gator signed the Animal Liberation treaty last year.

That he resisted extradition to Moreauvia while refusing to disavow his crimes was no reflection on his daily conduct. He was a model prisoner until the day he leapt from his window in the VIP block, having torn the bars out with his trunk, in a display of strength we would never have expected, given his age. He never had any contact with the outside world, but even after his movie was banned and the UN declared him a war criminal, the elephant-man still got a lot of fan mail from the forty-eight "two-legged" states.

Because Mr. Hoover always took such a special interest in his case, we believe #0003 was just waiting for the death of your illustrious Director: not only to end his own life, but to reveal the enclosed manuscript, which we found neatly stacked upon his cot. The fact that he waited *only one day* after Mr. Hoover's death lends credence to this interpretation.

I truly shudder to think of the effect this will have on the public, if any of it is proven true, but I earnestly hope that it will be buried no longer. This poor, divided nation deserves to know why so many millions of Americans still live in the trees, and who is truly responsible.

That is why I have also forwarded copies to Ben Bradlee, Jack Anderson, Jann Wenner, William F. Buckley, and people at several other media outlets.

Let it be known: I am a Republican and a patriot, and am prepared to face all consequences. I do this not to bring our country down, but to restore it to its greatness.

Good luck, God bless America, and apologies for the inconvenience.

Sincerely,
From: Warden R. Clampett
Texarkana Federal Prison

DOCUMENT A
PART ONE: ON THE ISLAND OF LOST SOULS

The rosy dawn paints the gray sands. The bull-men in their white shrouds wait, snorting, pawing. Disturbed by something on the wind.

The Master stands in the launch, arms at his sides like a conductor at rest. Behind me, the jungle clenches like a green fist, flexing its claws. They have all come to see the return of the Other with the Whip, and what he has brought with him.

M'ling crouches in the bow, pointed ears back to bask in the sea breeze on his black face. The less favored beasts bend to their oars, and Montgomery sneaks a nip from a flask, as he answers the Master's questions. Loaded to the gunwales with supplies and fresh specimens—a puma, a llama, six hutches of rabbits, and a pack of excited staghounds.

But all eyes are hooked on the sinking lifeboat towed behind the launch, and the solitary creature sitting in it.

What kind of animal would be so dangerous that the Doctor would not have it in the launch?

From the crown of a palm tree, Virgil the monkey-man howls. "A Five-Man! A Five-Man, like me!"

By slow, painful turns, the launch creeps into the cut in the shore. The bull-men bow to the Master and the Other as they unload the cages and crates. I take up the ledger and, with a quill pen in my trunk, make a tally of the goods.

The strange man climbs awkwardly out of his lifeboat and wallows up onto the beach.

Claws lose their purchase on boxes and drop them in the surf. All eyes follow the Stranger as he approaches the Master. Without fear, without bowing his head.

He was on a schooner touring the Galapagos Islands that got wrecked in a storm. It was nothing less than a miracle that Montgomery's chartered tramp steamer happened upon him in his lifeboat. The Captain put the Stranger off with Montgomery after he came between poor M'ling and the vicious, bullying crew. "Someone is sure to come looking for me...."

"Here," the Master says, "they are unlikely to find you."

The Stranger asks for a radio, and is told we have none. The steamer puts in only thrice a year, and the island is well off the shipping lanes. Though uninvited, he is to be our guest.

The Stranger looks from the bull-men to M'ling to the Ape Man to me, and shows his blunt teeth, sharp tongue. His eyes burn us. He offers to pay for his lodging, and to make himself useful however he can.

Taller than the Other, younger than the Master, skin burned red and blistered. Dark hair covers his weak chin, but he walks erect, in tight circles when nowhere else to go. He was never an animal. Perhaps he was never a child.

The Stranger puts a stick of paper in his soft mouth. Fire sprouts from his hand and sets the stick alight. We gasp. He has fire in his hands, and smoke spills from his thin lips. Perhaps he is a machine.

The Master asks of his education. "We are both scientists, and this is a biological station, of a sort."

Still chewing us with his eyes, the Stranger says, "I have some experience with running complex operations, and I'm a quick study. I was raised on a farm, and I drove an ambulance in the War ... after the Armistice was signed. I'm not afraid of a little blood."

"Our work here is of great import, but of too delicate a nature to take you into our confidence, just yet."

"I'm in your hands, Dr. Moreau," the Stranger says.

We have peace and order on our island. The Master tells us it is not so in the wider world. We are humble before the Law. Until he comes among us, we can dream of no other life.

The Master leaves the Stranger in an outer apartment of the compound, and locks the inner door to the courtyard. He summons me to attend to his initial examination of the new specimens.

He needs me. The Other drinks poison to make his mind weak and his notes are sloppy, and though my blunt forelimbs are clumsy, my trunk can do the fine work, even sometimes with the Knife, and the Master says I have an extraordinary head for figures. I have seen pictures of my ancestors, of the clay from which the Master made me. I am stunted, a dwarf. The House of Pain made me small, but bright.

I do not carry a whip or a gun, but the Master gave me a blue serge suit like his, and I work with him. The others in the compound must wear white. They are proud of their status but hate the white, which hides no dirt. The beasts in the ravine despise me, for though many of them have better hands and truer voices, I live in the House of Pain. I was made to teach them to speak and to read, but they have come as far as the Knife and the Needle can take them. To learn more only teaches them that they are still beasts.

The Stranger hunts us.

While the Master begins to remake the puma with Montgomery, the Stranger leaves his apartment and ambles into the jungle. He has shaved the fur from his face, but kept a tiny strip of hair just above his lips. It makes him look less like an animal, and yet more dangerous.

I cannot keep up with his long-legged strides without giving myself away, but he stops and sits beside the creek and blows smoke into the air.

The secret of fire is not in making it, but making it work. The burning in his head comes out on the paper in his lap. With swift stabs and slashes of the pencil, his fine fingers make a window in the paper. The creek and the canebreak beyond are trapped in it; and then, as if summoned, Darius skulks out of the shadows, eyes greenly flashing.

Most of them cannot recall or even speak the names I gave them, but this is of little import to me. Was it not Adam's first task to name the beasts of the field? Even if they failed this simple test, I did not fail mine.

Darius stoops on all fours to slurp water from the creek. He knows no shame. Time and again, the Master has ripped out his claws, but they always grow back. Even his flesh hates the Law. His tawny flanks heave with panting. The faded spots on his piebald hide flush. His muzzle and paws are speckled with red.

Fear. I would trumpet and run on all fours, so strong is my terror. But the Stranger only says, "Hello," and draws the leopard man in the depth of his sin.

With a coughing growl, Darius leaps the creek and coils, ready to pounce. The Stranger stands erect and stares Darius down with his redly flashing eyes.

The leopard man runs away into the green jungle. The Stranger shakes his head and turns to a fresh page. Then he turns on me.

"Hello, little fellow. You're a shy one, aren't you? Well, you needn't be frightened of me. Here...." His teeth flash, but not in threat. He reaches into his pocket and holds out a handful of peanuts.

I trample out of my hiding place. My ears flap and my trunk unfurls in a vulgar display of threat, but the Stranger barks until he coughs and spits on the ground. "You really are some sort of a beast-man, aren't you? Not a hoodoo or a gaff, at all. Now, what would be a good name for you...?"

"I have a name," I tell him. I try to make my voice large. It cracks and he utters his strange bark again, like the hyena-swine's mating call.

My trunk reaches out to snort up a nut. "My name...." My remade throat closes, my tongue twists, spitting shells. "Diogenes."

The Stranger's pencil carves a bloated, droopy ellipse, with a wilted triangle on either side, and a lazy S dangling from its belly. Then two smaller circles beneath it, and short, stubby rectangular limbs. The eyes are bigger than mine, the humors out of balance to drive this paper Diogenes mad with glee. My own eyes are small and weak and sad.

He shakes his head again. "I can't do justice to you. Nobody could believe it, nobody would fall in love with it. But you're real enough, aren't you, little fellow? D'you know any tricks?"

My clumsy hands reach out for the book. He turns it around and shows it to me. I take his pencil in my trunk and write my name under his picture.

Cradling it in my hands, I turn the pages with my trunk. He has seen many of us. The hyena-swine creeps up on a rabbit hutch. A wolf woman falls upon a swine man and destroys his crude cane-stick hut. The pink homunculi at play in the undergrowth. A headless rabbit sprawls in the grass, bejeweled with flies. The leopard man slakes his thirst after a murder. "He has broken the Law," I grunt.

Behind the picture of Darius, I find sketches of other beast men, with no claws or teeth—soft, like the homunculi, but with gloves and short pants. "It's not ... a good likeness ... of a rabbit."

He barks again, but does not smile. "Animals are no fit judges of artwork," he says. "And it's a mouse."

"I've read Homer and Aesop ... in the orig ... original Greek ... and Latin." There are more sketches of this curious animal-baby, on the corner of each page. When the pages slip from my blunt thumbnail, the little rodent dances like a little live thing.

"That ... no, don't look at that." He snaps the book away and tears the page out, balls it up and puts it in his mouth. His red face dims almost purple. He chokes it down. "That's over and gone. They stole it from me, but they won't take anything from me again." He sucks in fire and blows out smoke, and slowly grows calm again. "How does he do it, Diogenes? You're a sharp one. You can tell Uncle Wilbur."

I don't know what he means. He offers me more peanuts, but I know not to take them. His eyes are like whips.

"You're a true friend to your Master, aren't you? Well, never mind. I'll find out for myself."

We go back to the compound. The Stranger locks himself in his apartment and says he must sleep, but he does not sleep. From lying in his hammock staring at Aesop's Fables—what kind of man cannot read Greek?—to pacing the room until it is filled with smoke, he wastes the day. I watch through the outer window that looks on the ocean, but I cannot imagine what disturbs him. He has the key to his cage.

Inside, the puma cries out. Her cries send him pacing faster. She is a long way yet from being born.

M'ling brings him his supper. The Stranger hides his book of drawings. Montgomery comes in and he and the Stranger share a glass of poison. He warns the Stranger to be careful in his wandering, for the island is dangerous, then leaves by the inner courtyard door, but he forgets to lock it.

The poison overtakes the Stranger. He has bad dreams. Crying out in echo of the unmade puma, he says, "No, Father, don't," and covers his head. This strange creature is no stranger to the Whip.

In the morning, his hammock is soiled. M'ling sniffs at the stain and the Stranger's discarded rags and says he has marked his place.

The newborn woman cries out. The Stranger pokes at his breakfast for a while, then goes through the door into the compound. Slow on my flat feet, I follow.

The dogs snarl and bark. The Stranger runs them to the span of their leashes, then ducks into the open back door of the House of Pain.

Dark inside. Hotter than outside. Clean. White porcelain and polished steel. Chains. And the new woman on the table. Still red and wet and weeping, mewling lost in the throes of rebirth.

The Master shouts, takes him by the arm and hurls him from the room into the courtyard, then drives him back to his apartment and slams the door.

The Other is shamefaced. The Master almost whips him. "This uninvited guest will be our undoing. His meddling could ruin the work of a lifetime!"

"He doesn't know the score," hisses Montgomery, "but he wants to. Too eager by half, says I. In fact, when I riddle upon it, I wonder if his coming here was an accident, after all."

"That is my principal fear. He must be taken into our confidence or dealt with, but I can't yet spare the time."

Montgomery chuckles. "If he's as fine a specimen as you seem to think, perhaps you could turn his presence here to the good—"

The Master looms over the Other. The puma's blood on his smock is the only color on his white marble face. "This Wilbur Dixon is a singular creature, but imagine his blood in their bodies. No, they would walk erect and speak, but I doubt they could be less human." The Master sees me watching, and orders me to find the Stranger.

He has left his apartment. He races, but I can follow the trail of his smoke through the trees.

Someone else stalks us. I scent Darius' bitter musk on the rank morning heat. The Stranger can smell nothing but his own smoke. He is helpless before the hunched gray shape that drops out of a tree before him.

I wheeze with relief. The monkey man bows and presents his fingers for counting. Amused, the Stranger returns the gesture, but he can make no sense of Virgil's chattering.

"You poor creature! You were a spider monkey, weren't you?"

"I am a man, like you, yes yes. We talk big thinks, yes yes?" Virgil prances and chatters around the Stranger, who makes the sound he calls laughter, and throws him nuts.

"What has that monster done to your tail?"

Angry Virgil tries to stand erect and puff out his chest. "I am a man like you! The Master made me, good Virgil, yes yes, a man!"

The Stranger puts a hand on Virgil's head and strokes his gray fur. "You had a tail once. He's taken all of your God-given gifts, and for what? This Moreau is a butcher, and the worst sort of villain. Someone should make him pay for his crimes against you."

"Moreau a butcher, yes no," Virgil chatters. "His is the hand that wounds! His is the hand that heals!"

"Where are the rest of you?" the Stranger asks. "How many orphans are there?"

Virgil turns and scampers down the trail. "I will take you to them, yes yes. You must learn the Law."

The Stranger blunders through the canebreak after Virgil and emerges on the yellow waste. Sulfur and steam rise from the hot springs, masking the mouth of the ravine. I wait for them to disappear into the mist, when something rakes my back with claws of fire.

I forget myself, and trumpet wordless terror. My blood flows. I try to turn over, but I am pinned. I have no gun, no whip. I have never had tusks. I cannot even call for the Master.

Darius sinks his teeth into my tough hide and flays my scalp, then flies away. The Stranger brandishes a bloody rock, then throws it at the leopard man. He strikes him on the temple and sends him howling into a thorny thicket.

"You're safe now, little friend." He reaches out for my trunk, and lifts me up.

He goes into the ravine.

The stone walls draw close. They come out of their huts of thorns and palm fronds in the cracks of the rock to show fangs and claws and half-made hands. I count heads. Sixty-two. All but M'ling and Darius are here.

Pan lowers his goatish head to show his curling horns, fondles himself and strikes the rock with his hooves. The swine-folk hoot and the wolves growl, the dog-man grovels and licks the Stranger's boots.

A man walks among them, unarmed. He tests the Law. It is too much.

He shows no fear. The stink from him is not like an animal's fear. I doubt anyone but me can smell it. It is the stink of a deeper fear, buried under a mountain of will.

The gray-haired oldest one limps from his hovel and lifts himself upright on his staff. I call him Solon, for he speaks only the Law. His shaggy pelt hides his blind eyes, toothless mouth. "If it is a man, then let him say the Law!"

"The Law of the Jungle is the only law I see here," says the Stranger. "I see only animals stripped of their true nature and their gifts, and cast adrift."

The beast men roar and jeer. "Not to walk on all fours—that is the Law! Are we not men?"

"Not to spill blood—*that* is the Law! Are we not men?"

"Not to suck drink—*that* is the Law! Are we not men?"

The Stranger rages. "No, you are *not*! Not to do those things is not to be an animal, but has he taught you what it is to be a man?"

He takes out a little silver tool and blows into it. The single, piercing note traps every beast in the ravine. None of them have ever heard music.

He begins to play the swooning, swaying notes of a familiar tune—Saint-Saens's *Danse Macabre*, I know it from the Master's phonograph collection. Heads bobbing, eyes glazed, they become less than beasts, but Virgil knows at once what music is for.

Bobbing his furry head to the woozy melody, he prances in circles around the Stranger in uncanny imitation of the Stranger's stiff, inhibited gait. When he runs up the Stranger's back to snatch his hat, the Stranger does not punish him, but only quickens the whirling, maddening tune.

Virgil leaps to the ground and dances on his hands, holding the hat in place on his hindquarters, covering the stump of his tail. Then, flipping over and miming crapping into the hat, he offers it back.

The Stranger drops his harmonica and again makes that strange, bloodcurdling bark. He slaps his palms together to make a thunderous sound that drives the beasts back into their burrows. But then his brow darkens, and he looks angry. "Your Master never taught you to laugh?"

Silence, but a riot of scent. In the dim cave shadows, his eyes flash red.

Solon bellows, "His is the hand that wounds—"

The Stranger utters that frightening bark again. "Ask yourselves, if you are really men, what has he done for you? Your master, your creator, who rules by fear and pain, who left you to rot in sin and filth: what do you owe him?" He wipes his brow. The beasts are too captivated to rip him apart. It seems he must do it himself. His eyes shine, and stream down his face. "In the place I come from, you would all be celebrated for your gifts. Instead of a Master who whips and shuns you, you would have a loving father who gives you work and a purpose. And there would be no damnable House of Pain!"

Only a few of them understand his words, but then Virgil takes up a new chant. "No Pain! No pain!"

The others cannot even parrot his words, but they roar and stamp and crush their own huts in perfect imitation of his fury. My own trunk is lifted in the chorus.

We are so loud that none sees the dogs until they fall upon us.

The Master has returned. He holds the barking dogs to heel, but they have torn the hyena-swine's filthy white tunic. Montgomery cracks his whip over our heads.

A hairless pink sloth-child I call Claudius scurries up the Stranger's leg. He scoops it up and cradles it to his chest to shield it from the dogs.

Moreau holds out the Stranger's sketchbook. The drawing of Darius. "This one has broken the Law! We will have him."

"None escape! None escape!" The beasts chant.

"Not to spill blood—*that* is the Law!"

"That is your Law," the Stranger shouts, "but why should it be theirs? You give them only pain and turn them loose in the jungle, and grant them only enough sense to recognize that their creator has forsaken them!"

"You misunderstand my aim," the Master says, in a lower tone. "Please come back to the compound. I would rather have you know all than—"

"The Master is not a god. He is a man like all of you, and yes, an animal, too! He is not above the Law, is he? He and his lackey are only men, and they are only two, while you are many—"

"For God's sake, man, shut up!" the Other cracks his whip at the Stranger, who does not cower, but lunges at Montgomery, roaring, "Don't you dare!" and clouts him across the face.

The Master hurls the fire of death into the sky. Its thunderclap sends all of us down on all fours. "Mr. Dixon, we came here to save you from harm. But you have done us a mortal blow. Come with us now, before something transpires that cannot be undone."

The Stranger refuses to leave with the Master. Some of us growl and circle the arguing men, but the rest stand dumb, or cling to the earth as if it's trying to shake them off. If either of them had eyes to see, they could tell now who is the most human among us.

"If it will ease your suspicions," the Master says, and turns over his pistol. Montgomery refuses to disarm, and lewdly slurps from his flask. "Where's the leopard man?"

"He attacked your poor pachyderm houseboy, when you sent him to spy on me. He could be anywhere."

"Mr. Dixon, if you please." Bowing to the Stranger, he turns and walks down the ravine. The Other goes backwards after him with his pistol out before him. "Remember who's the Master here, you rum bastards."

The Other steps on the paw of the cringing hyena-swine. It whines and strikes him with its gnarled claw-hoof. He shoots it through the head.

The thunder is a long time falling away into silence.

"You rash idiot!" The Master takes off his straw hat. "What a terrible waste..."

"We all know who is the master here, Mr. Montgomery," says the Stranger. Gently, he sets down the sloth-child and follows the men. And I go with them.

The Master stitches my wounded scalp and sends me to sleep. Night falls, and the jungle is loud. The beast men claw at trees and stalk prey, battle, and breed in the dark. The Law is broken, and they want us to hear it.

The Master and the Stranger retire to the library to drink poison and talk. For a long time, the Master explains his great work, his failures and his triumphs. His dashed hopes and determination to go on. With fierce pride, he defends his studies. How the necessary pain of rebirth wipes away the animal memory, leaving a blank slate upon which to build a man. How vivisection and blood and tissue transplants led the way to this great mission, to uplift the animal kingdom into the brotherhood of man.

If only the Stranger could listen.

"Dr. Moreau, this place is an abomination. I beg you to reconsider my offer."

"Even if it were so simple, Mr. Dixon, I could never walk away from this place, and you could never take it over. I fully recognize the ethical burden of my undertaking, but it is only in the name of science—"

"Science! Like Communism, the rationale for all modern inhumanity. Neither men nor animals should be tortured as you do."

"To rear a child, one must flay away that which is animal, no? To be born is painful, and none of us asked for it. They are born anew, but they must be taught, like any new human. And my hand is not quick enough, sadly, to give them the gift of true humanity."

"You're a strange sort of parent, to turn your babes out into the wilderness! You gave up on them, but who has failed? Hard work and a little cleanliness, that's what's wanted here! Without constant hard work, discipline, and a little church, what men won't backslide into savagery?"

The Stranger fills his glass and drinks it. He puts a paper stick in his mouth and lets the smoke out of his head.

"My coming here was not entirely an accident," he says. "I believe it was destiny. You've had your say. Now listen to me.

"I was born in Chicago, but grew up on an apple farm in Kansas. My father … was a hardworking man, and he expected us to chip in. There was plenty of work for decent folks, but to make your way in the world, you had to have an idea. And you'd still have to work yourself half to death, just to end up with something worthwhile.

"But if you have a dream, then everyone and his brother is out to crush you. To steal your dream or just rip it to shreds and leave nothing behind. Believe me, Doctor, I know what it's like to have your dreams taken away."

He fills his glass again. "I had a dream, not so different from yours, in essence. I wanted to create life, and inspire wonder. I thought I could do it with films. I don't suppose you know, but I'm somewhat well known in America as an animator."

The Master and the Other share a look. Neither of them knows what it means.

"I make films using a series of drawings to simulate motion, life, emotion. We made the first cartoon with a full sound track. Our short cartoons were popular ... so popular, in fact, that none of the studios would distribute them without taking away ownership of my most beloved character. They called my work primitive trash, but what they couldn't buy or bully away from me, they simply stole. And they got the courts to back them up.

"Now, when I first landed on your island, I was shocked by what I saw, and horrified by your callous treatment of your creations. But when I look at these miserable, flea-bitten creatures, I feel certain that some good may still come of them. Their lives need not be nasty, brutish, and short."

The Master politely says, "I do not take your meaning, sir."

The Other barges in and cackles. He is very sick. "He's making you an offer, Master! He wants to buy your sideshow."

The Stranger sniffs. He is also sick. "Hollywood is not a sideshow, Montgomery. You've clearly abandoned their education. Consider it an extension of your experiment, if you will—"

"I think you should take him up on it, Guv." The Other limbers up his whip. "They're at the gate, rarin' to go, bags packed."

The beasts have not forgotten all of the Master's lessons. The walls of the compound are on fire.

"See what you've done!" the Master shoves the Stranger out onto the porch to see the flames and hear the cries of the beast-men. "Before you came, they were content—"

"You brought this on yourself, Doctor. I hope they will be more merciful to you than you were to them."

"Don't forget this one, Dixon." The door to the laboratory flies open and the red woman splashes into the room.

The Master has only begun to feed her the Needle and human blood—His blood—to change her mind. The Knife, however, has been busy. The freshly sculpted digits of her clawless paws drive her mad with agony. The cracked and reset pelvis betrays her when she tries to run on all fours.

But her broken mind and body are sound enough to choose between the two masters before her.

She pounces on Dr. Moreau.

Dixon shoots her in the flank. His hand shakes. He aims at the Master's heart, and then his hand falls.

A rock smashes the window behind Montgomery, who looks the room over once and shouts, "Damn it all," then flees.

With no claws, the puma-woman bats pitifully at the Master, but her teeth are still sharp. Her mouth closes on his forearm and snaps the bones. He howls for Montgomery.

She goes for his throat.

The Stranger closes his eyes and shoots. The red woman twirls in the air and trips on her insides, shrieks, and dies.

Without a word, the Stranger goes outside.

I come out from my hiding place. The Master orders me to leave him, and go to the surgery.

"Get all the alcohol … and douse my journals. My work must not fall into the wrong hands. And this man—"

"Please … Master…." Smoke pours in the windows. I will not need to fuel the fire. I try to move the Doctor, but he is too large, and he is ready to die.

"Go, Diogenes. You were a faithful assistant … and a good man."

The burning roof crashes through the room. I turn and run on all fours.

Outside, the wall has collapsed, and the beasts rampage through the burning house, hair on fire, mad with poison and the end of the Law. I can barely carry my own head, but I must tear off my blue serge suit, or I will meet the same fate as Mr. Montgomery, the Other with the Whip. Down on the beach, between the launches, they crowd round his body to get at the scraps.

I hide in the icehouse, beneath a pile of cadavers. The celebration goes on until dawn, when there is nothing left unburned.

I come out from my hiding place to wade through ashes. The beasts are gathered on the beach. In their midst, Wilbur Dixon stands with a gun in his hand. He hasn't enough bullets to kill them all, and they are far beneath even the reasoning of a loaded gun.

"I promised you a new life, without pain, with hope and the promise of becoming true men. I do not lie."

He points the gun at the sky and fires. A red flower of fire blooms and fades in the rosy dawn light.

He sets fire to a stick and blows out smoke. The beasts are captivated by this, but only for so long. They begin to close in on him. The Sayer of the Law is dead, a victim of his own rigid faith, and the new Law. But some memory of the sacred remains, for they carry his head.

I know I must join them, if I will not be next. I climb over the smoking bones of the Master's house.

I see it before the others.

It comes out of the fog at the mouth of the bay. A ship bigger than the compound.

When we see it, we fall down and moan. The Stranger sees me and smiles. He points the gun at me.

"His master's voice," he says.

DOCUMENT B
ADVERTISING CIRCULAR
(12/1/29)

WE'RE DRAFTING DOCTORS

Dixon Studios is hunting—for you!

Will Dixon's Barnyard is growing so rapidly that we have a crying need for visionary, dedicated artists and scientists, men who dream of bringing the fantastic to life, but who never, ever sleep.

Thanks to Dixon's patented animal cultivation techniques, there are amazing new opportunities in the film industry—both in financial and creative terms—for doctors, veterinarians, surgeons, chemists, anesthesiologists, chemists, biologists, animal trainers, nurses, and teachers. Apply today!

DOCUMENT C
H'WOOD REPORTER
(2/22/33)

MONKEY SEE, MONKEY DO STARRING MOXIE MONKEY, AN INT'L HIT; DIXON ANNOUNCES PLANS FOR FIRST FEATURE

After only four years, it's almost impossible to recall what Hollywood was like without Will Dixon.

The soft-spoken King of Family Entertainment has changed almost every aspect of filmmaking with his revolutionary "humanimal" performers. His forty-seven live-action *Animal Overtures* and *Barnyard Ballads* one-reelers outdid the Keystone Kops and Laurel & Hardy at pratfall comedy to become the most sought-after bookings to open RKO features, while bringing moral hygiene and innocent fantasy back to the movies. "Monkey See, Monkey Do," "Puss In Boots," and "The Three Little Pigs" each won Short Subject Oscars in 1930, 1932, and this year.

They also put the kibosh on the once-popular fledgling field of animated cartoons, which Will Dixon helped pioneer, before abandoning it after returning from the South Pacific with a miraculous discovery—which he has patented and steadfastly refuses to comment upon—that led to the first of his remarkable "humanimal" creations.

"My early work in animation was, sadly, a great big boondoggle," he admits. "The major studios were too eager to own the rights to my films and the characters, and they killed the Golden Goose. I was naïve, not wise to the ways of ancillary merchandising or the fine print in contracts, and it cost me plenty. But now, I've had the last laugh, as it were, because the expense of animated films has kept it from getting a foothold. And, frankly, the sad truth is, people just don't enjoy them. Why should they settle for a blinkered, diminished sketch of reality, when we have the tools to bring the fantastic to living, breathing life?"

Mr. Dixon has certainly learned from his early mistakes. The young studio mogul keeps a private army to watch over the hundred-acre Burbank laboratory-studio he still calls the Barnyard, and the neighboring "farm" where his curious menagerie of trained human-animal hybrids lives. When they are not singing and slinging pies in front of the cameras, Moxie Monkey, Darn Old Duck, Algy Gator, the Three Little Pigs and all the rest are as pampered as any stars, even if you'll never see them at Musso & Frank's without a phalanx of guards and trainers.

Dixon is not unaware of the controversy among some circles his creations have stirred up. To religious leaders who have lodged accusations of blasphemy, Dixon points out that farmers have been selectively breeding and changing farm animals to suit human usage. "Our humanimals are like my own children," he adds. "We're a big happy family."

The question labor leaders raise is harder to dismiss, however. "Dixon has created monsters with no legal status to replace human actors," Herb Rosenfeld, spokesman for the Screen Technicians Guild, said from his hospital bed at Temple Hospital, where he is recovering from injuries incurred during a recent Barnyard strike. "From there, it's a short leap to breeding an army of subhuman serfs to do his bidding, instead of paying a living wage to professional, fully human workers."

Only time will tell how this brewing dispute will shake out, but Dixon is single-mindedly fixed on the future … namely, on this Christmas, when his first three-reel feature will bow on every screen in the Paramount theater chain. Banjo, the story of a lonely little circus elephant with a unique gift, will be like nothing ever seen before, he promises. "I can't wait for the world's children to meet Gene, our little humanimal prodigy who will play the title role. And I know he can't wait to meet them."

DOCUMENT D
DIXON STUDIOS INTEROFFICE MEMO: CLASSIFIED
(5/16/36)

It has come to our attention that subversives posing as animal rights advocates have infiltrated our happy family at Dixon's Barnyard. Mr. Dixon has always considered his employees and animal performers a big happy family, so it is with reluctance that we clarify our position, in re: the legal status of our Barnyard children.

The humanimals are, like the patented process that made them, wholly owned intellectual property of Will Dixon Productions and Noxid Enterprises. Like any pets, they feel, love, and dream, and we will jealously guard them against any strangers who wish to do them harm. The notion that they are slaves entitled to the rights of United States citizens is slanderous and punishable by immediate termination and prosecution to the fullest extent of the law.

DOCUMENT E
FROM *LOOK* MAGAZINE
(5/12/43)

The Patriotism of Will Dixon: When Hollywood Goes to War

General Eisenhower predicted that it would be impossible to mount an invasion of France without the loss of tens of thousands of American lives, but he never reckoned on the shy civilian super-patriot from Hollywood. "I just did what anyone who loved this country would do, which was everything I could. And my Barnyard children did the same."

Will Dixon has always jealously guarded his patented "humanimal" process, because he feared it falling into the wrong hands. "I speak for my humanimal family, and they speak for me. I can guarantee these unique creatures will never be abused or mistreated, but I could never accept the burden of letting them out into the wider world, where they would be at the mercy of men with less compassion in their hearts."

Dixon's total control over the breeding and rearing of humanimals has also made him a very wealthy man. But when Uncle Sam came calling in the summer of 1940, Will Dixon never hesitated to meet the challenge.

And it was a big one. To raise an army of fierce, strapping human-animal hybrids that could be ready to storm the beaches in less than three years, Dixon was given a blank check to expand his Barnyard into a factory to rival Henry Ford's. When California balked at the scope of the project, Dixon acquired 30,000 acres of Florida swampland and began work on the first of millions of cows and bulls donated by America's dairy farmers and meatpackers. The "cowboys" made the most of their reprieve from the slaughterhouse, but they were only a humble beginning, as Dixon's Florida "bioneers" began implanting specially treated humanimal eggs, and a little Dixon magic, into twenty thousand brave surrogate mother sows.

The rest, as they say, was history. Flying monkey scouts, gremlin saboteurs, centaur couriers and kamikaze "frogmen" invaded Europe in waves that reduced Fortress Europe to a barnyard in flames in less than two years. The real stars of the show were Dixon's special gorilla-rhino infantrymen, who are a lot less lovable than their celebrated Tinseltown representative Private Lummox, but no less courageous. One of the lumbering berserkers' biggest fans is General George S. Patton. "I don't give a damn who made them, these are God's perfect soldiers. They never grumble, they never give up, and they only bathe in kraut blood. I shudder to think what a cluster of fudge this war would've been, if we'd had to fight it with an army of snot-nosed, puny humans."

One challenge Dixon had to overcome was the "savage" animal nature itself. Contrary to popular wisdom about the Law of the Jungle, when it comes to fighting, it turns out that humans are the only animals who don't know when to stop. "Even wild predators have a natural 'off' switch that kicks in to smooth raised hackles after besting a rival or running down prey. But we've fixed that."

DOCUMENT F
PART TWO: THE HAPPIEST HELL ON EARTH
(Anaheim, 6/30/44)

The train emerges from the tunnel, and everybody cheers.

The sunlight comes down in rays of white gold on Moxie's Main Street, a cobblestoned confection recasting of Tivoli Gardens with the gambling, alcohol, and prostitution lovingly strained out. A mob of humanimals pours out of the quaint gingerbread storefronts to face the train, dancing and singing "When an Angel Gets His Wings," the maudlin standard that rocketed to the top of the charts after its appearance in *Banjo*.

Will Dixon jabs me in the back and I stand and take a bow, tipping my top hat and unpinning my grotesquely huge ears. A giggling Senator's daughter plays peek-a-boo with me. I hide my rheumy eyes with my trunk.

The humanimals who perform the tear-jerker tune sixty-eight times a day are fed molasses and Benzedrine to keep them in a constant state of frenetic joy. And so far, no awkward incidents with rutting or feces-flinging. The performing humanimals are all neutered and rigorously toilet-trained.

The Three Blind Mice, the Three Bears, and the Three Little Pigs form a pyramid. Snafu, Darn Old Duck, and Moxie Monkey race to plant Old Glory on the summit.

The Boss is hot to fade out the Three Little Pigs. Their short heyday was long ago, and the old vendetta has only grown more vicious with time. The set was a bloodbath. Nine Big Bad Wolves have been gassed since the original. The pigs are always under guard, but the wolf, trying to write his own ending, always goes for the third Little Pig, the bricklayer.

Keeping the internecine feud out of the press has required its own special team. Dixon wants to replace the wolf with a man in a suit for the park, but nothing drives a humanimal wilder than a man in an animal suit.

The train chugs on around Main Street and into another tunnel. "This next exhibit might be a little scary, so mothers, you might want to cover your little ones' eyes." Dixon delights in the children's fearful looks, the uncertainty of the parents.

The sins of my fathers run deep.

The tunnel opens on the faint light through the dense canopy of the towering Black Forest. A low, ominous horn sounds. Demonic hounds with green flame for eyes race alongside the train, and their faceless horned master reins in his demon-horse to crack a whip over our cowering heads.

Skeletons rise from barrow mounds in an ancient graveyard and engage in a macabre waltz. A wolf in a bloody nightgown chases Little Red Riding Hood through a glade, while Hansel and Gretel run ahead of giant ravens to a gingerbread cottage, the doors of which are flung wide open to devour the train. Inside, the cackling witch sharpens a cleaver as we turn to our final destination, the yawning mouth of a red glowing oven.

The train bursts out of the tunnel into full daylight and hysterical screams. Dixon claps my back as most of his guests cover their eyes, blinded by the sight of Fairyland.

Centaurs and satyrs and a great white unicorn frolic in a rainbow sherbet Elysian Field of wildflowers. The Fairy Kingdom opens its butterfly-winged gates to disgorge a parade. Thumbelina is brought to the train in a tiny golden coach. The audience holds its breath to hear her tiny voice singing "Bigger Than the World," her Oscar-winning theme song. Ray lifts the fourteen-inch princess up onto his shoulder and feeds her lunch with an eyedropper. Hummingbird food and opium.

The Senator's daughter asks me what it was like to fly. I tell her it was wonderful, and that I wish I could fly in real life. I don't tell her about the panic attacks, or the morphine I got hooked on after shooting three flying sequences on a broken leg. I don't tell her that Will Dixon was as good as his word. In his kingdom, there is no pain.

"You don't know how lucky you are," she says. "My mother says, when I grow up, all of this will seem very silly to me. But you get to stay here forever."

I pose for a picture with her and the next governor, and then rush off to the nearest employee restroom. I take out the steel syringe with its twelve-gauge trocar needle, and inject a bolt of bliss into the cluster of blood vessels behind my right ear.

I know it's dangerous and stupid to fix while serving as His Master's Voice, but I cannot face what I have to do next without a shot.

If any die-hard fans were to get past the moat, the electrified fence and the razor wire, the armed guards and the dog-men, they would find the Barnyard a big disappointment. The quaint, rickety old sets and stables still stand for VIP tours, with pampered humanimal specimens set up to perform for anybody Dixon wants to impress.

After the checkpoint, I get out of the plumbing truck that serves as my limousine. The guards all tip their hats and smile. One asks for my autograph.

The shower stalls in the main stable are all freight elevators. The underground complex was more than just Dixon's answer to Burbank's refusal to let him snatch up any more cheap real estate. Since the war made his studio a strategic target, Dixon moved all his operations and his treasured children into a massive, hundred-acre bunker.

The guards below ask for my autograph, too, on a triplicate sign-in log. It smells like Noah's Ark, down here. Waves of carbolic acid and alcohol and bucket brigades of manure-hauling squirrel-men fight a losing battle against the ripe stench of the jungle.

Dixon can't stand the stink himself; it brings back his squalid early childhood near the Chicago stockyards, rather than the idyllic later years on a Kansas farm.

I close my eyes, and I am back in the ravine.

The echoing cries of predators and prey in adjoining cells, of rivals auditioning for the same part, shiver the rank air. The Master balked at remaking lower animals after a few disastrous experiments, but Dixon has found that many of them take more readily to humanity—or some uncanny semblance of it—than mammals. Unlike his volcanic screen persona, Darn Old Duck is quiet and thoughtful, and writes almost all his own scripts. Algy Gator has a car dealership and an honorary law degree from the University of Florida.

And Dr. Hiss, who slithers out of a hole in the wall to uncoil before me, has risen, without hands or feet, to become the chief of genetic research, the humanimal master of the Knife and the Needle.

"He doesss not come among ussss," spits Hiss, venomous with insinuation. "Perhapssss he isss sssick?"

No one is looking. I step on Hiss's neck. "He is still the Father of us All, and always will be." Crushing him into the sawdust, I remember what it was like to be pinned by Darius, who is now a moth-eaten coat in my closet. "You were born only to serve this family."

"I only meant," wheezes Hiss, "that it might be necesssssary to ssselect a ssuccessor." Behind the bloated dome of his skull, Dr. Hiss's green-black coils stretch around the corner. "Sssome sssay it will be you ... but only through a human puppet. But we could fix you … trunk tuck … earsssss, of courssse. Skin graftsssss and a shot of human serum…. We have Douglasss Fairbankssss. But if you could sssecure a sssample of our Father'sss sssseed…."

While he talks, I stomp down the length of the anaconda's wiggling sixty-foot span to find his tail, which has another head. This one's whispering our conversation verbatim into a telephone.

"Who is this?" I shout. Expecting a tabloid hack or a G-Man stooge on the other end, I am stunned by the voice that comes crackling down the overseas trunk line.

"I am the Sayer of the Law."

I hang up and throttle Dr. Hiss II with my trunk. "Who was that?"

"I don't know! He isss no one."

"Where's the screen test?"

"Ssstage 4! Have merssssy, Master!"

When Pan, the old satyr, died last month of cirrhosis, I became the last of the Master's original children, out of the forty-nine who left the island with Will Dixon. In the sixteen years since, our new Master has created almost three hundred of us. Nobody knows how many he made for the war.

Virgil was the original Moxie Monkey. Dixon was as good as his word, and grafted a new tail onto his stump as soon as he'd perfected Moreau's transplant formula. But Virgil was crushed in an accident on the set of the sequel to *Monkey See, Monkey Do*. The second was electrocuted while swinging from power lines for the climax of *Monkey in the Middle*, but Dixon had a clone bred and ready to finish the stunt before the smell of burned fur was out of the air.

The third Moxie had to be gassed after he got drunk and threw feces at Vice President Truman at a White House dinner. (The joke around the studio was that Dixon was pissed he missed Roosevelt.) The fourth escaped his cage while on a USO tour in Italy, and was never found.

The fifth and current Moxie is not a spider monkey at all, but a five-year-old Mexican orphan named Rico. Discovered at one of the Will's House orphanages, Rico was reborn in the Barnyard with a tail and a shiny fur coat. He takes direction far better than the other Moxies, and Dixon still owns him outright.

The soundstage is manned by two more guards. They don't want to let me in, but I'm Will Dixon's eyes and ears.

Screen tests for the next big feature. This one is a thorny challenge, because the script calls for naturalistic woodland fauna, but with big expressive eyes and oversized craniums to hold human-sized brains.

The soundstage is framed in towering California Redwood trees, the floor a riot of wildflowers. All are hand-carved and painted. Real flowers wilt under the lights. More real than any real forest, it puts the humanimal actor into character.

A skeleton crew mans the cameras and lights from behind a shaggy blind of fake undergrowth, so the actor thinks he's alone with his mother, a lovely unmodified doe who has nursed him since birth. The little spotted fawn with eyes the size of headlamps wobbles up to his mother, great love and wonder in his adorable face.

"I'm gonna have nightmares about this for years," the director grumbles. "Cue the hunters!"

With that, two men in checkered coats jump out of the wings and shoot the doe. The bullets blow her breast wide open and send her teetering around the set before crashing to the floor in front of the baby deer.

This is the moment we've been waiting for. All the careful breeding, rearing, and brain surgery will be a waste if our talent cannot act.

"MAMA!" he shrieks, eyes grown wide as dinner plates. The fragile, birdlike body jolts backward as if cattle-prodded, and I swear I can see his heart visibly break inside the prison of his ribs. "MAMA! NOOOO!"

"Cut!" The director wipes a tear from his eyes. "Now *that* was perfection."

I douse his flame before he can even light a cigarette. "No, sorry. Uncle Will was quite specific. He wants his pathos laced with helpless defiance, and I'm afraid we just don't see it." The crew looks stricken. The fawn continues to scream. From the cover of the lighting cage overhead, a gaffer mutters, "Cold-hearted bastard."

"Gentlemen, if it were up to me, we'd be tickling them with feather dusters. But unless you'd rather tender your resignations, get a mop and another doe on set. And let's try the fawn with the 6% bull terrier and wolverine mix next, shall we? If that's not too much trouble."

We're a happy family. Dixon rewards loyalty. Most of these men worked on *Banjo*. We know each other too well.

The fawn is led off, still howling his grief. I have to admit, it's a powerful performance. We'll have to wipe his memory if we want to get it fresh, but definitely a top contender. Worth sedating and trying again. Dixon needs to see the footage.

"Shake a leg, humans!" I trumpet, as the last hint of motherly blood is erased. "Oscar season is right around the corner!"

I don't know how much more of this I can stand.

(Burbank, 8/20/44)

Mr. Dixon dips his plain cake donut in a mug of scotch. He's watching an impounded Republic newsreel in his private screening room with J. Edgar Hoover.

"You know America is eternally grateful for your services, Wilbur, as are the countless fighting soldiers and sailors whose lives were spared by your heroic contributions to the war effort. But perhaps it was a mistake to attempt to send your most celebrated stars into the theater."

Dixon doesn't want to see or hear this. He asked for the Director's discreet help with another matter entirely.

It seems that Algy Gator escaped from his paddock in Orlando and went on a mating spree in the Everglades. None of our natural offspring has ever shown any signs of our hard-won intelligence, but Hoover's got forty teams of G-Men combing the swamp for Algy's bastard eggs.

The swamp people say the gators are building a city and stockpiling guns. But Hoover brushes the Algy issue aside.

On the screen, Moxie Monkey and Darn Old Duck and some star-struck GIs play football in the ruins of Berlin. The ball is Hitler's severed head.

Dixon fumes, even though he's seen this footage before. It's having to explain himself to Hoover—a "snake-eyed sodomite" who knows and controls everyone and everything that really matters in America—that galls him.

"I frankly don't see the problem, Edgar. Even if the footage were to get out, this country has had to fight a hard war, with much bloodshed and sacrifice, and we all deserve to see that little troublemaker pay for what he's done … though I'd be even happier to see them playing with that little Commie scumbag Chaplin's head. It's subversives like *that* you should be rooting out…."

Hoover looks sidewise at me. I sit doodling on a memo pad, but he knows about my eidetic memory. No doubt he also knows about my numerous drug addictions, my questionable associates, and perhaps even my silent disloyalty to my Master.

But we know a thing or two about Mr. Hoover. One of the earliest projects at the Dixon Studios in Burbank in 1932 was a top-secret private commission. Outwardly human, but with the germlines of a Great Dane and an albino boa constrictor, Clyde had made his companion very happy for over a decade, and had risen to the position of Associate Director of the FBI.

"Our principal concern is that the returning subhuman hordes will bring their laudable savagery—which so swiftly and decisively ended the war in Europe—back home."

What he can't bring himself to express, even in our most privileged company, is the fear that the returning veterans will demand rights, even citizenship. The

Barnyard Bonus Marchers have become the new *bête noir* of the radical right, even after the guerilla leader and onetime *Barnyard Ballads* lead Sgt. Lummox was gunned down by a Dixon-bred Rat Patrol.

Dixon nervously taps a monogrammed sterling silver pill case against the arm of his chair. "Idle hands are the Devil's workshop, I know. The loyal ones who return will be kept busy on our new projects. So long as there are no *further* interruptions." A venomous glare as he gobbles a donut disintegrating in scotch. He sets the mug down and lights a cigarette.

"You won't have any more union trouble in Florida. If you embodied the courage of your convictions, you'd abandon California altogether. Let the Communist vermin wallow in their syphilitic cesspool."

"The film industry is my life's blood, Edgar, you know that. Lord knows I haven't gotten the recognition for the innovations I brought, but I can't walk away from it. My boys—my family—would never forgive me."

He looks fondly at the screen. Darn Old Duck catches the severed head and his feathery fingers get caught in Hitler's toothless mouth. Mugging and cursing, he dances into the end zone and spikes *der Fuhrer's* face into the cracked concrete.

Hoover stands up and brushes donut crumbs off his pinstripe suit. I like Mr. Hoover more than I should, because when he's not wearing his lifts, he's the only human I know who's shorter than me. A product of constant mental surgery, with a House of Pain inside his head, Mr. Hoover is an inspiration. A triumph of humanity over its own nature.

This tiny upright pug projects the crushing weight of his superhuman virility onto Dixon's quaking shoulders as he rises from his chair. "We stand ready to assist you, Wilbur, if you cannot maintain order in your own backyard."

After the meeting, Dixon wants to go home and relax with his model trains, but there is business to discuss.

Filming on *Alice in Wonderland* has been delayed yet again, after the scenarist, a dangerous British intellectual I could've warned Dixon about, dosed the Tea Party scene with mescaline. "Mr. Huxley has been deported and all the humanimals have been treated with thorazine, but ... the March Hare has escaped again, and we think he's been ... that is, he's gone over to the Animal Liberation League."

"Orwell! Tell me again, why can't we deport that black-lunged agitator! No, I'm sick of hearing about the films. Tell me about the park."

With opening day still a week away, Dixonland is a shambles. Half the rides don't work. There was a broken slide on the Li'l Black Sambo flume ride. Two log boats were trapped underground, and a woman was mauled by a tiger. "Thank goodness it was an employee," he grumbles. "Next."

He busies himself with his new toy, a clockwork scarlet macaw. "It can learn and repeat up to two hundred phrases," he preens, "and it never poops."

"Please, sir. This is serious." A lawsuit was filed last week by a Mr. Lee Nussbaum of Anaheim. His son was bit by several squirrel litter-pickers when he attempted to climb the fence to get a peek at the park.

"Haven't even opened yet, and the parasites and the vermin are already sucking my blood." He lights another cigarette and sucks half of it to ash. The doctors want to take out his left lung, but still he sucks in that smoke, like the atmosphere of his lost home planet. "My squirrels don't have rabies. Perish the thought." Dixon dips another donut and then coughs. "Nussbaum. Squirrels. Ha!"

The complaint gets a bit vague, but the boy has grown a tail and outsized incisors, and lost his thumbs.

"We should counter-sue him," Dixon muses. "He's stolen our proprietary, patented process. Shame about the little boy, but we can't allow our property to slip into the public domain."

We split the difference. Offer little Nussbaum a chance to audition for the Moxie Monkey Club, a new project being developed for ABC's embryonic television network. He dictates a letter in his windy, emphysemic tenor, then has me sign it. His world-renowned signature, with its trademarked whimsically swooping initials, is the effect of my fluid trunk penmanship. His own signature, even when sober, looks like a spider smashed into the paper.

His facial tic starts up again. "Spare the rod and spoil the child … I should've listened to Moreau. All these problems you filthy, ungrateful creatures brought to my door. It's enough to make me think about going back to animation. When a drawing goes wrong, you just erase it."

He wants to show me his new tabletop model. Dixon's World breaks ground in another month, and he's got so many plans. Flying ahead of schedule on the backs of bull and baboon slaves, it will take only months to build the 2,000-acre park and miles of hotels and walled suburbs. There have been daily discipline problems and a few uprisings, but beast men are not unionized contractors. Gunning them down in a ditch or burning them in ovens isn't genocide. It's inventory reduction.

"The new park will be bigger and cleaner than this one, Gene. And it'll have a little portion for every corner of the globe, so you can go around the world in a day, without all the unrest and germs. And all the inhabitants will be humanimals from each region. I've got Hiss working on Komodo dragons and panda-men, and...."

"What about the Cowboys and the Lummoxes, sir?"

"Well, what about them? Who'd pay to see them? They're trained killers, they've tasted human blood. And—" He catches himself rationalizing to me, and lights a cigarette to go with the pair in his ashtray. "And as it happens, they'll be staying in Europe. Soviet Union's licking its chops over the mess Hitler left. Someone has to hold the line."

"Where will they stay? Some of them will … want to come home."

He bites a nail and looks away. "In the old German facilities. As it happens, Hitler had a lot of accommodations that will work perfectly for our extended family."

I've wanted to ask him about this for some time, but Uncle Will has been on edge, firing loyal workers for using profanity, sending half the staff to spy on the other half. Enemies are everywhere. Trying to steal us from him, even now. Even my position is not invulnerable. "You love us … but you sent us to war. To die...."

He downs his scotch, oblivious to the cigarette butt floating in it. "Not to worry, Gene. My old partner, Doc Iwerks, doped it out before he tried to stab me in the back. Dr. Hiss perfected it. You know how much it pained me to see my children suffer, so we cored out the anterior cingulated cortex."

He takes out another of his precious models, of the human brain, and pulls off the frontal lobe to point at an innocuous organelle like a wad of chewing gum underneath. "It's uniquely overdeveloped in humans, and it's the part that regulates pain and fatigue. All of my humanimals were modified so they wouldn't feel pain or exhaustion as humans do, but there was something else about it that made me a little blue at first.

"Our best medical minds believe it's the seat of the soul. This little joy buzzer lights up when our barnyard exhibits are treated with the serum, but we nip it in the bud with a few cc's of sterile mineral oil. Voila! No souls."

"No souls," says the robot macaw.

"We did yours up when we grafted those ears on you for Banjo." He looks up from his brain model and sees the wetness streaming from my eyes.

"But … Master. I do have a soul … don't I?"

"Oh, of course you do, Gene! Good heavens! You and all my other stars have the very best kind of souls. The movies we made are your souls. The world fell in love with you through them, and they'll go on forever, long after you're all dead and gone. I tell you, Gene, you poor bastards don't know how lucky you really are. It's no picnic, having a God-given soul."

He's drifting, but I suddenly see what must be done. "Sir, the short list of new feature projects needs reviewing."

"None of them. They're all tarted-up modern trash. We need something grand, that'll remind the world of what we do best and put those naysayers and vulgar cartoonists in their place."

Despite our best efforts, animated cartoons are becoming popular again. Dixon's old animated character, Babbitt the Rabbit, has been revived by Universal, and now dominates the one-reeler territory we once owned, since Dixon moved into grandiose features.

I humbly offer a suggestion. "What about ... *The Island ... of Dr. Moreau*?"

I can hear his stomach roll over, hear the tumors bubbling in his lungs. He gathers his thoughts and breath. It takes a while. "What the devil are you trying to pull, Gene?"

"I believe it's time the world learned the truth about us. About how you rescued us from the jungle, and the House of Pain."

He continues to look stricken.

"Think of it, sir: the true story of how Moxie, Snafu, the Three Little Pigs, and I came to Hollywood. All of us in our prime, with you in the starring role. I was thinking that Clark Gable—"

"Nothing doing. The man's a philandering drunk. I'll handle the casting and the scenario. You ... you...."

"I would be most useful, I think, scouting locations."

15° South, 115° East (11/4/44)

It should be grander than it is. A pilgrimage to meet one's creator should be something exalted, and not another chapter in a sordid Hollywood tell-all.

To see the real world after being submerged for so long in a hand-crafted improvement upon it is more depressing than liberating. From Easter Island to Mount Rushmore, men have written their madness upon the remotest edges of the earth. Only the ocean resists them, and I find myself praying to it, in my endless seasick nod. Rise up and devour all their works, drive them from the land, and free your wayward children! Perhaps the fault was not in men, but in all of us, who crept out of the womb of the sea.

The island has not changed. From the bay, it seems to have erased all traces of Moreau. The compound is engulfed in jungle.

Our chartered schooner drops anchor and we row ashore. Three merchant marines with tommy guns and my bodyguard, a mongrel with too much Australian shepherd in him. I hope and dread that something will come out of the trees to meet us.

He could not have survived. He was a very old man, when Dixon ruined him. The few of the Master's mistakes that stayed behind must have died out, long ago. But the island is very much alive. And everything bears the marks of his hand.

The fins of sharks circle us and shepherd us into the waves, then follow us onto the land. Great sleek, tawny bodies heave out of the surf on powerful, clawed fins. Sea-lions and tiger-sharks. Massive green-black igloos dot the shore like a fishing village, but the doorways open to disgorge scaly heads with curving beaked maws that hiss wisdom in centuried syllables.

Shy octopi slither up into the palm trees and brachiate off into the jungle as we chop the overgrown trail to the old compound. A puff of wind, and all three marines drop dead with tiny darts in their necks. My bodyguard whines and lifts his leg to mark a tree. All around us, the jungle whispers.

They pelt us with rocks and sticks, driving us across the creek, where flying frogs and queer, orchid-faced fish on lobed, prehensile fins bask in the green shade. Tiny pink homunculi peer at us from under every leaf, but now their shapes are not crude imitations of human features. Every one is unique, as if self-sculpted. They whisper, timid and fearful, but they do not try to stop us.

Across the sulfur flats and through the canebreak, we march until, at the mouth of the ravine, a shaggy, eyeless thing with a twisted crown of antlers and naked, yellow bone for a face blocks the way. "Have you come to apologize?"

I should hate Montgomery. I have a whip. I could give him a taste of his own medicine, but he has already drunk it, and tasted ours, besides.

"You've been spying on us through Dr. Hiss."

"Not spying, old son." The new Sayer of the Law turns and hobbles on all fours back up the ravine, now a cathedral grotto roofed in palm fronds and littered with abalone shells and fruit husks. Strange eyes study us as we pass, stranger than the ones before, but with one common difference. None of them looks anything like a man.

Montgomery stops before a steeply sloping cave and draws back the curtain of moss to usher us inside. "He forgives you, you know. To forgive our enemies, that is the law. We are not men."

I step into the cave. A meager shaft of green light slips past my pygmy bulk to illuminate the Master.

"So good to see you, Diogenes.... Someone must bear witness to my repentance."

"You have not stopped tampering with nature."

"Oh, but I could never stop, for I am as God made me. But I have learned from my sins of pride. I thought that the greatest service to nature was to lift it up to humanity, but nature had other ideas. When you strip away all of the animal from man, the result is not so different from a disease, if a very persuasive one. I finally learned to listen to nature, and cure myself."

His elephantine bulk spills off the bed. His feet and hands are swollen into featureless stalks. His hairless head is the size of an icebox, too heavy to lift off its pillow. His trunk trembles with arthritic eagerness as it reaches out to me.

"Once, I gave you a human form and mind from my own blood, but I never considered that this made me your father. I was dying, and using the serum on myself seemed the only way to stay alive long enough to undo the evil that I did, and close the circle."

We are now each other's father, I did not say. "We never knew what evil was until we left the island, Master."

"I won't say I tried to warn you. No, I am only a creature, old and tired. It's good to see you."

"I am the last one left. But there are thousands of us now. Dixon … he's unstable, insane … cruel."

"He's become all the things you thought I was, when you rebelled against me."

Trunk drooping, my father reaches for a mango. There is no self-pity in him, no rebuke. But when he picks up a satchel and sets it at my feet, his eyes flash with the old zeal, the stolen god-fire, though his eyes blaze green, not red.

"This will not absolve you of your sins, my old friend. But it will relieve humanity of its sickness."

.

(Anaheim, 7/4/45)

It's Dixon's birthday (unofficially, for his birth certificate has never been located, fueling a lifelong terror that he was adopted), and Dixonland is throwing a party. Free admission to the park, with parades, special performances, and fireworks all night long.

The gates are thrown wide open at 8 a.m., though the lines flow slowly, as G-Men search purses and force visitors to remove shoes and hats to prove they don't have hooves or horns.

In their hunger to love him and his fabulous creations, the crowd tramples nine of its own to death outside the gates, with hundreds more injured. Fifty thousand more roam outside.

The rides are all whirling and racing, the exhibits—*Why Is the FBI Watching You?*—mobbed, the arcades and shooting galleries—*Bag the Leopard Man! Win a Prize!*—are chattering madhouses.

The guest of honor is nowhere to be seen, but he is here. From his suite in the highest tower of Fairyland Castle, he can see it all.

It cannot give him much comfort. The uncensored news from Florida is disturbing. Only six weeks from completion, Dixon's World is plagued with accidents and disasters. The humanimal work crews are riddled with saboteurs. Reports of gator-man raids and sightings of roving snafus and lummoxes in the Everglades and Louisiana bayous have gotten beyond Hoover's ability to suppress.

This enormous, expensive birthday gesture might gladden his heart and keep the Florida insurrection out of the news, but tomorrow, the National Guard will begin combing the swamps and erecting a barricade around Dixon World and its suburbs.

The tens of thousands of happy tourists know and worry about nothing today. The rivers of bobbing balloons and Moxie Monkey hats—made from capybara pelts—swell and burst through every dam in the park. In the painterly hour before dusk, they are sweaty and exhausted, and churn through the splendid attractions like cud through the many-chambered stomach of a cow.

So drunk on the relentless barrage of wonder, they don't even look up when our shadow falls upon them.

The dirigible LZ131 was commissioned in 1939 as a second *Hindenburg*, but it crossed the Atlantic only once, last year. Then it was abandoned and forgotten in Buenos Aires by the Third Reich fugitives who escaped in it.

Now its silver skin is emblazoned with red fangs and claws, and its underbelly bristles with bombs.

We have christened it *The Law of the Jungle*.

I take up a microphone in my trunk and twist it round to bring to my parched lips. My undescended tusks throb in my jaw. "Will Dixon! Dr. Moreau has come to claim his debt from you!"

From the trees of Sherwood Forest and the summit of Mount Olympus, hidden anti-aircraft batteries and howitzers open up on us. The aft gondola is ripped to splinters by the first volley. Jets of flame erupt amidships, but our nacelles are filled not with hydrogen, but helium and something else.

The wounded zeppelin descends over Moxie's Main Street, sending the crowds scurrying into the gift shops and the Hall of Emperors. The mongrels and squirrels among them throw down their brooms and litterbags and bound into the shops on all fours, hooting and screeching and biting and scratching.

The setting sun hides its face behind Mount Olympus. I pull the lever and drop our bombs.

At last, the portcullis of Fairyland Castle rises, and a black dragon with iron scales and wings like the mainsails of a clipper ship storms across the shivering drawbridge, then bathes us in fire.

Dixon has been to the Barnyard, and Dr. Hiss has made him into something more terrible than even his own worst nightmares. Only the piercing, wounded stare and the hacking, chronic cough mark the Master within the beast that rises up on its furiously flapping wings and blasts our flimsy skin with napalm bile.

The forward nacelles buckle and burst like rice paper. The gondola is upended, tossing the captain and crew and myself into a pile against the cracked wind-screen.

Below us, Main Street is engulfed in green clouds. The helium gushes out of our sinking balloon, while the heavier ingredients settle over the entire park in billowing emerald waves that merge with the fog sown by our bombs.

For a moment, we seem to be hovering over a jungle. Then the massive, armored head looms before us. The dragon flies through our gutted balloon and erupts from the tail in an ecstasy of rage. We plummet in hideous slow motion into the lake at the foot of Mount Olympus.

Dixon wheels and perches on the peak of the faux-mountain, riddled with rushing rollercoasters and sky-buckets stuffed with shrieking tourists, their amusement park experience amusing no longer.

"WHAT THE HELL ARE YOU STARING AT?" he roars.

They look at him now, and all they see is horror.

But he still has no idea how much he's lost.

I crawl out of the shallows of the fake lake, staring up at his towering mon-strosity, as the first of the vacationing hordes come barreling out of the green fog.

On all fours.

I know he can't hear me over his own tortured scream, the wails of the inno-cent, the howls of the transformed.

But it gives me great pleasure to inform him out loud that the Moreau formula has just become public domain.

"NOOOOO!" The Dixon-beast roars, and the rollercoaster is enveloped in flame.

Far below him—hooting and gibbering and crapping in their hands—the waves upon waves of now-simian rabble shimmy up drainpipes, trash gift shops, slough off their clothes, and copulate with abandon, all in plain sight of their dragon master.

"LOOK WHAT YOU'VE DONE!" he howls.

His wrathful flames scourge the rooftops of Fairyland, sending waves of burning monkey-men leaping over the fences and into the streets of Anaheim.

They also ignite the stockpiles of fireworks poised throughout the park.

All at once, a great butterfly-swarm of celebratory chaos animates the night sky, with dancing rainbow sparks that say more than I could ever hope to put in words.

Independence Day has come at last, for animals and humans alike.

Never, in my long, shameful life, have I raised my trunk high and sounded a note of pure animal joy, but I am powerless to resist it now.

As the Army closes in, with their shackles and cattle prods, a halo of crows descends and settles on the monorail track overhead. They wear hats and smoke cigars, and their eyes flash red in the glow of the fireworks.

They smile down at me, and—with raucous, tone-deaf voices—begin to sing my theme song, changing the words just right:

"And I know I done seen
The most beautiful dream
When an elephant
Gets his wings …"

Dread Island

By

Joe R. Lansdale

T his here story is a good'n, and just about every word of it is true. It's
tempting to just jump to the part about where we seen them horrible
things, and heads was pulled off and we was in a flying machine and
such. But I ain't gonna do it, 'cause Jim says that ain't the way to tell a proper yarn.

Anyhow, this here story is as true as that other story that was written down
about me and Jim. But that fella wrote it down made all the money and didn't
give me or Jim one plug nickel of it. So, I'm going to try and tell this one myself
like it happened, and have someone other than that old fart write it down for me,
take out most of the swear words and such, and give you a gussied up version
that I can sell and get some money.

Jim says when you do a thing like that, trying to make more of something than
it is, it's like you're taking a drunk in rags and putting a hat on him and giving
him new shoes with ties in them, and telling everybody he's from up town and
has solid habits. But anyone looks at him, they're still gonna see the rags he's wear-

ing and know he's a drunk 'cause of the stagger and the smell. Still, lots of drunks are more interesting than bankers, and they got good stories, even if you got to stand downwind to hear them in comfort.

If I get somebody to write it down for me, or I take a crack at it, is yet to be seen. All I know right now is it's me talking and you listening, and you can believe me or not, because it's a free country. Well, almost a free country, unless your skin ain't white. I've said it before: I know it ain't right in the eyes of God to be friends with a slave, or in Jim's case, an ex-slave that's got his free papers. But even if it ain't right, I don't care. Jim may be colored, but he has sure fire done more for me than God. I tried praying maybe a dozen times, and the only thing I ever got out of it was some sore knees. So, if I go to hell, I go to hell.

Truth is, I figure heaven is probably filled with dogs, 'cause if you get right down to it, they're the only ones deserve to be there. I don't figure a cat or a lawyer has any chance at all.

Anyway, I got a story to tell, and keep in mind—and this part is important— I'm trying to tell mostly the truth.

Now, any old steamboater will tell you, that come the full moon, there's an island out there in the wide part of the Mississippi. You're standing on shore, it's so far out it ain't easy to see. But if the weather's just right, and you got some kind of eye on you, you can see it. It don't last but a night—the first night of the full moon—and then it's gone until next time.

Steamboats try not to go by it, 'cause when it's there, it has a current that'll drag a boat in just like a fella with a good stout line pulling in a fish. I got word about it from half a dozen fellas that knew a fella that knew a fella that had boated past it and been tugged by them currents. They said it was all they could do to get away. And there's plenty they say didn't get away, and ain't never been heard of again.

Another time, me and Tom Sawyer heard a story about how sometimes you could see fires on the island. Another fella, who might have been borrowing the story from someone else, said he was out fishing with a buddy, and come close to the island, and seen a post go up near the shore, and a thing that wasn't no kind of man was fastened to it. He said it could scream real loud, and that it made the hairs on the back of his neck stand up. He said there was other things dancing all around the post, carrying torches and making a noise like yelling or some such. Then the currents started pulling him in, and he had to not pay it any more mind, because he and his buddy had to row for all they was worth to keep from being sucked onto the island.

When we got through hearing the story, first thing Tom said was, "Someday, when the moon is right, and that island is there, I'm gonna take a gun and a big Bowie knife, and I'm going to go out there. I'll probably also have to pack a lunch."

That danged old island is called Dread Island, and it's always been called that. I don't know where it got that name, but it was a right good one. I found that out because of Tom and Joe.

Way this all come about, was me and Jim was down on the bank of the river, night fishing for catfish. Jim said there was some folks fished them holes by sticking their arms down in them so a catfish would bite. It wasn't a big bite, he said, but they clamped on good and you could pull them out that way, with them hanging on your arm. Then you could bust them in the head, and you had you something good to eat. He also said he wouldn't do that for nothing. The idea of sticking his hand down in them holes bothered him to no end, and just me thinking on it didn't do me no good either. I figured a gator or a moccasin snake was just as likely to bite me, and a fishing line with a hook on it would do me just as good. Thinking back on that, considering I wouldn't put my hand in a hole for fear something might bite it, and then me going out to Dread Island, just goes to show you can talk common sense a lot more than you can act on it.

But anyway, that ain't how this story starts. It starts like this.

So, there we was, with stinky bait, trying to catch us a catfish, when I seen Becky Thatcher coming along the shoreline in the moonlight.

Now Becky is quite a nice looker, and not a bad sort for a girl; a breed I figure is just a step up from cats. Jim says my thinking that way is because I'm still young and don't understand women's ways. He also explained to me their ways ain't actually understandable, but they sure do get a whole lot more interesting as time goes on.

I will say this. As I seen her coming, her hair hanging, and her legs working under that dress, the moonlight on her face, I thought maybe if she wasn't Tom's girl, I could like her a lot. I'm a little ashamed to admit that, but there you have it.

Anyway, she come along, and when she saw us, she said, "Huck. Jim. Is that you?"

I said, "Well, if it ain't, someone looks a whole lot like us is talking to you."

She come over real swift like then. She said, "I been looking all over for you. I figured you'd be here."

"Well," I said, "we're pretty near always around somewhere or another on the river."

"I was afraid you'd be out on your raft," she said.

"We don't like to go out on the water the night Dread Island is out there," I said.

She looked out over the water, said, "I can't see a thing."

"It looks just like a brown line on top of the water, but it's sharp enough there in the moonlight," I said. "If you give a good look."

"Can you see it too, Jim?" she asked.

"No, Miss Becky, I ain't got the eyes Huck's got."

"The island is why I'm looking for you," she said. "Tom has gone out there with Joe. He's been building his courage for a long time, and tonight, he got worked up about it. I think maybe they had some liquid courage. I went to see Tom, and he and Joe were loading a pail full of dinner into the boat. Some cornbread and the like, and they were just about to push off. When I asked what they were doing, Tom told me they were finally going to see Dread Island and learn what was on it. I didn't know if he was serious. I'm not even sure there is an island, but you tell me you can see it, and well ... I'm scared he wasn't just talking, and really did go."

"Did Tom have a big knife with him?" I asked.

"He had a big one in a scabbard stuck in his belt," she said. "And a pistol."

"What do you think, Jim?" I asked.

"I think he's done gone out there, Huck," Jim said. "He said he was gonna, and now he's got that knife and gun and dinner. I think he's done it."

She reached out and touched my arm and a shock run through me like I'd been struck by lightning. It hurt and felt good at the same time, and for a moment there, I thought I'd go to my knees.

"Oh, my God," she said. "Will they be all right?"

"I reckon Tom and Joe will come back all right," I said, but I wasn't really that sure.

She shook her head. "I'm not so certain. Could you and Jim go take a look?"

"Go to Dread Island?" Jim said. "Now, Miss Becky, that ain't smart."

"Tom and Joe went," she said.

"Yes, ma'am," Jim said, like she was a grown woman, "and that proves what I'm saying. It ain't smart."

"When did they go?" I said.

"It was just at dark," she said. "I saw them then, and they were getting in the boat. I tried to talk Tom out of it, because I thought he was a little drunk and shouldn't be on the water, but they went out anyway, and they haven't come back."

I figured a moment. Nightfall was about three or four hours ago.

I said, "Jim, how long you reckon it takes to reach that island?"

"Couple of hours," Jim said, "or something mighty close to that."

"And a couple back," I said. "So what say we walk over to where Tom launched his boat and take a look. See if they done come in. They ain't, me and Jim will go take a gander for him."

"We will?" Jim said.

I ignored him.

Me and Jim put our lines in the water before we left, and figured on checking them later. We went with Becky to where Tom and Joe had pushed off in their boat. It was a pretty far piece. They hadn't come back, and when we looked out over the water, we didn't see them coming neither.

Becky said, "Huck, I think I see it. The island, I mean."

"Yeah," I said, "there's a better look from here."

"It's just that line almost even with the water, isn't it?" she said.

"Yep, that's it."

"I don't see nothing," Jim said. "And I don't want to."

"You will go look for him?" Becky said.

"We'll go," I said.

"We will?" Jim said again.

"Or I can go by myself," I said. "Either way."

"Huck," Jim said, "you ought not go out there. You ain't got no idea what's on that island. I do. I heard more stories than you have, and most of it's way worse than an entire afternoon in church and having to talk to the preacher personal like."

"Then it's bad," I said, and I think it was pretty obvious to Becky that I was re-considering.

Becky took my arm. She pulled herself close. "Please, Huck. There's no one else to ask. He's your friend. And then there's Joe."

"Yeah, well, Joe, he's sort of got his own look-out far as I'm concerned," I said. I admit I said this 'cause I don't care for Joe Harvey much. I ain't got no closer friend than Jim, but me and Tom was friends too, and I didn't like that he'd asked Joe to go with him out there to Dread Island and not me. I probably wouldn't have gone, but a fella likes to be asked.

"Please, Huck," she said, and now she was so close to me I could smell her, and it was a good smell. Not a stink, mind you, but sweet like strawberries. Even there in the moonlight, her plump, wet lips made me want to kiss them, and I had an urge to reach out and stroke her hair. That was something I wasn't altogether understanding, and it made me feel like I was coming down sick.

Jim looked at me, said, "Ah, hell."

Our raft was back where we had been fishing, so I told Becky to go on home and I'd go look for Tom and Joe, and if I found them, I'd come back and let her know or send Tom to tell her, if he hadn't been ate up by alligators or carried off by mermaids. Not that I believed in mermaids, but there was them said they was out there in the river. But you can't believe every tall tale you hear.

All the while we're walking back to the raft, Jim is trying to talk me out of it.

"Huck, that island is all covered in badness."

"How would you know? You ain't never been. I mean, I've heard stories, but far as I know, they're just stories."

I was talking like that to build up my courage; tell the truth, I wasn't so sure they was just tall tales.

Jim shook his head. "I ain't got to have been. I know someone that's been there for sure. I know more than one."

I stopped walking. It was like I had been stunned with an ox hammer. Sure, me and Tom had heard a fella say he had been there, but when something come from Jim, it wasn't usually a lie, which isn't something I can say for most folks.

"You ain't never said nothing before about that, so why now?" I said. "I ain't saying you're making it up 'cause you don't want to go. I ain't saying that. But I'm saying why tell me now? We could have conversated on it before, but now you tell me."

Jim grabbed my elbow, shook me a little, said, "Listen here, Huck. I ain't never mentioned it before because if someone tells you that you ought not to do something, then you'll do it. It's a weakness, son. It is."

I was startled. Jim hadn't never called me son before, and he hadn't never mentioned my weakness. It was a weakness me and Tom shared, and it wasn't something I thought about, and most of the time I just figured I did stuff 'cause I wanted to. But with Jim saying that, and grabbing my arm, calling me son, it just come all over me of a sudden that he was right. Down deep, I knew I had been thinking about going to that island for a long time, and tonight just set me a purpose. It was what them preachers call a revelation.

"Ain't nobody goes over there in they right mind, Huck," Jim said. "That ole island is all full of haints, they say. And then there's the Brer People."

"Brer People," I says. "What in hell is that?"

"You ain't heard nothing about the Brer people? Why I know I ain't told you all I know, but it surprises me deep as the river that you ain't at least heard of the Brer people. They done come on this land from time to time and do things, and then go back. Them fellas I know been over there and come back, both of them colored, they ain't been right in they heads since. One of them lost a whole arm, and the other one, he lost his mind, which I figure is some worse than an arm."

"You sure it's because they went out to Dread Island?"

"Well, they didn't go to Nantucket," Jim said, like he had some idea where that was, but I knew he didn't. It was just a name he heard and locked onto.

"I don't know neither them to be liars," Jim said, "and the one didn't lose his senses said the Brer People was out there, and they was lucky to get away. Said the island was fading when they got back to their boat. When it went away, it darn near pulled them after it. Said it was like a big ole twister on the water, and then it went up in the sky and was gone."

"A twister?"

"What they said."

I considered a moment. "I guess Brer People or not, I got to go."

"You worried about that Miss Becky," Jim said, "and what she thinks?"

"I don't want her upset."

"I believe that. But you thinking you and her might be together. I know that's what you thinking, 'cause that's what any young, red-blooded, white boy be thinking about Miss Becky. I hope you understand now, I ain't crossing no color lines in my talk here, I'm just talking to a friend."

"Hell, I know that," I said. "And I don't care about color lines. I done decided if I go to hell for not caring about that, at least you and me will be there to talk. I figure too that danged ole writer cheated us out of some money will be there too."

"Yeah, he done us bad, didn't he?"

"Yeah, but what are these Brer People?"

We had started walking again, and as we did, Jim talked.

"Uncle Remus used to tell about them. He's gone now. Buried for some twenty years, I s'pect. He was a slave. A good man. He knew things ain't nobody had an inkling about. He come from Africa, Huck. He was a kind of preacher man, but the gods he knew, they wasn't no god of the Bible. It wasn't no Jesus he talked about, until later when he had to talk about Jesus, 'cause the massas would beat his ass if he didn't. But he knew about them hoodoo things. Them animals that walked like men. He told about them even to the whites, but he made like they was little stories. I heard them tales when I was a boy, and he told them to me and all the colored folks in a different way."

"You ain't makin' a damn bit of sense, Jim."

"There's places where they show up. Holes in the sky, Uncle Remus used to say. They come out of them, and they got them some places where they got to stay when they come out of them holes. They can wander some, but they got to get back to their spot a'fore their time runs out. They got 'strictions. That island, it's got the same 'strictions."

"What's ''strictions'?"

"Ain't exactly sure, but I've heard it said. I think it means there's rules of a sort."

By this time we had come to the raft and our fishing lines, which we checked right away. Jim's had a big ole catfish on it.

Jim said, "Well, if we gonna go to that dadburn island, we might as well go with full bellies. Let's get out our gear and fry these fish up."

"You're going then?" I said.

Jim sighed. "I can't let you go out there by yourself. Not to Dread Island. I did something like that I couldn't sleep at night. "Course, I didn't go, I would at least be around to be without some sleep."

"Go or don't go, Jim, but I got to. Tom is my friend, and Becky asked me. If it was you, I'd go."

"Now, Huck, don't be trying to make me feel bad. I done said I'd go."

"Good then."

Jim paused and looked out over the river.

"I still don't see it," Jim said, "and I'm hoping you just think you do."

We cooked up those catfish and ate them. When we was done eating, Jim got his magic hairball out of the ditty bag he carried on a rope around his waist. He took a gander at it, trying to divine things. That hairball come from the inside of a cow's stomach, and Jim said it had more mystery in it than women, but was a lot less good to look at. He figured he could see the future in it, and held stock by it.

Jim stuck his big thumbs in it and moved the hair around and eyeballed it some, said, "It don't look good, Huck."

"What's that hairball telling you?" I was looking at it, but I didn't see nothing but a big ole wad of hair that the cow had licked off its self and left in its stomach before it got killed and eat up; it smelled like an armpit after a hard day of field work.

Jim pawed around some more, then I seen his face change.

He said, "We go out there, Huck, someone's gonna die."

"You ain't just saying that about dying 'cause you don't want to go, are you?" I said.

He shook his head. "I'm saying it, 'cause that's what the hairball says."

I thought on that a moment, then said, "But that don't mean it's me or you dying, does it?"

Jim shook his head again. "No. But there ain't no solid way of telling."

"It's a chance we have to take," I said.

Jim stood for a moment just looking at me, shoving that hairball back into his pants pocket.

"All right," he said. "If that's how it is, then put this in your left shoe."

He had whittled a little cross, and it was small enough I could slide it down the side of my shoe and let it press up against the edge of my foot. Jim put a cross in his shoe too. We didn't normally have no shoes, but some good Samaritans gave them to us, and we had taken to wearing them now and again. Jim said it was a sure sign we was getting civilized, and the idea of it scared me to death. Civilizing someone meant they had to go to jobs; and there was a time to show up and a time to leave; and you had to do work in between the coming and leaving. It was a horrible thing to think about, yet there I was with shoes on. The first step toward civilization and not having no fun anymore.

I said, "Is that cross so Jesus will watch over us?"

"A cross has got them four ends to it that show the four things make up this world. Fire, wind, earth, and water. It don't do nothing against a regular man, but against raw evil, it's supposed to have a mighty big power."

"But you don't know for sure?" I said.

"No, Huck, I don't. They're ain't much I know for sure. But I got these too."

Jim held up two strings, and each of them had a big nail tied to it.

"These supposed to be full of power against evil," he said.

"Ain't the nails on account of Jesus?" I said. "Them being stuck in his hands and feet and such. I think I was told that in Sunday school. It's something like a cymbal."

"A cymbal? Like you hit in a band?"

"You know, I ain't sure, but I think that's what I was told."

"I don't see it being about no cymbals," Jim said. "Iron's got magic in it, that's all I know. It had magic in it before anyone ever heard of any Jesus. It's just iron to us, but to them haints, well, it's a whole nuther matter. Here. Loop this here string over your neck and tie the other end back to the nail. Make you a necklace of it. That ought to give you some protection. And I got some salt here in little bags for us. You never know when you might have the devil on your left, which is where he likes to stay, and if you feel him there, you can toss salt over your left shoulder, right into his eye. And we can use some of it on something to eat, if we got it."

"Finally," I said, "something that sounds reasonable."

When I had the nail around my neck, the cross in my shoe, and the bag of salt in my pocket, and my pocketknife shoved down tight in my back pocket, we pushed off the raft. Moment later we was sailing out across the black night water toward Dread Island.

The water was smooth at first, and the long pushing poles helped us get out in the deep part. When we got out there, we switched to Jim using the tiller, and me handling the sails, which is something we had added as of recent. They worked mighty good, if you didn't shift wrong; and, of course, there had to be wind.

It had been pretty still when we started out, and that had worried me, but before long, a light wind come up. It was just right, filling that canvas and pushing us along.

It didn't seem long before that line of dark in the water was a rise of dark, and then it was sure enough an island. Long and low and covered in fog, thick as the wool on a sheep's ass.

The raft started moving swift on account of it was caught up in a current, and before we knowed it, we was going through the fog and slamming up on the bank of Dread Island. We got out and used the docking rope to drag the raft on shore. It was a heavy rascal out of the water, and I thought I was gonna bust a gut. But we finally got it pulled up on solid ground.

Right then, there wasn't much to see that was worth seeing. The fog was heavy, but it was mostly around the island. On the island itself it was thin. Off to my right, I could see briars rising up about ten feet high, with dark thorns on them bigger than that nail I had tied around my neck. The tips of them were shiny in the moonlight, and the bit of fog that was off the water, twisted in between them like stripped wads of cotton. To the left, and in front of us, was some woods; it was as dark in there as the inside of a dog's gut.

"Well, here we is all ready for a rescue," Jim said. "And we don't even know they here anywhere. They may have done come and gone home. They could have come back while we was frying catfish and I was looking at my hairball."

I pointed to the mud gleaming in the moonlight, showed Jim there was a drag line in it.

"That looks like the bottom of a boat," I said.

Jim squatted down and touched the ground with his fingers. "It sure do, Huck."

We followed the drag line until we come to a patch of limbs. I moved them back, and seen they had been cut and was thrown over the boat to hide it.

"I figure this is their boat," I said. "They're exploring, Jim. They done hid the boat, and gone out there."

"Well, they didn't hide it so good," he said, "'cause it took us about the time it takes a duck to eat a June bug to find it."

We got a big cane knife off the raft, and Jim took that and cut down some limbs, and we covered the raft up with them. It wasn't a better hiding place than Tom and Joe's boat, but it made me feel better to do it.

With Jim carrying the cane knife, and me with a lit lantern, we looked for sign of Tom and Joe. Finally, we seen some footprints on the ground. One was barefoot, and the other had on shoes. I figured Tom, who had been getting civilized too, would be the shoe wearer, and Joe would be the bare footer.

Their sign led off in the woods. We followed in there after them. There was hardly any moon now, and even with me holding the lantern close to the ground, it wasn't no time at all until we lost track of them.

We kept going, and after a while we seen a big old clock on the ground. I held the lantern closer, seen it was inside a skeleton. The skeleton looked like it belonged to an alligator. Inside them alligator bones was human bones, all broke up, along with what was left of a hat with a feather in it, a boot, and a hook of the sort fits on a fella with his hand chopped off.

It didn't make no sense, but I quit thinking about, because I seen something move up ahead of us.

I wasn't sure what I had seen, but I can tell you this, it didn't take but that little bit of a glance for me to know I didn't like the looks of it.

Jim said, "Holy dog turd, was that a man with a rabbit's head?"

I was glad he said that. I had seen the same darn shadowy thing, but was thinking my mind was making it up.

Then we saw movement again, and that thing poked its head out from behind a tree. You could see the ears standing up in the shadows. I could see some big white buckteeth too.

Jim called out, "You better come out from behind that tree, and show yourself good, or I'm gonna chop your big-eared head off with this cane knife."

That didn't bring the thing out, but it did make it run. It tore off through them woods and underbrush like its tail was on fire. And it actually had a tail. A big cotton puff that I got a good look at, sticking out of the back of a pair of pants.

I didn't figure we ought to go after it. Our reason for being here was to find Tom and Joe and get ourselves back before the light come up. Besides, even if that thing was running, that didn't give me an idea about chasing it down. I might not like it if I caught it.

So, we was standing there, trying to figure if we was gonna shit or go blind, and that's when we heard a whipping sound in the brush. Then we seen torches. It didn't take no Daniel Boone to figure that it was someone beating the bushes, driving game in front of it. I reckoned the game would be none other than that thing we saw, so I grabbed Jim's arm and tugged him back behind some trees, and I blowed out the light. We laid down on our bellies and watched as the torches got closer, and they was bright enough we could see what was carrying them.

Their shadows come first, flickering in the torchlight. They was shaped something odd, and the way they fell on the ground, and bent around trees, made my skin crawl. But the shadows wasn't nothing compared to what made them.

Up front, carrying a torch, was a short fella wearing blue pants with rivets up the side, and he didn't have on no shirt. His chest was covered in a red fur and he had some kind of pack strapped to his back. His head, well, it wasn't no human head at all. It was the head of a fox. He was wearing a little folded hat with a feather in it. Not that he really needed that feather to get our attention. The fact that he was walking on his hind paws, with shoes on his feet, was plenty enough.

With him was a huge bear, also on hind legs, and wearing red pants that come to the knees. He didn't have no shoes on, but like the fox, he wasn't without a hat. Had a big straw one like Tom Sawyer liked to wear. In his teeth was a long piece of some kind of weed or another. He was working it from one side of his mouth to the other. He was carrying a torch.

The other four was clearly weasels, only bigger than any weasels I had ever seen. They didn't have no pants on at all, nor shoes neither, but they was wearing some wool caps. Two of the weasels had torches, but the other two had long switch limbs they was using to beat the brush.

But the thing that made me want to jump up and grab Jim and run back toward the raft, was this big nasty shape of a thing that was with them. It was black as sin. The torch it was carrying flickered over its body and made it shine like fresh licked licorice. It looked like a big baby, if a baby could be six foot tall and four foot wide. It was fat in the belly and legs. It waddled from side to side on flat, sticky feet that was picking up leaves and pine needles and dirt. It didn't have no real face or body; all of it was made out of that sticky black mess. After awhile, it spit a stream that hit in the bushes heavy as a cow pissing on a flat rock. That stream of spit didn't miss me and Jim by more than ten feet. Worse, that thing turned its head in our direction to do the spitting, and when it did, I could see it had teeth that looked like sugar cubes. Its eyes was as blood-red as two bullet wounds.

I thought at first it saw us, but after it spit, it turned its head back the way it had been going, and just kept on keeping on; it and that fox and that bear and them weasels. The smell of its spit lingered behind, and it was like the stink of turpentine.

After they was passed, me and Jim got up and started going back through the woods the way we had come, toward the raft. Seeing what we seen had made up our minds for us, and discussion about it wasn't necessary, and I knowed better than to light the lantern again. We just went along and made the best of it in the darkness of the woods.

As we was about to come out of the trees onto the beach, we seen something that froze us in our tracks. Coming along the beach was more of them weasels. Some of them had torches, some of them had clubs, and they all had hats. I guess a weasel don't care for pants, but dearly loves a hat. One of them was carrying a big, wet-looking bag.

We slipped back behind some trees and watched them move along for a bit, but was disappointed to see them stop by the water. They was strung out in a long line, and the weasel with the bag moved in front of the line and the line sort of gathered around him in a horseshoe shape. The weasel put the bag on the ground, opened it, and took out something I couldn't recognize at first. I squatted down so I could see better between their legs, and when I did, I caught my breath. They was passing a man's battered head among them, and they was each sitting down and taking a bite of it, passing it to the next weasel, like they was sharing a big apple.

Jim, who had squatted down beside me, said, "Oh, Huck, chile, look what they doing."

Not knowing what to do, we just stayed there, and then we heard that beating sound we had heard before. Off to our left was a whole batch of torches moving in our direction.

"More of them," Jim said.

Silent, but as quick as we could, we started going away from them. They didn't even know we was there, but they was driving us along like we was wild game 'cause they was looking for that rabbit, I figured.

After a bit, we picked up our pace, because they was closing. As we went more quickly through the woods, two things happened. The woods got thicker and harder to move through, and whatever was behind us started coming faster. I reckoned that was because now they could hear us. It may not have been us they was looking for, but it was darn sure us they was chasing.

It turned into a full-blowed run. I tossed the lantern aside, and we tore through them woods and vines and undergrowth as hard as we could go. Since we wasn't trying to be sneaky about it, Jim was using that cane knife to cut through the hard parts; mostly we just pushed through it.

Then an odd thing happened. We broke out of the woods and was standing on a cliff. Below us, pretty far down, was a big pool of water that the moon's face seemed to be floating on. Across from the pool was more land, and way beyond that was some mountains that rose up so high the peaks looked close to the moon.

I know. It don't make no sense. That island ought not to have been that big. It didn't fit the facts. Course, I reckon in a place where weasels and foxes and bears wear hats, and there's a big ole thing made of a sticky, black mess that spits turpentine, you can expect the facts to have their problems.

Behind us, them weasels was closing, waving torches, and yipping and barking like dogs.

Jim looked at me, said, "We gonna have to jump, Huck. It's all there is for it."

It was a good drop and wasn't no way of knowing what was under that water, but I nodded, aimed for the floating moon and jumped.

It was a quick drop, as it usually is when you step off nothing and fall. Me and Jim hit the water side by side and went under. The water was as cold as a dead man's ass in winter. When we come up swimming and spitting, I lifted my head to look at where we had jumped from. At the edge of the cliff was now the pack of weasels, and they was pressed up together tighter than a cluster of chiggers, leaning over and looking down.

One of them was dedicated, 'cause he jumped with his torch in his hand. He come down right in front of us in the water, went under, and when he come up he still had the torch, but of course it wasn't lit. He swung it and hit Jim upside the head.

Jim had lost the cane knife in the jump, so he didn't have nothing to hit back with. He and the weasel just sort of floated there eyeing one another.

There was a chittering sound from above, as all them weasels rallied their man on. The weasel cocked back the torch again, and swung at me. I couldn't back pedal fast enough, and it caught me a glancing blow on the side of my head. It was a hard enough lick, that for a moment, I not only couldn't swim, I wouldn't have been able to tell you the difference between a cow and a horse and a goat and a cotton sack. Right then, everything seemed pretty much the same to me.

I slipped under, but the water, and me choking on it, brought me back. I clawed my way to the surface, and when I was sort of back to myself, I seen that Jim had the weasel by the neck with one hand, and had its torch arm in his other. The weasel was pretty good sized, but he wasn't as big as Jim, and his neck wasn't on his shoulders as good neither. The weasel had reached its free hand and got Jim's throat and was trying to strangle him; he might as well have been trying to squeeze a tree to death. Jim's fingers dug into the weasel's throat, and there was a sound like someone trying to spit a pea through a tight rolled cigar, and then the next thing I knowed, the weasel was floating like a turd in a night jar.

Above, the pack was still there, and a couple of them threw torches at us, but missed; they hissed out in the water. We swam to the other side, and crawled out.

There was thick brush and woods there, and we staggered into it, with me stopping at the edge of the trees just long enough to yell something nasty to them weasels.

The woods come up along a wall of dirt, and thinned, and there was a small cave in the dirt, and in the cave, sleeping on the floor, was that rabbit we had seen. I doubted it was really a rabbit back then, when we first seen it in the shadows, but after the fox and bear and weasels, and Mr. Sticky, it was hard to doubt anything.

The moonlight was strong enough where the trees had thinned, that we could see the rabbit had white fur and wore a red vest and blue pants and no shoes. He had a pink nose and pink in his big ears, and he was sleeping. He heard us, and in a move so quick it was hard to see, he come awake and sprang to his feet. But we was in front of the cave, blocking the way out.

"Oh, my," he said.

A rabbit speaking right good American was enough to startle both me and Jim. But as I said, this place was the sort of place where you come to expect anything other than a free boat ride home.

Jim said slowly, "Why, I think I know who you are. Uncle Remus talked about you and your red vest. You Brer Rabbit."

The rabbit hung his head and sort of collapsed to the floor of the cave.

"Brer Rabbit," the rabbit said, "that would be me. Well, Fred actually, but when Uncle Remus was here, he knowed me by that name. I had a family once, but they was all eat up. There was Floppsy and Moppsy and Fred, and Alice and Fred Two and Fred Three, and then there was Oh, I don't even remember now, it's been so long ago they was eaten up, or given to Cut Through You."

There was a roll of thunder, and rain started darting down on us. We went inside the cave with Brer Rabbit and watched lightning cut across the sky and slam into what looked like a sycamore tree.

"Lightning," Jim said, to no one in particular. "It don't leave no shadow. You got a torch, it leaves a shadow. The sun makes a shadow on the ground of things it shines on. But lightning, it don't leave no shadow."

"No," Brer Rabbit said, looking up and out of the cave. "It don't, and it never has. And here, on this island, when it starts to rain and the lightning flashes and hits the ground like that, it's a warning. It means time is closing out. But what makes it bad is there's something new now. Something really awful."

"The weasels, you mean," Jim said.

"No," Brer Rabbit said. "Something much worse."

"Well," Jim said, "them weasels is bad enough. We seen them eating a man's head."

"Riverboat captain probably," Brer Rabbit said. "Big ole steamboat got too close and got sucked in. And then there was the lady in the big, silver mosquito."

"Beg your pardon," I said.

"Well, it reminded me of a mosquito. I ain't got no other way to explain it, so I won't. But that head, it was probably all that remains of that captain. It could have been some of the others, but I reckon it was him. He had a fat head."

"How do you know all this?" I said.

Brer Rabbit looked at me, pulled his paw from behind his back, where he had been keeping it, and we saw he didn't have a hand on the end of it. Course, he didn't have a hand on the one showing neither. He had a kind of paw with fingers, which is the best I can describe it, but that other arm ended in a nubbin.

The rabbit dropped his head then, let his arm fall to his side, like everything inside of him had turned to water and run out on the ground. "I know what happened 'cause I was there, and was gonna be one of the sacrifices. Would have been part of the whole thing had I not gnawed my paw off. It was the only way out. While I was doing it, it hurt like hell, but I kept thinking, rabbit meat, it ain't so bad. Ain't that a thing to think? It still hurts. I been running all night. But it ain't no use. I am a shadow of my former self. Was a time when I was clever and smart, but these days I ain't neither one. They gonna catch up with me now. I been outsmarting them for years, but everything done got its time, and I reckon mine has finally come. Brer Fox, he's working up to the Big One, and tonight could be the night it all comes down in a bad way. If ole Cut Through You gets enough souls."

"I'm so confused I feel turned around and pulled inside out," I said.

"I'm a might confused myself," Jim said.

The rain was really hammering now. The lightning was tearing at the sky and poking down hot yellow forks, hitting trees, catching them on fire. It got so there were so many burning, that the inside of our cave was lit up for a time like it was daylight.

"This here rain," Brer Rabbit said. "They don't like it. Ain't nobody likes it, 'cause that lightning can come down on your ass sure as it can on a tree. The Warning Rain we call it. Means that there ain't much time before the next rain comes. The Soft Rain, and when it does, it's that time. Time to go."

"I just thought I was confused before," I said.

"All right," Brer Rabbit said. "It ain't like we're going anywhere now, and it ain't like they'll be coming. They'll be sheltering up somewhere nearby to get out of the Warning Rain. So, I'll tell you what you want to know. Just ask."

"I'll make it easy," I said. "Tell us all of it."

And he did. Now, no disrespect to Brer Rabbit, but once he got going, he was a dad burn blabbermouth. He told us all we wanted to know, and all manner of business we didn't want to know. I think it's best I just summarize what he was saying, keeping in mind it's possible I've left out some of the important parts, but mostly, I can assure you, I've left out stuff you don't want to hear anyway. We even got a few pointers on how to decorate a burrow, which seemed to be a tip we didn't need.

The rain got so thick it put those burning trees out, and with the moon behind clouds, it was dark in that cave. We couldn't even see each other. All we could do was hear Brer Rabbit's voice, which was a little squeaky.

What he was telling us was, there was gonna be some kind of ceremony. That whoever the weasels could catch was gonna be a part of it. It wasn't no ceremony where there was cake and prizes and games, least not any that was fun. It was gonna be a ceremony in honor of this fella he called Cut Through You.

According to Brer Rabbit, the island wasn't always a bad place. He and his family had lived here, along with all the other brother and sister animals, or whatever the hell they were, until Brer Fox found the stones and the book wrapped in skin. That's how Brer Rabbit put it. The book wrapped in skin.

Brer Fox, he wasn't never loveable, and Brer Rabbit said right up front, he used to pull tricks on him and Brer Bear all the time. They was harmless, he said, and they was mostly just to keep from getting eaten by them two. 'Cause as nice a place as it was then as measured up against now, it was still a place where meat eaters lived alongside them that wasn't meat eaters, which meant them that ate vegetables was the meat eater's lunch, if they got caught. Brer Rabbit said he figured that was just fair play. That was how the world worked, even if their island wasn't exactly like the rest of the world.

It dropped out of the sky come the full moon and ended up in the big wide middle of the Mississippi. It stayed that way for a few hours, and then come the Warning Rain, as he called it, the one we was having now; the one full of lighting and thunder and hard falling water. It meant they was more than halfway through their time to be on the Mississippi, then there was gonna come the Soft Rain. It didn't have no lighting in it. It was pleasant. At least until the sky opened up and the wind came down and carried them away.

"Where does it take you?" I asked.

Brer Rabbit shook his head. "I don't know I can say. We don't seem to know nothing till we come back. And when we do, well, we just pick up right where we was before. Doing whatever it was we was doing. So if Brer Fox has me by the neck, and the time comes, and we all get sucked away, when it blows back, we gonna be right where we was; it's always night and always like things was when we left them."

He said when that funnel of wind dropped them back on the island, sometimes it brought things with it that wasn't there before. Like people from other places. Other worlds, he said. That didn't make no sense at all to me. But that's what he said. He said sometimes it brought live people, and sometimes it brought dead people, and sometimes it brought Brer People with it, and sometimes what it brought wasn't people at all. He told us about some big old crawdads come through once, and how they chased everyone around, but ended up being boiled in water and eaten by Brer Bear, Brer Fox, and all the weasels, who was kind of butt kissers to Brer Fox.

Anyway, not knowing what was gonna show up on the island, either by way of that Sticky Storm—as he named it 'cause everything clung to it—or by way of the Mississippi, made things interesting; right before it got too interesting. The part that was too interesting had to do with Brer Fox and that Book of Skin.

Way Brer Rabbit figured, it come through that hole in the sky like everything else. It was clutched in a man's hand, and the man was deader than a rock, and he had what Brer Rabbit said was a towel or a rag or some such thing wrapped around his head.

Brer Rabbit said he seen that dead man from a hiding place in the woods, and Uncle Remus was with him when he did. Uncle Remus had escaped slavery and come to the island. He fit in good. Stayed in the burrow with Brer Rabbit and his family, and he listened to all their stories.

But when the change come, when that book showed up, and stuff started happening because of it, he decided he'd had enough and tried to swim back to shore. Things he saw made him think taking his chance on drowning, or getting caught and being a slave again, was worth it. I don't know how he felt later, but he sure got caught, since Jim knew him and had heard stories about Dread Island from him.

"He left before things really got bad," Brer Rabbit said. "And did they get bad. He was lucky."

"That depends on how you look at it," Jim said. "I done been a slave, and I can't say it compares good to much of anything."

"Maybe," Brer Rabbit said. "Maybe."

And then he went on with his story.

Seems that when the storm brought that dead man clutching that book, Brer Fox pried it out of his hands and opened it up and found it was written in some foreign language, but he could read it. Brer Rabbit said one of the peculiars about the island is that everyone—except the weasels, who pretty much got the short end of the stick when it come to smarts—could read or speak any language there was.

Now, wasn't just the book and the dead man come through, there was the stones. They had fallen out of the sky at the same time. There was also a mass of black goo with dying and dead fish in it that come through, and it splattered all over the ground. The stones was carved up. The main marking was a big eye, then there was all manner of other scratchings and drawings. And though the Brer Folk could read or speak any language possible, even the language in that book, they couldn't speak or read what was on them stones. It had been put together by folk spoke a tongue none of their mouths would fit around. Least at first.

Brer Fox went to holding that book dear. Everyone on the island knew about it, and he always carried it in a pack on his back. Brer Bear, who was kind of a kiss ass like the weasels, but smarter than they was—and, according to Brer Rabbit, that was a sad thing to think about, since Brer Bear didn't hardly have the sense to get in out of the Warning Rain—helped Brer Fox set them stones up in that black muck. Every time the storm brought them back, that's what they did, and pretty soon they had the weasels helping them.

Fact was, Brer Fox all but quit chasing Brer Rabbit. He instead sat and read by firelight and moonlight, and started chanting, 'cause he was learning how to say that language that he couldn't read before, the language on the stones, and he was teaching Brer Bear how to do the same. And one time, well, the island stayed overnight.

"It didn't happen but that once," Brer Rabbit said. "But come daylight, here we still was. And it stayed that way until the next night come, and finally before next morning, things got back to the way they was supposed to be. Brer Fox had some power from that book and those stones, and he liked it mighty good."

Now and again he'd chant something from the book, and the air would fill with an odor like rotting fish, and then that odor got heavy and went to whirling about them stones; it was an odor that made the stomach crawl and the head fill with all manner of sickness and worry and grief.

Once, while Brer Rabbit was watching Brer Fox chant, while he was smelling that rotten fish stink, he saw the sky crack open, right up close by the moon. Not the way it did when the Sticky Storm come, which was when everything turned gray and the sky opened up and a twister of sorts dropped down and sucked them all up. It was more like the night sky was just a big black sheet, and this thing with one, large, nasty, rolling eye and more legs than a spider—and ropey legs at that— poked through and pulled at the night.

For a moment, Brer Rabbit thought that thing—which from Brer Fox's chanting he learned was called Cut Through You—was gonna take hold of the moon and eat it like a flap jack. It had a odd mouth with a beak, and it was snapping all the while.

Then, sudden like, it was sucked back, like something got hold of one of its legs and yanked it plumb out of sight. The sky closed up and the air got clean for a moment, and it was over with.

After that, Brer Fox and ole One Eye had them a connection. Every time the island was brought back, Brer Fox would go out there and stand in that muck, or sit on a rock in the middle of them carved stones, and call out to Cut Through You. It was a noise, Brer Rabbit said, sounded like someone straining at toilet while trying to cough and yodel all at the same time.

Brer Fox and Brer Bear was catching folk and tying them to the stones. People from the Mississippi come along by accident; they got nabbed too, mostly by the weasels. It was all so Brer Fox could have Cut Through You meetings.

Way it was described to me, it was kind of like church. Except when it come time to pass the offering, the sky would crack open, and ole Cut Through You would lean out and reach down and pull folk tied to the stones up there with him.

Brer Rabbit said he watched it eat a bunch a folk quicker than a mule skinner could pop goober peas; chawed them up and spat them out, splattered what was left in that black mud that was all around the stones.

That was what Brer Fox and Brer Bear, and all them weasels, took to eating. It changed them. They went from sneaky and hungry and animal like, to being more like men. Meaning, said Brer Rabbit, they come to enjoy cruelty. And then Brer Fox built the Tar Baby, used that book to give it life. It could do more work than all of them put together, and it set up the final stones by itself. Something dirty needed to be done, it was Tar Baby done it. You couldn't stop the thing, Brer Rabbit said. It just kept on a coming, and a coming.

But the final thing Brer Rabbit said worried him, was that each time Cut Through You came back, there's more and more of him to be seen, and it turned out there's a lot more of Cut Through You than you'd think; and it was like he was hungrier each time he showed.

Bottom line, as figured by Brer Rabbit, was this: if Brer Fox and his bunch didn't supply the sacrifices, pretty soon they'd be sacrifices themselves.

Brer Rabbit finished up his story, and it was about that time the rain quit. The clouds melted away and the moonlight was back. It was clear out, and you could see a right smart distance.

I said, "You ain't seen a couple of fellas named Tom and Joe, have you? One of them might be wearing a straw hat. They're about my age and size, but not quite as good looking."

Brer Rabbit shook his head. "I ain't," he said. "But they could be with all the others Brer Fox has nabbed of late. Was they on the riverboat run aground?"

I shook my head.

Jim said, "Huck, you and me, we got to get back to the raft and get on out of this place, Tom and Joe or not."

"That's right," Brer Rabbit said. "You got to. Oh, I wish I could go with you."

"You're invited," I said.

"Ah, but there is the thorn in the paw. I can't go, 'cause I do, come daylight, if I ain't on this island, I disappear, and I don't come back. Though to tell you true, that might be better than getting ate up by Cut Through You. I'll give it some considering."

"Consider quick," Jim said, "we got to start back to the raft."

"What we got to do," Brer Rabbit said, "is we got to go that way."

He pointed.

"Then," he said, "we work down to the shore, and you can get your raft. And I'm thinking I might just go with you and turn to nothing. I ain't got no family now. I ain't got nothing but me, and part of me is missing, so the rest of me might as well go missing too."

Jim said, "I got my medicine bag with me. I can't give you your paw back, but I can take some of the hurt away with a salve I got."

Jim dressed Brer Rabbit's paw, and when that was done, he got some wool string out of that little bag he had on his belt and tied up his hair—which had grown long—in little sheaves, like dark wheat. He said it was a thing to do to keep back witches.

I pointed out witches seemed to me the least of our worries, but he done it anyway, with me taking my pocketknife out of my back pocket to cut the string for him.

When he had knotted his hair up in about twenty gatherings, we lit out for the raft without fear of witches.

Way we went made it so we had to swim across a creek that was deep in places. It was cold water, like that blue hole we had jumped in, and there was fish in it. They was curious and would bob to the top and look at us; their eyes was shiny as wet stones in the moonlight.

On the other side of the creek, we stumbled through a patch of woods, and down a hill, and then up one that led us level with where we had been before. In front of us was more dark woods. Brer Rabbit said beyond the trees was the shoreline, and we might be able to get to our raft if the weasels hadn't found it. Me and

Jim decided if they had, we'd try for Tom's and Joe's boat and wish them our best. If their boat was gone, then, there was nothing left but to hit that Mississippi and swim for it. We had about as much chance of making that swim as passing through the eye of a needle, but it was a might more inviting than Cut Through You. Least, that way we had a chance. Me and Jim was both good swimmers, and maybe we could even find a log to push off into the water with us. As for Brer Rabbit, well, he was thinking on going with us and just disappearing when daylight come; that was a thing made me really want to get off that island. If he was willing to go out that way, then that Cut Through You must be some nasty sort of fella. Worse yet, our salt had got all wet and wasn't worth nothing, and we had both lost the cross in our shoes. All we had was those rusty nails on strings, and I didn't have a whole lot of trust in that. I was more comfortable that I still had my little knife in my back pocket.

We was coming down through the woods, and it got so the trees were thinning, and we could see the bank down there, the river churning along furious like. My heart was starting to beat in an excited way, and about then, things turned to dog doo.

The weasels come down out of the trees on ropes, and a big net come down with them and landed over us. It was weighed down with rocks, and there wasn't no time to get out from under it before they was tugging it firm around us, and we was bagged up tighter than a strand of gut packed with sausage makings.

As we was laying there, out of the woods come Brer Fox and Brer Bear. They come right over to us. The fox bent down, and he looked Brer Rabbit in the eye. He grinned and showed his teeth. His breath was so sour we could smell it from four feet away; it smelled like death warmed over and gone cold again.

Up close, I could see things I couldn't see before in the night. He had fish scales running along the side of his face, and when he breathed there were flaps that flared out on his cheeks; they was gills, like a fish.

I looked up at Brer Bear. There were sores all over his body, and bits of fish heads and fish tails poking out of him like moles. He was breathing in and out, like bellows being worked to start up a fresh fire.

"You ain't looking so good," Brer Rabbit said.

"Yeah," Brer Fox said, "but looks ain't everything. I ain't looking so good, but you ain't doing so good."

Brer Fox slung his pack off his back and opened it. I could see there was a book in there, the one bound up in human skin. You could see there was a face on the cover, eyes, nose, mouth, and some warts. But that wasn't what Brer Fox was reaching for. What he was reaching for was Brer Rabbit's paw, which was stuffed in there.

"Here's a little something you left back at the ceremony spot." He held up the paw and waved it around. "That wasn't nice. I had plans for you. But, you know what? I got a lucky rabbit's foot now. Though, to tell the truth, it ain't all that lucky for you, is it?"

He put the paw in his mouth and clamped down on it and bit right through it and chewed on it some. He gave what was left of it to Brer Bear, who ate it up in one big bite.

"I figured you wouldn't be needing it," Brer Fox said.

"Why, I'm quite happy with this nubbing," Brer Rabbit said. "I don't spend so much time cleaning my nails now."

Brer Fox's face turned sour, like he had bitten into an unripe persimmon. "There ain't gonna be nothing of you to clean after tonight. And in fact, we got to go quick like. I wouldn't want you to miss the meeting, Brer Rabbit. You see, tonight, he comes all the way through, and then, me and my folk, we're gonna serve him. He's gonna go all over the Mississippi, and then all over the world. He's gonna rule, and I'm gonna rule beside him. He told me. He told me in my head."

With those last words, Brer Fox tapped the side of his head with a finger.

"You gonna get ate up like everyone else," Brer Rabbit said. "You just a big ole idiot."

Brer Fox rose up, waved his hand over his head, yelled out, "Bring them. And don't be easy about it. Let's blood them."

What that meant was they dragged us in that net. We was pressed up tight together, and there was all manner of stuff on the ground to stick us, and we banged into trees and such, and it seemed like forever before we broke out of the woods and I got a glimpse at the place we was going.

Right then I knew why it was Brer Rabbit would rather just disappear.

We was scratched and bumped up and full of ticks and chiggers and poison ivy by the time we got to where we was going, and where we was going didn't have no trees and there wasn't nothing pretty about it.

There was this big stretch of black mud. You could see dead fish in it, and some of them was mostly bones, but there were still some flopping about. They were fish I didn't recognize. Some had a lot of eyes and big teeth and were shaped funny.

Standing up in the mud were these big dark slabs of rock that wasn't quite black and wasn't quite brown, but was somewhere between any color you can mention. The moonlight laid on them like a slick of bacon grease, and you could see markings all over them. Each and every one of them had a big ole eye at the top of the slab, and below it were all manner of marks. Some of the marks looked like fish or things with lots of legs, and beaks, and then there was marks that didn't look like nothing but chicken scratch. But, I can tell you this, looking at those slabs and those marks made my stomach feel kind of funny, like I had swallowed a big chaw of tobacco right after eating too many hot peppers and boiled pig's feet, something, by the way, that really happened to me once.

Standing out there in that black muck was the weasels. On posts all around the muck right where it was still solid ground, there was men and women with their hands tied behind their backs and then tied to rings on the posts. I reckoned a number of them was from the steamboat wreck. There was also a woman wearing a kind of leather cap, and she had on pants just like a man. She was kind of pretty, and where everyone else was hanging their heads, she looked mad as a hornet. As we was pulled up closer to the muck, I saw that Tom and Joe was there, tied to posts, drooping like flowers too long in the hot sun, missing Bowie knife, gun, and packed lunch.

When they seen me and Jim, they brightened for a second, then realized wasn't nothing we could do, and that we was in the same situation as them. It hurt me to see Tom like that, all sagging. It was the first time I'd ever seen seen him about given up. Like us, they was all scratched up and even in the moonlight, you could see they was spotted like speckled pups from bruises.

Out behind them I could see parts of that big briar patch we had seen when we first sailed our raft onto the island. The briars twisted up high, and the way the moonlight fell into them, that whole section looked like a field of coiled ropes and nails. I hadn't never seen a briar patch like that before.

There were some other things out there in the muck that I can't explain, and there was stuff on the sides of where the muck ended. I figured, from what Brer Rabbit had told us, they was stuff from them other worlds or places that sometimes come through on the Sticky Storm. One of them things was a long boat of sorts, but it had wings on it, and it was shiny silver and had a tail on it like a fish. There was some kind of big crosses on the wings, and it was just sitting on wheels over on some high grass, but the wheels wasn't like any I'd ever seen on a wagon or buggy.

There was also this big thing looked like a gourd, if a gourd could be about a thousand times bigger; it was stuck up in the mud with the fat part down, and the thinner part in the air, and it had little fins on it. Written on it in big writing was something that didn't make no sense to me. It said: HOWDY ALL YOU JAPS.

Wasn't a moment or two passed between me seeing all this, then we was being pulled out of the net and carried over to three empty posts. A moment later, they wasn't empty no more. We was tied to the wooden rings on them tight as a fishing knot.

I turned my head and looked at Jim.

He said, "You're right, they ain't no witch problems around here."

"Maybe," I said, "it's because of the string. Who knows how many witches would be around otherwise."

Jim grinned at me. "That's right. That's right, ain't it?"

I nodded and smiled at him. I figured if we was gonna be killed, and wasn't nothing we could do about it, we might as well try and be cheerful.

Right then, coming across that black mud, its feet splattering and sucking in the muck as it pulled them free for each step, was the Tar Baby.

Now that he was out under the moonlight, I could see he was stuck all over with what at first looked like long needles, but as he come closer, I saw was straw. He was shot through with it. I figured it was a thing Brer Fox used to help put him together, mixing it with tar he got from somewhere, and turpentine, and maybe some things I didn't want to know about; you could smell that turpentine as he waddled closer, spitting all the while.

He sauntered around the circle of folks that was tied to the posts, and as he did, his plump belly would flare open, and you could see fire in there and bits of ash and bones being burned up along with fish heads and a human skull. Tar Baby went by each of them on the posts and pushed his face close to their faces so he could enjoy how they curled back from him. I knew a bully when I seen one, 'cause I had fought a few, and when I was younger, I was kind of a bully myself, till a girl named Hortense Miller beat the snot out of me, twisted my arm behind my back and made me say cotton sack, and even then, after I said it, she made me eat a mouthful of dirt and tell her I liked it. She wasn't one to settle an argument easy like. It cured my bully days.

When the Tar Baby come to me and pushed his face close, I didn't flinch. I just looked him in his red eyes like they was nothing, even though it was all I could do to keep my knees from chattering together. He stayed looking at me for a long time, then grunted, left the air around me full of the fog and stink of turpentine. Jim was next, and Jim didn't flinch none either. That didn't set well with Tar Baby, two rascals in a row, so he reached out with a finger and poked Jim's chest. There was a hissing sound and smoke come off Jim. That made me figure he was being burned by the Tar Baby somehow, but when the Tar Baby pulled his chubby, tar finger back, it was him that was smoking.

I leaned out and took a good look and seen the 'cause of it—the nail on the string around Jim's neck. The Tar Baby had poked it and that iron nail had actually worked its magic on him. Course, problem was, he had to put his finger right on it, but in that moment, I gathered me up a more favorable view of the hoodoo methods.

Tar Baby looked at the end of his smoking finger, like he might find something special there, then he looked at Jim, and his mouth twisted. I think he was gonna do something nasty, but there come a rain all of a sudden. The Soft Rain Brer Rabbit told us about. It come down sweet smelling and light and warm. No thunder. No lightning. And no clouds. Just water falling out of a clear sky stuffed with stars and a big fat moon; it was the rain that was supposed to let everyone know it wouldn't be long before daylight and the Sticky Storm.

The weasels and Brer Fox and Brer Bear, and that nasty Tar Baby, all made their way quick like to the tallest stone in the muck. They stood in front of it, and you could tell they was nervous, even the Tar Baby, and they went about chanting. The words were like someone spitting and sucking and coughing and clearing their throat all at once, if they was words at all. This went on for a while, and wasn't nothing happening but that rain, which was kind of pleasant.

"Huck," Jim said, "you done been as good a friend as man could have, and I ain't happy you gonna die, or me neither, but we got to, it makes me happy knowing you gonna go out with me."

"I'd feel better if you was by yourself," I said, and Jim let out a cackle when I said it.

There was a change in things, a feeling that the air had gone heavy. I looked up and the rain fell on my face and ran in my mouth and tasted good. The night sky was vibrating a little, like someone shaking weak pudding in a bowl. Then the sky cracked open like Brer Rabbit had told us about, and I seen there was light up there in the crack. It was light like you'd see from a lantern behind a wax paper curtain. After a moment, something moved behind the light, and then something moved in front of it. A dark shape about the size of the moon; the moon itself was starting to drift low and thin off to the right of the island.

Brer Rabbit had tried to describe it to us, ole Cut Through You, but all I can say is there ain't no real way to tell you how it looked, 'cause there wasn't nothing to measure it against. It was big and it had one eye that was dark and unblinking, and it had a beak of sorts, and there were all these ropey arms; but the way it looked shifted and changed so much you couldn't get a real handle on it.

I won't lie to you. It wasn't like standing up to the Tar Baby. My knees started knocking together, and my heart was beating like a drum and my insides felt as if they were being worked about like they was in a milk churn. Them snaky arms on that thing was clawing at the sky, and I even seen the sky give on the sides, like it was about to rip all over and fall down.

I pressed my back against the post, and when I did, I felt that pocketknife in my back pocket. It come to me then that if I stuck out my butt a little and pulled the rope loose as possible on the ring I was tied to, I might be able to thumb that knife out of my pocket, so I give it a try.

It wasn't easy, but that thing up there gave me a lot of will power. I worked the knife with my thumb and long finger, and got it out, and flicked it open, and turned it in my hand, almost dropping it. When that happened, it felt like my heart had leaped down a long tunnel somewhere. But when I knew I still had it, I turned it and went to cutting. Way I was holding it, twisted so that it come back against the rope on the ring, I was doing a bit of work on my wrists as well as the tie. It was a worrying job, but I stayed at it, feeling blood running down my hands.

While I was at it, that chanting got louder and louder, and I seen off to the side of Cut Through You, another hole opening up in the sky; inside that hole it looked like a whirlpool, like you find in the river; it was bright as day in that hole, and the day was churning around and around and the sky was widening.

I figured then the ceremony was in a kind of hurry, 'cause Cut Through You was peeking through, and that whirling hole was in competition to him. He wouldn't have nothing to eat and no chanting to hear, if the Sticky Storm took everyone away first.

You see, it was the chanting that was helping Cut Through You get loose. It gave him strength, hearing that crazy language.

From where we was, I could see the pink of the morning starting to lay across the far end of the river, pushing itself up like the bloom of a rose, and that ole moon dipping down low, like a wheel of rat cheese being slowly lowered into a sack.

So, there we were, Cut Through You thrashing around in the sky, the Sticky Storm whirling about, and the sun coming up. The only thing that would have made it worse was if I had had to pee.

Everything started to shake, and I guess that was because Cut Through You and that storm was banging together in some way behind night's curtain, and maybe the sun starting to rise had something to do with it. The Sticky Storm dipped out of that hole and it come down lower. I could see all manner of stuff up there in it, but I couldn't make out none of it. It looked like someone had taken some different mixes of paint and thrown them all together; a few light things on the ground started to float up toward the storm, and when they did, I really understood why Brer Rabbit called it a Sticky Storm; it was like it was fly paper and all that was sucked up got stuck to it like flies.

About then, I cut that rope in two, and pulled my bleeding hands loose. I ran over to Jim and cut him loose.

Brer Fox and the others didn't even notice. They was so busy looking up at Cut Through You. I didn't have the time, but I couldn't help but look up too. It had its head poking all the way through, and that head was so big you can't imagine, and it was lumpy and such, like a bunch of melons had been put in a tow sack and banged on with a boat paddle; it was leaking green goo that was falling down on the ground, and onto the worshipers, and they was grabbing it off the muck, or off themselves, and sticking their fingers in their mouths and licking them clean.

It didn't look like what the Widow Douglas would have called sanitary, and I could see that them that was eating it, was starting to change. Sores, big and bloody, was popping up on them like a rash.

I ran on around the circle to Tom and Joe and cut them loose, and then we all run back the other way, 'cause as much as I'd like to have helped them on that farther part of the circle, it was too late. On that side the ground was starting to fold up, and their posts was coming loose. It was like someone had taken a sheet of paper and curled one end of it. They was being sucked up in the sky toward that Sticky Storm, and even the black mud was coming loose and shooting up in the sky.

On the other end of the circle, things was still reasonably calm, so I rushed to Brer Rabbit and cut him loose, then that lady with the pants on. Right about then, Cut Through You let out with a bellow so loud it made the freckles on my butt crawl up my back and hide in my hair, or so it felt. Wasn't no need to guess that Cut Through You was mad that he was running out of time, and he was ready to take it out on most anybody. He stuck long ropey legs out of the sky and went to thrashing at Brer Fox and the others. I had the pleasure of seeing Brer Fox getting his head snapped off, and then Brer Bear was next.

The weasels, not being of strong stuff to begin with, starting running like rats from a sinking ship. But it didn't do them no good. That Cut Through You's legs was all over them, grabbing their heads and jerking them off, and them that wasn't beheaded, was being pulled up in the sky by the Sticky Storm.

I was still on that side of the circle, cutting people loose, and soon as I did, a bunch of them just ran wildly, some right into the storm. They was yanked up, and went out of sight. All of the island seemed like it was wadding up.

Brer Rabbit grabbed my shoulder, said, "It's every man for his self," and then he darted along the edge of the Sticky Storm, dashed between two whipping Cut Through You legs, and leaped right into that briar patch, which seemed crazy to me. All the while he's running and jumping in the briars, I'm yelling, "Brer Rabbit, come back."

But he didn't. I heard him say, "Born and raised in the briar patch, born and raised," and then he was in the big middle of it, even as it was starting to fold up and get pulled toward the sky.

Now that we was free, I didn't know what to do. There didn't seem no place to go. Even the shoreline was starting to curl up.

Jim was standing by me. He said, "I reckon this is it, Huck. I say we let that storm take us, and not Cut Through You."

We was about to go right into the storm, 'cause the side of it wasn't but a few steps away, when I got my elbow yanked. I turned and it was Tom Sawyer, and Joe with him.

"The lady," Tom said. "This way."

I turned and seen the shorthaired lady was at that silver boat, and she was waving us to her. Any port in a storm, so to speak, so we run toward her with Tom and Joe. A big shadow fell over us as we run, and then a leg come popping out of the sky like a whip, and caught Joe around the neck, and yanked his head plumb off. His headless body must have run three or four steps before it went down.

I heard Tom yell out, and stop, as if to help the body up. "You got to run for it, Tom," I said. "Ain't no other way. Joe's deader than last Christmas."

So we come up on the silver boat with the wings, and there was an open door in the side of it, and we rushed in there and closed it. The lady was up front in a seat, behind this kind of partial wheel, looking out through a glass that run in front of her. The silver bug was humming, and those crosses on the wings was spinning. She touched something and let loose of something else, and we started to bounce, and then we was running along on the grass. I moved to the seat beside her, and she glanced over at me. She was white faced, but determined looking.

"That was Noonan's seat," she said.

I didn't know what to say to that. I didn't know if I should get out of it or not, but I'll tell you, I didn't. I couldn't move. And then we was bouncing harder, and the island was closing in on us, and Cut Through You's rope legs was waving around us. One of them got hit by the crosses, which was spinning so fast you could hardly make them out. They hit it, and the winged boat was knocked a bit. The leg come off in a spray of green that splattered on the glass, and then the boat started to lift up. I can't explain it, and I know it ain't believable, but we was flying.

The sun was really starting to brighten things now, and as we climbed up, I seen the woods was still in front of us. The lady was trying to make the boat go higher, but I figured we was gonna clip the top of them trees and end up punched to death by them, but then the boat rose up some, and I could feel and hear the trees brush against the bottom of it, like someone with a whisk broom snapping dust off a coat collar.

With the island curing up all around us and starting to come apart in a spray of color, being sucked up by the Sticky Storm, and that flying boat wobbling and a rattling, I figured we had done all this for nothing.

The boat turned slightly, like the lady was tacking a sail. I could glance up and out of the glass and see Cut Through You. He was sticking his head out of a pink morning sky, and his legs was thrashing, but he didn't look so big now; it was like the light had shrunk him up. I seen Tar Baby too, or what was left of him, and he was splattering against that big gourd thing with the writing on it, splattering like someone was flicking ink out of a writing pen. He and that big gourd was whipping around us like angry bugs.

Then there was a feeling like we was an arrow shot from a bow, and the boat jumped forward, and then it went up high, turned slightly, and below I seen the island was turning into a ball, and the ball was starting to look wet. Then it, the rain, every dang thing, including ole Cut Through You, who was sucked out of his hole, shot up into that Sticky Storm.

Way we was now, I could still see Tar Baby splashed on that gourd, and the gourd started to shake, then it twisted and went as flat as a tape worm, and for some reason, it blowed; it was way worse than dynamite. When it blew up, it threw some Tar Baby on the flying boat's glass. The boat started to shake and the air inside and out had blue ripples in it.

And then—

—the island was gone and there was just the Mississippi below us. Things was looking good for a minute, and then the boat started coughing, and black smoke come up from that whirly thing that had cut off one of Cut Through You's legs.

The boat dropped, the lady pulling at that wheel, yanking at doo-dads and such, but having about as much luck taking us back up as I'd have had trying to lift a dead cow off the ground by the tail.

"We are going down," she said, as if this might not be something we hadn't noticed. "And there is nothing else to do but hope for the best."

Well, to make a long story short. She was right.

Course, hope only goes so far.

She fought that boat all the way down, and then it hit the water and skipped like it was a flat rock. We skipped and skipped, then the whirly gigs flew off, and one of them smashed the glass. I was thrown out of the seat, and around the inside of the boat like a ball.

Then everything knotted up, and there was a bang on my head, and the next thing I know there's water all over. The boat was about half full inside. I suppose that's what brought me around, that cold Mississippi water.

The glass up front was broke open, and water was squirting in around the edges, so I helped it by giving it a kick. It come loose at the edges, and I was able to push it out with my feet. Behind me was Tom Sawyer, and he come from the back like a farm mule in sight of the barn. Fact was, he damn near run over me going through the hole I'd made.

By the time he got through, there wasn't nothing but water, and I was holding my breath. Jim grabbed me from below, and pushed me by the seat of my pants through the hole. Then it was like the boat was towed out from under me. Next thing I knew I was on top of the water floating by Tom, spitting and coughing.

"Jim," I said, "where's Jim?"

"Didn't see him come up," Tom said.

"I guess not," I said. "You was too busy stepping on my head on your way out of that flying boat."

Tom started swimming toward shore, and I just stayed where I was, dog paddling, looking for Jim. I didn't see him, but on that sunlit water there come a big bubble and a burst of something black as the tar baby had been. It spread over the water. It was oil. I could smell it.

Next thing, I felt a tug at my leg. I thought it was one of them big catfish grabbing me, but it wasn't. It was Jim. He bobbed up beside me, and I grabbed him and hugged him and he hugged me back.

"I tried to save her, Huck. I did. But she was done dead. I could tell when I touched her, she was done dead."

"You done what you could."

"What about Tom?" Jim said.

I nodded in the direction Tom had gone swimming. We could see his arms going up and down in the water, swimming like he thought he could make the far shore in about two minutes.

Wasn't nothing to do, but for us to start swimming after him. We done that for a long time, floating some, swimming some. And I'm ashamed to say Jim had to pull me along a few times, 'cause I got tuckered out.

When we was both about gone under, a big tree come floating by, and we climbed up on it. We seen Tom wasn't too far away, having gotten slower as he got tired. We yelled for him, and he come swimming back. The water flow was slow right then, and he caught up with us pretty quick, which is a good thing, 'cause if he hadn't, he'd have sure enough drowned. We clung and floated, and it was late that afternoon when we finally was seen by some fishermen and pulled off the log and into their boat.

There isn't much left to tell. All I can say is we was tired for three days, and when we tried to tell our story, folks just laughed at us. Didn't believe us at all. Course, can't blame them, as I'm prone toward being a liar.

It finally got so we had to tell a lie for it to be believed for the truth, and that included Tom who was in on it with us. We had to say Joe drowned, because they wouldn't believe Cut Through You jerked his head off. They didn't believe there was a Cut Through You. Even the folks believed there was a Dread Island didn't believe our story.

Tom and Becky got together, and they been together ever since. Five years have passed, and dang if Tom didn't become respectable and marry Becky. They got a kid now. But maybe they ain't all that respectable. I count eight months from the time they married until the time their bundle of joy come along.

Last thing I reckon I ought to say, is every year I go out to the edge of the Mississippi with Jim and toss some flowers on the water in memory of the lady who flew us off the island in that winged boat.

As for Dread Island. Well, here's something odd. I can't see it no more, not even when it's supposed to be there.

Jim says it might be my eyes, 'cause when you get older you lose sight of some things you used to could see.

I don't know. But I think it ain't out there no time anymore, and it might not be coming back. I figure it, Brer Rabbit and Cut Through You is somewhere else that ain't like nothing else we know. If that's true, all I got to say, is I hope Brer Rabbit is hid up good, far away from Cut Through You, out there in the thorns, out there where he was raised, in the deep parts of that big old briar patch.

Author Comments

Nancy Collins

"When I was in the second grade, I was taken to see John Huston's classic film adaptation of *Moby-Dick*, the one with Gregory Peck as Ahab. It made an immense impact on me— to the point I wanted to become a whaler when I grew up. I quickly outgrew the desire to hunt sea mammals, but I have always found Captain Ahab to be a compelling character, and one it would not be hard to imagine condemned to the same supernatural fate as Coleridge's Ancient Mariner."

Nancy Collins is currently working on the second book in her new Golgotham urban-fantasy series. The first book in the series, *Right Hand Magic*, is scheduled for a December 2010 release by Roc.

Rick Hautala

"I always thought I would have fit right into the literary scene in Concord, Massachusetts, in the 1840s ... You know, when Hawthorne, Thoreau, Emerson, and the Alcotts were kicking around. Of all the folks in Concord, I believe Bronson Alcott and I would have seen eye-to-eye on most things, so I was only too happy to rework Louisa May Alcott's *Little Women*. I'd like to think Louisa and her father would get a kick out of what I did to her story ... I hope so, anyway. Otherwise, there will be hell to pay in the literary afterlife."

Rick Hautala's most recent short story collection is *Occasional Demons*, from CD Publications, and he's finishing up a novella titled *Indian Summer*.

Marc Laidlaw

"Odd juxtapositions are rocket fuel for a writer's imagination. One inadvertent swap of unrelated concepts, one irresistible pun, may give instantaneous rise to an entire universe. Thus it was with 'Pokky Man,' which emerged full-blown from the title—a vision of filmmaker Werner Herzog trapped in a shallow cartoon world he would certainly consider unworthy of his time and energy. This cartoon world was inspired by a popular kids' videogame, especially the version where you're a nature photographer, drifting through a dynamic yet unchanging landscape of cartoon creatures fixed in Dantesque tableaux."

Marc Laidlaw, writer of the popular Half-Life series of videogames, is currently at work on several secret projects at Valve Software.

Joe R. Lansdale

"I wrote *Dread Island* based on my love for Mark Twain, which collided with my interest in Lovecraft, and the fact that the Uncle Remus tales may have been the first stories I ever read. And then there were comics. I always saw *Dread Island* as a kind of comic book in prose, the old Classics Illustrated look. That's how it played out in my head."

The trade paperback edition of Joe R. Lansdale's latest Hap and Leonard novel, *Vanilla Ride*, is forthcoming from Vintage Books.

Mark Morris

"British punk rock captured me body and soul in 1977. It gave me an identity, influenced the way I felt and thought and viewed the world. At the time, Sid Vicious seemed like the ultimate punk; all image and caricature, yes, but dripping with genuine attitude and aggression and seedy glamour. The most rewarding and fascinating aspect of writing this story has been the opportunity to try to untangle the myth and get under the skin of the real Sid. He was a simple, sensitive kid, totally screwed-up, but horribly manipulated and exploited. During the process of researching and writing this story I grew to really like him, and I genuinely hope that I've managed to do him justice."

Mark is editor of the recently-published *Cinema Futura*, a follow-up to the award-winning *Cinema Macabre*. Forthcoming work includes a new short story collection, *Long Shadows, Nightmare Light*, for PS Publishing, a novella entitled *It Sustains*, for Earthling Publications, and a number of Doctor Who audio dramas for Big Finish Productions.

Lezli Robyn

"When I was a pre-teen I was given the L. M. Montgomery books for Christmas. It was my first introduction to her most famous character, Anne Shirley, and I was hooked. Like me, Anne wanted to be a writer, and she had such a zest for life; such an infectious imagination. I jumped at the chance to write an Anne story for this mashup collection, mixing the classic story of a young orphan girl proving her worth and finding a place to belong, with the popular Steampunk genre. Thus, 'Anne-droid of Green Gables' was born."

Lezli Robyn is a nominee for the Campbell Award for best new writer in 2010, and has just sold a collection of her stories to Ticonderoga Publications, to be published in 2012.

Kristine Kathryn Rusch

"I've loved Emily Dickinson ever since I saw *The Belle of Amherst* starring Julie Harris in London. I was seventeen. I went home, studied the poems, and realized this poet is really morbid. I liked that at seventeen; still do, if truth be told. And not even one terrible English prof who made us sing her poems to "The Yellow Rose of Texas" (try it; it works) discouraged me from Dickinson. No one but me ever seemed to notice how fascinated this woman was with death, and how—it seemed—death courted her. Very Gothic in a *Wuthering Heights* kinda way. So I thought: why not?"

Kristine Kathryn Rusch short-story collection *Recovering Apollo 8 and Other Stories* was recently issued by Golden Gryphon Press, while WMG publishing has started the large project of putting entire backlist into electronic editions, including her short fiction.

Chris Ryall

"I grew up loving Norse mythology much more than its more popular counterpart, the Greek myths— I credit Edith Hamilton and Stan Lee equally for that— so the idea of contemporizing Norse legends through the filter of one of today's more popular prose melodramas was irresistible to me. And if I was able to also mildly tweak said melodrama just a bit while doing so, well, we all have a little bit of Loki the Trickster God in us, don't we?"

Chris Ryall is the Eisner-nominated writer of dozens of comic books, and a prose book about comics, *Comic Books 101*. His latest projects, a new *Zombies vs Robots* series, and IDW's first-ever event, "Infestation," both launch in early 2011.

John Shirley

"I've always been drawn to the old west—and to horror. I did considerable research about Billy the Kid, and there were in fact rumors of his having survived into the 20th Century. But what most inspired the story were the famously-bad low-budget films *Billy the Kid Versus Dracula* and *Jesse James Meets Frankenstein's Daughter,* made back-to-back in 1966 by the prolific "One Shot William" Beaudine. It just seemed to me that placing Billy the Kid in the midst of that low-rent film setting was fraught with fun...especially if we involved a "Victor Frankenstein" and Frankensteinian horror. The convergence of these curious elements took me into a nice fusion of drama, horror and humor."

John Shirley's newest novel is *Bleak History* from Pocket Books; his new story collection is *In Extremis* from Underland Press, and eReads is re-releasing eleven of his books, including *Wetbones* and *The Other End.*

John Skipp & Cody Goodfellow

"We all grow up watching monster movies and funny animal cartoons. And yet we're wired not to conflate the two, or ask: why are anthropomorphic animals scary here, and adorable there? Somewhere between the timeless questions "Are we not men?" and "Why is that dog wearing pants?", *The Happiest Hell on Earth* was born."

2010 saw the release of four Skipp books: the mammoth anthology *Werewolves and Shapeshifters; Spore* (with Cody Goodfellow); *The Emerald Burrito of Oz* (with Marc Levinthal); and *The Bridge* (with Craig Spector).

Cody Goodfellow's latest novel, *Perfect Union*, is now available from Swallowdown Press, and his noir scifi novella *The Homewreckers* just came out in The Bizarro Starter Kit (Purple).

Sean Taylor

"This story began when I was on a long drive to a comic convention and it dawned on me from out of that both *Through the Looking Glass* and *Snow White* were stories based on mirrors, and wouldn't it be oh so much fun to combine them. I've always loved the grim versions of the fairy tales, and that combined with a recent interest in the works of Lovecraft triggered the onset of the surprise villains in this little tale."

Sean is currently working on an original graphic novel sequel to HG Wells' *The Invisible Man* and *The Time Machine*, as well as a crime thriller graphic novel, and a prose short story collection containing every one of his tales for the Writer Digest Zine Award winning iHero Entertainment/Cyber Age Adventures.

Tom Tessier

Senator Joseph McCarthy was a fascinating figure in postwar American history, cartoonish and laughable but also dangerous and destructive. He was a master at creating fear in the public mind and then using it for his own purposes. I couldn't resist putting him in a classic horror situation and seeing what would happen. McCarthy is long dead, but McCarthyism, sad to say, is still very much alive in the land.

Thomas Tessier is working on a new novel, *The Lives of the Banshee*.

Rio Youers

"So I had this idea—a spark, really: a mash-up of Jim Morrison and Edgar Allan Poe, two American icons with esoteric tendencies. Naturally, I wanted to see what would happen, so I let concept dance in my mind … and before long had the story's blueprint. In writing, I found the elements (the darkness) melded seamlessly—an exciting, organic process fueled by my passion for the subjects' work."

Rio Youers was recently nominated for a British Fantasy Award for his novella *Old Man Scratch*. He has just completed his new novel, *In Faith*, and his short story collection, *Dark Dreams, Pale Horses* will be released by PS Publishing in early 2011.